Whirlwind

Mystical Elements 3

Meg Lynn

Copyright © 2025 by Meg Lynn

Cover by Moonpress Design / www.moonpress.co

Edited by Sydney Hawthorn.

All rights reserved.

No portion of this book may be reproduced in any form without written permission from the publisher or author, except as permitted by U.S. copyright law.

This is a work of fiction. The names, characters, events, or places portrayed in this book are the product of the author's imagination or used fictitiously. Any resemblance to actual persons, living or dead, events or locations are coincidental and not intended by the author.

GLOSSARY

People/Things

Elemental: A witch with the ability to control one of the five elements: water, fire, earth, air or spirit. Elemental power is regenerated to each Generation.

Generation: A group of five Elementals, each representing one element, born within five years of one another. A Generation is connected through their powers and are able to feel the other's powers when used.

Magister: The oldest of a living set of Elemental generations.

The Martyrs: Magisters to the Shepherds. The generation murdered by Erebus.

The Shepherds: The last known generation of Elementals before current times. The ones who sacrificed themselves and hid their magic in the talismans.

Seer: An Elemental who has visions of the future and is able to see into the past through memories of other Generations.

Feeler: An empathic Elemental, one who can sense other's feelings and cannot be lied to.

Talisman: An object thought to have magic abilities and bring good luck or protection to the wearer.

Archivist: A title passed down to witches that care for old texts and spellbooks, keeping them safe and the stories of the past alive.

The Coven: Audrianna Dansley and Amilia Burnett's group of friends, all witches, that grew up in Rifton together.

Erebus: The legendary leader of the Renati. A powerful witch who lived centuries ago that was banished to the Shadow Realm by the last known Generation of Elementals.

The Renati: A group of witches who believe Elementals are too powerful and therefore corruptible.

Shadows: Carnivorous creatures from the Shadow Realm.

Allurement: A concentration of magic that attracts witches, bringing them to one another and strengthens their powers.

The Key: The magical item required to access the Allurements.

Places

The Dark Star Forest: A massive forest that covers the majority of Western Oregon into the Cascade Mountain Range.

Falcon Bay, Oregon: A coastal city an hour and a half from Rifton.

Rifton, Oregon: A small town on the edge of the Dark Star Forest.

Pines Row: A neighborhood outside Rifton city limits where the Dansley siblings lived.

Diamond Gate: A gated community by the lake outside of Rifton where the wealthier families live.

Eagle Loop Trail: Hiking trail in the Dark Star Forest that leads around the local lake.

The Corner Cup: A local coffee shop in Rifton where Whitney works.

The Cottage: Whitney's boss, Amilia Burnet's, home.

The Hallow: A compound of witches hidden in the Dark Star Forest.

The Palace: A community of wealthy witches living in California's Bay Area.

The Shadow Realm: A dimension of darkness and danger that shares a veil with the modern world.

CONTENT

This book contains elements of
 death of a loved one (off page),
 mention of suicide and self-harm,
 mention of addiction,
 alcohol and marijuana consumption,
 cursing,
 blood,
 hospitalization,
 broken bones,
 explicit sexual scenes (MF) & (FF).

Listen to the playlist for Whirlwind here on Spotify!

To anyone who has ever watered themselves down or hid their true selves, never be afraid to live authentically and let your light shine. You will never be too much for those who love you.

Chapter One

Running Away

Whitney

Two bags sat on my bed; a floral overnight bag packed for a wedding and a dark blue backpack with supplies to run away.

My hands trembled as I packed clothes and gear into the never-ending backpack. Surely it had an end, but the enchantment gave me the ability to put everything I'd need for a month-long journey inside. Hopefully, we wouldn't be gone that long, but I wanted to be prepared just in case.

I only packed the necessities; sweaters, blankets, boots, thick socks, an insulated water bottle, on and on. I ticked off everything from the mental list in my head, not daring to keep it in my phone where it could've been found. Only one person knew of our journey, and he planned to stay behind.

Dominic's words from two nights ago echoed in my head.

Left at the waterfalls.

Do not get yourselves killed.

That pretty necklace of yours. It's our only chance.

I glanced down at the messy scribbles Nic called a map; the labels written out with shaky hands. Nic wasn't an artist, but I understood enough of it to feel confident that we could follow it. He drew a big circle around the part of the forest where he thought the shield reached, but he admitted he didn't know for sure. Nic hadn't been there in twelve years and his selective memory of that time made things tricky. A natural trauma response.

I wondered how much of this current time I'd remember. Would I lock every little detail in a box deep in my subconscious or would I cling to the memories, hoping they fueled me towards the end goal?

Tears blurred my vision as I processed the last few days. Warren's lifeless brown eyes staring back at me as blood trickled down from the glass in his neck. The sound of Harmony's screams as reality sunk in. Amilia's body falling to the ground as Erebus' killing curse struck her. The hate in his dark eyes as he squeezed on my throat.

The cottage had been our safe place, somewhere we could all be together and not worry about any outside dangers. Erebus and the Renati had broken through our defenses with ease and in doing so, shattered any bit of security I had left. If they were able to penetrate the cottage, would we be safe anywhere?

Leaving only a few days after the attack on the cottage was not ideal, but the girls and I needed to get to the Hallow. The compound of witches who lived in the middle of the forest were a group of Elemental supporters driven from their homes by the Renati. Erebus and his followers had hit us where it hurt, but if we could bring those witches back the Rifton...Well, hopefully we'd stand a fighting chance.

I finished packing and zipped up the enchanted backpack. I secured it to my back and grabbed the weekend bag, taking one last look around the bedroom I shared with Bryan. His poster of the Milky Way above the dresser. The photos of us on the bookcase next to pictures of my family. My candles and crystals on the dresser out in the open.

Home had always been a place I could be my true self, and living with Bryan had been no different. We had made this room our own and I hated to leave. I knew this wouldn't be the last time I'd see it, but I didn't know how long it would be until I snuggled back in this bed with his body pressed against mine. How long it would be until I heard him whisper good morning or get up before me to start the coffee pot.

My heart constricted in my chest but I swallowed, burying it deep down. If I lingered too much on what I left behind, I would never allow myself to go in the first place.

That and life as I knew it depended on me going.

I grabbed a sticky note from Bryan's stack of school supplies he'd left on top of his dresser and quickly jotted down the first thing that came to mind. A little something to remind him that I wasn't leaving *him* and that I would be back.

I stuck the note to the wall where I knew he'd see it. *I'll always come back to you* stared at me as I turned and left.

A silence hung in the air on the drive to Falcon Bay. I kept my focus on the road as the radio played softly in the background. Rayn sat shotgun, turned in her seat to chat with Brooke and Dmitri in the back. Dmitri had wanted to stay in Rifton with Abe. After the attack on the cottage, Abe decided he needed to face his parents. I didn't want to leave Dmitri in Rifton, so luckily Abe urged Dmitri to go to the wedding with us. Maybe if the girls and I weren't planning on leaving without his knowledge, I'd feel differently but I wanted to spend extra time with Mit. I hated keeping this from him, but if he knew, he wouldn't let us leave without him.

Dmitri stared out the window, his mouth a thin line and his brows furrowed. I could tell he didn't want to leave Abe behind. Finally going back home to see his parents was a big deal for Abe considering they thought he might be dead, and Dmitri wanted to be there for him. Even Dmitri had to accept that the conversation needed to be between the Roberts alone.

Brooke slouched in her seat with her head on the glass, watching the pine trees race past. She seemed to listen to us talk, but her heart clearly remained somewhere else.

"You okay, B?" I glanced in the rearview mirror.

Brooke sighed. "I'm worried about my parents, and I'm so pissed off at them. They did this to themselves. I know that. I still hate knowing how strained things are now. For me, at least."

"I'm sorry." Dmitri reached across the back seat for her hand. "I can't imagine how hard the last few days have been on you."

All of us may have gone through the attack on the cottage together, but Brooke's parents had her institutionalized. Her mom had caught her practicing healing magic on a self inflicted wound and well...we had to break Brooke out of the hospital. Our entire crew had been traumatized that night, but Brooke's heart had already been broken going into the worst night of our time in Rifton.

I chewed on my bottom lip. "Nicky promised he and Harmony would take care of things."

"Charming my parents?" Brooke lifted her head from the window. She licked her bottom lip and let out another sigh. "It's the only option, isn't it?"

"Nic would never hurt your parents, B." I wished I could turn to look at her, but I kept my eyes on the road. "Rose and Bryan weren't exactly comfortable with having to charm their mom after Christmas Eve but it ended up being the best option."

Brooke nodded. "At least Rose is an adult. Nancy can't lock her up when she doesn't follow their strict guidelines. I don't know how to feel. They're my parents, but they've really complicated things. I'm backed into a corner." She chewed on her thumb nail and blinked as if she held back tears.

"I'm sure they're just scared. Your dad is a cop and he sees the darkest parts of humanity." Dmitri tightened his grip on Brooke. "They didn't go about it the right way, but parents fuck up sometimes. It won't be like this forever."

I didn't know what to add to the conversation, so I turned my attention back to the highway as Rayn changed the subject to ask a question about the wedding.

We still had a few hours until the wedding ceremony began by the time we pulled into the parking lot of the hotel. The Grantman was a beautiful, historic hotel in Falcon Bay. The three story brick building overlooked the bay with a large peak in the roof above the entryway.

Lauren rode over with Ashley, and had sent a text that they were waiting for us inside. Bryan and Rose had come over the day before for the rehearsal dinner. Bryan had invited me, but I took the opportunity for some alone time to pack for the Hallow.

The hotel lobby was decorated with dark green paint and elaborately carved walnut trim. A massive chandelier made of antlers hung from the ceiling. The hardwood floors had long emerald green rugs with golden floral swirls that ran the walkways. I stopped and took in the massive wooden beams that ran across the tall ceilings and the roaring fireplace in the corner. Large pieces of natural stone ran up the length of the wall around the flames.

Ashley and Lauren sat close to the fire in forest green armchairs, chatting amongst themselves. They noticed us walk in and waved us over. Ashley gave a broad smile, bouncing in her seat. Lauren's makeup hid the dark circles under her eyes but the look of exhaustion lingered in her posture and heavy eyelids.

None of us had slept much since the attack on the cottage, but going out into the world and pretending that we weren't mourning remained the hardest part.

"You guys okay?" Ashley scanned each of us. "You're all so off today. It's a wedding!"

I faked a smile, knowing Ashley had taken a long weekend off work and had yet to notice Amilia's absence. I didn't know when Harmony planned to announce to my coworkers that our boss had died, but Ash had obviously not received that phone call yet.

"I'm tired," I answered nonchalantly. "Bryan drove over yesterday and I never sleep well when he's gone."

That wasn't a lie.

"I get it. You two have become nauseatingly adorable. Do you want to head up and get ready?" Ashley motioned towards the elevator. "Rose gave me her room key so you guys could get dressed when you got here."

After we got dressed, I put my hair up in a clip and Rayn did my makeup. She had done my makeup for every big event we'd ever gone to. It felt comforting to sit back and let her take care of me for a few moments, especially after the last few days.

As Rayn got herself ready, I put on my maroon lipstick in the floor length mirror. Rayn did an impressive job hiding the dark circles under my eyes, but no amount of makeup could hide the sadness in my gaze. I attempted to blink it away, but that would've been a fool's hope.

I wanted to be excited for the wedding. While Nancy made it clear on Christmas Eve that I wasn't her top choice for her son's romantic interest, I still had the opportunity to celebrate with my loved ones. But I had little to celebrate other than surviving. I grew tired of being relieved to live when not everyone I loved made it to the other side. I may have survived the attack on the cottage, but part of me died the night I watched Amilia throw herself in front of me.

"They're all set up in the ballroom," Ashley's voice startled me from where she sat on the bed next to Lauren. "Are you guys ready to head down?"

"I'm ready!" Rayn called from the bathroom. She bent down and flipped her hair, coating it in hairspray.

I nodded and mentally hardened myself. I could sit through this wedding and look pretty in the nice black dress I'd put on, but I wouldn't enjoy myself.

A damn shame, because the ceremony truly looked beautiful.

Nancy and Jack said their vows in front of a white sheer curtain with twinkling lights and strands of ivy hung behind them. Our crew sat on the bride's side of the room. Ashley sat with us but Emma and Troy sat a few rows up. Troy had waved when he saw us but Emma's polite smile barely felt genuine.

Bryan stood behind Jack as his best man, wearing a dark gray suit that fit his frame perfectly. His hands folded in front of him with his shoulders held slightly back, smiling at his mom. The heat in my stomach from seeing him swirled with the fear and regret of knowing this would be our last night together before the girls and I left for the Hallow. He had no idea.

As if he could tell I thought about him, his gaze shifted to me and a smile broke out across his lips. A real, genuine smile that showed off his perfect teeth. I smiled back, swallowing the tears that threatened to ruin the makeup Rayn had spent half an hour on.

Rose stood behind her mom, holding a beautiful bouquet of lilies. Jack's daughter stood behind Rose with her hand on her young daughter's shoulders. The little girl served as the flower girl for the evening, proudly holding her white, wicker baskets filled with cream-colored flower petals. I hadn't met either of them yet, but Bryan had mentioned them a few times in conversation.

Bryan turned his attention back to the preacher as they wrapped up the ceremony, asking Jack to kiss his bride while everyone cheered. I clapped and stood with the rest of the crowd, watching as bliss washed over Nancy's face. Part of me couldn't help but wonder if Bryan and I would ever have a day like this. If the threat of the Renati and the hunters would ever truly pass and we'd get to live somewhat normal lives. Or if Bryan would even want a life with me at the end of all this.

Mixed emotions swirled inside my chest. As I sat admiring Bryan on what should have been a night filled with joy, Amilia's vacant face flooded my mind every time I closed my eyes. As the small group of guests cheered for the happy couple, the screams inside my head drowned them out. Life didn't stop because Warren and Amilia were dead. No one in this room but us even knew they were gone. We mourned, but the world did not stop spinning for our grief.

Nancy and Jack headed down the aisle together as everyone continued to clap and cheer. Bryan offered his arm to Rose and the two of them followed behind the couple. Rose smiled at us as they walked past. After everyone cleared out of the ceremony area, we followed behind the crowd to the reception.

The small room had been filled with tables and a dance floor in the center. The tables were decorated with cream colored tablecloths and lit candles in small votives. The centerpieces were sliced pieces of flat wood with strands of ivy coiled around them, more candles sitting atop the slices of wood. Even though Nancy had been married before, they went fairly traditional with the whole ordeal.

I'd never been to a wedding before but I'd seen enough movies and had enough exposure to the internet to know what weddings typically entailed. Mom had been invited to a few over the years but she always declined. She'd send a gift and explain to my siblings and I that flying under the radar and not drawing attention kept us safe.

We found an empty table and took our seats as the guests filled the other tables, chatting and laughing with cups of wine in their hands. I recognized many of them from the Christmas Eve party at Nancy's home.

Rose walked over to our table and sat down in an empty seat next to Brooke, placing her bouquet down. "Hey, guys."

"You look so beautiful." Brooke leaned in and rested her head on Rose's shoulder. "I'm happy for Nancy."

"Me too." Rose let out a sigh as she looked around the room. "Everything turned out perfect. Luckily, Jack's daughter is an event planner, she did such a great job setting this place up."

"Hey, B, let's go get something to drink," Dmitri offered his arm to Brooke and the two of them walked over to the beverage table.

"When are we leaving?" Lauren whispered now that my brother stood out of ear shot. She scanned the wedding guests enjoying the reception.

"We probably won't be able to slip away until late." Rose furrowed her brow at Lauren's hurry.

"It doesn't matter as long as we're gone before everyone wakes up. We need to get a head start before anyone comes after us," I explained.

"You sure Bryan is going to take care of Dmitri?" Rayn asked, meeting my gaze. "He doesn't even know we're leaving."

"He promised." I shifted in my seat but remained firm in my words. I couldn't let the thought of Dmitri not being cared for take over. It wasn't a possibility. Bryan wouldn't let it happen.

Rayn tilted her head. "But he promised when you were frantic about Mia. He doesn't think he actually has to step up."

I glanced up to see Bryan crossing the room towards us.

"He will," Rose reassured, watching her brother.

As Bryan reached our table, a smile broke out across his face. A song began to play from the DJ booth and Bryan grinned wider, reaching for Rose's hand. She chuckled at the melody and took Bryan's hand. He lifted her arm above her head and spun her around as the music bounced off the walls. Rose Mary's name flowed from the speakers as the siblings moved to the center of the room and danced around each other. Bryan danced differently with Rose than he did when we all went out for Ashley's birthday. His movements were more reserved. The sway in his hips and shoulders were there, but they were conservative. They danced in circles around one another as if they had rehearsed a million times.

An air of innocence surrounded them as they spun around. I pictured the two of them as younger children dancing in the kitchen before the threat of our powers hung over them. Before they feared for their mother's safety.

The photographer quickly held up her lens and snapped photo after photo of Bryan and Rose. They laughed loudly as Rose grabbed Bryan's hand, reaching up on her tiptoes to spin him around. I felt privileged to witness such a sweet moment, but these moments made the knot in my stomach tighten. Thinking about leaving the people I loved behind broke my heart. The girls and I had been left with no choice, but for a split second, we weren't planning our departure. For a moment, we were a family celebrating our love for one another. For a moment, Rose was simply a girl, dancing with her big brother at her mom's wedding.

Rayn linked her arm in mine, reading my face all too well. "I know," she whispered.

Dmitri leaned over to Brooke. "Is Rose short for Rosemary?"

Brooke shook her head. "No, but her middle name is Mary."

The song came to an end and Rose threw her arms around Bryan's neck, holding him close. Her eyes shut tightly, holding back tears; no doubt in my mind the same thoughts buzzed around her head. Leaving Bryan would be painful for both of us.

The reception lasted for another few hours. After dinner, we stayed at our table chatting quietly. We hadn't discussed anything else about our plans for the night but we didn't need to. We needed to take a moment to appreciate the now. I sat next to my brother and we people watched, whispering to one another about the guests we recognized from Christmas Eve and the new ones we hadn't seen before. Bryan spent the evening floating around between our table, his friends and his mom. Ashley spent more time at our table than Bryan, but wanting to flirt with Lauren had a little to do with that. Emma kept her distance, barely making eye contact with me, but I couldn't blame her. Over the course of a few weeks I'd nearly killed her father and her twin sister. Things between Emma and I hadn't been the same since New Year's.

Bryan and Ashley danced in the middle of the floor, each holding a drink in their hands as they spun around one another. I wanted to join them, but I didn't want to bring them down to my level. Bryan laughed with his best friend and I couldn't bear to snuff out the brightness in his eyes. I had put him through enough.

He had been at the attack on the cottage, screamed my name when Erebus gripped my throat in his cold hands. He had watched Amilia fall lifelessly to the ground. Bryan remained right there in the thick of it with us, and I would forever be amazed at his ability to smile at the end of the wreckage.

As the song ended, Ashley returned to our table. She asked for the millionth time that night if Lauren was all right and retrieved her a glass of wine when Lauren lied that everything was fine.

"You know," Rose said, watching Ashley walk off. "I never in a million years would have predicted those two, but they're actually really cute together."

"They are," I agreed.

The DJ announced the final dance of the night, inviting all the couples to join the bride and groom on the dance floor.

Bryan placed a warm hand on my shoulder. His smile lit up the entire room. "Can I have this dance?"

My heart exploded in my chest, maxing out to capacity with love and admiration. Bryan took my hand and led me to the dance floor, spinning me around and pulling me close to his chest. He rested his hand on my hip as we swayed back and forth together, keeping the dance simple so we could lean in as close as possible.

"How're you hanging in there, baby?" Bryan whispered in my ear.

I shrugged against him. "I'm hanging."

"I appreciate you guys all still coming for this. It's trivial in the grand scheme, but I do appreciate it."

I glanced around the room at all the decor and guests. "I've never been to a wedding before."

"Seriously?"

"It's nice though, a nice distraction. And I'm happy to be here with you."

Bryan kissed my temple. "Sorry, I've been bouncing around so much tonight. Whenever I tried making my way back to you, something required my attention."

"Don't worry about it. I knew you'd be busy, you've had a lot of stuff to help with."

"But after this, I'm officially free for the night." He offered a coy smile. "And I've been daydreaming about taking you upstairs to unzip that dress."

Heat flooded my core and I smirked at him. "Well tonight is your lucky night, Bryan McClintock."

The song ended and Bryan lowered his face to mine, giving me a gentle kiss. Before I pulled away, he took my bottom lip between his teeth and nipped enough to send a chill through my body.

"I love you," he whispered as he pulled back, tucking a loose strand of hair behind my ear.

"I love you too."

Chapter Two

Awkward Silence

Lauren

I watched the guests spin around the dance floor. There weren't many of them but they knew how to have a good time. I always enjoyed watching people, seeing the joy on their faces and how they'd experience moments candidly. I could never do that, enjoy anything without worrying what everyone around me thought. I always used to care so much about fitting in. I wanted to be like everyone else because I knew under the surface, I was unlike anyone. Now that I'd been through some shit, I cared less about what everyone thought. I didn't have it in me anymore to worry about such trivial things.

As I scanned the crowd, my eyes fell on the one person whose opinion I did care about. Someone who made me self-aware of every little movement, every detail of my own body.

Ashley spun around with a glass of champagne in her hand, dancing with Bryan. The two of them moved in sync with one another without touching. They danced together without having to dance together. I had never seen two people so platonically in love. It made me jealous, not because I felt threatened by Bryan, but because I wanted to be the one dancing with Ashley.

I shouldn't, not when the girls and I were leaving so soon. If I cared about this girl at all, I'd stay far away from her. Why should Ashley let me into her heart only for me to turn around and leave. I wouldn't even be there when Ashley woke up in the morning, and the hours were quickly ticking away. Hanging out with Ashley had been a fun distraction, but I engaged my tunnel vision.

Nothing else should've mattered but getting to the Hallow. Getting to the witches in the forest was the next step in eradicating the Renati and ripping Erebus' head from his body. I made an oath to myself to stop him before anyone else I cared about got hurt. Then he stormed the cottage and killed Amilia and Warren in front of us. He needed to be stopped, and I wouldn't rest until I had avenged my mother, among everyone else who had been ripped from us.

The song ended, and as if Ashley felt the gravitational pull herself, she wandered over to the table and took the empty seat next to me.

"Are you okay?" Ashley asked. "You don't seem to be having fun."

"Oh, no, I'm okay. It's been a long couple of days, you know?" I forced a smile that I thought would be convincing but Ashley didn't seem to buy it.

Ashley glanced over to the bar. "Can I get you a drink? Maybe help you relax?"

Nothing sounded better but I shook my head. "That's okay."

"I'm getting you a drink," Ashley announced, leaping up from the table and heading straight to the self-serve bar.

I tried to speak up in protest but Ash already stood at the table pouring a glass of wine. I smiled as Ashley carefully walked the full glass back to the table and set it in front of me.

"Drink up."

"Thank you." I took the glass and sipped the white wine. "Go dance, I don't want to bring you down."

Ashley glanced across the way. "I've lost my dance partner."

Bryan had brought Whitney out to the dance floor as a love song played over the speakers. The final dance of the evening.

"They're really sweet," I muttered, watching them cling to one another. I didn't know what hit harder, holding back because we were leaving or giving in knowing it would be over soon. Though I didn't think Whitney necessarily had to worry about the latter. I knew in my heart that Bryan would be waiting for his girl when we got back.

"So, um, would you, uh, maybe want to dance with me?" Ashley stammered.

My face heated in a deep blush. I shouldn't. My inner voice screamed at me to say no, to politely decline but my head and my heart never agreed. Instead, I nodded and the two of us strolled towards the dance floor together.

Ashley offered her hand; her fingers trembled slightly as our palms came together. Ashley's other hand found my waist and I smiled down at her, never so aware of how much taller I stood. My height remained one of my greatest insecurities. Most men weren't attracted to taller women. I had only been with one other woman, who didn't want anyone to know about our relations regardless of physical appearances. But Ashley smiled up at me like no one else in the room existed and my heart squeezed. I smiled away my desire to let a tear fall and stared deep into Ashley's beautiful hazel eyes, admiring the little flecks of gold around her pupils.

Ashley had seemed so confident on dance floors. I had watched her on New Year's Eve, flinging her arms around as she sang at the top of her lungs. Even moments ago as she danced with Bryan, her hips naturally swayed to the beat as she laughed. I didn't think it was possible for Ashley to be nervous while she danced, but her palms were sweaty and her breath quivered as it filled her lungs.

I squeezed Ashley's hand, pulling her an inch closer. I wanted to make Ashley feel many different things, but nervousness and uncertainty were never on the list. I smiled at her and lifted our hands, spinning her around. Ashley giggled, coming back flush against my chest. We swayed together, lost in the moment as we floated on our own cloud until the song ended too soon and the other guests came back into view. The chandelier on the ceiling came back into my vision as I glanced up, realizing we were still on the dance floor in the middle of a semi crowded room.

"Let's go finish those drinks," I offered, leading the way back to their table.

One drink wouldn't be an issue.

I had four.

I giggled into my hand as Ashley and I leaned against the table, deep in conversation.

"Hey, we're going to bed soon," Rose put her hand on my shoulder. "The reception is over."

"Oh, mmhmmm." I stood up and swayed, Ashley quickly wrapping an arm around my waist to keep me steady.

"I've got you," Ashley laughed.

"Get some coffee and sober up," Rose whispered in a stern tone before she stepped away.

I grabbed my untouched glass of water and joined my friends as everyone stood in a circle chatting before they retired for the evening. I glanced across the way and caught Whitney sneaking off towards the elevators with Bryan. Ashley kept her arm around my waist as I caught eye contact with Whitney. She rushed over to our group and gave Dmitri a hug before she disappeared into the elevator.

"Can I show you something?" I turned to Ashley.

"Sure."

"Come on." I took Ashley's hand in mine and led the way towards a door across the room. I knew the door led outside, I'd been watching hotel staff go in and out all night.

The door led to an outdoor patio. Above us hung a blanket of stars twinkling millions of miles away. None of those stars had a care in the world. Tonight, I wanted to be one of those stars.

I sat down on a bench across the patio and patted the seat next to me. Ashley took the invitation and sat close enough for our thighs to touch.

"I wanted to say thank you," I said, my voice low and quiet. "You have been such a good friend through the worst time in my life, and I don't know how I would have handled everything without you to lean on."

Ashley smiled but her eyes reflected disappointment. "That's what friends are for."

Oh.

That did not come out right at all. I reached for her with trembling fingers and took Ashley's cold hand in mine. I gently rubbed the back of her knuckles and smiled into her gaze.

"You know, someone once told me that friendship was a really good starting point for when you don't know where your life is going. And I don't know what my life would look like, but all I know is…when I look into the future, I see you."

Ashley stared back at me, speechless, her eyes gazing down to my lips before looking back up. "Does this mean I can finally kiss you?"

I closed the space between us and crashed my lips to Ashley's. She received me warmly as Ashley wrapped her fingers in my hair and returned the kiss. Her lips were as soft as I had dreamed of and I could die happy knowing for sure. I wanted to lose myself in Ashley's embrace, the perfect place to get lost. Warm, soft, and safe. I tried to push everything else out of my mind, but a little voice in my head spoke treacherous words.

I was leaving in a few hours, and I didn't know when I'd come back.

To be completely honest, I didn't know *if* I'd come back.

I broke the kiss, pulling back slowly. Every inch I moved away from Ashley built up in my chest like an explosion, a lingering heart attack. The desire to grab Ashley's beautiful freckled face and kiss her again clashed with the temporariness of it all. Ashley wanted to kiss me right at that moment, but she would surely feel differently once I disappeared.

"Um, I should probably get to bed. It's been a long day." I stood up, smoothing out the wrinkles in my dress.

"Oh, okay, yeah. Me too." Ashley stood up and messed with her hair, both of us attempting to not look awkward but failing miserably.

"I had a really nice time." I mustered a smile. "Spending time with you is always my favorite part of any day."

"Mine too." Ashley's eyes glistened in the moonlight. "I, uh, I'm crashing at Emma and Byn's apartment tonight."

"Can I walk you to the car?"

Ashley nodded and offered her trembling hand. I clasped it tightly, lacing our fingers together. We walked in silence to the parking lot. A million different things ran through my head but I wouldn't dare speak any of them out loud. Ashley didn't deserve to be weighed down by me. She was a breath of fresh air. An open window on a beautiful spring day while the breeze blew in the scents of blooming flowers and songs of birds coming home from a long winter. I felt like a cellar that had been locked tight for decades, dark and deep. The door on the cellar may not have looked threatening, but the contents inside were best left locked up.

Ashley's car came into view and I cursed it as we came closer. I wished I could explain to Ashley that I had to leave for a while and would fight like hell to come back. How I would be counting the hours until we returned to Rifton and I could see that smile again but I chewed my lip instead.

"You said you have a ride home tomorrow?" Ashley asked again, even though I had told her twice on the drive over.

I nodded. "Yeah, I have plans with the girls tomorrow, but um…drive safe."

Ashley's lips curled but the smile did not reflect in her eyes. "I'll probably hang out here at the apartment. I took the whole weekend off."

"Good," I encouraged. "Enjoy it, you work too hard." I ran my fingers through my hair. "Um, I will text you okay?"

"Yeah, and I'll see you at work."

I fought off the urge to wince, the pain constricted through my body as I nodded. "Goodnight."

I turned and walked away before I came off any more awkward. I had already done enough damage, giving Ashley mixed signals. Kissing her only to disappear the next day. I shook the weight off my shoulders as I entered back into the hotel, heading towards the elevators. Rose had a room on the third floor for all of us, well, almost all of us. I assumed Whitney would be spending the first half of the night elsewhere.

Gently, I knocked on the door of room 319. Brooke opened it, her smile quickly fading as she saw my face.

"You okay?" She stepped back to let me inside.

"Are any of us okay?" I walked into the room.

This room didn't belong to a group of people who had just been to a celebration, it belonged to mourners. A heavy layer of sadness hung in the air and I choked on it, feeling the weight of the cottage's attack in my own chest. Everyone had changed out of their dress clothes and into more comfortable attire. Rose lay on one of the beds, her dress from the wedding replaced with a pair of yoga pants and a sweater. Dmitri sat next to her with his legs crossed, the two of them watching a movie on the television in silence. Rayn sat on the other bed with their spellbook in her lap, her eyes moving across the pages as she skimmed for something.

I flopped down on the bed next to Rayn and groaned into my arms. No one asked if I wanted to talk about it, they knew me well enough by now to know if I wanted to fill them in, I would.

Silence fell over the room but I welcomed it. What were any of us supposed to say?

I glanced up at Rayn, who stared down at the book with heavy eyes. I took Rayn's hand in mine and gave a gentle squeeze.

"I'm okay," Rayn whispered, turning back to the spellbook.

I nodded and pretended I didn't see the stray tear that Rayn quickly wiped away.

Chapter Three

Long Gone

Whitney

After the final dance, all the guests gathered by the doors to send off Nancy and Jack. The newlyweds waved goodbye to their guests and headed off to enjoy the end of their wedding day. The guests that knew one another stayed behind to mingle.

Bryan grabbed my hand and pulled me towards the hallway. "Can I steal you away for the night?"

I looked over my shoulder at our group. They all stood huddled together with Ashley, talking amongst themselves.

"One second," I told Bryan and made my way over. I slipped my arms around Dmitri's middle and squeezed, burying my face in his back.

Dmitri turned and put his arm around my shoulders. "You okay?" he asked.

"Just wanted to say goodnight." I blinked rapidly, keeping the tears locked behind my eyes. I squeezed them shut as I whispered, "I love you so much, Mit."

Dmitri patted my shoulder. "I love you too."

I gave him a final hug before I stepped back, meeting Rayn's worried, blue eyes.

Ray. I mentally said to my sister. *I'm going upstairs with Byn.*

See you in a few hours. She barely glanced my way, giving me a small smile.

I gave our group one final look, making sure I had eyes on everyone, when I noticed Ashley's arm around Lauren's waist. I smiled at my friends who finally decided to admit they were crazy for one another and buried the sorrow that tomorrow morning Lauren would have disappeared. I didn't know what she'd told Ashley, if anything. However Lauren decided to approach the subject was her choice.

After a quick elevator ride, Bryan slipped the key into the slot above the door handle. The light turned green, unlocking with a click. He pushed the door back, exposing a tidy hotel room with a giant king sized bed. The hotel had been newly renovated with dark gray carpet and cream colored wallpaper that echoed around the landscape paintings hanging on the walls.

"Troy, Emma and Ash are staying at the apartment tonight, so I wanted to get us somewhere more private." Bryan led the way further into the room. "I already brought your bags up from the car and grabbed your things from Rose's room."

A chill ran up my spine, sending panic through my veins. I had hidden the enchanted backpack in the trunk of my car. Air constricted in my chest as I asked, "My backpack too?"

"Yep, everything you had in the trunk." He gave a soft smile.

I slipped off his suit jacket and laid it carefully on the back of a green upholstered chair, doing my best to give off a calm facade. "Thank you, baby. You didn't have to do all this."

"I wanted to. Rose's room is down the hall for the girls and Mit to crash in so we can stay close and still have our own space." Bryan took a step towards me and rested his hand on my waist. "I've been going a hundred miles a minute since six am, and I could really use a shower," he paused and licked his bottom lip. "What do you think?"

I glanced over my shoulder towards the bathroom. I hadn't been under the water since I'd passed out after the cottage attack and woke up fully dressed in the shower with Bryan.

I pushed the thought of the flying debris and blood on the floor out of my mind. I wanted to get back into my element without thinking about everything I had lost. I wanted a new memory to replace the aftermath of the cottage attack. I needed something good to think about when I felt the water rain down on my skin. I wanted Bryan's warm body against mine and eager hands caressing every inch.

"I don't need convincing to get in the water." I waved my hand behind my head and the water from the showerhead rained into the tub.

Bryan's hands slid up to the back of my dress, skimming around for the zipper that he slowly pulled down, taking his sweet time. I took his face in my hands, tilting his head to look down at me. My fingers slid down his neck to the first button of his dress shirt.

"Promise me something," I whispered as I undid the first button.

"Anything."

"Promise you won't resent me when this is all said and done. I don't know what the future looks like or what is going to happen, but I don't want you to hold hard decisions against me." I knew as the words left my mouth I had no right to feel this way, to think I could do and say whatever I wanted because these were unprecedented times. I needed to know that he would still love me when I came back from the Hallow. I couldn't force him to forgive me, but I wanted to hear something I could hold on to.

Bryan studied my face as he ran his hands up to my shoulders, grazing his thumb along my jawline. "What are you really asking?"

"I'm scared of losing you in the midst of all this. It's chaotic and traumatizing and...I hope you still think I'm worth it at the end."

I looked up into his eyes, waiting for the words of reassurance to spill from his lips. I knew Bryan well enough, he would keep my demons at bay before he carried me into the shower. He would make sure he eased my mind before he turned his attention to my body.

"You know, I thought about us while I stood up there during the ceremony." Bryan's warm palm glided across my back.

"Me too," I admitted, relieved to hear that he still pictured that kind of future with me.

"And what did you see?"

I smiled, running my fingers through his hair. "A future that sometimes doesn't feel real."

"What do you mean?" he asked.

"With everything going on...losing my mom and Amilia and Warren. Life is fragile and the stakes are so high. Sometimes I wonder what things are going to look like after the dust settles."

"Hey, look at me." Bryan cupped my cheek, turning my face towards his. "No matter what happens or how things go, I'm going to be there at the end of it. I'm going to be there loving you. Nothing will ever change that, okay?"

I nodded and mustered a smile as he brought me into a gentle kiss. "So, shower?" I grabbed the front of his shirt and took a step backwards.

Bryan looked over his shoulder towards our luggage. "Let me grab a condom."

"No," I whispered. "I don't want anything between us tonight."

"Oh?" He raised his eyebrows in surprise.

"I've been diligent about my birth control, same time every day."

"In that case, why are my pants still on?"

I kissed him with force, gliding my fingers into his hair as he slid my dress down to my hips. His touch still lit a fire under my skin, no matter how familiar I'd grown with the feel. He took a step forward, walking us towards the running water of the shower without breaking the kiss. If this would be the last night I'd get with him for who knows how long, I planned to take full advantage of it.

We left the rest of our clothing in a trail to the shower. As we stepped into the water, I wrapped my arms around him, pulling his mouth back to mine. He pressed me against the cold shower wall, his weight pinning me into place as the water rained down on us. I jumped up against him and wrapped my legs around his waist as we deepened the kiss. Bryan lifted me with ease and ground his hips against mine as I played with his wet hair that slightly curled up at the back of his neck. His lips trailed kisses down my throat, causing my blood to spark with desire.

"I love you," he reassured. "I will always love you."

I rolled my hips against his erection that pressed hard against my center. His gasp turned into a groan that vibrated through his chest as my fingers met his wet skin. All the heat in my body pooled in my core hearing his response to me, feeling how rock hard he was when we had barely gotten started. I had been begging him for reassurance, for whispers of sweet words to cling to, but he needed something too. I wanted him to feel loved and cherished, to think back to this moment and know in his core that what we have is real.

I put my hand on his chest and gently pushed. Bryan set my feet down on the floor and created some space between us. I sank down to my knees before him, glancing up to meet those perfect green eyes. He looked down at me, his lips parted as he let out a breath, whispering my name like a prayer.

I grabbed the base of his erection and swirled my tongue around his tip. My name turned into a swear on his lips as his fingers tangled into my wet hair. He grabbed the back of my head as I slid his length into my mouth. I took him back as far as I could and he kept his hips still, letting me take my time. Letting me take full control.

My lips longed for his base, to take all of him and worship him like he had done for me so many times. I looked up, watching him come undone at my touch. His head tilted back and his groan echoed through the bathroom as I bobbed my head. I reached up and ran my fingers down his stomach.

He grabbed my wrist and looked down. As our eyes locked, his erection twitched against my tongue. Everything constricted inside of me; pins and needles across my skin. I wanted to egg him on, to feel him thrust in my mouth. I wanted to watch him lose control but he pulled away. He grabbed my shoulders and brought me to my feet, planting a gentle kiss to my lips.

"If I'm going to come inside you tonight, it won't be your mouth," he muttered. I melted, digging my nails into his skin as I grabbed him.

Bryan snaked his arm around my waist and picked me back up, pinning me against the shower wall. His tongue grazed mine and he took my bottom lip between his teeth, shooting electric shocks through my body.

I reached between us and helped him glide inside of me. He moaned into my neck as he tightened his grip on my thighs to keep me up against the wall, angling his hips to go deeper. I clung to his shoulders but he didn't seem to need help holding onto me as he thrust. His lips moved up my neck to nibble on my earlobe.

I loved how easily our bodies fit together; how he paid extra attention to the little things he knew made me tick. His hand slid down my thigh to grab my ass. His breath was warm against my skin as he said my name, whispering how he could die right there in that moment.

Being with Bryan and the energy from the water flowing through the shower revitalized me in a way I didn't think possible. All the sorrow and uncertainty I'd felt throughout the day washed away. All that existed in the entirety of the universe was Bryan's body moving in perfect sync with mine.

He didn't last as long without the condom. With a final thrust, he stayed buried deep in me. His groan vibrated against my neck as I clung to him, my fingers tangled in his wet hair. He slowly lowered my feet to the tub floor and peppered kisses over my face. I giggled as he nudged the tip of his nose against mine.

"I've never done that without protection before," he admitted. "That was...addicting."

I waited a moment, making sure I'd heard his soft voice over the noise of the shower. "Wait, never?"

He shook his head. "I've always been cautious, but with you I seem to throw caution to the wind. In this case, I think I'll keep the bad habits."

I laughed, kissing his shoulder. "Let's get cleaned up. Where are the little bottles of soap?"

After we actually showered, I stood next to the bed wrapped in a towel, drying my hair. I felt the swirl of adoration and lust from Bryan's emotions before he brushed against my back. He pressed his lips on my bare shoulder and the towel around my body fell to the floor.

"Back for more?" I joked, turning around to kiss him.

He pressed his body against mine and pulled me close. His fingers slid down my skin, leaving goosebumps. "I will *never* get tired of this."

He shoved me back onto the bed and buried his face between my thighs.

I waited until Bryan's breathing turned slow and deep. Once he started snoring, I took my chance to leave while I still had the nerve.

Carefully, I wrapped my fingers around his wrist and moved his arm off of me. He stirred for a moment, letting out a sigh before he rolled onto his back and settled in. I stayed still as a statue until I knew he'd fallen back to sleep. I had never gotten out of bed so slowly. Every variant in his breathing caused me to turn back to make sure I hadn't woken him. I tiptoed across the hotel room and gently opened the closet door, retrieving the backpack I had tried to keep hidden from him.

Stowed away in the front pocket were two envelopes, one with his name on it and the other for Dmitri. I couldn't tell them where we were going but at least I could let them know we were leaving. I took the envelopes from my bag and left them on the bedside table. The faint light from the alarm clock reflected off the diamond bracelet on my wrist. No way I could take this priceless gift into the woods with me. Swallowing the lump in my throat, I unhooked the bracelet from my wrist and lay it on top of the letter.

My eyes wandered over to Bryan and I froze, taking in how perfect he looked. His arm over his head with his face nuzzled into the pillow. His bare chest rising and falling with every breath. I wanted to reach out and touch him. One last touch to cling to.

"I'll come back," I whispered, swallowing my sorrow as a tear fell down my cheek. "I promise."

I closed the door behind me quietly, turning to see the other girls waiting for me in the hallway. They all had backpacks filled with the necessities; what we assumed would be necessities, anyway. A jolt went through me as I saw their eyes glued to my cheek. I wiped the tears away as quickly as I could, but they didn't stop coming.

"Aden is waiting at the trailhead." Rayn held onto the strap of her backpack. "Nic is coming to get the car, right?"

"Yeah, he said he'll be here on the first bus out. I left letters for Bryan and Dmitri both." I wiped away the last of the tears and cleared my throat.

"What do they say?" Rayn asked.

"I explained that we had to go and why we needed to go on our own. That Bryan and Nic would look after Mit until we got back."

Rayn nodded with heavy eyes.

I looked each of them in the eyes before I spoke again. "Ready?"

"Yes, let's go," Lauren answered quickly, tightening the strap of her backpack. She turned and headed down the hallway.

Brooke and Rayn followed Lauren, but Rose stayed put with her eyes glued to the door I'd come through.

"I didn't even think to write him anything," she muttered, tears stuck in her throat.

"I told him in my letter that we both loved him, more than he knew." Hot tears built in my own chest.

Rose nodded and held out her hand. "Let's go find the Hallow."

I mustered the most convincing smile I could and took her hand in mine.

Outside, the sun still slept behind the mountain tops, but we would be long gone before it rose into the sky.

Chapter Four
A Rough Start
Whitney

The night sky still hung over us as I parked my car at the trailhead leading up to Falcon Ridge. My knees trembled as I opened the door and stepped onto the asphalt. Aden waited for us by the bulletin board at the end of the parking lot, his backpack secured over his quiver of bolts for the crossbow.

Rayn waved to him as she got out of the car. I secured my bag and left the keys under the driver's seat mat for Nicky. My head tilted back as I attempted to look up the mountain. Even in the darkness, I could tell it stood much steeper up close than it had appeared from the kitchen window of Bryan and Emma's apartment.

"How the hell are we going to climb that thing?" Rayn asked my worried thoughts aloud.

In the days I had to prepare for our trek to the Hallow, not a single part of me wondered how I'd haul my out of shape body up the cliff. My heart sank into my stomach as I attempted to convince myself I wouldn't pass out in the first few hours.

"We'll be okay." I squared my shoulders.

Lauren glanced over at me, seeing right through my facade. Her face gave her thoughts away as she rolled her lips inward, though she didn't say a word.

"If you want to be out of town before the sun rises, I suggest we start climbing." Aden rested his hand on his hip, right above his pistol.

I wondered if Aden held the same gun he shot magic numbing darts at us, or if it was a new gun he acquired during his time away. Through everything we'd gone through, I never thought to ask. When the hunters abandoned him to die in the woods, they didn't leave him armed. Of all of us, Aden would be the one who could scale the entire mountain side without breaking a sweat. Being a genetically modified witch hunter had its perks, I supposed.

Rayn headed up the trail first, her long legs climbing the steady incline with ease. Rose put her arm around Brooke's shoulder and gave a gentle squeeze before they followed behind. Lauren stood next to the sign and stared behind us towards town, planted in place.

"Lo?" I asked, startling her. "It's time."

"Yeah, I guess it is." She moved past me and jogged to catch up with our group.

I took a deep sigh, giving the mountain one final glare before I took my first step up the trail. Aden waited until I began my climb before he came up the trail after me, staying a yard or so behind.

The first few hours of travel were brutal. My thighs screamed and my lungs squeezed, sending shooting pain through my chest as my breaths turned to pants. No one spoke a word as we moved; the further we went, the steeper it became.

The sun hung high in the sky when Aden came up next to me. "Maybe you should lead, since you have the map. And, um, so you don't get left behind."

"We don't have to rush." Brooke reached for her water bottle. "We haven't had any time to train for this."

"I'm sorry." Tears blurred my vision as I attempted to catch my breath. "I'm holding us back."

"No, we'll go at your pace. We have time," Rose encouraged. "We are following this same trail until the waterfalls."

Lauren nodded. "No one is following us, so no need to wear ourselves down."

"Okay." I pulled my water bottle out and took a long drink.

Brooke reached inside her bag, retrieving small vials with swirling bright green liquid inside. "We should all take some of the energy potion Rose created. This is the kind of event she made them for."

"Good idea." Rose took a vial from Brooke and tossed it back like a shot.

I uncorked the vial Brooke handed me and downed the liquid. The taste of lemonade coated my tongue. A jolt of energy shot through my body, perking my senses. I felt my posture straighten and the ache in my muscles vanished.

"What did you put in this?" I asked Rose, looking down my body.

Rose smiled. "Pretty cool, huh? Come on, let's take advantage of it."

I offered a small nod and led the way, following Nic's map as best as I could but his sloppy handwriting left much to the imagination. Aden brought up the rear, his head on a constant swivel looking at every bird in the sky as if they might attack us. He turned to listen to every little sound that echoed through the trees. This trail served as a main hiking trail, designed for those who desired a more challenging adventure. The chilling winter weather meant the chances of anyone else being on the trail was rare. The air lingered with a crisp cold that settled deep into my bones. I felt the snow approaching quicker than I had anticipated.

I couldn't tell if it was the moisture in the air perking my senses or the energy potion. The muscles in my calves strengthened with each step I took up the path. I reached out for a low hanging branch and pulled myself up to the top of the hill. Once I got to the top, I took a moment to look around and drink in the view.

All of Falcon Bay displayed out before us in a spectacular sight, blending into the coastline. Waves crashed up against the giant rocks that sat in the ocean. The water sprayed over the rough edges of the rocks as each wave rolled towards the shore. I could almost feel the salted mist on my face as I watched the waves dance.

"Wow," Rayn breathed, coming up behind me. "Look at that."

"I wonder if Falcon Bay has the same problem with Renati or if it's just Rifton," I asked.

"It's close to the Allurement so I imagine it does." Brooke huffed as she made it to the top as well. "The concentration of energy is supposed to call out to all witches, yeah?"

"That's how I understand it." I scanned the taller buildings of the city until my gaze landed on the university. Were my guys okay? Bryan must've found the letter explaining why we left them behind. How upset had Dmitri been? Endless questions flooded my mind, but I pushed them out. I didn't have the energy or the time to spare.

"Come on, little witches." Aden yanked on the strap over his shoulder, adjusting his backpack. "Let's keep going."

That night, the girls and I settled into our tent. The three person tent fit the five of us when we cuddled. I nestled between Rayn and Lauren, pulling the blanket down to cool off from Rayn's body heat radiating into my skin. It wasn't even the warmth that kept me awake, but thinking about the man who usually warmed me on a cold winter night. I laid on my back, staring up at the ceiling of the tent pretending the rock in the middle of my shoulder blades didn't bother me.

I sighed, listening to the sounds of the forest. The breeze blew through the branches, rustling the leaves and the insects chirped up at the moon. I hoped it would be a lullaby from mother nature to help me fall asleep. But the rustling in the leaves came with a set of heavy steps and I shot straight up in my sleeping bag. I reached out to shake my sister's shoulder as Aden's voice bellowed through the campsite.

"Move!" His scream dripped with urgency and fear.

"Wake up! Get out of the tent!" I shouted to the girls as I scrambled out of the sleeping bag. My knees trembled as I hurried, causing me to stumble.

I unzipped the tent so quickly the teeth of the zipped cut the palm of my hand. I had the flap half way open when my sister grabbed Brooke's shoulders and shoved her through. Rose and Lauren scrambled after her, tripping over each other to get out as quickly as possible. I pushed Rayn out of the tent before she had the chance to argue with me. I ducked under the flap to escape when the tent collapsed on top of me and a sharp pain pierced my calf. The searing sting exploded, soaring through my body as if my entire leg burned.

I released a scream and put up a shield. Giant hoofs attached to long skinny legs shredded the tent and trampled over the top of the shimmering energy force. If I didn't have the shield up, I likely would not have survived the attack.

"Whitney!" Rayn's cry echoed through the trees as shots from Aden's crossbow followed behind. Four bolts left the bow before Aden pulled his gun from his holster and shot into the night. The silencer on the end of the barrel muffled the explosions.

I kept my shield up, not knowing what came next and worried I'd get clipped by a stray bullet since whatever the hell Aden shot at remained close to my head.

Silence.

"Whit!" The girls all scrambled to me, four sets of hands tearing through the shredded tent, digging for me. I lowered my shield and whimpered. I tried to move my leg but pain shot through my body. Tears escaped my eyes and I trembled from the overwhelming burning.

"Whit!" Rayn pulled me close but I cried out again when she moved me.

"My leg," I hissed through my teeth. "What was that thing?"

"A moose," Rose answered, grabbing my hand. "Aden killed it."

"It stepped on me." I clenched my jaw, trying to focus on anything but the pain. The strong iron tinge of wet blood overwhelmed my senses.

"Oh," Brooke's voice whispered as she assessed my leg. "Don't move, Whit. No one move her."

I lifted my head but I couldn't get a good view of my wound in the dark. Through the tears in my eyes, I saw bright white reflecting against the moonlight.

"Is that–" I began to ask when Brooke held up her hand.

"I said don't move." Brooke placed her palms above my leg. Her magic left her hand in bright golden swirls, twirling down to my leg where my bone began to fuse back together.

Rayn's arms wrapped around me and I buried my face into her hoodie. The fabric stifled my scream to keep from drawing the attention of any other predators. We didn't need something else strolling over to kick us while we were vulnerable. Rose squeezed my hand and Lauren held onto my shoulders. Once the pain dulled down to a steady throb, I let out a deep breath and lifted my head.

"Are you okay?" Brooke asked, short of breath. She leaned back to sit on her feet and wiped the sweat from her brow with the back of her hand.

I nodded, daring to move my leg. The mobility returned, the white hot pain vanished completely. The skin had healed into a soft pink scar.

"That could have killed you." Lauren squeezed my shoulder as I sat up. "Good thinking on that shield."

"B, are you good?" Rose reached out for Brooke, who still struggled to catch her breath.

"Yeah," she gently nodded her head. "Just tired."

Aden approached us, his boots crunching foliage beneath him. "It's going to snow tomorrow night. We need to cover as much ground as we can."

"How can you tell?" Rayn glanced up at him.

"I checked the weather forecast before we left."

"I can feel it in the air." I got up on my knees, slowly daring to put weight on my leg. It felt good as new.

The moose's body lay motionless a few yards away, long legs twisted. A puddle of blood pooled underneath its massive body. Aden walked over to the moose and yanked the four bolts out of the carcass, cleaning them with a rag before adding them back into the black leather quiver strapped to his back.

I let out a deep breath, letting it vibrate past my lips as I assessed the damage done to our tent. Rose quickly waved her hand over the mess, stitching the tent back together and putting everything to the way it was before the moose attack.

We still had a long way to go before we reached the Hallow. The witches had hidden themselves deep in the forest after the Renati drove them out of Rifton. After everything I'd learned about our history and the Elemental generations before us, a part of me didn't blame the Renati for feeling the way they did. If I had been raised Renati and spent my entire life believing generations of my family that Elemental magic was corrupt and inherently evil, I would have feared for my life. Especially when eight Elementals appeared in Rifton within a few months of one another. But the Renati's hands were not as clean as they believed. They thought they were protecting their way of life and the future of their families, but Erebus had done nothing but kill innocent people.

Warren and Amilia's faced flashed to the forefront of my memory; their lifeless eyes staring back at me as each of them died. They were gone, and I hadn't been strong enough to protect them. The girls and I had failed so many people, let so much slip through our fingers. We had to get to the Hallow and find the missing pages of the Shepherd's book. We had to unlock the power trapped within our talismans and end this fight with Erebus once and for all. We owed it to everyone who had died protecting us.

I couldn't let their sacrifices be in vain. I couldn't let all of this end being taken out by a fucking moose.

After we had cleaned up the mess, the girls and I settled into our tent while Aden took care of the body. Rayn helped him by levitating it away from the camp to not attract animals coming for an easy meal. Aden repeated numerous times how the moose had been a waste of a beautiful creature. He didn't want its life to be lost in vain either, even if it had been the one who attacked first.

Slipping back into my sleeping bag as if I hadn't almost died felt surreal. This time, we put a shield up around the entire campsite. We would have to cover as much ground as possible tomorrow to try and get ahead of the storm. According to Nic's instructions, the Hallow shouldn't be more than a three day journey into the woods but a blizzard would definitely slow us down. I sighed and reached out for my sister, snuggling close to her back. She scooted closer against me.

"Any chance of us getting sleep tonight?" she whispered throughout the tent.

"Probably not, but we have to try," Rose answered from the other side of Rayn. "If you want, we can sleep in shifts. That way one of us is awake in case anything else happens.

I'll go first, you guys get some sleep. Especially Whit and B, you two need to sleep off that attack."

"Okay," I whispered, knowing Rose would keep a close eye out. I closed my eyes tight, pretending I lay in my warm bed next to Bryan and not crammed in a tent with my generation in the middle of the dangerous Dark Star Forest.

Chapter Five
Mental Check-In
Lauren

The next morning, I woke up to the sunrise. Slivers of light peeked through the mesh at the top of the tent. When I stirred in my sleeping bag, Brooke already sat up awake fiddling with her potion book. I stretched out the crick in my back, trying to release the tension in my muscles. My body felt still and rigid, like I'd aged five years in one night. Rose, Whitney and Rayn were fast asleep all huddled together. Rose nestled deep in her sleeping bag with the blanket up around her face, only tufts of messy brunette strands visible. Rayn slept with her arm covering her eyes, mouth hanging open slightly.

"We should get going." Brooke glanced at the girls.

I felt bad waking them when they were in such a deep sleep, but Brooke had a point.

"Whit, wake up." I gently shook her shoulder. When she didn't budge, I shook her a bit harder. "Whitney."

She jolted awake, shooting straight up in her sleeping bag with the back of her dark hair sticking in all directions. "What's wrong?"

"Nothing, I'm sorry." I rubbed her arm. "It's morning. It's time to get moving."

"Oh." She rubbed her face and sighed heavily. "Okay, yeah, I'm up."

The commotion of waking Whitney startled Rose and Rayn, warranting groans of protest. Rose stretched her arms over her head before she crawled out of her sleeping bag and rummaged through her backpack. She pulled out her toothbrush and left the tent without a word.

"How long have you been up?" Rayn asked Brooke, who still messed with little potion vials from her mobile apothecary.

In Brooke's lap sat a small wooden box that opened to layers of little drawers and compartments, similar to the book Amilia had given Rose. Only Brooke made this wooden box herself in woodshop. She had Rayn burn the Elemental symbol on the cover; the connected circles of the symbol took up the entire front plate of the box.

"A while," Brooke answered, handing each of us a small vial of energy potion. "Rose woke me up a few hours ago so she could get some rest."

"I'm hungry," Rayn said. "Any chance of getting some breakfast before we head out?"

"No," Aden's gruff voice answered from above our heads. I peeked out the tent's open flap to see big, black boots firmly planted on the dirt. "We should have left already."

Rayn groaned and began folding her blankets up to put into her pack. She shoved a thick quilt, sleeping bag, and her pillow all into her backpack without so much as a bulge in the fabric.

We got ready to leave in a hurry, quickly brushing our teeth and running a hair brush through our tangled manes. Once the tent had been packed up, we headed towards the waterfalls.

The rock formation of Falcon Ridge grew larger as we moved closer. The rocks were such a mystery. Everyone said the formation was natural but I saw no way these rocks eroded over the years to resemble a falcon on their own. The sharp rock break of the falcon seemed too perfectly pointed and the rocks curved into the wings too smoothly. It had to be magic.

"We're getting close to the falls," Whitney announced, motioning towards her right. "I can feel the water up ahead."

The closer we got to the falls, the louder the sound carried through the air, seeping into my bones. Lush green moss hung from the trees, covering the rocks and fallen logs that lay on the forest floor. The crisp air smelt of wet earth and I found it easier to take a deep breath here than down by the coast. How strange. Higher up in the mountains, I should have had a harder time breathing, but the altitude didn't seem to phase me a bit. Being an Air Elemental must have had something to do with it.

The white and dark blue water fell like a curtain into a pool that spilled into a roaring river. The river had cut its path in the dirt from years of erosion. Large rocks lay scattered in the river but the water didn't seem to mind; it pushed and crashed around the rocks with ease. Mist from the falls left droplets that slipped down the rock's sides and the mist rose up to where we stood, looking out over the scene.

A little bridge down the hiking trail allowed for a closer look at the falls, but none of us budged. I noticed Whitney inching close to the edge of the lookout as if the water lured her closer, but she remained with us.

I had been hiking up here a couple times before, I had stood in this very spot with my parents. They had taken pictures and helped me stand up on the railing to get a better look at the falls. My dad held my waist tightly as I reached out, feeling the mist on my face. My mom had run her fingers across the sword ferns and showed me all the various mushrooms she found growing at the base of the trees. My mom had put her arm around my shoulder and said, *we can't eat them, but aren't they so pretty in their own way?*

An ache grew in my chest knowing I'd never come back to this place with my mom again; she'd never see the falls or run her fingers along the bark of the tall trees. I turned away from the scene, blinking away the tears that threatened to overwhelm my system. I cleared my throat and gritted my teeth, only allowing one teardrop to fall.

Though this place remained a fond childhood memory, something about standing there with my generation felt different. As if I had been seeing the world for the first time.

"If I had to run away, I would definitely pick this place," Rose breathed.

After we finished admiring the waterfall, Whitney pulled out her map. I let out a sigh of relief that we had actually gone the right way following Nic's instructions. It had been so many years since he'd been to the Hallow, I wondered if his memory was on point. Since I'd been up here before, I could've at least gotten us to the falls, but my firsthand knowledge ended there.

Whitney smiled, pointing to the left. "This way."

"And just in time." Rose commented, holding out her hand to catch a falling snowflake.

I chortled. "We might need to take advantage of the hot springs if the snow keeps falling."

The storm had finally arrived. Snow flurried down all around us, sticking to the ground and our gear. I dug in my bottomless backpack for my white beanie and slid it on my head.

Aden huffed in irritation. "Where do you intend to camp for the night?"

"I don't." Whitney marched towards the side trail barely visible to the eye. "We need to keep going. According to Nic, we are approaching the edge of the Hallow's shield. We can make it if we keep going."

The rest of us all looked at each other. I side-eyed Brooke, silently asking if Whitney had finally lost her sanity.

"Whit." Rayn took a step towards her sister. "If the forest inside the shield is anything like Nic described, we should be rested to deal with it."

"But we're so close–"

"Yeah and once we get there it's all business and making first impressions." I buried my shivering hands into my pockets. "We want to give off strong, independent women vibes. They won't take us seriously if we show up half-dead."

Whitney sighed. "Okay, but we're going to get snowed in."

"We can put up a shield, it'll be fine." Rose's boots crunched in the newly-fallen snow. "My suggestion is to move further into this trail away from the waterfall and set up camp. Put up a shield that will block the snow and any other animals."

"Okay, yeah, good idea. Find somewhere you think looks decent." Whitney put her hand out to let Rose take the lead and fell towards the back of the group with me. Brooke and Rayn followed close behind Rose.

"You okay?" I asked once we began moving again. "I know that moose thing last night was crazy but your vibes are off."

"I'm worried about Mit and Bryan," Whitney admitted, staring off into the distance.

I chewed on my bottom lip. "They'll be okay. Dmitri's powers are growing stronger every day and Bryan is intuitive. They'll take care of each other. Plus the Magisters won't let anything happen to them." I paused, watching my breath fog in the cold. "Maybe after their attack on the cottage...maybe the Renati will–"

"Maybe they'll what?" Whitney cut me off. "Maybe they'll retreat after finally hitting us where it hurts? No, I don't think they will." She turned away from me. "I know we left the guys protected but it's hard not to wonder what is going on with us gone. If they panicked when we left or if they were relieved."

I stopped in my tracks, causing Aden to nearly run me over. Feeling Aden against my back, I started moving again. "Why on earth would your boyfriend and brother be relieved that you left?"

"I wonder sometimes." Whitney let out a quivering breath. "If their lives would be any easier without me around."

"Oh, Whit." I reached out and put my arm around her shoulder, giving a gentle squeeze. "I wish you could have seen the way you and Bryan looked on New Year's Eve. Confetti in your hair, smiling at one another like two goofy idiots in love. They're probably worried about us, but their lives are not easier without you. Especially Dmitri, you're his favorite sister."

"Hey!" Rayn turned around and scoffed at me. "I heard that!"

"I'm sorry," I chuckled. "Dmitri and Whitney get along better, you two are always fighting."

"They always have." Whitney reached up and grabbed my hand on her shoulder. "Ever since we were kids they've been at each other's throats."

"I still love him." Rayn crossed her arms. "I still worry about him. He's still my little brother."

I shook my head. "I didn't mean to hurt your feelings, Ray, I'm trying to cheer up your emo sister over here. Talking shit about how Bryan and Mit would be better off without her."

"You know better than that," Rose commented from the front of the pack. "And I think I found our campsite."

We followed Rose to a clearing off the faded trail. A few large rocks sat in the middle but she easily moved those aside with a wave of her hand. Once we had camp set up for the night, a wave of exhaustion crashed over me. I couldn't tell if the energy potion had worn off or if the events of the past week had finally caught up to me. It was smart to stop for the night and get to the Hallow rested.

The girls and I stood in a circle holding hands, erecting an energy shield around the camp. My generation's magic swirled together, weaving a perimeter. I felt confident it would hold throughout the night. There wasn't anything in this forest stronger than a complete generation of Elementals.

None of us spoke much as we ate sandwiches around a fire. The smoke rose up to the top of the energy shield and stopped, spilling back down around it.

"Should we open up part of the shield to vent the smoke?" Rose asked, glancing up at the dark cloud forming above us.

"Oh." Rayn looked up and waved her hand, allowing the smoke to pass through the shield.

"We can't let this fire burn for long. The smoke could attract someone," Aden warned, taking the last bite of jerky and wiping his hands on his pants. "Finish eating so we can put it out."

"How are we going to stay warm through the night without the fire?" I asked, watching Aden dig around in his bag.

"You have magical powers, you'll be fine." Aden set up his sleeping bag and crawled inside without another word.

We sat in silence for a moment, looking at Aden's back before I spoke again. "You know, for someone who has dedicated themselves to keeping us safe, he isn't very pleasant."

"He's nervous." Rayn ran her fingers through her bangs. "We're going to a colony of witches who won't be excited to see a hunter. He doesn't really know what to expect."

"That's understandable." Whitney nodded, watching Aden's steady breathing. "If we were walking into a hunter den with nothing but the word of a small group that we'd be safe, I'd feel the same way."

I wondered if he'd actually fallen asleep that quickly or lay there listening to our whispers about him. I sighed. "You're right. I'm sorry."

"Don't be, it's okay." Rayn stretched her arms over her head. "It's been a long week."

"It has." Rose hugged her knee to her chest. "Mental check-in. Where are you guys at? Are you okay?"

"Not really," Rayn answered without hesitation. "I can't believe Mia and Warren are gone."

"I'm sure Mom was happy to finally see them again." Whitney's eyes welled with tears.

Rayn nodded, wiping a tear from her cheek.

"We left quite the mess behind us." Brooke squeezed her eyes shut. "Harmony is probably pulling her hair out dealing with Amilia's affairs and…I don't even want to think about my parents."

"It's not unreasonable to think you'd run away after they locked you up in the psych ward like that." Anger flared in Rose's voice. "They pushed you away. We would've had to charm them either way with how they were abusing you."

I sighed, seeing my mom's face whenever I closed my eyes. "At least you have someone to worry about you."

"Nicky promised he would check on your dad while we're gone," Whitney offered, as if that would ease the tension building in my shoulders. "And he is going to charm Nancy and B's parents. There won't be a disaster waiting for us when we go back home."

I nodded silently in response, not wanting to argue.

"Byn is going to be so pissed off about our mom getting charmed again." Rose took a deep breath, the words catching in her throat. "I have no idea how he is going to deal with everything and take care of Mit while keeping himself afloat."

"Have we put too much on Bryan?" Whitney asked.

"He said he wanted to be part of it, this is being part of it. I know it sounds harsh but this shit is heavy. He knew that going into it." I rebutted.

"Dmitri..." Brooke sighed, covering her face in her hands. "I can't believe we left him behind."

"I didn't want to." Whitney's tone turned defensive. "At least he has Abe back."

Brooke turned to face her. "Whit, it's not a personal attack on your guardianship. I feel bad. He's going to take it personally."

"We all feel bad about leaving Mit." Rayn looked around at all of us. "None of us are all right but we are going to keep pushing forward anyway, okay? And that starts with getting some rest. We don't have to sleep in shifts tonight with the shield so–"

"So if you're done talking about your feelings, get some damn sleep." Aden huffed from his sleeping bag.

"Go to sleep, you big grump." Rayn stood up from her seat.

"Go ahead," I told the girls. "I'm right behind you."

"You sure?" Rose asked, hesitant.

"Yeah, yeah, I'll only be a second." I waved at them to go ahead.

The girls shuffled into the tent, leaving their shoes at the zipped door. I ventured to the edge of the shield and let out a deep sigh.

Whitney's earlier concerns echoed in my head.

What if everyone back home was better off without us?

What if Ashley was better off without me?

I may have convinced Whitney that those words weren't true, but now I began to have second thoughts about all of it. Not the hiking through the forest to find the Hallow part, that was a necessity. The Renati needed to pay for what they'd done and what they'd taken from me.

I began to second guess my personal choices. I shouldn't have gone to Falcon Bay for New Year's Eve. I shouldn't have spent my shifts chatting with Ashley, taking every little excuse I could to talk to her. I shouldn't have kissed her after the wedding. Worse, I kissed her and then skipped town. I had never been great at relationships, but I knew that had been a mistake.

I hadn't told any of the other girls about what had happened, especially not Whitney. It's not that I didn't trust her. I thought of Whitney as the closest friend I had in this world, but her opinion would be biased. She'd want Ash and I to be together. Whitney would want to go on double dates. And I wanted those things too, but something brewed deeper than my desire to finally kiss a pretty girl in public.

My hatred of the Renati.

I'd be damned if I gave them someone else to take away from me. But my heart and my brain were conflicted. With each step I took away from Ashley, the more I wondered if her life would be better without me.

My absence may have put my parents in danger, but they couldn't change their relation to me. Ash, on the other hand, could potentially move on with life as if we'd never met.

Before I headed back to the tent for the night, I took a moment to look up at the stars. The night appeared silent and peaceful, not a single pine needle out of place. I took a long moment admiring the moon, hoping that everyone back home stayed safe. Hoping our loved ones were looking up at the same moon and thinking about us. Not worrying if we're okay but knowing that we were capable enough to do this. No one had given us the opportunity to prove ourselves until now. This was our chance to show everyone back home how far we'd come since the girls and I stumbled into one another six months ago.

Chapter Six

Ambush

Whitney

"Are you sure we're going the right way?" Brooke asked, swatting a branch out of her face as we trekked further down the trail.

"I think so. I'm following Nic's map as best as I can." I took another look at the scribbled ink.

"And we trust the old flame gave us the right instructions?" Aden called up from the back of the group, keeping his crossbow close in his arms.

"With my life. Nic wouldn't send us on a goose chase through the woods," I defended over my shoulder. "He let me know there would be no trail for us to follow and that we would have to rely on Aden's tracking skills."

"There is nothing for me to track." Aden held his arms out in frustration.

"We all know Nic wouldn't lead us astray intentionally, but we should have found the edge of the Hallow's shield by now," Rayn said.

Point taken. I also grew nervous at how long we traveled past the waterfalls with no sign of this shield.

"Okay, let's take a break and figure out exactly where we are." Rose came up behind me and glanced at the map over my shoulder. She put her finger on the paper at the edge of where Nic had drawn a big circle to represent the shield. "We should be right about here, don't you think?"

"That's what I thought too but if that was the case, we should have found the shield by now." I scanned our surroundings for some sort of sign as to where we were. "Wherever it is, it's well hidden."

Rose nodded. "Either we took a wrong turn back there or Nic's memory is foggy. Both of those are pretty realistic possibilities."

I huffed in frustration. "This place has been pretty well hidden for fifteen years. I knew it wouldn't be easy to find, but I didn't think it would be this hard."

"Shh!" Aden spun in a circle, taking in our surroundings, looking for something I couldn't immediately see.

"I feel it too," Lauren announced in a hushed tone, her powers flaring under her skin. "Someone is watching us."

The girls and I immediately backed up to one another, our shoulders touching as we formed a defensive circle. Aden stood off to the side with a bolt loaded in his crossbow, ready to strike the moment something came into view. The feeling of all five of my generation's powers flurried underneath my skin as uncertainty pumped through my veins.

A man stepped out from behind a tree dressed in white and gray camouflage holding a familiar crossbow. Aden shot a bolt the moment the other man came into view but he ducked behind the tree and Aden's bolt struck into the wood.

Hunters.

"Do not let the darts hit you!" Aden quickly loaded and released another bolt behind me. A deep grunt echoed through the woods. Aden's shot struck one of the hunters.

Rose's powers unleashed first. Dark green vines broke through the snow and wrapped around two hunters coming towards us from my left, yanking them to the ground. Rose clenched her fists as the vines tightened around their necks. The two hunters clawed at their throats, gasping for air.

"You don't know when to quit, do you, Ezekiel?" Aden asked who I assumed to be the leader of the pack. I couldn't get a clear view of where Ezekiel stood. As I turned to scan the others, one of the other hunters had their gun pointed right at me.

I waved my hand, blocking the barrel with solid ice. The hunter attempted to pull the trigger but the bullet exploded inside of the barrel, taking off a few of the hunter's fingers. Crimson droplets splattered across the crisp white snow as the man fell to his knees, screaming in pain.

"You betrayed your family, Aden. Our entire way of life," the pack leader growled.

I turned around to see a man not bothering to wear the skull mask that covered the other hunter's faces. Ezekiel appeared older than I imagined him to be, with salt and pepper hair and a hardened face weathered from years of abuse.

"You're the one who has betrayed everyone. You've taken your bloodlust too far." Aden kept his crossbow pointed at Ezekiel's chest. Ezekiel kept his gun hanging loose at his hip.

Ezekiel's gaze traveled to the girls and I. "Seeing what has turned your loyalty, I understand your hormones have gotten the best of you. You could have been betrothed to a woman in the pack if you wanted something to put your cock in."

Aden shot a bolt at Ezekiel, but the old man dodged the attack with ease. I knew the hunters trained vigorously and altered themselves, yet it caught me by surprise to see a man with gray hair move so swiftly.

Aden looked shocked as well, glaring down Ezekiel with wide eyes and his mouth gaped. His breath formed into smoke before him from the cold. "Your alchemists are still tinkering with the serum, Zeke? You're stronger than last time."

"Maybe you're weaker. The more pack members you kill, the less redeemable you become. The monsters have put a spell on you with their siren song." Ezekiel brushed snow from his shoulder as more hunters came out from the trees behind him.

"Little witches..." Aden's voice shook with worry as a dozen more men came into view.

"We'll be okay," I assured.

Ezekiel had brought more hunters than when they came to our house looking for Aden. He must have expected to end things here and now. Maybe he wanted to make an example out of Aden, to show the others that this is what happens when you leave the pack and make your own path. This is what happens when you strike a deal with a witch. Either way, Aden looked nervous, and that scared the shit out of me.

Aden aimed his crossbow at Ezekiel, watching as the hunters surrounded us.

Whit. This is bad. Rayn's worried voice echoed in my head.

I know. I answered.

Aden turned to see the hunters gathered behind him, taking a step towards our group. His eyes glazed over in a mix of fear and hurt. These were his people. He had probably grown up with some of these hunters, and now they prepared to kill him solely because he chose to not murder us.

A crackle of energy shot through the field. At first, I thought it came from one of the girls, but I didn't feel any of them release their powers. An energy wave knocked over five of the hunters, putting them on their asses. Seeing their brothers knocked to the ground, the hunter closest to Ezekiel shot a bullet at us, but Brooke put up a shield around our group. The bullet bounced off the shield and went flying back towards the hunter, striking him in the shoulder. Another energy wave shot through the trees and took out three of the hunters on the other side of us, the impact from the magic knocking the wind out of them as they hit the ground.

I had no idea who sent these energy waves, but they gave us the perfect opportunity to hit the hunters while they were down.

I sent icicles flying through the air towards Ezekiel. If we were going to end this, I might as well cut the head off the snake. He dodged my attack with a swift roll through the powdered snow. My icicles lodged themselves into the armor of the surrounding hunters, splattering blood in their wake.

I hated this; hurting people. The attacks I sent out would likely kill them painfully but I had been backed into a corner. What was I supposed to do? Stand idly by and let them hurt my sister? Or Aden and my friends? I disassociated and put my mind elsewhere. This wasn't real. The screaming and the blood wasn't real.

One of the larger hunters took off sprinting across the clearing at us, running as fast as the snow would allow. Aden shot a bolt at him that lodged into his chest but didn't seem to pierce through his armor.

The hunter ripped the bolt from his chest plate and kept moving, drawing his gun and firing at Aden. Quickly, Rayn put up a shield around Aden before the bullet struck.

Lauren spun her hands above her head, the feel of her powers swirling through my body. The clouds above us boomed with thunder as a funnel formed. It descended slowly to the ground right on top of the sprinting hunter.

He tried to jump out of the way but the whirlwind became too strong. The powerful winds sucked him up, spinning him around in circles as he screamed. Lauren redirected the funnel to the other hunters, chasing them down as they retreated back into the forest.

Lauren's rage coursed through the sky at a mile a minute, making the funnel stronger than she may have intended. My body pulled forward slowly. A chill crept up my spine as I realized the funnel did not discriminate on who it sucked into its forces.

Brooke fell, sliding across the snow as her petite frame stood no chance against Lauren's anger.

I attempted to shield her but it still couldn't reach Brooke sliding across the earth. She cried out for help as Rayn and Rose joined their magic into my shield, expanding the perimeter to cover Brooke and Lauren.

At the realization of the shield over her, Lauren snapped out of her daze and her powers faded from my body. The funnel lost momentum and retreated back into the sky. The hunters who had been caught up in the funnel lay scattered across the field motionless. The others had successfully retreated into the woods and out of sight.

"Are you guys okay?" Lauren rushed to Brooke's side to help her up out of the snow. "I'm so sorry, B." Lauren wrapped her arms around Brooke and held her close.

"I'm okay." Brooke breathed into Lauren's chest, hugging her back.

"The coast isn't clear!" Aden barked, pulling his dart gun from his holster and aiming it towards the woods.

An older person dressed in a thick white coat with gray fur along the hood stepped out from the direction the initial energy waves had been released. They were tall, and even under the heavy coat I could see their broad shoulders and wide chest. They held up their hands at the sight of Aden's gun, silently telling us they were no threat and not to shoot. I motioned for Aden to lower his gun. He obeyed but kept both hands on it, ready to defend us if need be.

"Don't come any closer," I ordered, my voice leaving my body in a threatening tone.

They stopped, keeping their hands raised as a deep voice replied, "That's a funny way to say thank you."

"Who are you?" I asked, cautiously moving closer to get a good look at their face, but they were a stranger.

They stood their ground, unwavering. "I could be asking you lot the same question. State your business."

"We're looking for Roberta," I answered, not wanting to say the name of the Hallow in case this person couldn't be trusted.

They tilted their head in surprise and they lowered their hood. "Why?"

"We've come from Rifton with a message, but it can only be delivered to Roberta," I answered, choosing my words carefully.

The newcomer nodded slowly, chewing on their bottom lip. Their naturally tan skin was a contrast against their white coat and their dark brown eyes gave me a puzzling glance. "Well, you've come an awful long way for a simple message."

"We never said the message was simple," Rayn replied from my side.

"Then things are worse than we feared..." The stranger's voice trailed off as they scanned the treeline on the other side of the clearing. "Come, I will take you the rest of the way."

"You never gave us your name." I stood firm.

"No, I didn't, but I will take you somewhere you can speak with Roberta in private." They squared their broad shoulders and motioned over my shoulder towards Aden. "Leave the hunter."

"He goes where we go," Rayn answered firmly. "He's our protector."

"Elementals using witch hunters as their guardians. Now I have truly seen it all." They smirked. "Come, I will take you to the Hallow." Our new guide motioned for us to follow and led the way into the trees, off the path Nic had given me.

I looked back at the girls, waiting to see their reactions.

Lauren shrugged her shoulders and began to follow. "It's better than sticking around here waiting for the rest of the pack to come back," she replied, tightening the straps on her backpack.

Rose and Brooke both nodded, following behind Lauren.

Rayn turned to Aden, searching his face. "Are you okay?"

He huffed, putting his dart gun back in its holster. "Sure, why not."

"Okay." I grabbed a hold of my sister's hand for comfort. We followed the stranger into the thickness of the forest.

No one spoke a word, only the sound of boots crunching in the snow filled the silence that fell over us. Our guide stayed a few yards ahead. Every now and then they'd glance over their shoulder to see if we were still following but never spoke.

"Did you mean a literal guardian or is that a title like Archivist?" Rose asked after a while, speaking up so our guide could hear her.

"What?" They spoke over their shoulder, coming to a stop before turning to look at Rose. "We'll talk when we get to the Hallow. It's not safe until we are under the shield."

"Where is the shield exactly?" I asked, picking up pace to get close to our guide as they started walking through the snow again. "We've been following a map but it's not where it's supposed to be."

"How did you get a map to the Hallow?" they questioned, not bothering to look at me.

"Dominic Grant," I answered, hoping I hadn't made a mistake trusting this stranger with Nic's name.

That stopped our guide, their eyes wide as they met mine. They chortled as a small smile swept across their face. "He finally made it back home?"

I nodded. If this person knew Nicky, they must've known the other Magisters too. "He and Harmony are back in Rifton."

Raising their brow, our guide asked, "Just those two?"

"I won't say more until we speak with Roberta." I crossed my arms.

They slowly nodded before they continued once more. "We're almost there, have patience."

"You're awfully trusting, little witches," Aden spoke up. "He could be leading us into a trap."

"I am *not* a he," our guide gritted through their teeth.

"She brought up the Hallow, not us," Rayn comforted Aden in a whisper. "We'll be okay."

Our guide spoke over their shoulder again in a harsh tone. "Not a *she* either. Maybe you should be more concerned about keeping yourselves alive, which apparently you aren't very good at."

I wanted to rebuttal but who knew how our encounter with the hunters would've ended if our new guide hadn't intervened. Insead, I thanked them. "You saved us back there with those hunters, I appreciate your help."

"Mhhm," our guide responded. I guess that was their way of saying you're welcome.

I glanced back at Rayn, who had reached out for Aden's elbow in comfort and didn't let go as we continued on our path.

The friendship Rayn had formed with Aden still didn't sit well in my stomach. I trusted Aden. He had done more than enough to prove his loyalty to us and I felt protective over him as well. I would have buried every one of those hunters in the ground to keep Aden safe. He was one of us now.

Still, the way Rayn looked at him bothered me. I knew that look. I'd seen her flash that smile at countless guys before. Aden may have been the first one to actually deserve her batting eyelashes. If Rayn wasn't nineteen and still figuring herself out, maybe the eight year age gap wouldn't have been so unsettling.

Rayn denied it, but I saw what both of them refused to see. Aden looked at Rayn the way Bryan looked at me.

Bryan.

The sooner this stranger took us to the Hallow, the sooner we could speak to Roberta, get the pages, and get the hell back to Rifton.

Finally, we came to a stop and our guide held up their hand. The energy shield glimmered at their touch, glistening in the sunlight.

I reached out to touch the shield but our guide snapped. I jerked my hand away and stepped back, startled by their sudden movement.

"Don't touch it! It can only be opened or closed with certain magic. The shield doesn't recognize you. Have you been taught nothing? Elementals with no education?"

Rayn and I glanced at one another with furrowed brows.

The fuck? Lauren mouthed to me in silence.

Our guide turned back to the shield and waved their hand. An opening appeared for us to walk though. They went first, gesturing for us to follow. I took in a deep breath of courage and stepped through the shield with my generation and Aden close behind. Our guide closed the opening behind us. They glanced up at Aden, their lip curled in disgust as they side-eyed him. Shaking their head, they continued leading.

The atmosphere of the woods inside of the shield buzzed with energy, with magic. The pine trees towered over us. I thought the pine trees outside of Rifton were huge but these were double in size. How did they stay upright when they were so damn tall? Nic had warned me that the shield caused an increase in the oxygen level but I didn't think it would be this noticeable.

Remember what Nic said about your powers here. I told Rayn as I spun around in a circle, looking up to where the tops of the pines touched the sky.

I know, I'm on my best behavior. Rayn answered, taking in the sights as well.

A massive black swirl zoomed into my peripheral vision, causing me to duck on instinct. A buzzing filled my ears as if a hoard of insects hovered above me.

"The fuck is that?" Lauren's voice shouted behind me.

"A fly," our guide replied, unbothered.

"It was the size of a bird!" Rose uncovered her head.

"The shield." I glanced up at the sky. "Nic said the atmosphere is different here but holy shit, if that was a fly, how big are the birds?"

Our guide chuckled as they continued leading the way.

"Can we stop for a second?" Brooke asked, setting her bag on the ground. "I need to pee."

Our guide leaned against a tree trunk and waved their hand for Brooke to carry on.

I sat down on a boulder and attempted to steady my breathing. I didn't want our guide to know my pulse accelerated or that my lungs constricted from the pace they had kept. I didn't want them to think I was weak but I died inside. Deep and slow breaths in, deep and slow breaths out, no matter how badly I wanted to hyperventilate.

Rayn saw through my facade and handed me her water bottle. I took a drink and handed it back without looking at her, not wanting to see the sympathy in her eyes. As my pulse finally settled down, I took another look around. The massive pine needles on the trees towered above us. The blades of grass next to my shoe moved and I pulled my knees towards my chest in a startle. A massive beetle crawled out from the long blades, moving past us like we didn't exist, completely unbothered by our presence. I was unprepared for how big everything under the shield would be.

Taking another look around, it dawned on me how much my mother would have loved this place. She would have found the science behind all this completely fascinating. How long had the shield been up? How did Roberta and the other witches find out about it? Maybe my mom knew the answers to those questions. I'd never know. I'd never get the chance to ask her. I'd never get the chance to ask Amilia, either. Although I had a suspicion that neither of them would have told me the full truth.

It would be foolish of me to assume I'd know how either of those two would have reacted to anything. The time I spent with Amilia only taught me that I knew less than I thought about the woman who raised me as her own. The time I'd spent with Amilia also left a hole in my heart right next to the one my mother left behind when she took her final breath. My vision blurred as the lump in my throat grew. Despite the secrets, despite my anger, I missed them. They should both be here in the forest under the shield. They both should have been leading this crusade.

Two massive monarch butterflies landed on me, one on my thigh and one on my knee. I let out a gasp at their size; how delicate their massive wings were. How slowly they moved. A warmth flooded my soul as the two butterflies remained on my jeans. I dared inch my fingertips towards them. They didn't startle at my movement.

"Woah," Rayn breathed. I looked up at her as a tear slipped down my cheek and her eyes glazed over. "It's *them*."

Chapter Seven
The Labyrinth
Whitney

Finally, we reached a clearing in the forest. Once we walked into what initially appeared to be an empty field, we saw the Hallow.

A tall wooden fence surrounded the compound, protecting it from the dangers of the forest. Large wooden logs had been sharpened to a point at the top, making the Hallow feel like a fortress. The walls stood tall enough that everything behind it remained hidden. The massive wooden gates swung open, as if they waited for our guide's return. As we got closer to the open gates, I could see inside.

The Hallow displayed years of growth to meet the needs of the residents without anything excessive. Hearing how long it had been since the first round of families left Rifton, I easily wondered how they'd survived for so long in the woods. But these witches were resourceful.

There were wooden buildings everywhere. Smaller tiny homes that resembled cabins lined the far side of the area closest to the treeline. Two larger buildings took up the other side; a massive garden spanning in between them with four green houses in the back. Most of the garden beds were empty since I assumed the majority of the crops had been harvested for the year. A root cellar and separate shed that I imagined was used for food storage stood at the side of the greenhouses.

Three little kids ran through the garden, chasing one another as they kicked a soccer ball around, their laughter infectious. People came out of their little houses to stand on the porches and watch as our guide halted at the main gate. Everyone who lived in the Hallow's eyes were glued to us. Others gazes locked on our heavily-armed companion.

At the sight of Aden, a woman slowly backed up into her little house and firmly closed the door. These witches may not have been exposed to the world outside the shield in years, but the older ones knew a hunter when they saw one.

Aden halted, hesitant to step foot into the witches' compound beyond the gates.

"Leave your weapons here," our guide ordered him. "I mean it, you can't bring those in here."

"I am not disarming." Aden crossed his arms.

"Then you aren't coming in." Our guide planted their feet firmly on the dirt.

"Do you want to wait here?" Rayn asked, looking up at Aden. "The girls and I will be okay."

Aden sighed, scanning the village at all the prying eyes watching his every move. He put his crossbow into the holder and took a step backwards. "If you need anything, I'll be here."

"Give me your water bottle." I held out my hand to Aden. He retrieved it from his bag and used my powers to fill it up with water. If we were leaving Aden at the gate, I wouldn't leave him there without provisions. I turned to our guide. "He's one of us, I'd appreciate it if he was treated as such."

"He will be treated fine, but we have rules here that will be followed." Our guide waved for us to follow towards the two biggest buildings.

Following behind them, I continued to absorb my surroundings. The trees towering over the compound cast long shadows and the residents all stopped in their tracks as we passed by. "What is all this?"

"Do you want to speak with Roberta or not?" they asked over their shoulder, not slowing down.

We hurried after them up the stairs towards the big wooden doors of the first building. Our guide shoved the heavy door open and shouted, "Berta! Visitors!"

The room we walked into was lit by the windows cut high above our heads. The wooden shutters hung open on hinges as beams of light shined down to the floor. The ceiling peaked in the middle and the walls were decorated with hand-written pages. The rules of the Hallow hung up in a ceremonious reminder of the expected standards. A map of the entire plot took up one of the biggest walls, specifying which tiny house belonged to who and how much room they had to expand if need be.

I wondered exactly how the residents of the Hallow intended to pull this off long term. There were obviously children here but what happened when those children grew up?

Were they expected to have children with one another? Did they expect other witches from Rifton to join them here or were they waiting for the coast to clear in Rifton so they could go home?

A woman with dark hair tied up in a tight bun appeared around the corner, a thick book in her hands. Her face closely resembled our guide's; the same naturally tan skin and dark brown eyes. She looked each of us up and down, as if she knew who we were but not why we were there. "The newest generation?"

"Yes," our guide answered. "They brought a witch hunter as their guardian. He refused to disarm and is waiting at the gate."

"Thank you, Marin. I'll take it from here."

Marin smiled at Roberta and turned to the door. Their smile faded quickly as they passed.

Roberta took a step towards us and let out a short sigh. "Welcome to the town hall. My name is Roberta, but part of me assumes you already knew that. I am at a disadvantage, as I do not know your names."

"I'm Whitney," I spoke up. "This is my sister, Rayn. And our Elemental sisters, Rose, Brooke and Lauren."

"How do you know we are the newest generation?" Rose took a step forward to stand next to me.

Roberta gave a soft smile. "We may have left Rifton years ago but we still have ears and eyes in town," she paused, concern washing over her face. "Though our line of communication has gone dark the past few days. I imagine your arrival has something to do with that?"

The realization hit me like a ton of bricks.

"Mia is gone," I answered, barely recognizing my own voice. "The Renati attacked the cottage days ago. She...she didn't make it. Dominic Grant sent us here with urgency. We need—"

Roberta put up her hand to stop me, an icy gaze in her eyes. "You do not walk into my home and tell me one of my oldest friends is dead and then proceed to talk shop."

"I'm sorry," I apologized, tears welling in my eyes. "I just...I'm still in shock over it."

"You're Audri's girls?" Roberta waved her hand between Rayn and I as she sat down in a lone wooden chair, letting the book fall to the floor with a thud as she rested her forehead in her open hand.

"Yes," Rayn answered, her voice stuck in her throat.

Roberta nodded. "Of course they would all die and leave us with Maggie."

"Margaret Daniels as in the author of the Shadow Realm book?" Rose asked curiously.

Roberta shrugged. "She rambled on about many things." She waved her hand, as if dismissing the topic. "Enough about Maggie. Oh, my sweet Amilia. She suffered so much, but I'm glad to hear Nicky came back to Rifton before she died. Losing him and Abbie both devastated all of us, but it *broke* Mia. She was never the same after that."

"Warren also died in the attack on the cottage," Lauren sniffled, her shoulders hung in sadness. "The Renati killed him."

"Oh." Roberta took in a quivering breath, as if letting the information sink in and wash through her. She lifted her head from her hand and looked me in the eyes. "You were sent with urgency?"

"We need the missing pages from the Shepherd's book. The ones that tell us how to unlock the talismans." I straightened my posture, resting against the back of the chair. "If you were being kept in the loop by Amilia, you know Erebus is back and the Renati aren't going to stop with Rifton. The darkness will swallow the entire forest, the Hallow included, if we don't stop him."

Roberta lifted her eyebrows. "You may have the missing pages but they are worthless without the key."

"What key?" Lauren deadpanned.

"The key to unlock the labyrinth," Roberta answered simply. "The missing pages are not instructions to unlock the talismans, but how to access the labyrinth. The talismans can only be unlocked in the center of the Allurement, and if the legends are true, there is a great trial awaiting you."

I turned to look at the girls with wide eyes. Amilia may not have mentioned it but surely Nic would not have kept this information from me. Would he?

"Why is this the first we're hearing of it?" Brooke asked, as if reading my mind. "We know Amilia kept plenty from us but this is pivotal information."

Roberta chuckled to herself. "If I knew my dear friend, and I certainly did, she had her own motives. She convinced herself that her daughter's generations would be able to unlock the powers. Even after the deaths, she held onto the hope that the talismans were out there waiting for her kids. She didn't count on you five showing up." Roberta licked her bottom lip. "I think she was afraid if you knew too much, your generation would break the same way. But the talismans seem to have a mind of their own, and the Shepherds chose you."

"So what exactly is the labyrinth?" Rayn glanced around the room. "Is there anywhere we can sit? We've been walking for three days straight."

"Oh dear, excuse my manners. We aren't used to company." Roberta waved her hand and five wooden chairs floated over from the other side of the room. A small round table accompanied the chairs and settled down before us. The girls and I all took a seat, waiting for Roberta to say something that made sense. "From what my archivists have collected, the Seer of the Martyr's generation had many visions of our time. He saw the rock formation of Falcon Ridge and jotted the map down, assuming it would have importance someday. The Shepherd's Seer wrote in their book about it, saying that each Allurement is linked together, one massive portal in the center."

I sat up straight. "The Allurements are portals? To what?"

"The labyrinth. The Shepherds kept this information between themselves and one trusted Archivist. The same Archivist who took the talismans and separated them, ultimately losing them but in doing so, kept them safe." Roberta wrung her hands together, staring down at her fingers. "The Shepherds intended to use the trials of the labyrinth as a method to unlock their powers from the talismans, but only to those who could prove themselves worthy." She glanced up at us. "Five separate trials for five Elementals. In doing this, they prevented Erebus from unlocking their power as he would be unable to perform all five trials at once."

"So, there's no way for Erebus to unlock the powers without the trials?" I asked, scooting towards the edge of my seat.

Roberta shook her head. "*A* method to unlock the magic in the talismans, not *the* method. Magic always finds a way and Erebus is a determined old goat."

"Is Erebus an Elemental?" Rayn leaned forward. "He has our powers."

Roberta shrugged her shoulders. "I don't know who Erebus was before, but he carries the powers of the Martyrs in his veins. He did indeed steal your magic."

"Wait." Lauren rested her elbows on her knees and furrowed her brow. "The labyrinth isn't the only way to unlock the powers? Then why do we have to go through it?"

"Because the only other known way to free Elemental power from its host is a blood sacrifice. How Erebus absorbed the powers in the first place," Roberta explained. "I suppose the choice is yours but if you plan to build a better magical world than the Renati, I believe the labyrinth is your best bet."

"Who exactly would we have to sacrifice?" Lauren asked curiously.

Roberta paused, almost surprised that Lauren would even bother to consider that option. "The ones you love most."

"Oh." Lauren paused, running her fingers through her blonde hair. "Labyrinth it is, then."

"Do you have the key?" Rose turned to Roberta. "The one that unlocks the Allurement?"

Roberta shook her head. "No, I only have the pages."

"Of course you do," I mumbled. "Let me guess, you broke the key apart and distributed it to trusted Archivists to keep it safe."

"Are we so predictable?" Roberta licked her bottom lip. "A piece with Amilia, a piece with Maggie, and a piece with Bonnie."

"Who is Bonnie?" Brooke tilted her head to the side.

"Bonnie was a dear friend, the first of our coven to fall to the temptation of the Renati. She went undercover when we were in our twenties. We learned so much from her until...well, until she converted. She joined forces with them and her piece of the key went with her. Where they keep it now, I'm not sure."

"Wait!" Rose shot up onto her feet. Her eyes wide in shock. "Bonnie *Drake*?"

"Her married name." Roberta nodded.

"Henry Drake's wife?" I shouted as my blood ran cold.

Roberta turned away, anger rising in her voice. "She betrayed us."

Serenity and Emma's mother had been a member of the coven. My mother's friend. The feud between Serenity and I felt much more personal knowing it ran as deep as a betrayal between our mothers.

"We took the ledger from Drake and destroyed it, we could easily steal the key fragment back." Lauren held her head high with confidence. "They took my talisman and we got that back too. We have a good track record with this type of thing."

"You destroyed the ledger?" Roberta shot out of her chair so quickly it fell to the ground behind her. "The tracking ledger?"

I smiled. "Yes. That's the other reason we came. It's safe to return to Rifton."

Roberta leaned against the table and rested an open hand over her beating heart. "How on earth did you girls pull that off?"

"It wasn't easy. I got into Drake's home office and grabbed it but we almost had our heads bitten off by a massive winged shadow," Brooke explained. "We were able to destroy it but it took a lot of power from the Flame Elementals."

Roberta caught her breath, steadying herself. "Even if the ledger is gone, Rifton is no safer than when I left. More dangerous with Erebus back and winged shadows lurking about."

"But we destroyed the ledger so you could come back. So we could have more support in town. We can't do this by ourselves!" Lauren raised her voice. "We did it for *you*!"

Roberta hardened her gaze. "Your intentions may have been admirable but the act remains a selfish one. If we wanted to return to Rifton, we would have. It's not safe there."

"So you'll leave us to fight this battle alone? It's your war, too." I pointed towards Roberta.

She stared down at my finger before she met my gaze. "I will provide you with the pages you came for and the knowledge I have of where the missing key fragments are but I will not subject my family to fight in this war." Roberta folded her hands. "I have gone to great lengths to protect these people and I will not endanger them now." She turned away. "I'm sorry."

We haven't proved ourselves yet. Rayn's voice popped into my head. *Remember that. We have to show them we are trustworthy before we ask them to follow us into battle.*

I nodded, knowing she had a point. I needed to slow things down.

"I understand. Thank you for helping where you can." I relaxed my shoulders and let out a short sigh. "Would it be possible for us and our guardian to stay here before we head back to Rifton?"

"You may stay as long as you like." Roberta offered a smile.

"Thank you."

"I asked your friend who brought us here but they refused to answer any questions...what is a guardian?" Rose asked.

Roberta chuckled. "Marin is a tough one to impress. My sibling does not trust easily. Long ago, Elementals had witches who served as their personal protectors. Though they were powerful enough to defend themselves. It's more of a status, an honorable title to be given to someone you trust above all others. Someone who would lay down their life before the Elemental had to think twice about defending themselves." She crossed her arms and raised her brows. "A witch hunter is an interesting choice for a guardian. You'll have to tell me the story of how that came to be."

Rayn ran her fingers through her hair. "The pack attacked us in the woods outside of Rifton. Aden saved us and led his pack away. Their leader has gone rogue and is killing witches in a sadistic fashion. Aden couldn't stand it. They found out he let us go and nearly killed him, leaving him in the woods to die. We found him and nursed him back. He's been loyal to us ever since."

Roberta shifted her weight. "That is quite the story. Not many have faced a hunting pack and lived to see another day. But I suppose the hunters in these woods haven't faced an entire Elemental generation in quite some time."

"They were surprised by our powers, like they'd never seen an Elemental before," Lauren explained.

"They probably hadn't. We have never seen a hunter in these parts. The shield keeps them at bay and they take their hunts elsewhere." Roberta glanced over to the list of rules on the wall. "Never put the community at risk, it's the first rule. We have taught our young ones of the hunter's existence and we remain alert to their presence. Those of us who grew up in Rifton know they are in the forest lurking. One of the many dangers. You will have to understand the tension having one with you will cause here."

"Aden has more than proven himself to us," Rayn defended him once more.

"I'm glad he has earned your trust, but to those who call the Hallow their home, that man is a dangerous stranger." Roberta motioned towards the direction of the gates. "A threat they have not yet seen with their own eyes until today. The Dark Star Forest was a much different place before the Renati slithered into power."

"I have so many questions for you," Rayn hesitated, letting out a deep sigh. "We had a million questions for Amilia too when we first met her but she kept so much from us."

Roberta's shoulder fell as she offered a soft smile. "I have no reason to lie to you. Not as the keepers of the Shepherd's lost talismans. Not when Erebus has returned and more shadows than ever are crawling through the woods. I may not be able to help you physically in the war but I can provide the knowledge I have." Roberta bent down and picked up the book she had dropped on the floor. "I am going to take some time to let the news you've shared sink in, but after you've gotten something to eat and rested, we will talk more. I will answer your questions."

"Thank you." I returned a small smile.

We had been in the Hallow for all of five minutes and we knew exactly what Roberta had to offer. She set her boundaries, and now the girls and I knew what our next step needed to be. We had to find the pieces to that fucking key, and of course a third of it was already with Bonnie Drake and the Renati. Which meant they were one step ahead on completing the key and getting to the Allurement. If they got their hands on the talismans and we would truly be fucked.

"In the meantime, I suggest you girls take a look at our library. Our head Archivist is there now with her mentee. It's not much but she does have the missing pages you seek under a protection spell. Perhaps Amanda and Jake will have some knowledge to share, and of course they would love to meet you." Roberta waved towards the door. "It's the building right next door, you can't miss it."

"Oh, okay." I stood up as Roberta excused herself. Her shoulders hung low, heavy with the information we'd given about how dire things had gotten in Rifton. I hoped the information about the ledger being destroyed for good would have gone over differently, but maybe Roberta needed time to come to terms with the situation.

"What an info dump." Rose ran her fingers through her hair, blowing air through her lips. "Do you think Mia and the Magisters knew about this key?"

"I hope not," I answered, leading the way out of the building. "If Nic knew about it and didn't tell us, we're going to have some problems when we get home."

"You guys go ahead to the library, I'm going to check on Aden," Rayn announced, heading out the door before any of us could respond.

"Hey, about that," Rose said in a hushed tone after Rayn moved out of earshot. "What's going on there?"

"I don't know, to be honest. I want to talk to her about it, but I'm trying to figure out how I want to approach it. She got so defensive last time I brought it up." I looked over my shoulder in case Rayn came back.

Rose put her hands up. "I'm not judging. Aden has proved he isn't a bad guy, but after everything with Tom…"

"No, I totally agree, I can see it too." I nodded, realizing I would have to talk to Rayn about the whole Aden thing sooner than I had wanted. "I'll talk to her tonight."

"I don't want her to think that we're all in her business but I don't know, we're all kind of in each other's business." Lauren crossed her arms. "She felt the pull and I support that, but our decisions affect all of us. Even your decision to be with Bryan, Whit. We all support you and love him, but bringing someone into the inner circle is probably something we all need to sign off on."

"Isn't Aden already in the inner circle?" Brooke tilted her head. "He's here with us when no one else is. And I don't remember us taking a vote about Bryan. Or whatever Lauren has going on with Ashley, for that matter."

I glanced at Brooke sideways, wanting to rebuttal but she had a point. "Touche, but this is a slightly different situation, don't you think? Aden is...was a hunter. I already told Aden to back off but he's clearly protective over her, more so than he is the rest of us."

"He's in love with her," Brooke answered simply. "He doesn't hide it, but he is cautious." Brooke glanced towards the gate and sighed. "We'll deal with that later. Let's go talk to their Archivists."

Lauren, Brooke, Rose and I headed next door to the library. When we left the town hall's front steps, there were more community members gathered to see the mysterious Elementals who had arrived unannounced. There were about a dozen people watching us carefully from afar; no one wanted to come too close or be the first to talk to us, like we weren't people. I waved, scanning the crowd but no one waved back. Some even broke eye contact when they noticed we were looking back at them.

In reality, we weren't just people. We were Elementals, and to these witches who had been hiding in the forest waiting for someone who could take down the Renati, we were the promise of a better future.

Looking out past the crowd, Rayn came into view walking back from the main gate alone. I guess Aden still didn't want to disarm himself, but Rayn looked calm.

"Aden okay?" I asked as my sister approached us.

Rayn nodded. "Irritable but okay. I think he's hangry."

"Aren't we all," I muttered. "Come on, let's go to the library."

Chapter Eight
The Archivists
Whitney

I walked into the library first. It wasn't as large as the town hall, but it had more natural light coming in through similar wooden windows. Three tall bookcases were lined up along a wall with two more in the back, some with thick leather covers while others were newer and bound in cloth. They still looked hand bound but done by someone who knew how to hardcover a book. The spines had the titles handwritten in a beautiful cursive script.

"Oof!" A voice echoed through the library from the back. "Jake, watch out! Those books are heavy as fuck."

"Hello?" I called out, following the direction of the voice to the far corner of the library.

"Yeah? Who is it?" the feminine voice replied as a brown-haired head poked out from behind a massive bookcase. Blue eyes widened in confusion as her pupils dilated. "Who are you?"

I cleared my throat and took a step forward. "Um, hi. Roberta sent us over to talk to you. I'm guessing you're Amanda?"

She nodded. "And you are?"

"The Elementals," Lauren answered from behind me.

"Wait, wait, wait." Amanda set down the book on a small wooden desk and put her hands up. "What Elementals?"

I forced a smile. "My name is Whitney. We came from Rifton to update Roberta on some events." I motioned towards the direction of the town hall building. "We just met with her and she said to come speak with you about some information you have on the Shepherd's talismans and the labyrinth."

"Holy shit, you're *those* Elementals?" Amanda let out a deep breath and rubbed her arm. "So I guess we're finally here, huh? Okay, cool, cool, this is super cool." She turned and shouted over her shoulder. "Jake, get over here!"

A teenage boy came up from behind Amanda. He towered over her with wide shoulders and short black hair. He carried a stack of books in his arms.

"Jake, these are...put those down." Amanda moved her hands as she spoke, flustered.

Jake set the stack of books down on the small desk and brushed his hands off on his pants. "Sorry, did I hear you say Elementals?"

"*The* Elementals. The whole ass generation. Do me a favor and grab those books in the case, the ones about the Shepherds," Amanda instructed Jake before she turned back to us. "I'm sorry, I am not prepared at all for your arrival. I had no idea you were coming."

"We didn't exactly send notice." Rose scanned the library, her eyes moving down the wall of books. "We weren't expecting anything, we knew we'd be surprising everyone."

"That's an understatement," Amanda muttered under her breath. "It's okay though, everything is fine. Amilia always said the purpose of the Archivist is to prepare for anything and keep everything because you never know what's going to be important in the future."

"You knew Amilia?" Rayn asked, perking up at the mention of Mia's name.

Amanda nodded. "I was sixteen when we left for the Hallow, and she wanted to make sure we had an Archivist on the compound, so here I am." Amanda opened her arms and turned to face Rayn. Her arms dropped to her sides as she raised her brows. "Wait, what do you mean *knew*?"

Rayn looked down at the ground, her eyes quickly misting over in sadness.

"Oh fuck." Amanda's shoulders fell as Jake came up behind her with two large books in his arms. "She's gone, isn't she?"

"I'm so sorry," my sister muttered, wiping away a tear from her cheek.

Amanda let out a deep breath, trilling her lips as Jake handed her the books. "She always said it would take a swarm of those bastards to take her down."

"Definitely a swarm," Rose answered in a small voice. "They attacked the cottage."

Amanda rubbed her face. "Well, shit. And you're here to tell us it's safe to go back, I imagine? Amilia said she'd send someone when the ledger was finally fried."

"Dominic Grant sent us," I told Amanda. Nic's name immediately changed her tone.

"Oooh." She blushed, quickly turning away. "I don't know what's more of a surprise...Losing Mia or Nic finally going back. I always thought he'd sooner die." Her shoulders fell and she closed her eyes. "Oh, Mia...I know she's out there in the ether watching over us. She's finally with her family."

Lauren tilted her head to the side. "You knew the Magisters?"

Amanda glanced at Lauren and furrowed her brow. "The who? Oh, wow, yeah I guess they would be the Magisters now that you guys are here." She cleared her throat and awkwardly shifted the books in her arms. "Yeah, I knew them. I knew Abbie really well, she was only a year older than me in school and we both grew up in Rifton. Our moms were friends. We had only been out here for about a year when Marin showed up in the middle of the night with Nic, all fucked up and crying." Amanda glanced off to the bookshelf, breaking eye contact as she spoke. "I wasn't supposed to overhear what happened but I figured an Archivist is supposed to document that sort of stuff. He is an Elemental after all, you know? Anyway, I eavesdropped when he told the story to Roberta. The Renati kidnapped them, he burned the place down with Abbie inside." She paused, chewing on her lip as if she questioned whether to continue. "He, uh...he wasn't doing well after that. Tried to, you know...tried to off himself. We kept him here until he seemed more stable but I don't think he'll ever be right again." Amanda finally met my gaze. "Crying shame too because he is quite fun to look at, isn't he?"

The vision I saw at the Corner Cup before the Magisters came into the picture washed over me. Nic burning down the house, screaming into the night for help though no one heard him. How he passed out in the grass from exhaustion and shock. He was so young, still a kid and had already seen so much death and destruction.

Hearing he tried to kill himself after he arrived at the Hallow ripped a hole in my soul. I closed my eyes, wishing I could pull Nicky into a hug.

"Nic's okay, he doesn't really talk to us. He's in love with Whitney though." Brooke spoke for the first time since we'd walked into the library.

"No, he isn't," I snapped. Why couldn't I love Nic platonically without it being questioned?

"Ooh, is he?" Amanda opened up the book and began flipping through the pages. "Lucky you."

"No," I repeated. "It's not like that at all. I have a boyfriend."

"Since when has that ever stopped a man?" Amanda ran her finger down the page looking for something specific.

Rose crossed her arms. "Whitney is dating my brother."

"Oh, well, that makes for fun family dinners doesn't it." Amanda flipped to the next page. "Here it is." She set the book down on a side table and spun it around so we could read it. "This is everything I have on the Shepherd's talismans and the labyrinth. It's not much but it's a place to start."

Rayn and Rose leaned forward to read from the page but I turned my attention to Amanda. "We need the pages that were taken from the Shepherd's spellbook. Roberta said you had them?"

Amanda froze in place. "Oh, um, you can't have those."

"What? Why not?" Lauren asked, confused. "They're centuries old, very delicate." Amanda crossed her arms.

I stammered for a moment, unsure of how to approach the Archivist without exploding. "But we have the Shepherd's *and* the Martyr's spellbook in our backpack."

Amanda huffed. "I'll believe that when I see it."

I glanced over my shoulder at Brooke, who already slipped the straps of her backpack down her arms. She unzipped it and dug around for a moment before pulling two spellbooks out. "Satisfied?"

Amanda furrowed her brow and took a step towards Brooke. "I'm supposed to believe you have two of the rarest and most coveted books in the entire magical world?"

Brooke flipped the Shepherd's book open to the page with their names listed. Amanda's eyes widened as it dawned on her that we indeed held the Shepherd's spellbook.

She whispered, "Oh shit."

I crossed my arms. "We have their talismans. We aren't some strangers off the street."

"No offense, but that's exactly who you are." Amanda glared at me.

"We need the pages so we can find the labyrinth," I explained. "Roberta already told us about the key and said you'd give us the missing pages."

"Well then she can come over here and tell me herself." Amanda stepped back. "I need to speak with her. Jake here will show you whatever books you want to look at, but I'm not giving you those pages."

Before any of us could protest, Amanda spun and left the library.

Jake stood awkwardly, rubbing his arm. "Well," he finally spoke up. "Amanda can be a lot, so sorry about her. She doesn't really know how to turn it off, you know?"

"Could you show us the missing pages we need?" I asked, hoping that this kid would be more helpful than the Hallow's Archivist.

"I don't have access to them, unfortunately. I'm not actually an Archivist yet, still in training. And Amanda is taking her sweet time on the training, keeps saying I'm not ready yet but she doesn't want to share the title, I think." Jake shrugged and set the book down on top of a random shelf.

"How fortunate," Brooke muttered.

"Do you really have the Shepherd's lost talismans?" Jake asked cautiously, wringing his hands together.

I nodded, motioning to the pendant around my neck. I left it out, resting against my hoodie. I didn't see much point in hiding it from a compound of Elemental followers.

"Holy shit," he breathed, leaning in for a closer look. "My mom used to tell stories about them when I was a kid, how someone would find them one day and restore the imbalance. You don't think big events would happen in your lifetime but you–"

"Jake! Come here!" Amanda's voice echoed through the library, cutting him off.

"On my way!" Jake answered and turned to us. "Uh, don't start going through stuff. Amanda has a very specific organization method. Maybe, uh, maybe go check out the garden and I'll come find you in a bit."

The girls and I watched Jake scramble out of the library before we exited the building ourselves. The garden beds were pretty barren, only winter plants were thriving in the uncovered soil. The greenhouses, on the other hand, were impressive. On the outside they looked like little sheds but on the inside, there were at least three levels. A wooden staircase led up to a top story and another down to plants that had been buried underground.

"Wow." Rose turned in a circle to take it all in. "They certainly are resourceful, I'll give them that."

"It's hard to grow in the winter. If we didn't have the greenhouses, we wouldn't survive out here." Marin's voice startled me.

I turned to see them standing in the entryway, watching us closely, still wearing their heavy white coat.

"I could help with that." Rose offered. "I love to garden, and I could help with any plants that are struggling."

"You must be the Dirt Elemental," Marin replied. "If you want to help, it would be greatly appreciated."

"Yes, absolutely." Rose smiled and looked over her shoulder at Brooke. "Dirt Elemental. I'm not a fan of that."

"Dirty Rose," Brooke chuckled, gently touching the massive leaves growing off of a head of broccoli.

"We are having issues on the bottom level of the neighboring greenhouse, if you don't mind taking a look now." Marin motioned towards the doorway.

"Of course, lead the way." Rose walked over to Marin. "You can call me Rose, you don't have to use titles. Though Earth Elemental sounds much better, don't you think?"

"It's your title, you can change it if you please," Marin replied and they left the greenhouse together.

Rayn smiled at the doorway even after they'd left. "That's really nice of Rose to offer, and very smart. I bet if we put in some work around here, they will have more reason to trust us. It'll give us the chance to show them we are serious about being worthy leaders."

"I agree." I walked down the rows of planter boxes. "I'm sure there's something here for each of us to help out with. We'll stay a while and make sure we have enough time, if they let us."

"I can't believe their Archivist straight up told us no about the Shepherd's pages." Lauren crossed her arms. "It's not her decision to make, or even Roberta's. They technically belong to us. We have the talismans."

"If you look at the reincarnation of Elemental power, technically we are the Shepherds," Brooke pointed out.

"Exactly," Lauren replied. "The pages are ours."

"I know, but I'm trying not to pick fights when we just showed up. I think having Aden with us startled them," I said.

"Aden wouldn't harm anyone here," Rayn defended him.

"We know that, but they don't. Roberta made that pretty clear," Brooke explained. "They've been out here in the forest on their own for a long time. Hunters are nothing more than a faceless danger. And now they have a face to associate with those that have been hunting us for generations. Unfortunately, that face belongs to Aden."

Rayn tapped her fingers against her jeans. "And Aden not wanting to disarm probably wasn't a good look."

Lauren nodded. "Probably not, but they'll come around, I think. The Renati aren't going to leave them much choice."

As the sun began to set, the witches of the Hallow began lying down wood and kindling in a massive fire pit towards the center of the compound.

"Would you like some help lighting the fire?" Rayn approached one of the men who positioned logs.

"Oh, um, I don't know," his voice shook. He stood up and took a step backwards for every step Rayn took towards him.

When she realized, she stopped. "It's okay if not, just wanted to offer my assistance. I'll be over here if you change your mind." Rayn smiled and joined us off to the side. "Wow, they are really skittish."

"They've seen an Elemental before. Nic stayed here years ago when he left Rifton," I whispered.

"Maybe they didn't know him? Or didn't know he was here?" Brooke shrugged. "People are hard to analyze sometimes."

Rose and Marin came back from the greenhouses after hours of work. Rose's hands were clean but she had dirt under her fingernails and a smile across her face.

"Thank you, for all your help. I...I don't know if those crops would have survived without you," Marin's tone sincere.

"I'm happy to help, if there's anything else that needs attention, please don't hesitate to ask," Rose offered to Marin before she joined us. "Their potatoes had root rot. It was awful, I think I saved all of them."

"Good job, Mother Earth." Brooke nudged Rose with her elbow. "Ray tried helping them start that big fire over there but they turned her down."

"Oh." Rose glanced over at the bonfire. "They have reason to be cautious, I suppose. I'm trying really hard not to feel everyone's fear and concern, but I don't know how to turn this empathy off. I'm kind of overwhelmed by it." Rose let out a deep sigh. "We startled them by showing up the way that we did." She glanced up at the shield protecting the Hallow. "I wonder how the smoke is venting out? All of our shields end up suffocating us when we try to light fires."

"I wonder the same thing." Rayn motioned behind me. "We should ask Roberta."

Almost as if summoned by her name, Roberta walked up to us with a soft smile. "Are you girls hungry? We will be starting dinner soon."

"You all eat together around the fire?" I watched the witches of the Hallow gather on the massive logs placed around the fire for seating.

Roberta nodded. "Yes, we have a wonderful sense of community here."

Rayn glanced up at the night sky. "We have a question about the smoke and your protection shield, if you have time." Rayn took a step towards Roberta. "How does the smoke ventilate out?"

Roberta began explaining the magic to the girls but my mind drifted off elsewhere as I scanned the entirety of the Hallow. Everyone here had a routine they seemed to stick closely to. The Hallow remained peaceful as the community gathered around the fire in preparation for dinner; everyone pitched in to get the food served. The trees surrounding the compound stood tall like the outer stone wall of a castle. The perfect protection barrier. The shield remained but the forest itself made me feel safer. I understood why these witches left Rifton when they did, especially if their lives and families had been threatened. I could easily stay out here forever too with the woods surrounding me and the vast sky above my head.

It made me forget the dangers of the outside world. A false sense of security, maybe. It was easy to forget Erebus lurked out there somewhere. Every day that passed he only grew stronger and the Renati tightened their grip on the town.

I didn't know what they had planned, but I knew in my bones that they didn't intend to stop at Rifton. Why would an evil as powerful and ancient as Erebus return from the dead to run a small town? No, he wanted to wipe the Elementals out and take power over the witches. I think he wanted to drive the powerless from the Dark Star Forest and rule over the Allurement himself. Once he had all three manifested generations of Elemental magic coursing through his veins, he could do anything he wanted. Erebus would have no problem unlocking the labyrinth through the blood sacrifice, though it remained a mystery what exactly he loved most in this world. Whatever, or whoever, would be cast aside without a second thought.

The witches of the Hallow didn't care about Erebus and the Renati, and they didn't care about the urgency of our mission because they didn't see the threat, therefore it didn't exist. If the girls and I were going to pull this off, we would have to show them the threat. Getting them to trust us might not work, but the truth might scare them enough to join us.

"Whit?" Rose's voice behind my shoulder startled me back into the moment. "You hungry?"

I nodded. "Yeah, we should probably eat." I turned to face a pair of worried green eyes that made the homesickness burn in my soul.

"It is something out here." Rose looked around at the tall trees and then back at me. "Are you planning something? I can feel the wheels turning."

"Maybe. Depends how the next few days go," I replied. "They don't care about Erebus because they haven't seen him. They haven't dealt with the Renati in over fifteen years. They are out of touch with reality."

Rose nodded. "They won't go back to that reality without a fight. For right now, let's get some dinner. I'm getting hangry."

"Yeah, me too."

"Hey, I miss Byn too." Rose put her hand on my shoulder. "And I miss Dmitri. But they're okay. They will be okay until we get back."

"Nicky promised," I answered. "He won't let anything happen, as long as Bryan doesn't completely shut him out."

Rose chewed on her bottom lip. "Byn is smart and more importantly, he isn't spiteful. He won't turn down help when he actually needs it."

A wave of relief washed over me. I knew Bryan well enough but Rose had grown up with him. She knew versions of him that I would never meet and I took comfort in her words.

Chapter Nine
SPOUT OF FIRE
Whitney

I took the bowl of beef stew handed to me with a smile, pretending not to notice the trembling fingers of the witch who served the meal.

"Thank you," I said and followed behind my sister to an empty log by the fire.

We sat on a massive log, big enough for all five of us; which came in handy because none of the other Hallow citizens offered for us to join them. But I tried not to let it bother me as I nestled in with my girls and the scent of the stew wafted up from the bowl, making my mouth water. I decided not to worry about the sideways glances from the other witches and took a spoonful. The warm food and snuggling between Rayn and Brooke warmed my soul, thawing me out enough that the sore muscles under my skin ached a little less.

"I need a shower," Lauren muttered, taking a big bite from her bowl. "Do you think the guest cabin has a shower?"

"They should have something, if not then we'll improvise," I said in between chews. "We'll make it work."

"I want to wash my hair too," Rayn agreed with a nod. "I think I've gone nose blind to myself but I'm sure it's bad."

Rose laughed. "We were only in the woods for two nights, we used to go camping for a week at a time and didn't think twice about it. Granted, we were swimming in the lake everyday but I guess it mentally prepared me for this."

"My mom never took us camping but we'd sleep outside in the backyard a lot. Looking back though, I guess we missed out." I took another bite of stew.

"You *never* went camping?" Lauren asked in surprise.

"Mom never took us anywhere." Rayn set her spoon down in the bowl. "But wrangling three kids by yourself is hard. Make those three kids witches and I probably wouldn't have taken us anywhere either, to be honest."

"I don't know how people have kids at all, let alone more than one," Brooke admitted.

"Me either," I agreed.

Rose leaned around Lauren to look at me with furrowed brow. "I'm sorry, *what*?"

"Whitney doesn't want to have kids." Rayn spoke for me, taking a bite of her stew.

Rose's shoulders fell in disappointment. "You don't?"

I shook my head. "Sorry."

"No, it's okay. I understand. It's your life." Rose let out a sigh. "I just always wanted to be an auntie and you're kind of dating my only sibling."

"You'll be my kid's auntie." Rayn smiled at Rose. "You all will be. My kids are going to have the whole damn village. I'm determined."

"They will. I can't wait to be the gift-bearing, wine aunt." I smiled at my sister. Even amongst all the bullshit going on in our lives, all the uncertainty, we could still look towards the future and dream.

Soon, everyone finished eating, though they continued to chat around the warmth of the fire a bit longer before they slowly began to retire for the night. Amanda and Marin stood off to the side; arms crossed as they whispered to one another, no doubt talking about us. Scowls and concern covered both of their faces.

I tried not to read too much into it, but their immediate distrust of us was certainly unsettling to say the least.

"Whitney, Rayn?" Roberta's voice came up behind us, startling me. "May I speak to you two alone for a moment?"

Rayn and I left our bowls with the girls and followed Roberta off to the edge of the dinner crowd.

"I have questions about your mother, if you don't mind me asking..." Roberta paused, taking a seat on a stump. "When we both left Rifton, we decided it would be safer to cut contact, even though it broke our hearts to do so. We wanted to stay hidden. Though, I think she kept in contact with Amilia." She offered a smile, but sadness reflected in her misty eyes. "I always wondered what her life looked like after she left Rifton." She glanced up at us with sorrowful eyes. "Where did you live?"

"We lived in Kansas," Rayn answered, sitting down on the ground. "Mom and Dmitri moved there and found us a few years later. She was our foster placement but she decided to adopt us when she...because of our powers."

I felt awkward standing there while both of them sat, so I joined my sister in the dirt.

"Was she happy?" Roberta asked, her eyes glistening with the threat of tears.

"I think so," I replied, wondering how true my words were. "Maybe not all the time. Looking back, I think she was lonely. I think raising the three of us on her own was tough and we didn't always make it easy on her, but we were happy. She laughed a lot."

Roberta let out a sigh of relief. "Your mother was a good woman, and a good friend. I'm devastated at the loss of my coven sisters but I know I will see them again one day. We will meet again in the next life."

Rayn tilted her head to the side. "What exactly do witches believe to be the afterlife?"

"There isn't one. Our energy recycles into the next life and our essence is reincarnated to a new body. Our face and our names may be different, but the heart remains. When we feel the pull, we know we've found a loved one from a past life. I felt the pull when I met your mother. Audri was very intuitive, very knowledgeable for someone raised in a powerless family."

"Mom never spoke about the family she left behind. I know that her mother died a few years ago but not much else," I replied.

"Well," Roberta sighed. "Your mother left to start a new life and you can't start over while holding onto the past. When she let her old life go, she let her family go too."

"Yeah, we know a thing or two about starting new lives." Rayn picked at the loose strands around the knee of her jeans. "We want to make an impression here, Roberta. We want to make things better for you guys here at the Hallow, however we can."

Roberta nodded. "First, tell me something. Tell me the truth about Rifton. You say it's safe to go back but you also say you need support in fighting Erebus and the Renati. Both cannot be true."

I stared at her for a moment. "It's safe in the sense that the ledger is gone, but–"

"I removed myself from that ledger long ago." Roberta cut me off. "It hasn't been a threat to me in years, but what *is* a threat is getting back into the sight of the Renati. They burned down my home and destroyed my family business. They all but carried me from town themselves. Why would I go back to that?"

"Don't you feel any allegiance to the town?" I asked. "Don't you feel any need to protect the people who are still there?"

Roberta scoffed. "If any Elemental support remains in Rifton, they are not very bright. They sat back and watched the Renati rise to power and did nothing." She crossed her arms. "Why wait until Erebus is resurrected and the Renati hold so much in their hands to fight back? You girls are a day late and a dollar short."

"But the Elementals are back, *we* are back." I pleaded on my knees, but the hardened look on Roberta's face didn't change.

"We had a generation of Elementals before I left town and they did nothing to protect us. I don't see how it can be any different now. I'm sorry girls, I wish I could help you, for the love I hold for your mother."

"Maybe you still can," Rayn said, looking up at Roberta. "Amanda won't give us the pages you said we can have."

Roberta nodded. "Yes, she is being rather protective of them."

"But you said we could have them, I don't understand," I admitted.

"They aren't mine to give. Those pages belong to the Archivist and Amanda takes her job very seriously."

I stood up from the dirt. "They don't belong to Amanda or any other Archivist for that matter. Those pages are from *our* spellbook, and while I appreciate you keeping them safe for us all these years, we have come to take them back."

Roberta sighed. "I will have another discussion with Amanda. I'm sure you girls are in a hurry to get back to Rifton. You wouldn't want to leave the town unprotected for too long."

"We didn't leave it unprotected. Harmony and Nic are there." I crossed my arms, struggling to hide my irritation. "Is that all you wanted to ask us?"

"Yes, that's all. I'm sorry if I intruded." Roberta held out her hand towards the fire. "I'm sure Amanda would love some help in the library during your stay, that may soften her up. For now, I will let you return to your dinner."

I helped Rayn off the ground and walked back towards the fire. Every conversation I had with one of my mom's old friends left me more puzzled than the last.

The members of Mom's coven are something else, Rayn's voice replied in my head.

I know. They all acted like they loved each other so much but didn't see each other for over a decade. Now they won't help us even though they claimed to care about Mom, I answered.

Rayn shrugged, looking around at the smaller buildings that made up the compound. *I thought it was just Mia, but Roberta gives off the same vibe. I wonder if Maggie is the same way.*

I'm sure we'll find out eventually. If she really does have a piece of the key, then we'll be paying her a visit too.

Rayn nodded but said nothing else. When we got back to the girls, she took one look at her half empty soup bowl and let out a harsh sigh then announced, "I'll be right back."

Where are you going? I asked her telepathically but she didn't reply as she stormed away.

"She's mad." Rose watched Rayn walk away. "Not at us, but she's mad."

Brooke shook her head. "I bet she's going to argue with Aden. To try and convince him to stay in the guest house with us and get some dinner but he's a stubborn ass."

"I don't know why he's so concerned with having to leave his bow when we have literal weapons weaved into our DNA." Lauren shrugged. "He's way too attached to those things."

"I'm going to check on them." I left the fire and walked down the main pathway to the gates.

The noise of chatter and dishes clinking together faded behind me as I walked further away from the center of the compound. A throbbing pain rushed through my skull, stopping me dead in my tracks. I leaned against a nearby building, gripping tightly onto the wood as my stomach churned and my vision went black.

When my surroundings finally blurred back, a glowing orange lit up before me. Heat radiated against my skin as the row of small cabins burned to the ground. The two large buildings across the way blazed into the night, the flames reaching up to the sky.

I recognized the two larger buildings and the row of small cabins.

Flames overwhelmed the Hallow.

I tried to run back to the girls, to the library to save the Shepherd's pages. I opened my mouth to scream out for my generation or call for Roberta, but I couldn't move. I couldn't make a sound.

I held my hands up, channeling all the moisture in the air in an effort to extinguish the fire but my magic did not answer the call.

This wasn't real.

This was a vision.

I stood frozen in place, watching the smoke billow up to the clouds. Screams of the Hallow residents echoed off the trees, their cries of terror filled my head. As I breathed, the smoke filled my lungs and I coughed, my throat constricting from the ashes.

The witches ran from the fire with children in their arms, but not everyone made it. People pounded on doors from the small cabins. I recognized Amanda's voice from inside of the burning library, screaming for help.

Shadows crawled around the grounds, snarling and biting at those trying to escape. They attacked, tackling witches to the ground as children screamed. Large wings opened wide as they pounced, their fangs and talons dripping with blood.

The clouds above the Hallow began to spin and a funnel cloud formed, touching down in the midst of the chaos. Pieces of burning wood and charred branches lifted into the air, combining with the whirlwind. The funnel cloud looked like a massive spout of fire, spinning through the compound and destroying everything in its path.

I watched helplessly as everything around me collapsed. The flames spread to the surrounding trees and the funnel cloud carried embers through the air. Everything burned to the ground, and I couldn't do anything to stop it.

When I came back into my mind, I had fallen to my hands and knees, barely keeping myself off the ground. The smell of smoke still lingered on my clothes, but that could have been from the campfire. Gazing around at the buildings of the Hallow, everything looked how it had been. The only fire came from the center of the compound where the citizens gathered for dinner and warmth. The only shadows were cast from the light of the flames and the moon shining down on us.

This vision complicated things. Had I seen something that would literally happen or another metaphoric view into a potential future? How could I get the pages we needed and walk away from these people knowing that they could be left vulnerable to an attack? The Hallow couldn't possibly be destroyed by a storm if the girls and I were still here. Rayn and I would never let a fire get that out of hand. Lauren would never let a tornado rip the buildings apart.

I huffed out a deep breath. I wish I could have brushed it off as stress; that everything caused me so much anxiety I created problems in my mind. But I knew in my heart that wasn't the case. Lifting myself off the ground, I wiped the dirt from my knees and headed to find Rayn at the gate.

With the light from the fire far behind me, I couldn't see much in the dark. Hushed conversation floated through the air, both voices clearly irritated as they exchanged short sentences and scoffs.

Ray? I asked, staying a few yards back from the gates. They had been pushed open far enough for a person to slip through. I didn't want to scare Aden if he was on edge and still armed.

"It's my sister," Rayn said to Aden with a sigh. "We're just talking, you don't have to hide, Whit."

"I'm not hiding," I answered, coming into view. Rayn and Aden stood under the moonlight, both of their arms crossed against their chests. "Didn't want to interrupt. Everything okay?"

Rayn scoffed, turning to Aden. "I don't understand why he's making things so complicated."

"We don't know these people. If we trust everyone we come across, we're going to get ourselves killed," Aden argued back.

"They're witches. Roberta knew Amilia and my mom. These are our people." Rayn motioned towards the compound behind her.

Aden clenched his jaw. "The hunters were once my people."

Rayn dropped her arms to her sides and brushed past me, entering back into the safety of the Hallow. "Maybe you can talk some sense into him."

I looked up at Aden, his demeanor hardened and irritated. "You know if anyone tried to hurt us, you included, I'd flood this place without thinking twice." I studied his face.

Aden's shoulders fell and his face softened. "I believe you."

"So what's really going on?"

"It's best I keep my distance." Aden glanced over to the gate. "In all regards."

"When it comes to my little sister, yeah sure, but you need to eat and you need somewhere warm to sleep. There's a guest house we're going to stay in tonight. Sleep on the damn floor for all I care, but you're not sleeping outside and you're not starving yourself."

"I'm not starving myself." Aden shook his head.

"You can't live off beef jerky, Aden." I gently reached for his elbow. "Come get some stew, it's actually really good. Take it to the guest house if you want." When he didn't reply, I decided to take advantage of the privacy. "Look…Rayn is incredible. She's the best person I know, she's everything. But she's got a muddy history with guys. She still has so much to figure out, you know? The last guy she took a chance on nearly killed us and considering you still have that hunter mark on your back–"

"I'm a grown man, Whitney, I don't need to be coddled." Aden cut me off. "I'm a hunter surrounded by magic. I'm completely rewiring everything I've ever known. Have some patience." Aden took his crossbow off his back and unbuckled his holsters. "Where am I supposed to store this for the duration of our stay?"

"I don't know, but we can go ask Marin." I motioned towards the gate. "Let's get some rest."

Aden nodded, following behind me as we reentered the Hallow.

When Aden and I got back to the fire, the girls had already retired for the night, but Marin and Amanda were still off in the corner talking. I cleared my throat as I approached them, giving warning that Aden and I were walking over.

"I see your 'guardian' got tired of the cold?" Marin asked, using air quotes when they said guardian.

"Where do you want Aden to keep his weapons while we're here?" I asked, ignoring their attitude.

Amanda's wide eyes were glued to the crossbow Aden held loosely at his hip, finger off the trigger.

"There is a locker in my home," Marin answered. "That should be sufficient."

"Aden?" I asked, looking up at him to make sure he agreed with the arrangement.

"Very well." He nodded. "But I get them back the moment we leave."

"I have no reason to hold onto such barbaric items," Marin scoffed, excusing themself to Amanda and motioning for Aden and I to follow.

After Aden and I dropped off his weapons at Marin's cabin, we walked to the end of the row of tiny houses to the guest home. I didn't think the Hallow intended to have any guests. The extra house must have been for when the children grew older and needed their own space. I wondered if Jake had his own little house or if he still lived with his parents. He couldn't have been more than eighteen years old.

"Do you think these witches can survive out here long term?" I asked Aden, filling the silence that had fallen between us.

He scanned the row of houses. "They seem to be doing fine. The hunters live out in the woods for months at a time."

"In compounds like this?"

"The dens are very similar to this, yeah." Aden cleared his throat. "But we don't live at the dens full time. Only for training and hunting."

"Gotcha." I opened the door to the guest house and announced, "It's us."

Rayn smiled softly as we walked into the tiny house and took off our boots at the door. Aden sat down at the little table with his bowl of stew and ate quietly.

"I had another vision," I announced to the girls now that we were safely secure in our cabin away from prying ears.

Aden's spoon clattered against the side of the bowl where he dropped it. "A vision?"

"What did you see?" Brooke jumped up from her seat.

"The Hallow…This whole place went up in flames and a tornado came through…it destroyed everything," I explained.

The girls were silent for a moment, staring back at me.

"Obviously not from our doing, I hope," Lauren spoke up first.

I shook my head. "I didn't see any of us in the vision."

Brooke cleared her throat. "So, someone attacks?"

I shrugged. "I'm guessing?"

"What else could that mean?" Lauren slid to the edge of her seat.

"The visions are metaphoric, aren't they?" Rose asked, chewing on her bottom lip.

"Mia said they can be, not that they always are. I don't know. I'm exhausted, but it happened while I went to see Rayn and Aden, so I wanted to tell you guys as soon as possible." I folded my arms tightly across my stomach.

"We'll dissect it more tomorrow." Rayn yawned. "Right now, we need to get some sleep."

Rose, Rayn, and I climbed up into the loft, ducking our heads as we crawled into the narrow space where a queen-sized mattress lay. It was claustrophobic, like the walls would inch in on us to trap us. Aden already lay in his sleeping bag on the floor, snoring. He must've been more tired than he admitted. I got into bed and closed my eyes, not wanting to see the inches between my face and the ceiling. Rayn lay down between Rose and I, humming as she got comfortable. We were already getting minimal sleep, but I promised the girls I'd talk to Rayn about Aden tonight, and now may have been my only chance.

What's up with you and Aden? I asked Rayn mentally after everyone settled into bed. I didn't want to be rude and talk about him like he wasn't in the room, even if he already slept.

Nothing? What are you talking about? Rayn answered, turning on her side to face me with a furrowed brow.

You can see the silent pining from a mile away.

Rayn sighed and closed her eyes. *I like seeing him happy, so I make an extra effort to get rid of those rain clouds over his head.*

Yeah, that's what people do when they love someone.

I never gave you a hard time about Bryan, Whit. Even when your relationship drove a rift in our generation, I still stood by you. I still defended you to Rose and did my best to convince her that you weren't doing anything wrong.

Bryan isn't a hunter.

Neither is Aden, not anymore.

I paused, unsure of how she'd react to my next sentence. *We're hesitant after everything with Tom.*

So that's what this is about? You don't have a perfect track record with guys either but I don't hold that over your head. Plus, nothing is going on between us. Aden has made it pretty clear that he isn't interested. Rayn curled her lip as she silently stared at me.

I bit the inside of my mouth. *Brooke is convinced he's in love with you.*

Rayn lifted her brow. *B also thinks something happened between you and Nic before Bryan came back, so...*

Okay, point taken. I looked away from her.

Listen, I've got a handle on it, okay? I'm a nun now. Call me Sister Rayn because I've sworn off men for a long time. The situation with Tom will never happen again, nor will the situation with Jon. I've learned my lesson. I don't want you to be lonely.

Rayn shrugged and rolled onto her back. *I'm not, not really. I have plenty of things in my life to make me happy and plenty of fires to put out to keep me busy. I'm okay.*

I believed her. *I'm only looking out for you.*

I know, but don't worry about it. We have plenty of other shit going on, okay? Goodnight.

Yeah. Goodnight.

Chapter Ten

ENTERTAINING ROBBERY

Lauren

I laid awake on the couch when the sun finally began to shine through the curtains. I stared at the ceiling, wondering what happened back in Rifton. Would my dad ever wake up? Did the Corner Cup stay open without Amilia? Was Ashley angry or driving herself mad with worry? Did she care at all? Did a part of Warren exist out there in the ether, looking down on me? Endless questions without a single answer.

"Are you awake?" Brooke asked from the armchair in the corner.

I nodded. "How'd you sleep?"

"Better than I did in the tent, but we are swapping out who gets to sleep in that bed."

I chortled, looking up at the narrow loft. "Agreed." I glanced across the room at Aden. He did push ups on the floor. Shirtless. His bedding had been folded neatly and put in the corner, out of the way. I stared at the black tattoo on his back. The markings resembled tree roots, stretching up from in between his shoulder blades to the nape of his neck.

Was that a tattoo? I had never seen anything like it, but chose not to make that comment aloud. "I think you've slept less than any of us, Aden." Astonishing, since I'd barely slept an accumulative full night since the wedding.

Aden huffed, continuing his exercise. "I've slept enough."

The girls up in the loft began to stir at the noise from the lower level.

"I missed sleeping in a bed," Rose mumbled above my head. "Is anyone else awake?"

"Yeah," I answered. "I've been up for a while."

"You've barely slept since we left Rifton." Rose's voice dripped with concern as her head appeared over the side of the loft.

I shrugged, sitting up on the couch. "I'm fine."

Rose's mouth twisted in concern before she climbed down the ladder. Whitney appeared over the edge of the bed and climbed down after her. They both glanced over at Aden, who hadn't stopped lowering himself inches from the ground and lifting himself back up.

"We have a lot of work to do if we are going to get what we came here for. They have no intention of helping us." Whitney crossed her arms.

Rayn's muffled voice came from the loft. "I think Roberta has good intentions."

"Yeah, but she's not the only one in charge here." My gaze met Rayn's as she peeked over the edge of the bed.

"We'll keep helping out. Maybe we can find something for Aden to do and everyone will stop pissing themselves over him being here." Rayn slipped from the bed and climbed down the ladder. She stopped and stared at Aden's bare back.

Rose cleared her throat. "We have to remember who we are, and remind them." Rose reassured the room. "We are the only complete generation of Elementals holding the lost talismans of the Shepherd's. We gotta pull that card out more often."

Brooke nodded. "Let's get out there and show them the Elementals are back for good."

Aden finally finished his routine and hopped onto his feet. He stretched out his arms over his head, arching his back. "Aren't you supposed to be their leaders?"

"We...we used to be, but that was a long time ago," Rayn explained to him, her eyes wandering down.

Aden nodded but didn't reply as he reached for a clean shirt.

Marin stood waiting outside the cabin when our group emerged. They eyed Aden carefully with annoyance before they turned to speak to Whitney. "Now that you've spoken with Berta and our Archivist, what are your intentions here?"

"You mean how long do we plan to stay?" Whit clarified.

Marin's silence answered the question.

"We are in no hurry to leave as long as we are welcome. We'd like to stay and help where we can before we go. That is the role of an Elemental, isn't it? To take care of their people?"

"Hmm." Marin crossed their arms. "Are you bringing your 'guardian'?"

"Aden goes where we go," Rayn stated, not budging on the issue.

"Okay, then, follow me." Marin turned and walked down the path towards the center of the compound.

I glanced over my shoulder at Aden, stiff as a board. He looked more uncomfortable at the compound than any of the witches here felt around him. Rayn stayed close to his side as we all followed behind Marin. Three people stood waiting for us at the center. Roberta, Amanda and another woman we had yet to meet but I recognized her from last night's dinner.

"Rose, this is Jennifer, our master herbalist. I'm sure there is something she could use your skills for." Marin waved a hand at a dark haired woman, who smiled warmly at Rose.

"I'd love for you to take a look at our stock in the apothecary," Jennifer offered.

Rose lit up. "Apothecary?"

"Ooh, I'm coming with you." Brooke invited herself.

Roberta smiled at us. "We are also making some repairs to one of the family's homes today."

"I'm, uh, I'm familiar with home repair," Aden offered with a quivering voice.

Rayn stood close to him, her hand almost touching his. "Aden and I can help with that."

Roberta hesitated, though she seemed to make a genuine effort not to show it. "E-excellent. Thank you."

A tall man with a lanky build and wide blue eyes approached us cautiously. He spoke with a shaky voice as he kept his distance. "Whitney, isn't it? The, um, Stream Elemental?"

"Yes?" Whit turned to face him.

"Oh, hello, um. I hate to be a bother, but I heard you ladies asked if you could help with anything around the compound and well, you see, our water filters and storage system have been giving me some trouble," the man stammered uncomfortably.

Whitney gave him a soft smile. "Of course. Show me what we're working with."

"If it's not too much trouble, that is." The man put up his hands.

"No trouble at all. We are here to help."

"Thank you so much." His shoulders relaxed a bit.

I took a step forward. "I know a thing or two about filtration systems. I grew up in a hardware store. Maybe I could tag along?"

"Oh, yes, thank you. Please, follow me." The man motioned for us to follow.

Whitney and I accompanied the man to the other side of the compound. Hopefully, this would all be enough to help convince these witches to trust our generation. They reminded me of a group of mice. Nestling in where they felt safe and then scattering at the first sign of trouble.

The man spoke again. "It's so kind of you to come all this way. I understand it was a long journey."

"It wasn't easy, but definitely worth it. We had heard a lot about the Hallow and we wanted to come see it for ourselves," Whitney replied.

"It's been a long time since we left Rifton, so I imagine it's a completely different town now." The man offered out his hand. "I'm Lenny, by the way."

Whitney flashed a smile and took Lenny's hand. "It's nice to meet you. This is Lauren, our Air Elemental."

Lenny smiled and shook my hand. He led us into a clearing with massive water tanks set up across the way. I squinted my eyes in an attempt to get a better look at the various PVC pipes and storage containers.

Twigs broke as someone walked into the clearing with us. I expected to see one of the girls when we turned around, but Jake – the Archivist trainee – came out from the treeline and waved at us.

"I believe you met my son, Jacob, yesterday in the library," Lenny replied.

"Jake is your son?" Whitney asked Lenny and waved back at Jake.

Lenny smiled. "He's a good kid."

Lenny and Jake were definitely related. They both had the same long build and dark hair, and their noses hooked into the same shape.

"I heard you guys were out here messing with the water filters so I wanted to come see if you needed any help." Jake buried his hands in his pockets to keep them warm.

"Aren't you needed in the library?" Lenny asked his son.

Jake shook his head. "Nah, I'm done over there for the day."

That didn't surprise me. From what we'd witnessed yesterday, Amanda didn't let Jake do much of anything but household chores.

Lenny rustled Jake's hair. "I'm proud of this one. Being given the task of Archivist is an important role and requires a lot of trust. Jake has given so much of himself to the job already. It's a serious job, especially now that the Elementals have returned. The generations from the past put an immense amount of trust and responsibility on their Archivists. The talismans would have been lost forever without them, along with all the books. It's a tedious job but probably the most important of them all."

"If only I was actually allowed to do the job," Jake muttered as we followed behind his dad to the water system.

Lenny approached three massive plastic water tanks on the edge of the compound. Each tank had a spicket on the bottom, and containers on top of each tank. He patted the side of one of the tanks. "We collect rain water and purify it using a charcoal system, which has worked well over the years when the stream runs dry. We don't usually have to use these in the spring or summer but during the colder months the stream is unusable. Lately, we haven't been able to keep the tanks clean. We have had a lot of wasted water. The tanks will be fine for a few days and then the water that comes out is gray. We've washed them numerous times but I can't figure out what is going wrong."

Whitney stared back at him with wide eyes, chewing on her bottom lip. " Um. I could get the stream flowing for you again. Would that help?"

"It would definitely be a short term solution but it will dry again next year, so we have to do something about the tanks," Lenny replied.

Whitney nodded. "I can definitely help with the stream."

I took a step towards the filters. "What kind of adhesive did you use for the pipes?"

"Standard PVC cement," Lenny answered.

"There's a lot of joints. The more joints, the more places it could leak. Something must be cracked if debris keeps getting into the tank." I walked around the base of the tank, analyzing every connection. "I don't see any purple primer?"

He furrowed his brow. "Um, I don't believe we used any?"

I got down on my knees and inspected the pipes further, feeling around each of the joints to see if any of them were wet. Finally, I found a small bead of water gathered where the pipe went into the tank. "Bingo. Lenny, there's a crack in this pipe. It's small, but big enough that it can mess with the entire system."

Lenny joined me in the back of the tanks and kneeled down next to me. "How did you find that? I've checked these pipes a million times."

"This black plastic isn't the same kind of material, they need different adhesive." I put my hand on the pipes. "They probably didn't seal together."

Lenny let out a huff and nodded his head. "Joe, the guy who set all this up…he passed away over the summer. He was an older man, hell of a plumber. I've been doing my best to take over, but he left some big shoes to fill."

I offered a soft smile. "This stuff isn't easy, it takes a lot of practice. I can help you repair it. Where are the spare parts?"

"There aren't many... We've been working with scraps all summer trying to get ready for the winter," Lenny explained.

Whitney furrowed her brow. "No one ever goes back to Falcon Bay for supplies? Isn't that the closest city?"

Lenny shook his head. "No one has left the compound in years. We haven't had a reason to."

"I know the whole point is to hide away from the Renati, but these mechanics don't last forever. It's plastic, and plastic breaks or wears down in the weather. It's only a matter of time before you guys have to get more supplies or this whole thing will fall apart."

I noticed Whitney and Jake glance at one another in surprise at my knowledge of the pipes. Those looks were nothing new. I got them frequently from customers who weren't regulars at the hardware store. The customers who weren't used to me being one of the employees who could actually help them fix a household issue.

The regulars knew my dad. They knew TJ Thaner, the licensed contractor. They understood I actually knew what I talked about. I didn't particularly have a passion for this kind of thing, it wasn't my favorite way to spend my time. But being with my dad was one of my favorite past times and he taught me everything he knew.

Lenny let out a deep sigh. "I'll show you what we have left in storage and maybe we can go from there? See if there is any chance of fixing this thing?"

"Yeah, I can definitely help with that."

"Thank you, Lauren." Lenny smiled. "In the meantime, the dried stream bed is right over here, Whitney."

Whit stood at the edge of the dried stream and looked down at the barren ground. She got down on her knees and waved her hand, reaching out as if she were looking for something to hold onto. I felt the rush of Whitney's magic flow through my body as water began to trickle down the frozen dirt. It pulled the fallen leaves and branches with it, carrying them along as more water flowed down the river.

"Wow," Jake breathed. "That's amazing."

"Maybe I can make the stream run all year round." Whitney reached out and dipped her fingers into the cold stream as the water rushed past.

"Wait, really?" Lenny knelt down next to her. "Could you do that?"

"I could try." Whitney turned her attention back to the flowing stream.

She slipped her hands back into the cold water. I closed my eyes and listened. The water crashed over the tops of the rocks, the droplets trickling against one another. I smiled at the comforting feeling of my friend's magic. When I opened my eyes, Lenny and Jake stared at Whitney in wonder.

"Did it work?" Jake whispered.

"Time will tell." Whitney leaned back, balancing on her bent legs. "Think you can fix the pipes, Lo?"

I nodded. "If we have the proper supplies."

Lenny led the way to a smaller wooden shack with no windows and a makeshift door. Lenny waved his hand and lifted the protection spell keeping the shack's contents safe from the elements. He rummaged through a few piles of various items before he pulled out a wooden box and placed it at my feet.

"This is everything?" I asked, skimming over the various pipe connections.

Lenny nodded. "Everything Joe left behind."

My heart sunk in my chest. Most of the pieces were cracked or the wrong size. The glue had already dried up. I glanced up at Lenny, trying to break the news as gently as possible. "We need to restock these supplies. All of this is too old to hold up any repairs we could attempt."

"Well, damn..." Lenny glanced over to the flowing stream. He chuckled. "Well, at least we have flowing water now. I can't believe the help you two have provided, you have no idea how much this means."

I returned the smile, relieved to hear we were one step closer to gaining the Hallow witches' trust. It felt good to help. These people needed more assistance than they were willing to admit.

Lenny and Jake escorted us back to the compound, telling us all about how they began building the Hallow when they first came to the clearing.

"Did you know the clearing was here before you left Rifton?" I asked Lenny as we approached the town hall building. "Or did you come out here hoping to find somewhere?"

"We planned for a long time before we finally left Rifton. We met in secret, making sure we had the right supplies and people to make this sustainable. The last thing we want to do is have to retreat back to Rifton. We wanted to disappear into the night and never be seen again." Lenny looked around at the compound. "I'm very proud of the life we have built here."

"They still tell stories about you all in Rifton," Whitney told Lenny, causing him to smirk. "Stories about a group of people who all moved away at once. One of my friends back home told me the story, Troy thinks you all were taken by the witches who haunt the woods."

Lenny chuckled. "Little do they know, we are the witches who haunt the woods."

"It's amazing how well you've done out here."

"Well, it helps to have magical powers. We may not have been as successful if we were powerless, but thank you." Lenny held his hand over his heart. "And thank you again for your help today. I heard your fellow Elemental did some remarkable work in the greenhouses last night, and saved our entire crop of potatoes. I hope you all know how much it means to us."

A woman walking the same path as us spotted Whitney and I. She slowly backed away, taking the long way around us to her destination. I kept my eyes on the woman, trying to meet her gaze so I could smile and show the stranger that we meant well, but she kept her head down.

"Not everyone seems to be happy we are here," I dared say aloud.

Jake sighed. "I don't think they're unhappy. I think they're just nervous about what newcomers, especially Elementals, means for the future of the Hallow."

Lenny hummed in agreement. "We have been out here for a long time, and they are skittish about an unknown future. With news that Erebus has returned and then to have an entire generation of Elementals show up on our doorstep, it's a lot to take in. Everyone here thought we had left our problems behind us."

"I understand. Thank you for talking with us. You two have been the friendliest witches and we won't forget that." Whitney smiled at the two men.

We bid one another goodbye as Whitney and I met up with the other girls and Aden outside the library.

"Hey, everything okay?" Whitney asked as we got closer.

Rayn shrugged. "Aden tried to help with those cabin repairs and it didn't go well. They were super suspicious of him and wouldn't give him any tools."

Aden huffed. "I disarmed. What more do they want from me?"

"We made some headway with Lenny, he's in charge of their water system and he's Jake's dad." I glanced over my shoulder at the two still chatting in the middle of the compound. "I think we need to get on the good sides of a select few members and they'll convince the others."

"I'm doing more damage than good." Aden scanned the compound. "I shouldn't have come."

I met Brooke's eyes as she chewed on the side of her mouth. None of the girls protested, not even Rayn.

"There's nothing we can do about it now." Whitney rested her hand on his elbow. "You're not a hindrance, Aden. We wouldn't have made it here without you."

"How was the apothecary?" I asked Rose and Brooke, changing the subject.

Rose's eyes widened and a smile broke out across her face. "Do you want to see it?"

Rose led the way to a small building next to the greenhouses. Aden waited outside by the door as we went in. It looked to be the same size as the tiny shack by the water filters but when we stepped inside, the building became much larger. Rows and rows of narrow shelves lined with tiny colorful glass bottles. Bundles of dried herbs and strings of garlic hung upside down from the ceiling. The light from the window shone through the tiny leaves and stems onto a wooden counter.

Sitting on the workstation were different sized mortars and pestles along with tiny mixing bowls. A small stack of books and pens sat in the corner. One of the walls was lined with little tiny drawers that resembled the inside of Rose and Brooke's traveling apothecaries. The little knobs were all lined in neat rows and labeled by hand. Vines grew up the walls from the cracks in the floorboards and framed themselves around the edge of the window, growing towards the light.

I laughed, taking in the sights as I turned to Rose. "Are you sure they didn't make this place for you?"

Rose returned the smile. "Isn't it beautiful? When we get back home, I'm going to make sure Amilia's stock stays well taken care of."

Whitney turned to her sister, seeming to want to take advantage of the privacy. "Did you get the chance to talk to Amanda at all?"

"I didn't even get the chance to bring up the Shepherd's pages before she kicked me out of the library and said we weren't getting them. I could strangle her." Rayn rolled her eyes.

"How much time are we going to give it?" I asked. "I know we can't burn our bridges down here but we are giving them too much power over us."

"It's delicate, Lo," Whitney answered.

I shook my head. "Amanda isn't the key here, it's the other one. Jake already trusts us. We convince him to get us the pages, or to convince Amanda before we have to rob them."

"Lauren's right, you know." Rose ran her fingers through her brown hair. "There is a time limit on this mission. We can't stay gone forever. Everyone we love is back home practically unprotected. I know Nic and Harmony are there but they can't be with everyone all at once. The Renati know that everyone we love is there without us, we can't risk it for much longer."

"Nic has charmed Brooke's parents by now," Whitney pointed out. "Nancy too, for that matter."

Brooke trilled her lips, letting out a deep sigh. "It's for the best. I don't want them home freaking out over me."

"It's only been a couple days." Whitney seemed to convince herself as much as she attempted to convince the rest of us. "Give it a few more, and then we will start entertaining the idea of robbery."

Chapter Eleven
Archivist's Notes
Whitney

Nearly a week had passed, and the witches of the Hallow stopped flinching when they saw us, but we still didn't have the missing pages. The girls, Aden and I had spent every day since arriving at the compound working. Rose and Brooke spent countless hours in the greenhouses and the apothecary. Lauren and I did the best we could patching the leaking pipes of the water filtration system, but Lo didn't seem optimistic about the longevity of the repairs. Rayn and Aden finished the repairs on the tiny houses. The witches levitated the heavy pieces of lumber up and Aden used hammers and saws without speaking a word to anyone.

In the afternoon, I decided to take advantage of some downtime and browse the library. It reminded me so much of the books back at the cottage. How many of these books once sat on those very selves? The Magisters had talked about a fire that destroyed many of the books the coven had been keeping, but there were so many books still around. How many did the coven initially have?

I ran my fingers along the spines, taking comfort in the familiar covers when a voice spoke up behind me.

"Looking for something specific?"

Unfortunately the voice did not belong to the Archivist in training.

I looked over my shoulder at Amanda and gave her a soft smile. "Nothing specific. I like old books. They remind me of home."

"Hmm." Amanda walked up next to me. "Me too, even before I was named the compound's Archivist. I had expected the title before I got it, but now that I've worn it for a while...I think it means more now than it did at first, you know?"

"Yeah, I can understand that. I kind of feel the same way about my position as an Elemental." I touched the next book's spine on the shelf. "Which one is your favorite?"

"The one you're trying to take home with you." She glared at me sideways.

"Ah, so it's personal then." I turned towards her.

Amanda took a step back. "Isn't it always?"

"Amanda," I sighed, leaning my shoulder against the bookcase. "You know we can't unlock the talismans without those pages, and you know if we don't defeat Erebus then the Hallow won't stand. You have to understand that."

She squared her shoulders, looking down at me. "I understand that you're a stranger waltzing in here expecting me to hand over the most precious piece of information I have. Do you have any idea how long Archivists have been protecting those pages? There is a reason we didn't leave them in Rifton."

I softened my stance. "You've been protecting it so that one day I could walk into this room and it would still be here for us to use," I pointed out. "And I'm not a stranger. You've met Harmony Vasquez."

"So?" Amanda raised her brows. "I've met Harmony, not you."

I smirked. "Hmmm, and I thought you understood how Elemental magic works."

Amanda chewed on her bottom lip. "We always thought it would be them."

"Who?" I tilted my head.

"The generation before you." Amanda began to walk down the row of books. "We all thought they would be the ones to fight back, to protect us when the Renati killed our loved ones and burned our houses down. They couldn't protect us, and neither can you."

Oh.

I followed behind her. "I understand, but we have something the Magisters didn't. We have the talismans." I yanked on the silver chain around my neck and exposed the aquamarine to Amanda.

She turned to face me and watched the white ink swirling inside with wide eyes. "Are you a hundred percent certain that is the actual talisman of the Shepherds? It doesn't look as old as it should."

"As an Archivist, you should know about the cloaking spell put on the talismans to help keep them hidden." I held the gem in my hand, glancing down at the simplicity of its design.

Amanda cleared her throat and shifted uncomfortably.

"Don't you want to be part of the reason we save our world?" I let the talisman rest against my chest and took a step towards her. "Don't you want to be one of the Archivists who gets to experience this firsthand and write about it for those who come after us? I know it's scary, but we're all scared. If we come together, it'll be a lot less scary than if we continue to isolate ourselves." I motioned between the two of us. "We're stronger together. That's the one thing the Renati have on us. They are united and they have something to die for. We'll never stand a chance if we don't let one another in."

"We only have one shot at this," Amanda snapped back. "Once I hand those pages over, that's it. You fuck up and they are gone. Generations and hundreds of years wasted. I will not be the Archivist who ruins that legacy."

I let out an irritated sigh. "You will be if you don't help us."

I left the library with trembling fingers. That speech had been building inside of me for over a week and Amanda needed to hear it. Hopefully my words resonated and she would let us in, because if she didn't then we were all dead in the water.

) ·) · ● · (· (

That night at dinner, Roberta sat next to Rayn answering every little question my sister had for her. Roberta had years of experience conjuring powerful shields and surviving in the forest. We could definitely learn a thing or two from her.

Roberta explained how energy from the Allurement had already created the base of the shield that stood about us today. I was intrigued by the information but my attention pulled elsewhere.

Jake and Amanda sat a few yards away, whispering to one another. Amanda didn't look very happy but Jake only appeared to be half listening. He glanced my way and lifted his brows when our eyes met. Amanda made a closing statement and walked off, leaving Jake alone.

"Hey," Jake whispered, barely getting my attention. He nodded at the greenhouses and slowly stood up, making his way towards the gardens. I waited a few minutes before I followed.

I'll be right back. I told Rayn telepathically and left the fire.

I wandered through the dark past all the planter beds where the greenhouses stood at the edge of the compound. The bright moon reflected off the remnants of snow, acting as a guiding light. "Jake?" I whispered.

"Back here," he answered from behind the structures.

My power bubbled under my skin, ready to strike, but this kid didn't feel threatening. "What's going on?" I asked when I finally found him, far from any eavesdroppers.

"Amanda told me about the talk you two had in the library today." Jake looked around to make sure we were truly alone. His voice lowered to a whisper. "She's starting to give in, I think, but not soon enough. She is wasting time and she won't listen to anyone. She's clinging too tightly to her role as Archivist, hindering the cause. She's afraid to make the wrong choice and be the one responsible for blowing the whole thing up." Jake let out an irritated huff.

"And what about you?" I lifted an eyebrow.

"I want to make a difference," Jake answered, meeting my gaze. "I want to be the Archivist who writes about this firsthand. The return of the Elementals to end Erebus once and for all? This is the kind of shit they'll talk about for centuries. It's important. If this is really the second coming of the Shepherd's, why wouldn't we step up and do everything we could?"

"Fear," I replied simply.

Jake nodded. "The only thing I'm afraid of is not doing enough."

"I wish Amanda shared those same concerns." I glanced over my shoulder.

"She's not trying to be deceitful for anything. She doesn't know you and once those pages are gone, that's it. There's literally nothing else, no other back up."

I grit my teeth and spoke through a clenched jaw as anger bubbled under my skin. "I can't believe how many times I've had to explain that they are *our* pages to begin with and we are the only ones who can unlock the talismans. Have we not made that clear enough?"

"I hear you. I see you." Jake took a step towards me. "I want to help you."

"Do you know how the key works?" I attempted to relax my shoulders.

"It's supposed to work on any of the Allurements, but I honestly don't know if the door that they documented was metaphorical or a literal door." Jake handed me a book, one with a cloth cover that had clearly been bound by hand. "This is mine. I've been compiling information on the Allurements for years now. I find them fascinating."

I glanced down at the book with wide eyes. "Wow, this could be really helpful."

Jake smiled. "I hope so. Read through it and see if there's anything in there you can use."

"Thank you." I took the book from him and slipped it into my bag. "I'll show the girls tonight after everyone goes to bed. Why did I have to meet you all the way back here? Why not give this to me by the fire?"

"I don't want to get in trouble, honestly," Jake admitted, shifting his weight. "I know Amanda will help you eventually, especially if she listens to Roberta. But you have to understand that everyone here has been isolated for so long. They get kind of skittish around new people, especially Elementals."

I nodded. "Your dad seems to trust us."

"My dad likes you a lot. He talked about what you and Lauren did for our water source all week." Jake looked away and cleared his throat. "The stories we are told about the Elementals are mixed."

"But one of them stayed here for a year." I studied Jake's face as he let out a deep sigh.

Jake tilted his head. "I've heard it mentioned a few times, but I was too young to remember him. A Flame Elemental?"

"His name is Nic. He's..." I paused, feeling his absence weigh heavy on my heart. "He's a good friend. He's helping keep Rifton safe."

"I want to go back to Rifton. I hate it here." Jake ran his fingers through his dark hair and began to pace. "I hate being stuck in the middle of nowhere, hiding away while you guys fight the real battles." He gestured towards the trees. "I want to be out there in the world."

I nodded, wondering what it would be like to grow up in the middle of the woods with such limited contact with the outside world. From my understanding, Roberta had been the only one still in touch with anyone in Rifton and it was only updates on the town from Amilia.

Jake had probably never spoken to anyone outside of this tiny community. He probably daydreamed about the towns and cities. How the glow of the lights from town reflect off the night sky after the sun sets. Little things, like stopping by the grocery store when you're out of milk or getting a coffee while you're running errands. So many things I didn't realize I had been taking for granted. Yes, they were protected here in the Hallow but they had given up so much for that safety net.

I skimmed over Jake's words in my head and something stuck out. "You said you were told mixed stories about the Elementals?"

"Yeah," he paused. "Marin, Roberta's sibling...they didn't go as far as thinking you guys are evil or anything, but they think Elementals are trouble."

"Trouble," I repeated. "Because of the Magisters?"

"Who?"

"The generation before us. Amilia Burnett's daughter and her friends. Nic is one of them," I specified, realizing we were the only ones who knew them as Magisters.

Jake shrugged. "I think so? Marin never gave names or details, just the witches had always been pulled into the Elemental's orbit and that means the good *and* the bad."

"Aren't witches pulled into each other's orbit anyway?" I tilted my head. "The Allurements and all that?"

"We do, but Elementals have much more power than the rest of us," Jake paused and chewed on his lip. "It's not a secret that power used to get abused."

I sighed. "I can see how they would feel that way. We aren't here to start trouble though, we are here to end it."

"Trust me, I'm on your side. I think standing up to the Renati is brave. Braver than my dad, running away to hide in the forest while someone else fights the war."

I paused. "I'm sorry if this is intrusive, but is your mom here?"

Jake turned his head away. "Just me and my dad. We lost her before we left Rifton." Jake briefly closed his eyes and shook his head. "Another reason I want to end the Renati. I don't want to be on the sidelines, I want to be on the frontline."

My heart broke at his words. "I'm so sorry, Jake." I reached out and placed my hand on his shoulder, giving a gentle squeeze. "Thank you so much for your notes. I'll get your book back to you before we leave."

"You aren't staying much longer?"

I shook my head. "We have to get the missing pages from the Shepherd's book and head home. We have people waiting for us."

"Who?" Jake turned his head and blushed. "Sorry if that's an intrusive question. I want to know as much about the world as I can. What it's like to have someone...to have a life out there."

"I have my boyfriend and my brother. Rose and Brooke still have parents who worry when they don't come home at night." I trusted Jake enough to tell him the truth. His brown eyes were sincere, hopeful that we were going to fix this mess.

He almost made me believe I was capable of pulling it off.

Jake sighed. "I wish I could go with you." I opened my mouth to speak but no words came. Jake spoke again before I could think of how to reply. "It's okay, I'm not inviting myself. I know I'm staying. I wish I could get the hell out of here."

"You will," I promised. "We'll come back. I don't know when but we will."

Jake smiled. "Come on, we should head back before someone notices we're here conspiring."

I waited a few moments after Jake left before I headed back to the fire to avoid anyone asking questions, not wanting them to think I went behind Amanda and Roberta's backs. I genuinely wanted to do this the right way. I wanted to earn their trust and prove to Marin and whoever else felt we were trouble that we wanted to be better than the ones who came before us.

"Where have you been?" Brooke asked as I sat down on the log next to her.

"I'll tell you later," I whispered, setting my bag down on the ground.

When we got back to the cabin, I retrieved the book Jake had given me and laid it out for the girls.

"What's this?" Rose leaned forward for a closer look.

"Jake asked me to meet him behind the greenhouses and let us borrow this. He's been compiling information about the Allurements for years, he said it may help us with the labyrinth."

"Glad to see someone around here is willing to help." Lauren sat on the floor. She leaned back against the couch and pulled her legs on her chest. "You know, the way the Magisters talked about the Hallow, they made it sound like these people were on our side."

"They are," Rose answered, looking over her shoulder at Lauren. "They're hesitant."

Lauren shook her head. "They won't even give us pages from our own book, let alone come back to Rifton and help us fight the Renati. They want us to do all the hard work so they can come back to town once the coast is clear. They want the Renati gone but won't do anything to help us get there."

"It's annoying," Brooke agreed. "Everything we went through to burn the ledger, and they still won't help us. We're going to get ourselves killed if we're the only ones fighting."

"Jake wants to come back to Rifton with us. He said he knows he'll have to stay here in the immediate future but he wants to fight." I sat down on the couch, my knees resting against Lauren's shoulder. "I guess Marin and some of the other witches have been skeptical of Elementals for a while, saying we're trouble."

"Oh, that's a great sign." Rayn ran her fingers through her hair. "Even after everything we've already done to help out here."

"Who knows." Rose sighed. "Tomorrow is a new day. Maybe they'll come around sooner than we think."

Aden chortled but didn't share his opinion out loud.

We took turns reading aloud from Jake's book about the Allurements as we brushed our teeth in the sink and got dressed for bed. Apparently, the Shepherd's missing pages may have explained *how* the key unlocked the labyrinth. Jake had been filling in the gaps of where it actually hid. We compared Jake's notes to the Shepherd's book but anything about the labyrinth had been torn out.

Aden sat quietly in the corner, chewing on a piece of beef jerky. Rayn sat on the floor at his feet. Brooke ran her fingers over the pages torn from the Shepherd's spellbook

"I wonder if I'll get any visions about the labyrinth. You'd think if we're the ones who are meant to go through it that I'd get some kind of heads up." I watched Brooke with the Shepherd's book as I braided my hair. "I have to get some control over my visions."

"That would be helpful." Brooke glanced up with an encouraging smile.

Lauren tapped her thigh, deep in thought. "So Jake wants to help us, but he can't hand over the pages because he's only an Archivist in training?"

"That's my understanding of the situation, yes." I nodded. "Amanda must have a protection spell on them that only she can break."

"I think we should take him back home with us," Lauren said. "Whoever wants to help should come back and fight."

I turned to look at the girls. "I told him we would come back. I don't want to leave him locked up here forever, not when he can help."

"He may not be the only one. I bet there are younger members here that don't want to be stuck in the forest waiting for Erebus to find them," Rayn agreed, hugging her knees to her chest.

I chewed on my bottom lip, deep in thought. I had gotten into Nic's mind without even trying. Our pull was so strong, but he couldn't be the only one I could reach. If all Elementals were reincarnated from past lives destined to find one another for the rest of our existence...couldn't I reach them?

"I want to try and trigger memories," I announced to the girls.

"A memory or a vision?" Rayn specified.

"Both? Nic told me about this really cool ability Abbie had. She was their Seer, remember? She could look into memories. We think the vision I had of him burning down that building had been me subconsciously accessing one of his memories," I explained. "Nic showed me a memory of Mom and I'm thinking I should be able to do that with other Elementals too."

Rayn tilted her head. "Can you do that?"

"I'm going to try. I got into Nic's head without trying, and if we are all connected...I don't know, maybe I can reach memories of the past generations and get some firsthand information on this Seer who drew the Hallow map. Maybe they have more to offer than the witches who actually live here."

"That would answer a lot of unknown questions we have about the Elementals who came before us. What a hell of a power," Lauren praised.

"That would be amazing," Rose breathed. "How are you going to do it?"

"I have no idea. I got into Nic's head without even trying."

"Yes, but that's different. He stood right in front of you," Lauren pointed out.

I chewed on my lip. "Not when I saw the first memory of the fire that killed Abbie." I turned to Lauren. "I hadn't even met him yet."

Brooke nodded. "It's worth a try. I'm desperate enough for anything at this point."

"Me too," I admitted, silently worried how far that desperation would push us.

Brooke's eyes widened. "Wait! Can you pick which past Elemental you can see or is it random?"

"I don't know, honestly." I shrugged.

"You have to go back to Gabriel's memories!" Brooke exclaimed. "Literally anything you'd be able to learn would be helpful. He's already taught me so much about my powers through his writing. It would mean the world to me, Whit."

"Okay," I agreed. "That at least gives me a starting point."

"Plus, it might answer some of our questions as to what happened with the rise of Erebus. Why the Elementals fell. Knowing what happened could help us deal with where we are now." Rose pointed out. "Since they were members of the Martyrs."

Rayn reached out for my hand. "How can we help? What do you need from us?"

"I don't know," I admitted and took her hand in mine. "The memories I've seen so far have been involuntary. Even Dmitri showed me the memory of him and Abe at the lake. I didn't initiate it. When I saw Bryan's conversation with Serenity, he already thought about it."

"All you can do is try." Lauren climbed up into the loft bed. "Preferably tomorrow, because I'm going to pass out."

"Me too." Brooke climbed up the ladder behind Lauren.

"Yeah," I agreed, plopping down on the small couch. "Maybe I can practice. Go off into the woods to meditate and see if I can trigger something."

"If anyone can do it, you can." Rayn smiled at me encouragingly.

Chapter Twelve
Memories and Tea Leaves
Whitney

I had no idea if my theory about triggering past memories would work, but I had to find out. A few nights later, I took some supplies and left the bustle of the compound. The sounds of voices from the dinner crowd carried off into the trees, but I ventured far enough out that I could concentrate.

Of course I didn't go alone. Aden stood guard a few yards behind me. He gave me enough space to practice my craft but stayed close enough that he could defend me if he needed to. I had assured Aden I would be fine out here on my own, but he insisted.

It warmed my soul to see how protective he had grown. At first, I thought his loyalty only extended to Rayn, but his dedication appeared to be an umbrella that covered all of us.

Even in the darkness, the forest looked different than it did around Rifton. It felt different. The fern at the base of the nearest redwood spanned out the size of a dining room table. The long, thin leaves of the sword fern reached out as if it intended to say hello.

I knelt down in the cold dirt and lit a candle with a match. I watched the flame dance in front of me, letting my body relax.

Fire had always brought me comfort and familiarity. Getting to relax in a warm shower and enjoying a hot cup of coffee at the end of a long day. Fire was Bryan, his heat radiating into my very being as he showed me I was easy to love. Fire was Rayn, holding my hand through the hardest times of my life. Fire was Nicky, showing me parts of his soul he had kept locked away for years. Fire felt like home, and a good place to start this experimental exercise.

I closed my eyes and took in a deep breath of the cold forest air. Water droplets clung to the moss that grew on the sides of the trees. I concentrated on the water that hung in the air and let it course through my bones. While my element stuck out to me the most, I became hyper aware of the other elements surrounding me. The dirt held firm below me, the air filled my lungs. The fire before me and the very spirit in my body. All connected, each of them part of me. The elements were not separate entities but intertwined, one unable to exist without the others.

My girls and I.

I took in the sounds of the forest; the leaves rustling against the branches in the soft breeze. Even the chirping crickets were louder under the shield. I let myself go and became one with the forest. My shoulders relaxed and my breathing steadied. I unclenched my jaw and the weight I had carried for months lifted off my body. I felt like my body floated off the ground, above the clouds to that beautiful waxing gibbous moon in the sky.

I thought about Gabriel, the Spirit Elemental from the Martyrs who had taught Brooke so much through his writing. She had blossomed into such a capable witch and healer, inspired by his words. I focused on his name, silently calling out with my magic, reaching out a hand.

Suddenly, my stomach dropped and churned, spinning my head. For the first time since my visions began in Amilia's office all that time ago, I felt relief in the oncoming sickness. I rubbed my eyes and gave them time to adjust but the darkness overwhelmed my blurry vision.

A man's voice muttered from across the way. I moved closer to the sound though I could barely see, almost as if the room was thick with smoke or I had something over my eyes. The outline of a man hunched over a desk came into my hazy vision. A table, maybe? Blurs of glass orbs sat all around him. Bottles? He muttered to himself, scribbling in a book chaotically, or at least I think he did based on how quickly the quill danced across the page. He shot onto his feet and dashed out of sight. I wanted to follow him but I felt myself slipping back into my body.

As my vision became clear again, I returned to the forest with the half-burnt candle before me. Raindrops pattered down from the sky, sprinkling over me. I threw out my arms and welcomed the cold water.

A laugh escaped my lips and I threw my hands over my mouth. I did it! I had triggered a memory of generations past. I don't know who I saw or what they were doing, but it didn't matter.

I had never felt more powerful in my life.

I blew out the candle and gathered my things, rushing back to Aden.

He took a good look at me and replied, "You seemed frazzled. Did it work?"

"It worked! Let's go tell the girls." My heartbeat pulsed through me like pop rocks.

Aden followed me to the guest cabin where the girls waited. I played with the rain falling from the sky, alerting the girls that Aden and I were the ones bursting through the doors.

Rayn jumped up from her chair as we entered. "Did it work?"

"Yes!" My voice filled the small cabin as Aden and I shed out wet jackets. "Kind of. Everything was fuzzy and I don't really understand what I saw, but I definitely triggered a vision."

"Do you know who you saw?" Brooke jumped to her feet. "Gabriel?"

My smile widened. "I think so. A man wrote in a book with glass bottles and jars all around him, an apothecary maybe."

Brooke lept in the air. "This is amazing! We are going to learn all kinds of things about him! And other generations too."

"I hope I can do it again," I admitted.

"We have faith in you." Rose put her hand over mine.

"It was so easy getting into Mit, Nic, and Bryan's memories back home, but I thought that was only because I knew them, and they let me in. I didn't know if I'd be able to reach across generations to those who had already passed on," I paused. "Should I try another generation? The Shepherds? Maybe I can see what happened when Erebus rose to power."

"It's definitely worth a try," Lauren agreed.

A few evenings later, Roberta invited me into her tiny home. It was smaller than Marin's, with a sitting area and two chairs on either side of a little table. Both of the chairs had blankets draped over them. A kettle sat on a single burner connected to the solar panels on the roof. Steam rose up from the kettle and two tea cups sat next to the burner, waiting for the water to boil. The earthy fragrance from the tea sitting in the cups wafted through the air.

I peaked around at the rest of the tiny house. Roberta's bed sat up in a loft, a small ladder hanging off the edge. Quilts and throw blankets were thrown on every surface, giving the small area a cozy and welcoming vibe.

Raindrops pattered against the roof as Roberta poured the water and offered me a cup of tea. "I wanted to apologize if I came on too strong about your mother when you first arrived, asking questions you and your sister weren't ready to answer. I understand how difficult her loss must have been for you."

"Thank you." I took the tea cup and sipped the warm liquid. The Hallow didn't have any coffee and I missed it, but the tea still spiked my senses. The blend of spices tickled my throat as I swallowed. "So, Dominic stayed here for a while when he was younger?"

Roberta nodded. "Why do you ask?"

"He's my friend. Amanda made a comment that he tried to hurt himself. I worry about him, even now." Nic had done a great job keeping himself together, considering everything, but I hadn't forgotten about him crying on the floor over his sister or the pain in his voice when Warren was killed. "I know there are years of distance, but sometimes I still see that damage in his eyes."

"I have always worried about him. He and Finn, their Spirit Elemental. The two of them were always so...unbalanced. Their magic too chaotic for their personalities."

My shoulders fell. "Finn died of a drug overdose, from what I've heard."

Roberta shook her head. "I am not the least bit surprised, unfortunately. Amilia always wore rose petal glasses with the Flame Elemental. He was a sweet little boy, he wanted to try. He didn't use his magic for seven months while he stayed here, but he worked hard when I had him. I hope he grew into a somewhat stable man."

"He has his moments." I ran my fingers around the rim of the teacup. "Were the Hallow residents weary of him too?"

"At first, but some of the adults knew him already, and one Elemental is not five." Roberta paused as her gaze met mine. "You and the girls are an entire generation with a hunter in tow. They will be skittish no matter what."

"I understand. We disrupted the peace, even though we didn't mean to." I chewed on the inside of my cheek. "Can I ask you something?"

"Of course, dear." Roberta took a sip from her cup.

I pondered asking this question, but I'd never know if I didn't. "Do you know much about Seers?"

"I'm familiar with the concept, if that's what you're asking?" Roberta tilted her head.

I took a deep breath. "Do you know of any Seers who were able to trigger their visions or memories?"

Roberta pondered and then slowly shook her head. "Not that I've read of, but many things happened in the past that were not documented. Why do you ask?"

"I'm trying to better understand my visions," I admitted, telling a half-truth. "Sometimes I don't always understand what I see. They aren't usually specific, even the memories."

"Is there something in particular you saw that is bothering you?" Roberta rested her elbows on the table.

I let out a sigh. Roberta deserved to know what I saw about the Hallow's future, she was their leader and if I could do something to protect these people we needed to act.

"I saw the Hallow...on fire."

"Oh..." She paused, wide eyed. "That is worrisome."

"I don't know how, or who, or when...or even if," I admitted. "But I saw it burning."

Roberta pursed her lips. "Have you had visions like this before?"

"The only other true vision I've seen was of Rayn being kidnapped. I saw where she would be held by the Renati, but my vision showed me as the one taken. So they aren't always exact," I explained. "When I saw the Hallow burning, a tornado spread the flames and destroyed everything as shadows attacked the witches."

Roberta remained quiet for a moment. "A fool's hope to think we could last out here forever."

"You truly have built a remarkable community," I encouraged. "I know you didn't plan on us showing up, or Erebus for that matter."

"No," Roberta whispered with heavy eyes. "But life is full of moments we do not anticipate."

I took a final sip from my cup and set it down on the table. Roberta didn't hesitate to reach across and pick up the cup, studying the contents. She turned the delicate china in her hands, analyzing the inside of the cup. Roberta's brow furrowed and she finally tilted it towards me, showing me the loose tea leaves at the bottom.

"What do you see?" I asked, familiar with the practice.

Roberta cleared her throat. "What do *you* see?"

I paused, hesitant to have any insight for our future. What if I saw how this would all end and we were not victorious? I wasn't sure how that punch to the gut would affect my generation's morale. But I took the cup anyway; if I could get some kind of insight on our future, I'd be an idiot not to take it.

I tilted the cup and peered inside. The loose tea leaves were scattered throughout the bottom. I turned the cup, waiting for a clear sign, but only an x.

"I see a cross," I told Roberta. "It reminds me of the Renati symbol."

"Trials and great suffering," Roberta replied. "The symbol is to the right of the handle, meaning it lies in the future."

I scoffed, not the least bit surprised. "Fitting."

"Futures are never written in stone, but pain and suffering is part of everyone's journey. The ability to feel is what makes us human."

I shifted my weight as my own words came back to bite me. "I gave this speech to my brother not long ago but it feels empty being on the receiving end of it."

Roberta smiled. "Dmitri. He's nearly a grown man now."

I glanced up from the cup to meet Roberta's gaze. "He's tall."

"I'm not surprised. Kyle was a tall man."

"You knew him?"

Roberta sighed. "Unfortunately. I'm sure by now you know the sad tale of him and your mother?"

I shook my head. "She never spoke about him. I didn't even know his name until we moved to Rifton after she died."

"Audri probably wanted to move on as if it never happened." Roberta nodded and took the tea cup back from me, giving it another glance.

"What else do you see?" I asked.

"To the left of the cup are symbols of the past." Roberta handed the cup back to me. "What do you see?"

I focused on the cup, waiting for something to stick out. Three little circles all linked together sat at the left side of the handle. I pointed them out. "These circles are like the Elemental symbol, only there aren't five of them."

"What else do you think they could be?"

"Bubbles?"

Roberta smirked. "Chain links?"

"Chains," I echoed, squinting my eyes at the three circles. "Chains in the past, or chains of the past?"

Roberta leaned back in her chair and took another sip from her cup. "I'm curious to know how *you* interpret them."

"Both," I whispered. "Losing my mom weighs heavy on me every day. Amilia sacrificed herself to save me. Both of their deaths are the direct result of my actions. I don't think I'll ever get over that."

Roberta let out a sigh. "Surely you know nothing is that simple."

"You weren't there," I snapped, sliding the tea cup across the table. "Suffering and more suffering. Thank you for the reading."

Roberta sighed and shifted her weight in the seat. "Being an Elemental is a burden, one that I know you didn't ask for. I know the generation who came before you wasn't ready for what they faced."

I blinked at her, not sure if I should be offended or not. "They've been through a lot."

"They have." Roberta nodded. "Chains of the past are heavy for the reincarnated Elementals. Do you feel the weight?"

Staring down at the tea cup, I let her question sink in. "Somedays are better than others."

Roberta put her hand on top of mine. "I hope your generation is ready for what you will face, Whitney."

I opened my mouth to defend myself, but stopped. Instead, I took in a deep breath and collected my thoughts. I didn't want to hear it, but the truth in Roberta's words remained. The girls and I had been through so much together. Our powers and our bond as a generation had grown stronger because of it, but we carried a lot on our shoulders.

"It's heavy," I admitted. "But I'm not carrying it alone. My generation is strong, and we are supportive of one another. Together, we're capable of whatever our futures hold."

Roberta smiled. "I believe you."

Chapter Thirteen
COWARDS
Whitney

A woman dashed into Roberta's home, panting heavily like she had run a marathon to get there. "Roberta!"

Roberta stood from her seat, gripping the edge of the table. "Tell me."

"There's something around the perimeter. Something is attacking the shield." Fear echoed in the woman's eyes as she spoke.

"Renati?" Roberta's voice cracked.

The woman shook her head. "There aren't any people, they're...animals. I don't know what they are. They look like cougars. Like...demons."

"Shadows." I let out a short breath and turned to Roberta. "They're Shadows."

"They can't penetrate the shield." Roberta sat back down. "There's no way they can get past our defenses."

"Are we going to risk that? Are we not going to prepare for that possibility?" I asked.

"It isn't a possibility." Roberta returned to her tea.

Something in my gut told me otherwise.

The pull.

"Yes, it is." I jumped up from my chair and rushed past the scared witch. When I got to the porch, most of the Hallow residents were outside. They talked amongst themselves in hushed whispers, looking to one another for answers. Their eyes darted across the compound, searching in the darkness. A woman picked up a small child and held them to her chest. They looked terrified.

As they should be.

I found the girls, standing by the gardens with Aden only a few steps away. He watched the impending chaos bubble around us with a watchful gaze.

"Shadows," I whispered when I got to the girls. "There are Shadows attacking the shield."

"Can the shield withstand them?" Rose scanned the panicked witches.

"Roberta thinks so, but I don't," I answered, my heart thudding in my throat.

Lauren nodded with wide eyes. "I feel it too. I don't know what they did when they created the shield, but they did it to keep Renati and wild animals out, the Shadows are neither."

"Shit," Rayn hissed, balling her fists. "They're going to get through."

"We have to stop them before they can." My hands trembled as I swallowed the lump in my throat.

The witches of the Hallow didn't realize they were being faced with a real threat. Part of me wondered if any of them had ever seen a fully formed Shadow, if they understood what knocked at their front door.

"How many Shadows are there?" Brooke turned to the open gate at the entrance. "Can we even take all of them?"

"Only one way to find out." Rayn started towards the main gate and glanced over her shoulder. "You guys coming or not?"

"I need my weapons." Aden stepped towards us. "I cannot help defend this place with my bare hands."

"Where is Marin?" I searched the residents who had gathered around us, but Roberta's sibling was nowhere to be found. I approached the nearest witch. "Where is Marin?"

"I-I don't know," they answered with a shaky voice. "I haven't seen them for hours."

I groaned and went back to the tiny house where Roberta still sat with her tea. "Where is Marin? Aden needs his crossbow."

Roberta rested her elbows on the table. "Whitney, the Shadows will not penetrate the shield." She attempted to ease me down but I fought back.

"They will! I told you about my vision. I told you I saw the Hallow on fire. I won't let that happen!" My voice echoed throughout the tiny room. "Aden needs his weapons. *Now*."

Roberta shook her head. "Whitney, I cannot arm a witch hunter in the middle of the compound. It's not safe."

Rage boiled my blood but this time I didn't swallow it. "Aden is not a threat, I've told you a million times! He will fight to defend the Hallow but you have to get his weapons. Marin has them locked in their cabin. Roberta, search your gut, you know I'm right. You know the pull when you feel it."

Roberta hesitated before she let out a sigh and stood up. "All right."

"Thank you." I breathed in relief.

I followed Roberta out of the building and waved for Aden to come with us. He trailed eagerly behind as we made our way to Marin's cabin. Roberta waved her hand over the locker and a bright light shone around it, breaking the spell that kept it locked. Aden didn't hesitate to grab his crossbow and pistols, quickly securing them to his body.

"Whitney, we–"

"Get everyone back inside their cabins." I cut Roberta off. "Put up a shield around the compound itself. I don't care what you do, Roberta, but do something. We'll take care of the Shadows."

I tried to straighten my back as I walked away, attempting to keep the shaking in my knees unnoticeable. I didn't want her to see me falter, even in the slightest. I wouldn't risk our moment to prove ourselves to the witches of the Hallow.

"Are we good?" Rayn asked as Aden and I approached the group.

"Yes," we both answered. I wasn't sure who she had asked, but we all took off out the gate nonetheless.

The massive wooden gates creaked as they closed behind us. I let out a short breath of relief seeing that Roberta listened, at least partially. She wasn't stupid. Roberta had done an amazing thing bringing all these witches out here and keeping them alive for so many years, keeping them safe.

"Where are these Shadows?" Lauren asked as we jogged away from the compound.

I realized I didn't know.

Rose pointed off to our left with a trembling hand. "This way. I can feel them digging in the dirt."

"Are they trying to dig under the shield? How deep does it go?" I wondered out loud.

"Let's go find out." Rayn motioned for Rose to lead.

We followed Rose through the trees. I didn't look back at the Hallow as we disappeared into the forest. The girls and I had dealt with Shadows before, we knew their weaknesses and how to defeat them. The witches at the compound didn't have the same firsthand experience and I didn't want to find out how they'd fare against the demons.

We trudged behind Rose for a while, all of us staying on high alert. We couldn't afford to be caught off guard by a fully-formed shadow.

Lauren spun around in a circle. "No one is watching us."

"I don't feel the Shadow's eyes on us either." Rayn picked at her nails nervously.

Rose huffed. "But I feel them in the dirt still. We are getting close to the edge of the shield."

Aden held his loaded crossbow in both hands, ready to strike at a moment's notice. "Can you tell how many?"

Rose shook her head. "No, but I do feel there is a lot of digging. I'd guess a dozen, maybe more."

A dozen of them. Six of us. At least two Shadows for each of us.

I hardened my second ice skin, not wanting to get tackled without it. This time, I'd be prepared. We moved towards the edge of the shield together as a group.

"Do you think–" A snarl behind us cut Brooke off.

The Shadows had made it through the shield.

"Shit." My blood ran cold as I turned around to face a familiar winged Shadow that I swore we had left behind in Rifton. The only positive of seeing Big Boy in front of me: knowing he was nowhere near my loved ones back home.

Flames erupted from Rayn's hands as she went to throw a fireball at the winged shadow. As her flames grew three times their normal size and caught a fern next to us ablaze, I remembered Nic's warning. The oxygen levels under the shield were higher than the rest of the forest.

Tell Rayn to watch her fire or she'll burn the whole place down.

"Put it out!" I ordered my sister, stepping away from the spreading fire to assess the damage.

"Fire is the only thing that will stop the Shadows," Rayn protested over her shoulder.

"Ray, it's spreading. Put it out," Rose echoed my concerns. She buried her hands in the dirt, trying to create a barrier around the flames to stop them from leaping to the next tree.

I conjured the biggest thunderstorm I could, focusing my power above the foliage that burned. But our attention was split. While Rose and I did our best to keep the forest from burning down, the Shadows circled us.

Aden shot a bolt at one of the Shadows but it bounced off of their rock-hard skin.

Brooke closed her eyes and let out a deep breath, drawing my attention away from putting out the fire. Why the hell would she put herself in danger? Surely the Shadows would attack knowing she had her eyes closed, unable to see them sneaking up on her.

Before I could call out to her, the fire crackled and I turned back to it. The rain had put out the bigger flames but the wood split from the shock of the heat. Rayn brought her hands together and the flames shrunk with her movements. The embers had already reached the base of a neighboring redwood. The flames licked at the bark, catching the bark aflame.

"Brooke?" Lauren shouted, sending a chill up my spine.

Rayn and Rose shifted their attention from the burning tree. As the rain from my thunderstorm poured down onto the fire, I turned back to where Brooke stood. Where she *had* stood.

"B?" I called out, scanning the forest for her. "Where's Brooke?"

"She disappeared!" Lauren held her hand up in the air, and quickly closed her fist. One of the burnt branches snapped off the tree and hurled through the air at the Shadows. Two of them knocked back from the impact.

The Shadows hissed, letting out a gut-wrenching scream that would haunt my dreams. The embers from the branch Lauren threw at them seemed to be enough and they didn't get back up for a second attack. My attention had been so focused on the Shadows that Lauren took out with the burning branch, I barely noticed the one sneaking up behind her.

"Lo!" I shouted, getting her attention as the Shadow swiped at her with its paw.

Lauren's feet left the ground and she levitated away from the snarling Shadow, but its claws still caught her arm.

I threw an energy wave at the Shadow at the same time Lauren used her powers to lift it into the air. My attack sent the Shadow flying into the burning tree trunk. It screamed as the flames took them.

"Are you okay?" I dashed to Lauren's side, looking up at her.

"I'll be fine." Lauren remained in the air, turning her attention to the other Shadows as blood trickled down her arm.

"Where the fuck is Brooke?" Rose shouted, panicked.

Big Boy lurked towards me, his wings pulled close to his body. His ears bent back as he snarled. I readied myself for an attack when Brooke appeared out of thin air. She caught the winged Shadow off guard and hit him with an energy wave so strong, it fell onto its back.

With Big Boy down and distracted, Rayn hit the Shadow hard with a roaring fireball. Her attack collided into his side, singeing the scales on its body. The winged Shadow let out a yelp of pain and scrambled back to its feet.

By the time it got its bearings, Rayn prepared another strike. She hit it with another fireball in the face as beads of sweat fell from her brow, all her focus on containing her flames. Big Boy shook his head, as if attempting to shake off the attack but the second blow to the face did some damage. The Shadow kept one of its eyes closed as it backed up away from us, pawing at its face.

It leapt into the air and spread its wings, flapping hard to get airborne. The wind stirred up from his massive wings whipped dirt and leaves around. I covered my face as little particles found their way into my eyes. I used my powers to flush the debris from my eyes with water as Big Boy disappeared into the sky.

The remaining Shadows took off sprinting towards the Hallow. My vision of the compound up in flames washed over me and I ran after them, the others close behind. Aden's long legs carried him faster than my short, thicker frame and he soon passed me.

Even with his hunter abilities, the Shadows outran Aden. By the time we got back to the Hallow, massive claws scratched against the wooden gates.

Roberta hadn't put up a fucking shield.

Rayn's powers tingled under my skin as she prepared to unleash on the Shadows, but the flames roared out of control. Her magic extinguished.

"Ugh!" Rayn yelled out in frustration. "What the hell am I supposed to do? I can't contain it!"

Screams from the other side of the tall fence erupted as the Shadows tore at the wood, chipping away at it with their talons. I mustered all my magic and shot an energy wave at the row of demons. They faltered as the attack knocked them off balance, but it didn't stop them.

"I have an idea!" I shouted, turning to the girls. "Rayn, launch a fireball at the Shadows. The rest of us will contain the flames around a shield. We'll trap them."

Rayn's powers warmed in my stomach before I finished my sentence. Rayn nodded and held up her hands. "I'm ready!"

The rest of us stood our ground, preparing to catch the flames in the shield before they touched the wooden fence around the Hallow. Rayn snapped her fingers, sparking flames in both of her hands. She combined them into a fireball that grew faster than she seemed comfortable with. She regained her balance and threw it, levitating the fireball towards the center of the Shadow pack.

The moment it left Rayn's hands, the four of us cast a shield above the Shadows. The flames struck one of the smaller Shadows in the middle, and it cried out in pain as the shield touched down in the dirt. Fire danced behind the glimmering barrier and the cries of the Shadows muffled. Smoke filled the shield quickly as Rayn's magic joined with ours. We contained the Shadows until their cries and growls fell silent.

Once I felt the compound was truly safe from the attack, I lowered my hands. We dropped the shield and held our breaths, waiting for another attack. The smell of sulfur filled the air, but none of the Shadows budged. I scanned the row of limp stone bodies, searching for wings, but Big Boy was not amongst the dead monsters.

"How did he get away?" I whispered to myself, taking a brave step forward. I stopped to scan the tree line around the compound. He still lurked out there somewhere. I knew it. If the Hallow was lucky, he headed back to Rifton. That possibility left a knot in my stomach. I wanted to end things with that demon right here, prevent him from hurting anyone.

"Oh, Lauren, you're still bleeding." Brooke reached out and took Lauren's hand in hers, healing the gashes from the Shadows. Thankfully, Elemental magic protected us from the poison in the demon's talons. The witches of the Hallow wouldn't have died right away, but it would have definitely begun to shut their bodies down.

Flashes of Bryan being attacked by the Shadows came to the forefront of my memory. The fear that swam through him as his lungs constricted. The way his pupils dilated as he struggled to breathe. I shook my head and reminded myself that Bryan had survived.

"Is everyone all right?" Rose called out, shoving the wooden gate open. Part of me hoped she had unlocked the gate with her powers but I never felt them.

I inched past her and entered back into the safety of the Hallow. Everyone hid inside the various buildings. I don't know why Amilia and the Magisters were so insistent that we impress these witches. They were all cowards.

How could they possibly help us fight Erebus and the Renati when they wouldn't even defend their own home against a group of Shadows?

Chapter Fourteen

OVERSTAYED WELCOME

Whitney

I stood in the center of the Hallow with my arms crossed, glaring at each of the shut doors until someone finally dared show themselves. One of the cabin doors creaked open and a man stuck his head out. Seeing us standing next to the town hall building, he stepped out onto the tiny porch.

"Are they gone?" he called out.

"No thanks to you," Lauren muttered with her hands on her hips.

I chortled and nodded at Lauren, silently agreeing. "Yes!" I shouted across the way. "Come see for yourself. There is a pile of charred Shadow remains by the gates."

The man stood on his porch, frozen in fear. Steps echoed behind me as Roberta finally emerged from the town hall building. She wrung her hands together, scanning the Hallow as if she expected there to be damage or casualties. She let out a sigh and turned to me with a smile in her eyes that I did not return.

"You didn't put up the shield," I hissed through my teeth.

"I–" Roberta paused as more of the compound's residents came out of their houses. "Show me these remains."

Without another word, I led a group of witches to the gates. The girls and Aden followed close behind. The witches kept their distance from Aden and he must've noticed. He put his weapons away in their holsters but kept them loaded.

The charred pile of Shadows were still smoking when we approached. Mouths gaped open to expose rows of stone teeth, their long, skinny tails wrapped around their legs. Their paws lay limp but their razor sharp talons still sent a chill through my body.

One woman gasped, covering her mouth at the sight of them. "Don't let the children see!" she cried out.

Amanda spoke with her hand over her chest, "What the fuck are those things?"

"Demons," Roberta answered. "Monsters from the Shadow Realm."

"We were able to close the portal to the Shadow Realm, but it took longer than we would have liked," I explained, staring down at the steaming Shadows. "Shadows came through into our world. There shouldn't be as many now, but the ones here are getting stronger by the day."

"It's true!" a woman cried from the crowd forming around us. "Erebus has truly returned."

"Are you fucking kidding me," Lauren muttered under her breath.

Rose announced to the crowd, "This is what we have been trying to tell you!"

Amanda's eyes locked into mine as I turned to her. Her pupils dilated, and the bottom of her eyes lined with tears. "Okay."

"Okay what?" I turned to her and shrugged.

She cleared her throat and wiped away a stray tear. "I'll give you the pages."

I couldn't keep the laugh inside my chest. "It only took Shadows attacking the Hallow's gate for you to give in?"

"It doesn't matter." Amanda shook her head and turned away from the Shadows. "Take the pages and do what you have to do."

"Thank you."

About fucking time.

As infuriating as this whole thing had been, Amanda only did what she felt would protect her people. At the end of the day, that's all I tried to do. I didn't think it would take a pack of Shadows attacking the Hallow to get the missing pages we had come for, but at least we had gotten through the event unscathed.

An unsettling realization churned my stomach, looking around at the Hallow still intact.

None of this explained my vision.

"I cannot thank you enough." Roberta turned towards us. Her gaze traveled up to meet Aden's eyes. "And you too, thank you for defending us. I...I cannot explain how the

Shadows penetrated the shield but we will fortify it as best we can. In all the years we have been here, nothing has ever threatened the shield until…your visit."

I knew what Roberta had insinuated without her needing to spell it out. We are getting the pages. The Hallow remained safe. Time for us to go home.

"You think the Shadows came because of us." Lauren crossed her arms.

Roberta sighed. "Personally, I believe it was only a matter of time before something found its way here. But there will be many residents who believe the Shadows followed you here."

I couldn't help but roll my eyes. "We'll leave now, then."

"Now?" Rose turned to me with wide eyes.

I shrugged. "All we need to do is open a portal and go home."

"It might not be a bad idea," Brooke agreed. "Get the pages and leave before anyone gets too upset over this attack."

"Wait." Roberta held up her hand. "A portal? You aren't going back to Rifton through the woods?"

"Absolutely not." Lauren shook her head. "It took us days to get here and the woods are littered with things trying to kill us. A portal is the safest way home."

"But…to open a portal means breaking the Elemental Code," Roberta informed us.

It took me a second to realize Roberta meant it. I wondered how she'd feel if she knew how many times the girls and I had broken the Elemental Code in the last several months.

"We don't follow the Code," Rayn answered, simply.

Roberta lifted her brow in surprise but she didn't say much. "I see."

I narrowed my gaze and studied her expression. "But the Elemental Code was established to keep witches from exploring dark magic, to protect them. So what is wrong with us? Is that what you're thinking?"

Roberta's shoulders fell as if she had been defeated. "It's a slippery slope between the Elemental followers and those loyal to Erebus. The Code is all that separates us."

"There aren't two sides of magic, there's only magic. We have never used our powers with ill intent," Brooke informed her.

"But the Elemental–"

"We *are* the Elementals." I cut her off. "We decide the Code, and we have decided not to adhere to old, outdated laws."

"Very well," Roberta whispered. "It is your Code to follow or break, after all."

I turned to the Archivist who had grown very silent during the end of the conversation. "Amanda, we'll follow you to the library."

"We'll go get the Shepherd's book," Brooke said as she and Rose took off towards the cabin.

Amanda nodded and led the way to the back room of the library. She hesitated briefly, then lifted her hand and waved it at the wall. A glow of bright gold light shone as the charm broke and the wall opened.

Amanda stepped inside and we followed close behind. In the back lay a pedestal that reminded me of the one that the Renati ledger sat on during Founder's Day. Amanda picked up the stray pieces of parchment and stared down at them before she handed them over.

"They are protected like the other old texts. They look old but they are pretty resilient. They won't age or fade. If you put them against the book where they were been ripped from, they should reattach themselves," Amanda explained.

"Thank you." I breathed in relief.

Brooke and Rose rushed into the library with the thick, leather-bound book in Rose's arms. The book began to tremble in her hands and it flew open, pages flapping after one another. Once it got to the end where the jagged remains of the pages attached to the spine it stopped.

I slipped the pages into the book and a bright light exploded in the room, blinding me. I closed my eyes and turned my head away, waiting for the light to diminish. Even behind my eyelids, it shone as bright as the sun. When it dimmed, I opened my eyes to a complete book. The pages bonded back into place as if they had never been removed.

Amanda chewed on her bottom lip for a moment. "Please don't forget about us."

"Why would we?" I turned to look at her.

"Just..." Amanda stared down at the ground with tear-filled eyes. "Now that you have what you wanted from us, please don't forget about us in this whole thing. I hate to admit it, but after the attack today...I think we are more defenseless than any of us would care to admit." She glanced up to meet my gaze. "It would be easy to leave us defenseless."

Rose stepped forward. "We won't forget, and you won't be defenseless. If you ever need our help, all you have to do is ask for it. But protecting yourselves is a necessity you have to get comfortable with."

"But that goes both ways," I reminded Amanda. "We will also call on you."

She nodded. "I understand. We'll answer."

"Thank you." I let out a short breath of relief as Brooke gently closed the spellbook.

We gathered our belongings from the guest cabin and tried to ignore the glances of the Hallow residents as we walked to the main gates.

Considering we had saved the entire compound from a Shadow attack, they didn't appear to be grateful for our help. After everything we had done, they were still afraid of us, or at the very least apprehensive. I didn't know if we would ever fully gain their trust and that unsettled my nerves.

Jake met us by the gates with a soft smile, though his eyes were heavy with sadness.

I handed his Allurement book to him. "I believe this belongs to you."

He took the book from me and stared down at the cover. "I hope something in there helped."

"You were beyond helpful. You have no idea how your work has paid off."

"In that case, a parting gift." Jake handed his Allurement book back to me, his smile widened.

I took the book from his hands. "Are you sure?"

"Totally. Bring it back to me when you return," he paused. "You are actually planning to come back, aren't you?"

I nodded. "We are. We aren't going to ghost you guys, I promise. This isn't the Elemental's fight against Erebus, it's all of us. Everyone is going to be affected by it."

"I couldn't agree more." Jake surprised me by leaning down and giving me a hug. "Stay safe out there."

"Thank you. We'll be okay, we've survived this long." I rubbed Jake's back and lowered my voice. "I'm coming back for you. You'll leave the Hallow with us the next time I visit, I promise."

I heard the smile in his voice. "Thank you, Whitney. I'm really looking forward to that."

Jake stepped back from the hug and gave the other girls and Aden one final wave before he went back inside the library.

"Thank you, for letting us stay and for feeding us." I took Roberta's hand as she and Marin escorted us out of the compound. "Do you want help fortifying the shield before we go?"

"No, we can take care of that ourselves, but thank you," Marin answered, crossing their arms.

"Are you sure?" Rayn asked but Marin shook their head.

Lauren narrowed her gaze on them. "Where were you, Marin?"

"Excuse me?" Marin raised their brows.

"When the Shadows attacked. Where were you?" Lauren asked again.

Marin scoffed and let out a laugh. "I was moving the children to the underground bunker. Don't come into my house and question my loyalty. I don't care what kind of witch you are."

Roberta put her hand on Marin's elbow. "It's a genuine question, Mar, I don't think they intended to be accusatory." Marin gave a slight nod as Roberta cupped my cheek. "It was a pleasure having you girls and getting to know you. I see Audri in your spirit." She looked over at Rayn. "In both of your hearts."

Tears caught in my throat as I smiled at her. "Thank you. Meeting all of our mom's old friends has been...I feel like we know her better." I reached into my pocket and handed Roberta one of the blue lace agate communicators that Abe had given me. "Here, in case you ever need to get a hold of us."

Roberta smiled down at my hand and took the crystal. "Thank you, girls."

Rayn nodded. "It's been an honor, truly. Thank you for everything." She stepped forward and gave Roberta a hug. "Even you, Marin, thank you."

"Thank you for helping us against the Hunters. You're a badass," Lauren said to Marin. "If you ever need anything, let us know."

Marin smirked. "Sure."

"Ready, girls?" Brooke asked.

"Question." Aden stepped forward, gripping the strap of his bag. "This...portal. How does it work? I...I think I'd rather go through the woods."

"Not alone," Rayn disagreed. "You'll be fine, I promise. Portals feel kind of like roller coasters."

"I hate roller coasters," Aden huffed.

Rayn smiled. "You're safe with me, I promise."

Aden only nodded, securing the buckle between his backpack straps across his chest.

Rose emptied a potion vial onto the ground and pulled a dagger from her backpack. Seeing it glisten in her hand sent me back to the night we closed the Dragonfly Mystic portal that led to the Shadow Realm.

"Whit?" Lauren brought me back to the present, holding the handle of the dagger towards me. "Ready?"

I hadn't realized everyone had already cut their hands and were waiting for me. I took the dagger from Lauren and sliced through the meaty part of my palm, over the tiny white scar that remained from the last two portals we had performed. I wiped the blood off on my jeans and tucked the dagger into my bag, letting the blood from my wound drip down into the dirt.

Soon, the energy before us began to swirl and bend. The ground creaked and shifted as the portal became visible, swirling around like a whirlpool.

"I can't go in there." Aden took a step back, his eyes wide with fear.

Rayn reached out and took his hand in hers. "You're safe with me. I have done this before."

Aden wrapped his fingers around the back of Rayn's hand and closed his eyes. With a nod from him, Rayn stepped forward to the edge of the portal.

"Ready? On three," Rayn said to Aden, looking up into his scrunched face.

I had a hard time imagining a massive witch hunter with altered DNA afraid of anything, but I had never seen Aden this scared before.

"One, two," Rayn paused, readjusting their hands so that Aden's fingers were laced with hers. "Three."

The two of them stepped forward and through the portal, disappearing from sight.

Rose and Brooke clasped hands and went next.

Lauren glanced over at me with a sad smile. She held out her hand. "Are you ready to go home?"

"Yes." I clasped her hand in mine and gave a gentle squeeze. "We have people waiting for us."

Lauren nodded and whispered, "I hope so."

We both stepped off solid ground and into the whirling portal.

Chapter Fifteen
Homecoming
Whitney

The swirling magic of the portal opened up right where we intended – the cottage. We had only been gone for two and a half weeks but it already looked different. The flowers near the back garden had all wilted and most of the once lush plants had been ripped from the planter boxes. The lights inside the house were dull and the air smelled too plain; no scents of fresh herbs or baked bread wafting through the air. Smoke came up from the chimney but the house had been stripped of everything that made it feel alive.

I stood in the backyard, waiting to see a silhouette in the window. Waiting for someone to come out onto the porch and see us. Did I go to the front door and knock like a guest? Did I walk up the back steps and stroll into the kitchen like I owned the place?

I reached my emotions into the house but I couldn't feel anything. Bryan wasn't there, but why would he? He'd be in Falcon Bay. Even if he had been in Rifton, I couldn't imagine why he'd come to the cottage without us there. Still, my heart grew heavy at the thought.

"Feels so much longer than eighteen days." Rose's voice broke the silence, looking around at the barren garden.

"Are we going in or are we sleeping outside?" Rayn marched up the back steps. She opened the back door and shouted into the house. "We're back!"

"Ray?" Dmitri called from inside.

I rushed up the stairs at the sound of my brother's voice. Shoving the door into the kitchen all the way open, I collided into him and Rayn hugging. I threw my arms around both of them as tears stung my eyes. Dmitri wrapped an arm around my shoulders and pulled me against his chest, holding Ray and I each in one arm.

"What the fuck?" He finally stepped back and dropped his hands around his hips. "Seriously, guys, what the actual fuck?"

"I'm sorry." I wiped a tear from my cheek with the back of my hand. "We didn't know what we were going to come across in the forest and we wanted to keep you safe."

Dmitri scoffed at our excuses. "Typical bullshit. You two never fucking listen to anyone. Two weeks? You disappear for two and a half fucking weeks?"

"We got the missing pages from the Shepherd's book," Rayn explained, as if her words would ease the tension in Dmitri's shoulders.

"Oh, thank fucking god for that." Dmitri spat out sarcastically and crossed his arms. Hurt washed over his face as his eyes softened. "I didn't know if you were ever coming back."

"I told you in the letter we would." I reached out for his arm but he pulled away.

Dmitri glared at me. "You never do anything you say you will, so what was I supposed to think?"

"I'm sorry, Mit." Brooke came up behind us, awkwardly rubbing her arm. "You have every right to be furious with us."

"Trust me, I am." Despite his anger, Dmitri put his arm out and welcomed Brooke into a hug. "Stupid. You're all so stupid."

"Good to see you too, bud." Lauren patted Dmitri on the shoulder as she walked into the house. "Where are the Magisters?"

"Harmony said she'd be back soon. She's been at the Corner Cup all day," Dmitri answered, pulling Rose into a hug as well.

"Where's Nicky?" I glanced down into the living room as if I'd hear his bedroom door at any moment.

Dmitri shrugged. "He does whatever the hell he wants. No wonder you two get along so well."

I opened my mouth to shoot back at my brother but I bit my tongue. He had spent the last eighteen days worried about us; wondering where we were, if we were safe. Wondering if we were ever coming back. He deserved to be mad, and I wasn't going to tell him to get over it when he was entitled to those feelings. I'd be furious if he had disappeared.

"Bryan promised he'd take care of you if anything happened to us." I watched the fire behind Dmitri's eyes ignite.

He lifted his brow. "And you think *I'm* mad at you..."

My heart skipped a beat, sending a chill through my body. "What does that mean?"

"You heard me." Dmitri turned and walked out of the kitchen. "I have homework to finish. If you decide to skip town again, maybe give me some warning before you leave." He stopped in the entryway leading to the living room and turned to look over his shoulder. "I'm glad you're home."

I glanced over at Rose, who already met my gaze, chewing on her bottom lip. "Do you think he's really that mad?"

"Who?" Rose asked. "Your brother or mine?"

"I need to go see him." I dropped my bag on the kitchen floor and stepped onto the porch. "Wait, where are my car keys?" I went back into the house, shuffling around in the fruit bowl where Amilia always kept her keys. "Dmitri, where are my keys?"

"What are you going to do, drive to Falcon Bay tonight?" Dmitri came back into the kitchen and frowned. "Shouldn't you at least call the guy first?"

"I didn't ask for your opinion, Mit, I asked for my keys." I dumped the bowl out on the counter, but the keys to my Eclipse weren't there.

"Whit." Rose placed a gentle hand on my shoulder. "He should be coming back to Rifton the day after tomorrow."

"No. I've already made him wait too long." I turned to Rose as tears blurred my vision. "What if I made him wait too long?"

Rose let out a short sigh. "He's patient."

"Should you even be driving? You haven't really slept in days," Lauren pointed out with concern. "Maybe you should wait until you've calmed down a bit."

"I am calm," I snapped, knocking the fruit bowl over on its side. "Where the fuck are my keys?"

"Whit, it's getting late. You won't get there until way past dark." Dmitri took another step towards me, his voice and demeanor calmer. "If you insist on going, go in the morning." He looked me up and down. "At least take a shower first."

I glanced down at myself, mildly offended, but I also knew how long it had been since I properly bathed. My shoulders fell. "I don't want to let more time pass."

"One night isn't going to make a difference," Rose replied warmly. "Trust me. He isn't going to dump you on the spot."

"I'm leaving first thing in the morning." I picked up my bag and headed to the bathroom.

"Um, no you aren't." Harmony's voice filled the room. "You're not going anywhere, Whitney."

"Oh, sorry, *mother*." I turned to face her. "I forgot you were the boss of me."

"What a fuckin' brat." Harmony looked over her shoulder. "Your child is a fucking brat."

Nic walked up behind her, and shrugged. "A trait that carried over from the previous generation." He smiled at me with relief in his hazel eyes. "Welcome home, did you get the pages?"

"Brooke has them." I motioned towards the girls. "I'm going to Falcon Bay in the morning. I have to see Bryan."

Harmony slammed a stack of files down on the dining room table. "You and Lauren are working shifts at the Corner Cup tomorrow. I need an opener and a closer. You have no idea the shit I've been putting up with trying to cover your damn hours." Harmony pointed to her head. "Did you ever stop to think about the colossal mess you left us all in when you bounced without a second thought? You irresponsible little shit heads."

"While we're yelling at each other, thanks for telling us about this fucking key we need to unlock a labyrinth!" I shouted at Nic and Harmony. Disbelief brewed under my skin at everything they had kept from us.

Rayn crossed her arms. "Seriously, what the fuck you two?"

The Magisters glanced at one another before Harmony spoke. "We weren't going to let you march off to the Allurement without explaining everything. We needed the pages to even know how this would all work."

"There's always a catch. Always something you're keeping from us." I moved closer to them as I continued to shout. "Did you know the key is broken up into fragments?"

"Yes," Nic answered in a soft voice.

"Did you know that one of those fragments is currently being held by Bonnie fucking Drake?" My voice vibrated off the walls.

He nodded.

"Where are the other two pieces? With Maggie, who no one has spoken to in years?" I crossed my arms and glared at my friend. "Where is Mia's piece, Dominic? Roberta said Mia had part of it."

Harmony pointed towards my chest. "All *you* needed to worry about was getting those damn pages so we could plan our next move. Do you think Nic and I are incompetent? Of course we know about the key fragments! We were here when they broke the damn thing up!"

"Fuck off." I pushed past them with a scoff, smacking my shoulder into Harmony.

"Hey, hey, hey." Nic came after me, reaching out to grab my arm. He followed me down the hallway and stopped me in front of the bathroom. "Talk to me, Goose."

"What?"

"Oh, I'm old. Nothing. It's from a movie." Nic rubbed his face. "What happened? Why are you so freaked? Did something happen at the Hallow? How is Roberta? You gotta give me something, kiddo."

I ran my fingers through my tangled hair. "I have to talk to Bryan."

"And you will." Nic put his hands on my shoulders. "Listen, I saw him on Sunday, he's fine."

"He's mad at me."

"He'll get over it. You have to focus on what's in front of you." Nic took my bag off my shoulder and set it on the ground. "Let's go sit down. I need to know what happened at the Hallow. Are you hangry or something? Get some food and take a deep breath. You have a boyfriend, and you'll still have one in the morning, okay? Focus, Whit."

I took a deep breath and let the tension leave my body as the air left my lungs. "I'm leaving first thing in the morning."

"I heard you." Nic offered a soft smile.

"I'm not working a shift at CC tomorrow."

"I will work your goddamn shift like I have been for the last eighteen days but you will be gone one night, and then you're coming home to help fix this cluster, okay?" Parent Nic was out in full force, giving me a long enough leash to satisfy my anxiety but reeling me back in when he needed me to behave.

"Okay," I whispered, accepting the terms.

"I'm really glad you're home." His thumb rubbed gently against my hoodie.

I nodded.

"I missed you."

The tension left my shoulders and I pulled Nic into a hug. "I missed you too."

"What do you want to eat?" he muttered into my shoulder. "I'll make you something. Go sit down."

I went back down the hall and slumped onto the couch next to Dmitri, hugging a leg to my chest. "A grilled cheese."

"You got it. You guys hungry?" Nic asked the girls as he strolled into the kitchen.

"Yeah, a grilled cheese sounds good." Rayn eyed me carefully as she sat down on the couch. *You're losing your mind.*

I need to see him.

You will, I promise. Rayn nodded and turned to face Aden. "It's too cold for you to sleep in the shed." She glanced over at Harmony. "I know this isn't an easy ask, but...is Warren's bedroom still open?"

Harmony's shoulders fell and she let out a short sigh. "Yes."

Rayn's eyes glistened as she looked at Aden. "Move into the house, please? There's no reason for you to sleep outside."

Aden tensed, and his lips turned to a thin line. For a moment, I thought he might decline the invitation. He finally asked, "Are you sure?"

"You've more than proved yourself, Aden," I encouraged him. "You're one of us now."

The whisper of a smile curved up the corner of his lips. "Thank you."

Nic stepped into the entryway between the kitchen and the dining room. "Thank *you* for keeping the girls safe."

Aden gave him a slight nod in return.

Dmitri stirred next to me, letting out a short sigh. His shoulders remained tense as he stared off into the corner of the room. He still seemed angry at us for leaving.

"Hey." I reached out to my brother, grabbing his hand. "I won't go to Falcon Bay if you need me here, Mit."

"No, you should go see Bryan," Dmitri said, his voice heavy.

"I want to be here for you."

Dmitri turned to look at me. "Bryan matters too. He's been...Abe and I couldn't have gotten through the last few weeks without him."

Of course he stepped up. I knew when I'd asked Bryan to look out for Dmitri that he would follow through. Bryan already treated Dmitri like his brother, his own flesh and blood. He was the kind of person my brother needed in his life. Dmitri had us but he'd never had a man to look up to, someone who could relate to him on a level that we never could. My eyes welled with tears that I quickly blinked away.

"Is Abe doing okay?" Rayn asked.

"Going to see his parents was nerve wracking at first, but they were so happy to see him. He finally believes that we can protect all of them from the Renati," Dmitri explained.

I swallowed, hoping that still held truth.

Harmony scoffed and sat down at the dining room table. "We've been fine here, thanks for fucking asking. Lauren's father is still unconscious in the hospital. We've been slaving away keeping the doors of the Corner Cup open in your absence. It's been fantastic."

I curled my lip at her sarcasm.

"Things haven't been going well with Amilia's...estate?" Rayn spoke as if her words were acid, wrinkling her nose.

Harmony leaned forward, glancing through the kitchen as if she looked for Nic, but her attention quickly returned to me. "Amilia left me the Corner Cup and the bank accounts. I knew I was the beneficiary on the accounts, but I didn't know about the coffee shop."

"What about the cottage?" Rayn asked.

"I'm getting there." Harmony ran her fingers through her wavy brown hair. "Audri remained the beneficiary of the house. She used to be the beneficiary of the Corner Cup but Mia changed it after the accident. I thought she had changed the house too, but apparently she didn't."

"But Mom....What does that mean for us?" Rayn blinked at Harmony.

I knew. I had dealt with enough legality settling everything after the car accident to know the line of succession.

"That means the house is ours," I announced.

Harmony nodded.

"Wait, all of ours?" Rayn clarified. "Not just Whitney's? Because when Mom died, the house went to Whit."

"That's probably because Audri specified the house would go to just Whitney," Harmony explained. "Since Mia had Audri as the sole beneficiary, the house equally belongs to all three of you. Dmitri too. I had to charm a notary and forge some signatures, but the paperwork is done."

"Hang on though, how can we afford that? I had to give our old house back to the bank before we moved here," I pointed out.

"The cottage is paid off, there is no bank. You own it outright. I think there's enough of us living here now that we can pull off utilities and food. That is if we can keep the Corner Cup going, since we all fucking work there now." Harmony huffed and paced across the room.

My mom was Amilia's beneficiary. How different our lives would be right now if Mom still lived when Amilia passed. Would Mom have decided to come back to Rifton to deal with all the hardships Harmony was now facing? Would she have taken over ownership of the Corner Cup? We may have moved back here anyway, and I'd have the same job I do now. I could have still met Bryan. I trapped myself inside of that daydream, checking out of the conversation until Brooke put her hand on my shoulder.

"Did you hear that, Whit?"

"Sorry, no. What?" I looked up at her worried gaze.

"Here's your sandwich." Brooke handed me a plate with a golden brown grilled cheese.

Dmitri cleared his throat, his voice broke as he talked. "That's not everything Amilia left us."

"What do you mean?" Rose sat down on the floor and placed a gentle hand on Dmitri's knee.

"Mia was an Archivist. It's a title that passes down, and the Archivist chooses who will take over for them when they die." Dmitri took in a deep, shaky breath. "Mia chose me."

"Wait." Lauren put her hand up. "You're our new Archivist, Mit?"

Dmitri nodded. "I have no clue what I'm fucking doing. She never said a word to me about it." He glanced over at the bookcases. "All I know is that those books are mine now."

Rayn and I looked at each other with wide eyes.

"Are you okay?" I asked my brother.

Dmitri shook his head. "Not in the least."

I wrapped my arm around his shoulder and pulled him close to me, trying to comfort him even though he towered over me. Dmitri snaked his arm around me and held me in place.

Rose tilted her head, deep in thought. "So, what exactly does this mean, Dmitri being the new Archivist? He is responsible for keeping the spellbooks safe?"

"It's more than that." Dmitri stood up and crossed the room towards the bookshelves. "I can feel them, like they're vibrating. They…call out to me." He ran his fingers along one of the spines. "I started to feel it after the cottage attack, but I didn't know what it was at first, not until I read Mia's letter."

I slid to the edge of my seat. "Mia's letter?"

Dmitri nodded, staying close to the bookcase. "It appeared on the dining room table…as if it were charmed to appear after she…" Dmitri cleared his throat. "Anyway, it explained everything. I don't know. I don't think I'm ready to accept it."

Brooke turned to me. "We should've brought that Archivist in training from the Hallow with us. Did you bring home the book Jake let us borrow?"

I nodded and set my plate on the side table. "It's in my backpack."

"Who is Jake?" Nic settled down in one of the arm chairs and glared at me. "Eat your damn sandwich, Whitney."

"He's their Archivist in training." I picked the sandwich back up and took a bite. "He hates it at the Hallow and wanted to come with us, but...You're right, B, we should've brought him."

"If he is the Archivist in training, who is their actual Archivist?" Dmitri asked, finally turning away from the bookcase.

Rose answered, "Her name is Amanda and she took a lot of convincing to trust us. I'm still not sure she does. Jake seems to like us though, he has been collecting information on the Allurements for years and compiling it in a separate book."

I swallowed my next bite. "He thinks he knows where the center of the Allurement is, but he isn't sure how the key works. That's what the Shepherd's pages are for, right?"

Harmony nodded from the dining room table.

"You'd think if they're supposed to be big magnets pulling on our magic, they'd be easy to find," Lauren replied.

"I know what you mean, but if it's powerful enough to do what everyone thinks then that kind of magic wouldn't be easy to find." Rose chewed on her bottom lip, deep in thought.

"And we can't exactly wander around the forest until we feel the pull of the magic," Brooke said.

"No, if it were that easy, the Renati would have found the Allurement already." Harmony ran her fingers through her long hair again. "We were always told the Dark Star Forest was an Allurement and not much else, but the forest is massive. It takes up a huge chunk of the state."

"The location is pointless if we don't have the key," I announced, taking the final bite of my sandwich.

Dmitri nodded slowly. "Then let's find the key and get this over with."

Everyone seemed to say everything they needed to and one by one, they trickled out of the room. Rose and Brooke went home, eager to see their parents and to sleep in their own beds. Lauren and Rayn went to their bedroom while Harmony and Dmitri wandered into the kitchen.

"So, Roberta is okay?" Nic lingered behind.

I nodded. "She seemed fine, yeah. Happy to hear you came home. Amanda had a lot to say about you."

"Like what?" Nic lifted an eyebrow.

"That you were kind of a wreck the last time she saw you. That she knew Abbie." I paused, wondering if I should say the rest but if I were Nic, I'd want to know. "She told us that you, um, tried to hurt yourself when you were there."

Nic chewed on his bottom lip. "Kind of personal."

"I'm sorry." I studied his face, his expression void of any emotion though a heavy gaze took over his eyes.

"Did she say that in front of everyone?"

"Me and the girls."

Nic huffed. "Fuckin' Amanda. She could never keep her damn mouth shut." He ran his fingers through his dark hair, grabbing at the roots. "I'm glad you made it there without any issues."

"A moose almost killed me." I leaned back on the couch, getting comfortable. "And Shadows penetrated the shield, but we killed them."

Nic's head shot up. "I'm sorry, *what?*"

I told him about the moose trampling the tent; how it crushed my leg and Brooke fused my bone back together. I explained what had happened earlier that day with the Shadows, how we left before the Hallow residents accused us of leading the Shadows there.

"Jesus Christ, Whitney." Nic looked at me with heavy eyes.

I put my hand up to stop him. "I'm okay now, but we got off to a rocky start. The map wasn't…it wasn't super accurate."

He groaned. "Shit. I'm so sorry."

"It's okay." I shrugged. "We're home now, we got what we went for."

He winced and let out a deep sigh. "It's not okay. I'm the one who sent you in my place. I told you how to get there. I could've gotten you killed. Fuck, I almost did." Nic looked towards the fire, the flames reflecting in his eyes. "I'm sorry, kiddo. Things have been…not great here either."

"Harmony's losing her mind." I glanced over my shoulder towards the kitchen.

Nic nodded. "She is slowly going insane, yes. She's stretched so thin, it's only a matter of time before she snaps. We really have to step up now that you and the girls are back." He glanced back my way. "Unless we close the Corner Cup."

"I don't want to do that." I shook my head, not even wanting to entertain the thought.

"Neither do I, but we can only do so much." Nic's shoulders tensed as he spoke. "There's a black cloud over Rifton, and it's growing darker every day."

"I was afraid of that," I admitted. "I had to keep reminding Roberta that an actual threat existed. The Hallow witches have grown too comfortable in hiding."

"I'm not surprised, but it's time for them to step up. Roberta and Marin had so much fight in them before their house burnt down. I hoped seeing you girls would light a spark in them," Nic paused, shifting his weight. "There was a Shadow in the back lot of the Corner Cup."

I sat up straight. "Did it attack anyone?"

"Nope, just enjoying a leisurely stroll. Dmitri and I think it was doing surveillance, but it walked right past us without a care." He chewed on his bottom lip. "I don't know how much time we have left but Erebus is stronger than ever."

I hugged my knees to my chest as a chill ran over my body. "Have you seen him since the attack?"

"Yeah," Nic hesitated. "I've had a pit in my stomach ever since."

"Nic, I–"

He cut me off with a small, fake smile. "Be careful in Falcon Bay tomorrow. Make sure nothing follows you over there."

"So, the Shadows have gotten worse?" I dared to ask, bringing the conversation back to my fears.

"Killing us has gone to the back burner," Nic answered, his eyes wandering off to a spot on the floor. "Erebus won't be happy until he's run us all out of Rifton, until he has a new haven to rule over. I don't think he'll stop at the city limits."

I stared back at my friend, seeing his fear paralyzed me. "How the fuck are we going to stop him in time?"

"I don't know." Nic's honesty rattled my core.

"I'm scared, Nicky," I admitted as the threat of tears built in my chest.

Nic looked at me, his eyes glazing over. "Me too."

Chapter Sixteen
Mutual Respect
Whitney

I left my car in Rifton and took the first bus of the morning to Falcon Bay. I hoped Bryan and I would make up and I'd ride back to Rifton with him the next day. And if we didn't, well...I guess I hoped that wouldn't come to fruition.

I spent the entire bus ride with my headphones in, listening to Bryan's main playlist on his Spotify account. My forehead rested against the cold glass of the window, watching the pine trees zoom by until the bus reached the coast. Salt water engulfed my senses the moment I stepped off the bus in front of Falcon Bay University. The waves splashed against the rocky shore line, echoing through the air and calming my nerves.

According to Bryan's class schedule, he currently sat in History 338: The United States in World War II; the last elective of his undergraduate career. I scanned the giant campus map posted at the bus stop and found the nearest coffee shop. It was only nine in the morning but I didn't have time to grab coffee before I left the cottage and my vision had begun to blur. I ordered myself a quad iced coffee and a warm chai for Bryan. Hopefully, showing up bearing gifts would soften the blow of disappearing for two and a half weeks.

I double and triple checked the photo of the map I took to make sure I stood in the right courtyard, but I still wasn't satisfied. "Excuse me?" I asked a student walking past. "Is this the Umpqua Building?"

"Yep," they answered and went on their way.

Okay, right place at the right time. Now to hope Bryan walked through this courtyard when his class ended. I closed my eyes, taking in a steadying breath. Everything would turn out okay. I loved Bryan and he loved me and he'd be excited to see me, right? Yes, I had a lot to apologize for but if the roles were reversed, I would forgive him. Wouldn't I?

I was pretty positive I would. I had gotten mad at him in the past but I had gotten over it. It's easier to forgive someone when you love someone with every fiber of your being.

I kept my senses on high alert, waiting to feel any extra emotion. Any kind of indication that Bryan was close by. After what felt like an hour had passed, I checked my phone again. Bryan's class had ended five minutes ago, and still no sign of him, visually or emotionally. I took the last sip of my coffee and plopped down on a bench, letting out a defeated sigh when a spark erupted in my chest.

Sadness.

An all too familiar sadness stirred under my skin, causing the hair on my arms to stand straight up. Bryan felt more than sad, he was worried. I jumped up from the bench and turned in a circle, doing a full scan of the courtyard. My pulse rushed through my body with anticipation and nerves when I couldn't find him. Finally, I glanced up the stairs leading to the second story of the building and saw him.

Bryan wore a navy blue and dark gray hoodie. His hair had been brushed back out of his face, probably from raking his fingers through it during class. His black-rimmed glasses made their appearance as they did when he felt too tired to put in contacts. The girl he walked with was all smiles, chatting away about something. I recognized her as the bartender from New Year's Eve.

Though Bryan actively engaged in conversation, his mind appeared elsewhere. The way Bryan glanced down at his black and white vans, the way his hands were buried into the front pocket of his hoodie. He replied to Lana but his eyes were anywhere but her, until finally they were on me.

Bryan froze three steps from the bottom, locked at me as if I were a mirage, a figment of his imagination. Something he'd pictured in his mind so many times that he began convincing himself I couldn't be real.

I gave a small smile and waved, barely moving my trembling fingers. The moment of truth. He would either turn and head back up the stairs or meet me at the bench. I held my breath, waiting for him to make a decision.

Bryan turned to Lana and mouthed something, waving goodbye to her as he trotted down the last three steps and jogged towards me. Tears sprung from my eyes as I left my belongings on the bench and met him halfway. I leapt into his arms and he caught me, pulling me close to his chest. He lifted me up and I wrapped my legs around his waist, tightening my grip on him. I couldn't hold my emotions in. I buried my face in his neck and let the sobs leave my lungs as I soaked his hoodie in tears.

"I missed you." He nuzzled his face against the side of mine.

"I'm so sorry," I sobbed, grabbing fistfuls of his hoodie as I clung to him for dear life. "I'm so so sorry, I hated leaving but I–"

"Shhh." He ran his fingers through my hair and tightened his grip around my back, holding me up with one arm. "Can we get into all that later? Right now I want to be happy you're back. You are back, right?"

I nodded into his neck. "I'm not going anywhere."

"Good." He gave me one last squeeze before he lowered me to the ground, my feet resting on the concrete. Bryan cupped my cheek and wiped a tear away with his thumb. He gave a half-smile and lowered his mouth to mine, pulling me into a wet and desperate kiss.

I racked my fingers through his hair, deepening the kiss with open lips. I had dreamed of this moment every night since we'd left Rifton but nothing my mind came up with compared to the real thing. He was excited to see me. He didn't hate me. He wasn't mad.

"When did you get back?" Bryan asked as he pulled away, keeping a hand on the small of my back.

"Last night. I came here on the first bus of the day," I answered, gently grabbing his arm. I didn't want to let him go.

His heart weighed heavy in his chest. "Is Rosie okay?"

"Rose is fine." I tightened my grip on him. "Everyone is safe, we all made it back okay."

Bryan nodded and let out a sigh of relief. "And you already saw your brother?"

"Yeah, at the cottage last night."

"Good, I'm glad you saw him first." Bryan glanced over his shoulder. "I have to turn in a paper for my next class but after that I can ditch the rest of the day."

"Oh, I didn't even think about you having a busy day. I didn't intend to make you miss class." I chewed on my bottom lip.

"Fuck class." Bryan leaned down and gave me another quick kiss. "Let's drop off my paper and then we can go somewhere to talk."

"Okay, um, wait. I got you some tea." I went back to the bench and handed him the cup. "It's probably cold now, I'm sorry."

"Don't be." Bryan took the cup and sipped, not even making a face when the chilled chai touched his lips. "I like iced tea as much. Thank you."

I picked up my bag and secured the straps on my shoulders.

"Ready?" He held out his hand.

I nodded and mustered a smile as Bryan laced his fingers in mine and led the way out of the courtyard.

"Why did you take the bus?" He asked as we fell in line with the rest of the students traveling the pathways through campus.

"I hoped things would go well and I'd ride back to Rifton with you."

Bryan glanced over at me. "Why wouldn't things go well?"

I looked away, watching the people in front of us. "Dmitri said you were pissed."

He sighed, tightening his grip on my hand. "Doesn't mean I'd make you walk all the way home. I still love you."

"I love you too, I just–"

"Can we please get into it later?" Bryan winced as he looked at me.

"Yeah, I'm sorry."

"No, it's okay, we're okay. I just...give me a minute?" He brought my hand to his mouth and kissed my knuckles.

"Okay...I'm sorry, I've been going over what I wanted to say on the ride here and there a million things I want to say to you."

"We have all day, so don't stress about it. I want to show you around, is that okay?"

"Oh, yeah, around campus?" I scanned the bustling college.

Bryan nodded. He gestured across the lawn to the massive building towering over all the others. "That's the bell tower. It rings every hour, which can be kind of annoying but you get used to it. During orientation they let you go inside, not all the way up but still pretty cool. It's the tallest point on campus. And across there on the other side, the building with the four points in each corner is the library. There's a basement where all the older volumes are kept. I had a class down there my sophomore year. And over there next to the Umpqua building is the main hub of the English department. That's where I spend a lot of time."

"And your next class?" I asked. "Romance?"

"Romantic Literature, yeah. The novels are better than I thought. Part of me expected a semester of Jane Austen."

"Not a fan?"

Bryan shrugged a shoulder and took another drink. "Not my favorite."

When we got back to the apartment, Bryan kicked off his shoes and headed straight for his bedroom. I followed, leaving my sneakers by the front door. I took a quick glance around the dark apartment. Emma must have been in class.

Bryan tossed his backpack on a chair in the corner of his room and sat down on the edge of the bed. He grabbed my waist and pulled me between his legs. He tightened his arms around me and held me close to him, burying his face into my chest.

"It's been a long couple of weeks," he muttered into the fabric of my hoodie.

"For me too, believe it or not." I ran my fingers through his hair. "Leaving wasn't exactly easy."

"And you went anyway."

My heart skipped a beat. "I had to, Byn. I know it doesn't seem like it but we had no other choice."

"Can we lay down?" he asked. When I nodded, he picked me up and laid me down, climbing into bed next to me. He rested his head on the pillow and closed his eyes, his glasses slightly skewed to the side.

Mixed emotions swirled under his skin. Happiness of my return. Sadness that I'd left in the first place. Irritation that I'd left the way that I did. Worry that I would probably leave again without saying anything to him.

He fell silent, drumming his fingers on the bed. His mood had shifted as I assumed the excitement of seeing me wore off and the reality sunk in that I'd left in the first place. A tinge of anger lingered under his skin.

I sat up in bed and criss crossed my legs. "Look, I know it was a lot to dump Dmitri in your lap, and I know you only agreed because the cottage had been attacked and we'd watched Amilia and Warren...I know you didn't actually plan on having to and–"

"I'm not mad about Dmitri." He cut me off.

"I know you guys get along and all that, I just...I figured he already lived at the house and–"

Bryan propped himself up on his elbow. "I'm not mad that you left Dmitri with me. I'm mad that you left."

"We had to go to the Hallow. The Magisters weren't going to let us go at first, and then at the last minute Nic gave us directions. We had to take our opportunity before it passed." I picked at my cuticles as I explained everything I didn't write in the letter. "We needed missing pages from a book, and Roberta, who is the head witch of the Hallow, gave us the exact information we needed. There would be no next step if we hadn't gone when we did."

Bryan let out a deep sigh. "That's great and all, Whitney, but you didn't have to leave in the middle of the night. Do you have any idea how fucking terrifying it was to wake up in that empty bed not knowing where you were? Left with nothing but that bullshit note where you apologized a million times but did you actually mean it?" Bryan sat up and looked me stone cold in the eyes. "Dmitri had a panic attack. I didn't know what to do. I eventually talked him down but he had himself convinced that you and Rayn were gone for good. Went on about how he'd lost everyone that he'd ever loved. Dmitri lost your mom, too, Whit. He had to watch Warren and Mia both die right in front of him too, and then he woke up and his sisters up and left him behind."

Hurt overwhelmed my core. Bryan spoke as if I hadn't been riddled with guilt over leaving Dmitri. "I talked to my brother. He let me know how he felt and I apologized to him. I came out here to apologize to you, to set things right so we can move past it."

"The world doesn't revolve around your family, you know. Do you think it was easy to watch Nic charm my mother?" Bryan narrowed his gaze. "They had to charm Jack too because he lives there, of course he noticed Rose wasn't home. There are so many people affected by your actions but none of you stop to think about any of us, do you?"

"All I do is think about you!" My voice dripped with hurt as I defended myself. "That's why I came here to see you instead of waiting for you to come back to Rifton. I couldn't let this go another day, Bryan!"

Bryan's voice broke and he rubbed his face with his open hand. "You take advantage of our relationship."

"What?" I snapped. "Take advantage?"

"Yes!" He raised his voice as a pang of anger broke free in his chest. "You do whatever you want, convinced that I'll still be here whenever you decide to get back, and fuck, Whitney, I want to be but you push me too far sometimes."

I blinked at him before I spoke. "This is a matter of life and death, Bryan, I wasn't on vacation."

"Don't pull that." He shook his head and put his hand up. "I understand the severity of our situation. I am not dense. I lived through the cottage attack too. But you cannot up and leave us in the middle of the night. You can't keep pushing me away and expecting me to wait around like a dog." Bryan sighed and took my hand in his, rubbing my knuckles with his thumb. "We're supposed to be partners. I don't want to be in a relationship where I'm not an equal part of it, where I'm not respected or considered. You have to trust me, baby. You should have told me where you were going."

"You would have tried to come with us." I stared down at our joined hands.

"Probably." He nodded, his temper plateauing. "But I also might have agreed to stay back and help hold down the fort. You don't know what I would have done because you never give me the chance. You didn't give Dmitri a chance either. Haven't we been through enough together by now that you don't have to keep me at arm's length? I've more than proven myself, Whit."

"I do trust you, but we had to-"

Bryan put up his free hand. "If you say keep us safe, I'm going to snap." He tightened his grip on me. "We promised we wouldn't push each other away."

I chewed on the inside of my cheek, breaking eye contact. "I didn't know what we were going to find out there, so I figured it would be better to take as few people as possible." I finally looked back into his green eyes. "I should have told you. I'm sorry about the letter. I thought it was better than leaving without saying a word. I at least wanted you to know we were planning on coming back and not being gone forever. But I guess things in Rifton have gone downhill the last few weeks?"

"The air is heavier," he admitted, reaching out to turn my face towards his. "It's hard to breathe when you're gone."

"I know, I hated being away from you. I'm sorry."

"Next time you go somewhere, Dmitri and I will be kept in the loop. I'm not asking."

I nodded. "Okay. We opened up a portal between the cottage and the Hallow that only we can open, so..."

"Why didn't you do that to get there in the first place?"

"I didn't know how to get there. Nic barely knew where it was and he's the one who drew the damn map." I tightened my grip on his hand. "It'll be easier to travel back and forth now, and we will have to go back. I promised them we would. Roberta gave us the missing pages but they won't help us fight the Renati."

"Why the hell not?" Bryan furrowed his brow.

"I think they're scared. You should have seen the way they looked at us, like we weren't even human...It was surreal. We have to show them that fighting is the only option."

"That makes sense. Sometimes I want to run away too," Bryan admitted, and it surprised me.

"You do?"

He nodded. "Oh yeah, I think about it all the time. Pack what we need into our cars and leave, throw a dart at the map and run. Go somewhere the Renati can't follow."

I scooted closer towards him. "You know, someone very handsome and wise once told me that running away from your problems doesn't work because you take them with you."

"Hence the fantasy." He forced a smile. "I know it's not realistic, but a guy can dream, right?"

"Tell me more about this dream." I leaned into him, hoping that we were past the argument. I heard him. I loved and respected him enough to understand I had fucked up.

Bryan wrapped his arm around me and pulled me back onto the pillows. "Something about a porch swing."

I leaned up and kissed his cheek. "Hey, I do love you, and I do respect you. It wasn't you, it's all of it. Losing my mom and Mia and the weight of it all seemed too heavy."

"It's too heavy because you're carrying it all alone." Bryan paused, deep in thought. "Wow, your magic really is regenerated from past generations."

"What?" I glanced up at him.

"You and Harmony...She is drowning and won't let anyone help her settle things with Amilia's death. She will let people take shifts at the Corner Cup and that's it." Bryan shifted his weight, tucking me under his arm. "Nic has argued with her incessantly and she won't share the load. She decided she's in charge and you do the same thing with us. You decided it would all be on you and you barely let anyone in. You barely let *me* in."

"I–" I stopped as his words sank in. I buried my face into his chest and squeezed my eyes shut. "Fuck."

He rubbed my shoulder and held me tight. "I admire your dedication, baby, I do. You're the strongest person I know, but you aren't alone. You have an entire crew of people here to help, me and Mit included."

"Thank you for sticking with me through all this. I don't know what I did to deserve you."

He leaned in and gently pressed his lips to mine. "Tell me about the Hallow."

I told Bryan about the compound, about the tiny homes and the greenhouses. How they use magic to sustain themselves and live off the land. The apothecary and the shield over their section of the forest, how no one knows how old it is and how it changes the oxygen level. How much bigger the animals were. I conveniently left out the hunter attack and getting trampled by a moose, but he definitely seemed intrigued by the witches who hid out in the forest.

"That's insane. Troy talks about how those people abruptly left Rifton. It's crazy to think about how much he knows without even realizing what is going on under the surface."

"So, how exactly has Troy been with Emma for so long and not learned the truth about her family?" I asked.

"Emma doesn't want to tell him, and I guess being powerless makes it that much easier. There aren't any slip ups for him to see. She keeps her family at arm's length anyway, so Troy assumes they have regular family drama and doesn't ask too many questions about things he knows she doesn't want to talk about. Especially after her falling out with Serenity."

I paused, wondering if I should even ask, but I needed to know. "Speaking of, has there been any new developments on that front? Nic said something about Erebus but conveniently left Serenity out of the conversation."

Bryan shook his head. "I've seen her around but she doesn't speak to me, big surprise there."

I lifted an eyebrow. "Serenity said she was going to kill you."

He scoffed. "If Serenity wanted to kill me, she would've done it when they attacked the cottage." Bryan met my gaze as nerves swam through his veins. "I think they're planning something big."

"Something big?" My heart skipped a beat.

Bryan nodded. "They have to be. Why else would they attack the cottage and then back off? Why would they have let you guys leave town, not follow you and on top of it, leave us alone while you're gone? Lauren left town and they killed her mom but your entire generation leaves for weeks and they don't lay a finger on us?" He licked his bottom lip. "It doesn't make sense. I'm kind of nervous."

"Well, now that we have the missing pages from the Shepherd's book, we can move onto the next piece of the puzzle." I nuzzled into him. "We're one step closer to blowing the lid off this thing."

"And what is the next puzzle piece?" he asked into my hair.

"A key. Apparently there's a trial we have to go through to open the powers locked in our jewelry, and this key is the only thing that will open the portal. It's broken up into pieces though," I explained.

"Oh, cool, a scavenger hunt," Bryan sarcastically sighed. "We don't have time for this."

"I know, but one of the pieces is here in town."

His interest piqued. "You have it already?"

"No," I paused. "It's, uh, with Bonnie Drake."

A jolt of panic shot through him. "Em's mom? Are you joking?"

I shook my head. "I wish, but that's what the people at the Hallow said. I guess Bonnie used to be part of my mom and Mia's coven before she got together with Henry. She was my mom's friend and she betrayed them, taking the key with her."

"We barely got away with destroying the ledger, how do you think we're going to pull off stealing from the Drake's again?" Bryan tilted his head.

"I honestly don't know yet, but we'll come up with a plan. Tomorrow we'll go home and figure something out over the weekend." I lifted my head and kissed him. "I have to work to make up for being gone the last few weeks but we will have meetings in the evenings. The Magisters might be able to give some insight. Roberta talked about this key like we all knew about it, and go figure they didn't tell us."

Bryan tightened his arm around me. "Emma isn't a factor in stealing this key. She has to stay neutral, for her own safety."

"I know." I settled against his chest and ran my fingertips up his arm to his shoulder. "I promise I won't drag Emma into anything again."

"Thank you." He pressed a kiss into my hair. "So, um, while we are catching each other up. You need to keep an eye on Dominic."

"Why?" I glanced up to meet his gaze. "What happened?"

Bryan let out a sigh. "We were downtown and...*he* was there. Erebus. In the middle of the fucking day. I had to physically restrain Nic from getting himself killed. He lost it, and burned me when I grabbed him." Bryan showed me the palm of his hand where the skin had been slightly discolored, as if it had scarred. "It was an accident. I'm okay now, but he, uh, he is reckless and I don't want you to get hurt because he can't control himself."

"Oh." I ran my fingers over his palm, a mix of anger and concern washed over me. "He burned you?"

"It wasn't intentional. He had literal steam rising off him and I grabbed him anyway. But I think if he charged like he wanted to, Erebus would have killed him right there in the street." Bryan wrapped his hand around mine. "He had some potion that took care of the blisters, but...I did not enjoy it."

"Blisters..." I tried to shake the mental image away. "I'm so sorry."

"He's not a bad guy. We actually spent a lot of time together while you were gone. He was a big help with Dmitri." Bryan paused, as if choosing his next words carefully. "But, he's not a stable person. Not right now, at least."

"I already knew that," I answered. "Thank you for holding him back."

Bryan nodded and offered a small smile. "If you care about him, then I do too."

I nuzzled in further, getting as close as I possibly could without crawling under his shirt. I had finally made it back home. I closed my eyes and inhaled the familiar scent of cedarwood and vanilla as I drifted off to sleep. Whatever we were up against, at least I'd always have this to retreat into.

Chapter Seventeen
Just Friends
Lauren

Walking up to the doors of the Corner Cup used to be what I looked forward to the most, but not this morning. I dragged each step, taking my time getting to the doors. It had been nineteen days since I had talked to Ashley Turner, let alone seen her. My heart ached to be close to her again but the knot in my stomach weighed heavier. With Whitney on a bus to Falcon Bay to reconcile with Bryan, I had no buffer zone to make this interaction with Ashley any easier.

The lights already lit up the coffee shop and Ashley stood behind the counter fiddling with the espresso machine. The air left my lungs as I stood on the sidewalk and watched. That moment could very well be the last time I could look at Ashley and smile, so I wanted to soak it up.

As if Ashley could feel eyes on her, she lifted her head and looked at me standing on the other side of the glass. Ash perked up, her eyes widening as a smile took over her face. She left the espresso machines and skidded around the counter, fumbling with the keys to unlock the door.

I took a step back, unsure how to feel. Ashley looked far too happy to be greeting someone who kissed her and then ghosted for damn near three weeks. No calls, no texts. I didn't even think to leave a letter like Whitney had done for Bryan. I felt awful about it, but I also understood that the...whatever I had...with Ashley, was different from what Whitney had with Bryan. I had watched them with jealousy for weeks, how they looked at one another. Bryan dropped literally everything the moment his girl needed something. I wanted to feel that kind of commitment for someone and have them return it.

Ashley threw the door back and stepped out into the cold, launching herself into my arms. I caught her and held her close. I could have floated, making a conscious effort to keep my feet on the sidewalk. The anxiety that weighed down on me the entire drive here drifted off into the atmosphere as Ashley rubbed my back and broke the embrace.

"Are you okay?" Ashley took a step back.

I chortled. "Me? Are *you* okay? I am so sorry, Ash, I...I should have been in touch. I should not have left without a word. That wasn't fair and I feel like shit over it."

Ashley brushed me off with a wave of her hand. "You didn't plan for your grandmother to break her hip. I understand. You don't owe me anything. We aren't...we're friends, right?"

I paused, wetting my bottom lip. "Yeah."

"Is she okay?" Ashley tilted her head. "Your grandmother?"

Who the hell told her my grandmother had been hurt? I had to remind myself to breathe. At least I didn't have to lie about everything. "Yeah, my grandmother is fine. She's safe at home in Idaho."

Ashley let out a sigh of relief. "I'm glad you're back. Whitney and Rayn home too?"

I nodded, blinking back the tears threatening to form.

"What a relief. Things have been so weird around here without you guys." Ashley pulled the glass door back and held it open for me to follow behind her. "Not like this place has been the same since Amilia passed." She quickly blinked back tears and cleared her throat. "I've really hated coming to work, to be honest."

I stood on the curb for a moment in utter shock. I grabbed the door right before it closed and followed Ashley into the coffee shop. This didn't make any sense. Ashley wasn't the least bit mad that I had disappeared after the wedding? That hurt more than if Ashley had come at me swinging. I would have preferred Ashley had screamed or threatened me. Something. *Anything*. At least then I would have something to fight for. Every day spent at the Hallow, I fell asleep dreaming of curly red hair and freckled skin. I made myself sick wondering if Ashley was safe in Rifton. If the Renati would dare touch her. If they would take away another person I cared about.

"Hey," I caught Ashley before she disappeared into the break room. "Uh, about the wedding. I–"

Ashley cut me off. "Oh! Don't think twice about it. We were at a wedding. I always get drunk and end up kissing people I shouldn't at weddings."

Everything inside of me exploded, shredding my heart to bits. "You do?"

"Yeah, it's not a big deal. Like I said, you and I are friends and I am perfectly content with friends. You said it yourself, you've got a million things going on in your life. Who am I to complicate things for you?" Ashley put her hands up as if she surrendered. "So, I am officially friendzoning myself and we can go back to being work buddies who got drunk at a weekend shindig."

"Is that what you want?" I asked, forcing the words to leave my lips.

Ashley nodded with a bright smile. "Totally. Everything is fine. Hey, after you clock in, do you think you can do a quick clean up of the dining area? Whoever closed last night did a shitty job."

"Sure thing." Tears stung my eyes as I brushed past Ashley to the break room. I threw my bag into my locker with a loud thud.

I collapsed into one of the folding chairs at the small table and buried my face into my hands. I wanted to break down and hyperventilate. I wanted to scream and throw things, but I swallowed the cries and locked them away in the smallest box I could find in my heart.

Clearing my throat, I buried my emotions and built the walls of my fortress around me. I rubbed the goosebumps on my arms and went about my day as if I wasn't dying inside. I could think of only one explanation as to why Ashley would act so nonchalant about my return, and I intended to deal with it after I clocked out for the day.

) ·) · ● · (· (

I took a deep breath, trying to calm myself as I drove home with no success. I parked crooked in the driveway and slammed the car door behind me as I marched up the walkway to the cottage. He better be there. I didn't feel like having to hunt him around town. Balling my fists, I knew I couldn't kill him. He was as powerful as me so he would be difficult to kill but I mostly didn't want to piss Whitney off. Though if my closest friend didn't have such an attachment to this asshole, I probably would send him flying through the nearest window.

I waved my hand and the front door flew open, banging against the wall. The photos on the walls rattled as I marched into the cottage. He sat in the nearest arm chair.

Dominic flinched at the crash of the front door, sitting up. He relaxed when he saw my face.

He had nothing to feel at ease about.

"Bad day?" Nic asked, turning to face me.

Without a second thought, I mustered all the energy I had and shoved both hands towards Nic. The chair went flying out from underneath him, sending Nic tumbling to the floor. His feet flew up over his head as his back hit the wood floor.

"The hell, Lauren?" he demanded, remaining on the floor.

Fight back. Stand up and face me like a fucking man, you coward.

"You charmed her!" I spat out, sending a stack of papers on the coffee table spinning above our heads. "How fucking dare you get into Ashley's mind! You had no right, you entitled son of a bitch!"

Nic covered his head with his arm as the force of the wind no doubt stung his eyes. I didn't feel a thing other than the anger coursing through me.

"I had to!" Dominic shouted over the whistling of the wind. Books on the shelves flew open and pages ripped from the spine, joining the funnel that spun above them. "Lauren, stop!"

Rayn ran into the living room from our bedroom, but the wind pushed her back. She grabbed the corner of the wall and pulled herself into the room. "Lo!" she yelled. "Lauren, calm down!"

My point had been made. I lowered my hands as my pulse throbbed through my body. My knees trembled from the adrenaline but I stood my ground. The loose papers floated to the ground. The living room was wrecked. The books were destroyed. I didn't care.

"What happened?" Rayn asked, taking a step towards me.

I ignored Rayn, my attention still locked onto the other pyro in the room. "Stay the fuck out of Ashley's head or I will hurt you. I don't care how much Whit loves you. I will end you, Dominic."

Nic sat up on his elbows. "Ashley asked too many questions. She knew something was wrong and she worried about you. I did her a favor." He raised his shoulders and shook head. "What would have happened if she kept asking around for you? I did it to keep her safe. I promised I would hold things together here for *all* of you. I did you a fucking favor, Lauren."

"A favor?" My scream echoed off the walls. "She's completely indifferent. I'll never know if she actually cares that I'm back or if it's your mind magic blocking her true feelings. When I left, she wanted me. You fucked everything up!"

"Oh," Nic whispered, guilt heavy in his gaze. "I didn't charm her feelings. I charmed her concern. I told her you had a family emergency and would be back, that she wouldn't worry or ask questions. I never charmed her to be indifferent about you when you came back."

Rayn stepped further into the living room, coming up next to me. "Lo, you know Ash cares about you, regardless of Nic's actions."

"She called us friends," I muttered.

"Aren't you?" Rayn glanced up at me with confusion.

"I...I don't know." I brushed past Rayn and hurried down the hall to our bedroom. I hoped for some privacy to collect myself, but Rayn followed close behind.

"Hey, what even happened? Did you and Ashley get into a fight or something?"

I thought about closing the bedroom door in Rayn's face but stopped myself. That would have been mean. Rayn didn't deserve that. She only tried to help. I closed my eyes and plopped down on the edge of my bed. Rayn closed the door behind her and stood across the room, probably waiting for me to explain.

"I wanted a fight," I admitted, looking up at Rayn. "I wanted her to be upset that I left. I wanted her to care that I had been gone or question where I had been but nothing...she hugged me, said things were weird at CC without me, and went about the shift like I had never left. It was like I never left, Ray."

"You wanted to fight with her?" Rayn clarified, not understanding.

I huffed, rubbing my face. "At least I would have known she cared enough about me disappearing to fight with me."

"Oh, babe." Rayn crossed the room and sat down next to me on the bed. "If she didn't care about you being gone, Nic would not have had to charm her. You heard him right? Ash asked so many questions about you, she worried about you. He would not have had to silence that concern in her mind if she didn't care about you being gone."

"I guess I'll have to take his word for it."

Rayn rubbed my back. "Nic wouldn't lie about this."

"What makes you so sure?" I glanced over at her.

"Because I would never lie about this, and Nic and I are kind of a lot alike." Rayn put her hand on my shoulder. "I'm sorry things didn't go how you planned with Ashley, but she does care."

"We kissed after the wedding."

Rayn smiled. "Then she definitely cares."

I sighed. "What do I do? She's so…She should not get wrapped up in all this and I knew that. I *knew* I had to leave her out of this. I thought we could be friends because she and Whit and Byn are all friends. She and Emma are friends. She's already in it, right? But I didn't want to make things more complicated."

"Whitney used to say the same things about Bryan and look how that turned out." Rayn rubbed my back again. "They tried to stay apart, but the pull is too strong. If it's meant to work out, it will. Nic's actions aren't going to change any of that."

My shoulders fell. "I hope you're right."

"Lauren, just because we have a lot of heavy shit going on doesn't mean you don't deserve happiness. We all deserve someone who makes this life easier to live and if Ashley is that person, you better hang on to her. Don't let the Renati or our powers get in the way of your happiness. There will be a life after this, I promise. We need something to fight for."

Tears blurred my vision as I wrapped my arms around Rayn's shoulders and pulled her into a hug. Rayn held me back.

"Is Aden that person for you?" I whispered into Rayn's shoulder.

Rayn paused before she answered. "I know you're all worried about him. I won't do anything to jeopardize our generation."

"That isn't what I asked, Ray." I pulled back and looked her in the eyes.

Rayn sighed. "I don't know, to be honest. I want him to be, but I don't want to put all this pressure on it. He doesn't have anywhere else to go and I don't want to confuse him staying because he has to with him staying because he *wants* to."

"Have you asked how he feels?"

Rayn nodded, pulling out of the hug. "He said he wants to be here, but the reality remains…Where else would he go? He can't go home. He's kind of stuck with us." Rayn rubbed my back and pulled away. "Besides, this isn't about Aden and I, this is about you and Ashley. Ashley isn't the only one who got charmed while we were gone. Brooke's parents and Rose's mom did too. Hell, even that guy Nancy married had to get charmed.

No one had their feelings about their loved ones changed, just the fear of us being gone put at ease."

"Did I ruin the books?" I changed the subject.

Rayn shrugged. "Probably not. I'd be surprised if the mess isn't already cleaned up."

"I'm not apologizing to Dominic," I stated.

"No one expects you to."

"Will Whitney be mad at me?" I had a hard enough time accepting my situation with Ashley, I didn't want to be at odds with my best friend too.

"No, I don't think so. I think she's too distracted with Bryan. Besides, if the roles were reversed and Nic had charmed Byn, I think Whit would have knocked the old man on his ass too." Rayn smiled.

I rubbed my face, pressing the balls of my palms against my eyes. "I'm so tired...I need to go see my dad."

Rayn reached out and took my hand in hers. "Want some company? I am officially unemployed, so I don't really have anywhere to be."

"Out of a job?" I leaned back. When did this happen?

She shrugged. "Giani's fired me while we were gone, but I'll figure something out. I just feel awful that Bryan went out of his way to get me that job and I made him look bad." Rayn lifted her brows. "So, want me to come with you?"

I squeezed her hand. "Thank you, but I think I need to go on my own. It won't be very eventful since he's just lying there but I need to go."

"Nap first?"

"I'll be okay." I shook my head. "I drank an entire pot of coffee to myself at work, so I'm too jittery to sleep anyway."

Rayn smiled at me again as I hopped off the bed and left our bedroom. Rayn was right. Nic had cleaned up the mess I made in the living room but he was nowhere to be found. I didn't necessarily think he deserved an apology, but I would have at least thanked him for fixing all the books I destroyed.

) ·) · ● · (· (

I hesitated outside of my father's hospital room. I couldn't wrap her head around why I felt so nervous to go inside. He lay asleep, deep in a coma. It's not like he would have questioned where I'd been or why I hadn't been by to visit in the last two and a half weeks. With a deep sigh, I crossed the threshold.

The monitors beeped at his bedside. I watched his heart rate bounce up and down on the screen, little peaks and divots proving that he still lived. He may not have been awake yet, but the signs of life were enough for now. He still hung on. I still had something to dream about.

I sat in an empty chair next to the bed and slouched down, crossing my legs. I rested my head on the back of the chair and breathed. In and out. I focused on the beeping monitor, letting my breathing follow the same pattern. I listened to the nurses chatting outside the door. The sound of footsteps on the floor down the hall. One of the doors to a neighboring room opened and closed. The intercom beeped and a voice came over, paging one of the doctors.

"I'm a witch," I finally spoke. "I have powers. I've always had powers but I hid them from you and Mom. Grandma's bracelet that Mom gave me? Yep, that's all part of this too." I let out a harsh sigh and hid my face in my hands. This felt ridiculous, talking to my dad like this. I had heard that people in comas could sometimes still hear their loved ones, so I continued. "And there's this girl, her name is Ashley and...I think I'm in love with her. She's kind and smart and everything I imagine a good partner would be. I know it's not what you and Mom had in mind when you pictured my future, but she makes me happy."

I stared at my motionless father and wiped away the tear that fell down my cheek. When my parents heard the rumors about Layla and I in high school, my mother had lost it. She barely made eye contact. She wouldn't discuss the possibilities that there could be any truth to the whispers going around town. My mother could not bring herself to even entertain the idea.

My dad on the other hand...he never actually said anything about it. He didn't react, he didn't miss a beat. I always wondered if my father was a typical man who buried their feelings and never let them brew to the surface or if he genuinely didn't care. A small glimmer of hope burned in my chest that maybe my dad would have been fine with it if my mom wasn't so loud about her disapproval.

I'd never know, because my mom was gone and my dad may have been breathing on his own but his eyes were still closed. He still lay still in this hospital bed with a feeding tube and more wires connected to him than I cared to count.

Maybe it didn't matter. I had finally looked one of my parents in the face and told them the truth about myself and I never thought I'd have the strength to.

Chapter Eighteen
Healing Waves
Whitney

I didn't realize I had fallen asleep until I opened my eyes to the dimly lit room. A thick comforter had been tucked around my chin, but Bryan wasn't pressed up against my back where he normally slept. Instead, he sat up with a book in his lap and his glasses on. I studied his face while he read. How his eyebrows furrowed slightly, how his lips parted and slowly moved along with the words flowing through his head. It wasn't until I shifted that he realized I woke up.

He turned and smiled at me, closing his book with his thumb keeping the page. "Hey, baby."

"Hmm, I missed hearing that." I reached out and scooted closer to him, nestling against his side. He tucked me under his arm and gently rubbed my back. "What are you reading? Something for class?"

"Nope, this is for pleasure, believe it or not. It's a high fantasy. Dragons and big castles." Bryan kissed the top of my head.

I closed my eyes, listening to the beating of his heart. He no longer felt angry, and his pulse steadied as we cuddled. It seemed the pent-up feelings he had released earlier hadn't returned, not yet anyway. "Sounds like a good book."

"I like it so far. The magic system is cool. I think this one mage is my favorite, though." Bryan tilted the book to show me the back cover. A witch stood with her back facing the reader, commanding the sea to crash over a massive ship.

"You have a type, I see," I teased him.

"I have a thing for dark-haired, smart-mouthed witches." He smiled and checked the time. "Hey, since we're up so early...get dressed."

"Why? What time is it?"

"Early. Come on." Bryan jumped out of bed and pulled on a pair of jeans.

I got up and reached for my pants. I turned to ask Bryan another question. He stood perfectly still, staring at me. "You okay?"

"Yeah, sorry." He cleared his throat. "You still look so good in my clothes."

I glanced down and smiled at the dark green shirt I'd stolen from him the first night we'd spent together. It hung low on me but I filled it out easily. Bryan may have been taller but my body was wider than his. Still, he looked at me as if I were the sun, the center of the entire solar system.

We finished getting dressed and slipped out of the apartment into the darkness. As Bryan warmed up his Jeep, I finally got a look at the time.

"It's six fifteen in the morning." I groaned, resting my head against the window.

Bryan nodded. "We should still catch it."

I turned to face him. "Catch what?"

Bryan only smiled as he pulled out of the apartment complex and turned right. Bryan drove around Falcon Bay with ease, knowing exactly where he wanted to go and how to get there. He clearly wanted this to be a surprise, so I didn't say anything when I felt us approaching the ocean. The waves called to me. I heard the crashing of the water against the beach before we pulled into the strip of parking. Bryan put the car in park and killed the engine.

He turned to me and smiled. "I promised that I'd bring you to the beach. I'm sorry it took so long, but we're in time to catch the sunrise."

I leaned across the center counsel and pressed my lips to his. "I love you," I whispered and jumped out of my seat.

We walked towards the water together. I had already ditched my shoes, but Bryan kept his on.

"It's far too cold to take anything off," he had said with a shiver.

The cold winter mist kissed my face as we strolled through the wet sand, hand in hand. The tide was low and we were able to move out pretty far before we met the waves. I had seen an ocean before. Mom took us to the Gulf of Mexico when we were younger. But Bryan had been right all those months ago, nothing compared to the Pacific Ocean.

Waves crashed up on the massive rocks that sat out on the coastline away from the beach. Pine trees lined the steep cliffline behind us, standing high up around the edge of the city. I glanced up at Falcon Ridge, amazed that only a few weeks ago the girls and I were setting out on our journey to the Hallow.

Out past the endless ocean, the line of sky that met the water turned from dark blue to a soft pink as the sun began to peek up. The clouds hung low over the water, but they couldn't hide the bright colors that came with the sunrise. I felt the freezing air in my bones but I never shivered. I barely noticed a difference at all. It comforted me. Right there on the chilly coast was where my soul had always longed to be. I inhaled a deep breath of salty air and reached for Bryan, sliding under his arm.

He kissed the top of my head and held me close as the sun continued to rise, lighting up the sky as it came further up. The pinks turned into oranges and yellows that reflected across the water. Soon, the warm colors took over the entire ocean, reaching out to us. The sun shone through the early morning fog to gently wake up the sleeping people of the bay.

"I planned to bring you here for Valentine's Day." Bryan tightened his grip on me.

Oh shit...Valentine's Day.

"Babe, I'm so sorry." I glanced up to meet his gaze, worried I'd see irritation in his eyes even though not a pang of anger echoed in his chest.

He smiled and kissed my forehead instead, holding me close to his chest. "This is exactly what I had planned, sunrise on the beach. I wanted to surprise you."

"I am definitely surprised," I whispered, grabbing Bryan's cold fingers in mine. "This is everything, being here with you. I wish we could get in the water."

Bryan chortled. "I'd catch hypothermia, but you'd probably be fine."

"It feels weird being out here without at least going to say hi."

"Then let's go say hi."

He walked with me to the edge of the water, pausing where the waves almost reached him. Bryan reached down and dipped his fingertips into the edge of the tide. "Holy shit, it's freezing."

I marched right in. The cold water shocked my legs at first but I acclimated quickly. I went all the way to my knees as the waves crashed up around my legs, soaking my jeans. I could almost feel the tears in my soul healing as the ocean kissed my skin. The anxiety left my shoulders and I breathed easier. Before I could pause and give it a second thought, I dove in.

Fully submerged, I cleansed myself in the Oregon coastline. Bryan yelled something but his voice was muffled under the waves. I closed my eyes, feeling the tiny bubbles floating up around me. When I did come up for air, I could hear Bryan laughing. A large wave crashed over me, causing me to stumble but I quickly regained my footing. The ocean woke up with the sunrise and the daylight unfortunately meant I needed to return to Rifton. I needed to return to real life.

I trudged through the waves back to Bryan on the beach. He smiled at me, not the least bit surprised that I'd jumped in. "I should have known. I didn't think to bring a towel."

"I can change my clothes when we get back to the apartment," I paused. "Oh, I'm sorry. I'm going to get the seat of your Jeep soaked."

Bryan reached for my wet hand and laced our fingers. "I don't care about that. You look happier."

"I feel happier, that was rejuvenating."

He leaned in for a kiss, gently holding my face in his hand. "Seeing you smile like this is priceless."

Bryan and I left Falcon Bay after a shower that took longer than we initially planned. The drive back to Rifton seemed shorter than the bus ride, but I felt much more relaxed with Bryan's fingers on my thigh.

We got into town in time for my shift at the Corner Cup. Bryan dropped me off in the back parking lot and headed to our place so he could change into his work clothes and get a few things done before his shift at Giani's.

It felt bizarre to be back in the old routine. Kissing Bryan goodbye knowing he would only be two doors down and would eventually wander over on his lunch break to see me. The weight of my diamond bracelet finally back on my wrist. The memory of how his body moved against mine that morning in the shower. I could have lived in that memory all day but the air around Rifton filled my lungs with a thickness I didn't recognize. The energy felt heavy; the town didn't seem right. There were less people out and about, as if they felt the difference and stayed away.

I strolled into the Corner Cup as the familiar little bell dinged above me. Lauren and Robby were at the counter while Ashley chatted with a customer in the far corner of the dining area. Everything looked normal and calm, almost as if the girls and I hadn't been gone for weeks.

Almost as if Rifton didn't have a metaphoric black cloud lingering in the sky. Almost as if Amilia and Warren hadn't died.

Lauren gave me a soft smile as I walked in, waving her fingers. I smiled back and went through the employee only doors. I stopped at the sight of Amilia's office door wide open. Harmony sat at the desk, fistfuls of her hair held tightly at the roots. Papers were strewn everywhere, filing cabinet doors left open with more files resting on them.

"Hey." I stood in the open doorway.

Harmony looked up at me, moving her hair out of her eyes. "Hi. Thanks for showing up."

"I'm sorry Lauren and I left you high and dry on coverage. We'll make it up to you."

"Yeah, thanks. Dmitri has been a big help. Rayn is going to start tomorrow."

"Here at CC?"

Harmony nodded. "Yeah, guess Giani's fired her. We charmed a lot of people to convince them your sudden disappearance wasn't suspicious. I honestly forgot Rayn worked there."

Neither Bryan nor Rayn had mentioned anything about it to me. "Oh, shit."

"Works out though, I guess. We have spots to fill and Rayn needs a job."

"What's with all the papers?" I glanced over the mess that had taken over the office.

Harmony stared down at the pages and let out a deep sigh. "I'll tell you about it later. You need to clock in."

"Right, okay. Let me know if you need anything."

Harmony nodded again, going back to the stack of papers in front of her. I didn't know if what she stressed over had anything to do with the Corner Cup but I decided not to press the issue.

"Holy shit, you're alive!" Ashley's voice bellowed through the dining area as I walked back out onto the floor. She pulled me into a hug and patted my back. "Byn told me about the family emergency back in Michigan that you and Rayn had to deal with. Is everything okay?"

"Yeah," I nodded. "It's fine."

"God, I can't even wrap my head around everything that's happened. Amilia having a heart attack? Lauren's grandmother being hospitalized. You and Rayn suddenly losing your aunt. Mercury isn't even in retrograde."

"Amilia was too young." My chest constricted around my heart. If I kept talking about Amilia, I'd break down.

"Ugh, I cried for days when her niece first broke the news to us. What do you think about the niece? Kind of a bitch isn't she?" Ashley glanced past me towards the employee only doors.

"Niece?" I asked, slightly confused.

"The one in Amilia's office going over paperwork. The new owner of CC. You met her right?" Ashley tilted her head.

"Oh, yeah, duh. Yes, I know Harmony. She's uh, she's stressed out, but I would be too if I inherited as much as she did out of nowhere."

"I guess, but it's not anyone's fault." Ashley shrugged and put her hand on my shoulder. "Anyway, glad you're home safe. Glad Lauren is back. Maybe we can find some sort of normalcy in all this."

"That would be great." I forced a smile.

I didn't really know what to say to Ashley. I didn't know how to express that Amilia's passing broke me. I couldn't tell Ashley that Mia had died right in front of me, sacrificing her life for mine. That she gave her final breath to keep me safe. I didn't know how to go about my day pretending I hadn't spent the last eighteen days in the woods. That the girls and I had almost died, *twice*.

Now I had to slap a smile on my face and serve coffee like the end of the fucking world didn't sit on the horizon. Like I wasn't one of the few people who could stop it from happening. If we didn't stop Erebus' impending reign of terror, it wouldn't matter that we worked our asses off to keep the Corner Cup open. It would go down in flames with the rest of the Dark Star Forest.

Hours later, Lauren's shift ended and she stopped by the counter on her way out. She slipped her arms into her sweater and asked. "Are you coming over tonight?"

"Yeah, I'll be there. Make sure the girls are too, we need to have a meeting."

"Agreed." Lauren gripped the strap of her purse and sighed.

"Hey, are you okay?" I reached out to stop her. "You're sad."

Lauren glanced back into the supply room where Ashley stood. "Didn't come home to what I'd hoped for."

"Oh." My shoulders fell. "I'm really sorry." I wanted to ask for details but this felt like a private conversation.

Lauren cleared her throat. "I'll see you at home."

Ashley and Robby weren't far behind, clocking out soon after and heading out the front door. I glanced around the dining room at the few customers left sipping from their mugs when I realized none of the other employees were on the floor. Had Harmony scheduled me to close alone? I stepped away from the register and peaked at the daily schedule taped to the stockroom door, running my finger down the list to the closers.

Whitney. 12 pm - 8:30 pm

No one else.

The bell above the front door jingled. I let out an irritated sigh, ready to tell the customers wandering in to get out because I wouldn't run a one woman show.

"Hey, kiddo." Nic walked around the counter. He reached into the stock room to pull a spare apron off one of the hooks and put it on.

"Are you closing with me?" I leaned against the counter.

"Yep. I've been filling in here and there."

I crossed my arms. "I'm really confused why we are so short staffed. When the girls and I left, we never had gaps in coverage."

"Harmony had to let two people go."

"What? Why?"

"Because we couldn't afford to keep them. This place is dangerously close to closing its doors, unless Honey can pull a miracle out of thin air. Mia was in debt up to her eyeballs."

I widened my eyes. "She never said anything."

"No, she wouldn't have." Nic shook his head.

"How is Harmony affording to pay you?"

"She isn't." Nic patted his chest. "I'm here out of the goodness of my heart."

I furrowed my brow. "If Harmony isn't paying you, how are you affording to live?"

Nic chortled. "Don't worry about little old me, I have money. Did your trip to Falcon Bay go okay?"

"Good, everything is good."

Nic grabbed a mug off the shelf and poured himself a cup of coffee. He smiled as he took a sip. "I'm glad, genuinely. Any ideas on the key?"

I shook my head. "I hoped we could get together tonight at the cottage and figure something out."

"We don't even know if Bonnie still has the key, and even if she does there's no way the Drakes keep it at their house." Nic took another drink. "After we swiped the ledger they would have moved anything of value elsewhere."

I nodded as the wheels in my head turned. "Process of elimination, then. I don't know if you and Harmony heard me the other night, but Roberta said that Amilia had a piece of the key."

"Oh, yeah?" Nic lifted his brow.

My shoulders fell. "You honestly don't know anything about it?"

The corner of his lips curved into a tiny smile. "I think we should focus our attention on the two pieces that are in enemy hands." Nic set his coffee cup on the counter.

"The last piece is with Margaret Daniels, I thought she was part of the coven." I moved on.

Nic shook his head. "Mia hadn't spoken to her in a decade. She's in California last I checked."

"You didn't see her while you were there?"

Nic scrunched his face when he looked at me. "It's a big state, Whit. I lived in SoCal. I'm sure she's still in the Bay Area though. Hard to pick up and move the palace."

"The palace?" I leaned against the counter and crossed my arms.

"That's what we call it. There's a community of witches there that have more money than God, but that's future us's problem." He waved his hand, brushing off the conversation. "We have plenty to keep us busy in the meantime. Like coffee, want some?"

"Sure." I grabbed my favorite mug from the wall and Nic poured me a cup. Amilia let us have drinks behind the counter but it had to be in a to-go cup with a closed lid and we had to be discreet. I'd never taken a mug off the wall and leisurely drank while on the clock. Another reminder that we were living in a world without her.

Harmony came out of the employee hallway and set a stack of papers down on the counter. She turned to me and asked, "Did the bagel guy come yet?"

I shook my head. "Not since I've been here."

Harmony groaned and pulled out her cellphone. She tapped the pages while she dialed. "Take a look at this." She crossed the room and leaned against the wall.

I grabbed the first page from the stack to take a closer look. "This is not about the Corner Cup."

Nic took the paper from my hands, his pupils growing larger the further down he read. "This is about the Drake estate."

"Why is Harmony looking up info on the Drake estate?" I studied his wide eyes.

"I don't know, we'll ask her later, but maybe she's onto something." Nic put the paper on the counter and pointed to the center of the page. "Look at this, it's a list of the properties Henry Drake owns."

I ran my finger down the list. "This is Emma and Bryan's apartment in Falcon Bay, but what's this other property on the coast?"

"Whatever it is, it's worth looking into. Maybe they're keeping their key piece in the bay."

"Are there a lot of Renati in Falcon Bay?"

Nic shrugged a shoulder. "There didn't used to be, but I wouldn't be surprised if there are now. Things have changed a lot since I lived here."

The last customer in the dining area packed up their books and left, giving us a polite wave as they did. Nic rushed to the door and locked it behind them, flipping the open sign to closed. "Let's close down for the night and get back to the cottage."

I finished off the coffee in my mug and began closing out the till for the night. I took the cash to the back office and settled everything money-wise while Nic cleaned up the dining room. We both rushed through our tasks and met in the breakroom when we finished.

"Where are you two going?" Harmony leaned against the door frame of the breakroom.

"We're going to the cottage to get a plan together." Nic shoved his hands into his pockets. "Don't stay here all night banging your pretty head against the wall. Come home."

Harmony let out a sigh and glanced behind her at the open office door. "I'll be there soon."

"Soon as in half an hour or soon as in before midnight?" Nic tilted his head.

Harmony rolled her eyes. "Half an hour."

I stared at the two of them, wondering when they stopped threatening to kill one another.

Nic nodded, as if accepting her response, and left the breakroom. I followed behind him, waving to Harmony as we left.

"So you and Harmony are getting along now?" I questioned.

Nic glanced at me over his shoulder. "My charm is irresistible, even to the strongest of wills."

I chortled. "Well, that's good. Part of me worried you two would have a huge blow out fight while I was gone."

"Oh, we did." Nic shoved his hands back into his pockets.

"Over?" I tilted my head.

"Uh, well," he paused. "She told my mother I was back in town. That wretched woman ambushed me on the sidewalk and it didn't go well. I swear Honey enjoys torturing me."

I chewed on my bottom lip, processing his words. "Your biological mother?"

He shrugged. "It's over and I haven't seen my mother since, so I'm trying to put it behind me."

I wet my bottom lip and turned to him. "Is that when you burned my boyfriend?"

Nic trilled his lips. "I already apologized for that. It won't happen again."

"It better not." I shook my head and changed the subject. "Do you think we may have to close this place down?"

"I hope not, but you know, if we could take something off our plates then I wouldn't complain," he answered.

"But, all of us work here. We'd literally all have to find new jobs."

Nic huffed. "How shitty is it that the fucking world could be ending and we still have to pay taxes and buy groceries? I can't believe Mia didn't have any sort of life insurance."

"To be fair, my mom didn't either."

"Those stubborn women. Did they think they were going to live forever when they both had targets on their backs? They should have known better, especially Audri. She had three kids to take care of and didn't think about life insurance?"

"Do you have life insurance?" I nudged him with my shoulder.

"Why? Planning to off me for it?" He smirked.

I chortled. "Because I think it's kind of a luxury, personally. I don't have the extra money to pay for fucking wi-fi, let alone life insurance."

"I guess."

I stopped Nic on his way out the front door. "For the record, I'd be completely and utterly lost if anything ever happened to you."

He froze in the doorway, his hand up on the frame. "Well, I'm not dying tomorrow. Hurry up, we have a heist to plan."

Chapter Nineteen
Family Business
Whitney

When Nic and I got to the cottage, everyone but Harmony sat in the living room next to the fire. The girls were scattered across the room. Rose and Rayn leaned over the missing pages we got from the Hallow while Lauren and Brooke sat at the dining room table scrying with a crystal dangling over a map. Bryan and Dmitri were looking through the book Jake had lent us about the Allurements. Everyone busied themselves doing something to help us win this stupid fight we didn't ask for.

"How did things go with your parents?" I asked Brooke.

She shifted in her seat uncomfortably. "It's really weird how indifferent they are. Before we left, they were literally locking me up and now…" Brooke chewed on her thumbnail. "I walked in through the front door expecting this big, blow out fight. But they hugged me and welcomed me home. My mom asked what I wanted for dinner and never said another word. They don't even ask where I'm going when I leave the house now."

"I mean, that's good isn't it?" I didn't know what else to say.

"It's *easier*, but it's not great." Brooke glared at Nic over my shoulder. "They aren't themselves. I did get them to sign some paperwork so I can go to the same charter school at Mit. That should make my life easier."

"Oh, good, I'm glad you did that." Rose turned to face us. "Mom was weird too, she didn't ask a single question. She told me all about the trip she and Jack took to Canada for their honeymoon and that's it. It's like I never left."

Bryan let out a deep sigh. "I hated doing that to Mom, but it was for the best. She would have called every single person she knew looking for you. She would've called Dad."

Rose cleared her throat. "I know, I'm glad you did. The aftermath is just…different."

I went to Bryan and pressed a kiss to his cheek, reading over his shoulder to see what he and my brother had been focusing on. The top of the page had "The labyrinth?" written in big block letters.

"You get off work early?" I asked Bryan, who should've been at work for another hour.

"They overscheduled and sent me home," Bryan explained.

I blinked at him. "Sent *you* home? Don't you have seniority?"

He shrugged. "I'll talk to Angela about it later. What's going on?"

I showed him the paper from Harmony's stack. "Do you recognize this address?"

Bryan squinted, taking a closer look. "No." He shook his head. "Hang on, let me see where that even is." He pulled out his phone and looked up the address. "It's barely in the city limits, look."

The property sat south of town; near the coastline but far from the main road that took travelers into Falcon Bay from Rifton.

"It looks like a regular house. Maybe a rental property?" Dmitri suggested, glancing over Bryan's shoulder.

"Maybe," I replied. "I don't know. It stuck out to me."

"I can check it out. I'll drive by or something, see what I can figure out," Bryan offered.

"Thanks, babe, that would be huge." I gave him another kiss.

"Cool." Nic crossed his arms and leaned against the wall. "That's a lead on the mystery property. It's the only one not in Rifton, so if the key truly is outside of town, it might be there. Unless Drake is hiding it right under our noses at your apartment."

"I highly doubt that." Bryan shook his head. "He doesn't trust Emma with anything Renati related."

Nic shrugged. "Maybe that makes her the perfect hiding place. The last person you'd expect to have something of value."

Bryan chewed on his lip. "I don't think so. I've lived there for years."

"It wouldn't be out in plain sight, it would be cloaked," Nic said.

"We could search the house with magic," Rose suggested. "Search every corner while Emma is in class using that powder Amilia gave us to find the ledger. We have to at least look. We don't have the luxury of crossing it out as an option without looking first."

"Okay," Bryan agreed. "I'll give you Em's class schedule."

"In the meantime." Nic turned to face me. "Let me see the Shepherd's missing pages."

I took a seat next to my sister on the couch. "I haven't gotten a good look at them either."

Rayn slid the book into my lap and motioned for Nic to join us. He sat down on the other side of me and leaned in for a closer look, reaching out to turn the page when I stopped him.

"Wait," I whispered. "Is that…my talisman?" An elaborate drawing stared back at me from the page, but it looked nothing like the aquamarine that hung from my neck. The chainlinks braided together and the setting around the gemstone swirled like little waves crashing up around the blue stone. "They really are enchanted to change their appearance, aren't they?"

Rayn leaned over my shoulder and nodded. "They used to be kind of extra, don't you think?"

Nic still held the corner of the page in his fingers, glancing over at me with wide eyes. "Can we move on?"

"Yes, sorry." I leaned back in my seat. "I know you've seen these before, but I haven't."

Nic turned the page. "What the talismans used to look like is not as important as how the labyrinth works."

Rayn crossed her arms. "And how exactly did the Shepherd's know about the labyrinth, let alone how it works?"

"This may come as a shock, but I don't actually have all the answers." Nic glanced up from the pages to look at her. "Everything written about the Dark Star Allurement was documented by Seers, like Whit. They wrote that Elementals used to access the labyrinth to enhance their magic, but that was long before the Shepherd's time."

"Okay," I paused. "How exactly does the labyrinth work?"

"The Allurement can't be accessed without the key," Nic explained. "The key surpassed the Shepherd's by…I don't know how long actually. Elementals stopped going into the labyrinth when the Allurement started to weaken."

"I thought the Allurements were portals?" Lauren asked.

"That's what I've been told." Nic nodded. "According to what they documented, all the Allurements are connected. They all lead to what is called the labyrinth which apparently presents itself as a unique challenge for whatever witch finds themselves there." He tapped the page with his finger. "When the Shepherd's locked their powers in the talismans, they did so with the intention that they'd only be accessed in the labyrinth."

"Roberta vaguely went over all of this." I stared down at the drawing of the Allurements, a swirling portal of blues, greens and purples. "If Elementals hadn't gone into the labyrinth in so long, how did the Shepherd's know so much about it?"

"Spellbooks and visions, I imagine." Nic leaned back in his seat. "You've seen stuff before it happened, so it makes sense that they would too."

"All of my visions have been random though, except for the little memory glimpse I triggered in the woods, but I didn't see much," I explained.

Rose put a comforting hand on my elbow. "You're just getting started though, I'm sure in time your visions will become clearer." She turned to Nic. "Whit told you about the vision she had at the Hallow?"

His gaze widened as he smiled at me and blinked. "No, she did not."

Letting out a sigh, I shared the fire and the tornado I had seen ripping the compound to shreds. Nic and Bryan both tensed as I shared my vision and they glanced at one another with their brows raised.

Bryan let out a breath. "And how many visions have you seen that didn't come to fruition?"

"None yet." I met his dilated pupils. Bryan's fear swam in my stomach, blending with my own. I stood up and sighed, closing the spellbook still in Nic's lap. "None of it matters until we have the key."

"Don't get too discouraged. We have learned so much in the last few weeks, my head is still spinning." Bryan moved to my side and laced our fingers. "What are we going to do in the meantime?"

"Bury Mia," Nic announced, hugging the spellbook to his chest. His words caught me completely off guard. Every hair on my body stood on end. "Her remains were cremated, so we didn't need to rush. We wanted to wait until you guys were back from the Hallow. Now that you're here, we can plan the funeral. She was a well-loved member of the community, people will come."

Bryan tightened his grip on my hand in comfort as the room fell silent. Nic looked around at all of us, waiting for a response. When he didn't get one, he continued.

"Harmony and I will take care of it. She raised us, so we owe it to her." Nic sighed, running his fingers through his messy hair. "But if you want to help with anything, I'd appreciate it."

"I'll take care of the flowers," Rose announced. "I want to do something special in that regard, since she loved them so much."

Nic nodded silently.

"What about Warren?" Lauren asked in a somber tone.

"He has family up in Portland. It's up to them, and they haven't decided to share any official details with us." Nic glanced over at the fireplace. "We'll do a more private memorial on Ostara, but Mia deserves something public."

"I think we should have a reception at the Corner Cup," Brooke suggested. "Some way to honor Mia's legacy and all the hard work she put into the place. Maybe bring in some business."

"It's a great idea but I'd feel awful inviting people to a celebration of life to charge them to eat and drink," Rayn pointed out.

"Can we do both?" My voice sounded foreign as I spoke. "Have a celebration of life at the CC but maybe we can do a fundraiser too? Same day or a different day, I don't know. We need to bring money into the place or we're going to lose it."

"If you're worried about feeding people for the services, I can talk to my boss about donating something," Bryan said. "She and Amilia were friendly from my understanding, plus I could present the angle of free publicity for the restaurant."

I leaned down and kissed the top of his head. "Acoustic Nights always brought in a lot of business. What if we did another one, but a weekend long event? We could include raffles, giveaways, that kind of thing. Instead of it being a free event, we could charge a cover fee? I don't know."

"That's actually a brilliant idea, Whit." Nic smiled. "I like that a lot."

"I could make a cool flier," Dmitri added. "The kind you see advertising weekend-long music festivals. A 'Save the CC Acoustic Weekend'."

That was it. We all had our tasks, all of us using our skills and talents to do one last thing for Amilia. To thank her for all the guidance she had provided us. Even though she had her own way of doing things and we didn't always agree with her methods, we wouldn't be there without her. Mia saved Rose's life when she had been possessed by the vengeful spirit. Mia saved us Halloween night from our injuries we sustained in the Dragonfly Mystic basement. She healed Bryan from the Shadow attack. She housed us, fed us, employed us. She had given so much and never expected anything from us in return. The least we could do is keep the family business going.

A slight wave of relief washed over me as I walked into the Corner Cup a few mornings later. The smell of coffee and Bryan on my sweater calmed my nerves, seeing Dmitri and Lauren put me at ease. Ashley blew me a kiss as I came into view. Abe sat at a table in the corner of the room with his feet up on an empty chair and a book in his lap. Dmitri conveniently cleaned the tables closest to him, the two of them deep in conversation.

Ashley and Lauren were busy catching up on to-go orders, focused on work with little time for pleasantries. Once I clocked in, I got to work helping Mit in the dining area. Half of the tables were covered with used napkins and dirty dishes. Thankfully, Luke caught up on dishes in the back so I handed off the tub to him and joined the girls behind the counter.

Ashley disappeared into the back room and Lauren came up next to me, probably taking advantage of the privacy.

"How's everything going?" I asked her.

Lauren lowered her voice. "Grady was in here earlier. He didn't stick around long but he's making his presence known again."

I scoffed. "Grady is flirting with the whole hiding in plain sight thing again, isn't he?"

"But we know who he truly is, why would he keep coming at us when we could expose him?" Lauren asked.

"We'd have to expose ourselves to do so." I shook my head. "He's only here because of our powers. I don't understand what the hunter's motives are, but they are unwanted guests in the equation."

"Speaking of unwanted guests." Lauren raised her voice, loud enough for the next customer in line to hear us.

"What do you want?" I moved to the register and gripped onto the sides.

"Coffee, obviously. Something sweet." Serenity Drake tapped her chin with black fingernails and looked over the menu as if she wasn't there to taunt us.

If I didn't steady myself, I would leap over the counter and strangle her with my bare hands. I hadn't seen her since the attack on the cottage, but no amount of time could heal the wounds that event left behind.

I caught Dmitri and Abe tense across the room from the corner of my eye. Abe lowered his feet to the ground and shoved his back against the wall. Dmitri moved closer to him, crossing his arms as he glared Serenity down.

"You need to leave," I ordered, my knuckles turning white.

"Is my money not green?" Serenity smirked.

"You're not welcomed here," Lauren hissed through her teeth.

Serenity's gaze wandered across the room. She gave a sly smile to the guys and waved. "Funny seeing you out and about, Abraham. Feeling brave, today?"

"Back off." Dmitri stepped in front of Abe, who remained planted in his chair.

"Mmm, you know holding grudges is a lot like drinking poison and expecting the other person to die." Serenity's smile widened.

"If only it were that easy." I hardened my gaze.

Serenity continued to Abe, "It's a bit pointless if you ask me. Kind of like waltzing about town as if you aren't a dead man walking. You owe us your life, Roberts. Good thing I know where you live. We have some experience breaking your attempts at protection."

"Get out!" I shouted, causing the few customers sitting in the dining area to look over at me like I had lost my ever loving mind.

Serenity took a step back with wide eyes, placing her hand dramatically over her chest. "Well, this is the worst customer service I've ever received. I'll make sure to leave a review online."

"Everything okay?" Ashley came out of the back and stood next to me at the register. She watched Serenity turn and slither out the door.

"I'm sorry. I know I shouldn't have reacted, but I can't stand her."

"Go take a break," Ashley said in a soft tone and put her hand on my shoulder. "I already told her to stop coming in here. I don't know what else to do."

"I know, I'm so sorry." Tears welled up in my eyes. The nerve of Serenity to come in here and threaten Abe.

"Hey, it's okay." Ashley pulled me into a hug.

"I'll be back in a few," I muttered into Ashley's sweater and broke the hug.

Sitting in the breakroom and drinking some water didn't do anything to help chill me out. Anger dripped off of me, but instead of letting it control me, I would get Serenity back for everything she had done. For trying to kill Dmitri and Abe. For helping kidnap Rayn and trying to kill us. For helping Erebus storm the cottage and taking Warren and Amilia from us. I ran my fingers over the scar on my forearm.

I left the break room with a groan, determined to finish the rest of my shift without another incident. When I got back behind the counter, Nic chatted quietly with Lauren.

"Feel better?" Lauren asked, crossing her arms. "Serenity is such a bitch."

"I'm fine." I leaned against the counter.

"I'm here, you can go home if you want." Nic offered. "It's not really busy enough to justify all of us being here anyway."

I paused. "You know, usually I'd stay and get all the hours I could, but leaving early sounds like a blessing."

"Good. Get out of here." Nic waved towards the door. He turned to the register where a customer waited, but froze in place when he saw a tall, dark-haired man smiling. "What, uh, what can we get started for you?" Nic nearly tripped on his way over.

Lauren met my gaze with furrowed brows, as confused as I felt. She leaned in and whispered, "This guy has been coming in here almost every day."

Taking a better look, I recognized him from the crowd of faces I interacted with over the last week since we'd been back in Rifton. The customer ordered a plain black coffee to go. After he picked up his coffee, he set a piece of paper on the counter and slid it towards Nic.

The customer smiled as his cheeks heated in a blush. "Thanks."

Nic didn't move a muscle as he watched the customer leave. Once the door closed behind him, the whisper of a smile came over Nic's lips as he grabbed the piece of ripped paper. I caught a glimpse of a phone number before Nic shoved it in his pocket.

"Uh, hang on. I'm sorry, what was that?" Lauren motioned between Nic and the door.

Nic cleared his throat. "My good looks are hard to ignore."

"Are you going to call him?" Lauren's eyes widened with excitement.

"I haven't decided yet." Nic turned away from us.

"Wow. No, sorry, not wow. I just...I didn't think he was your type? I didn't think men were your type?" Lauren's gaze wandered over to me as she spoke.

Nic smacked his hand down on the counter, his stupid skull ring clinked against it. "What about me screams straight man?"

Lauren glanced from Nic's hazel eyes to his black Vans. "Now that you mention it. Nothing."

"He always set my radar off a bit," Dmitri called from across the room. "Strong bi vibes."

Nic winked at him. "Pan, actually."

Lauren turned to me. "Am I the only one who's excited and a little surprised about this?"

"I had no idea, but nothing he does surprises me anymore," I laughed. "Good for you, Nicky. Get some."

A pang of heat stirred in my chest. An angry pounding against my rib cage that swirled in my stomach.

Jealousy? I had absolutely nothing to be jealous about. Nic was my best friend. I loved him but there were no sparks or burning desire in my chest. I chewed on my lip, unsure where these conflicted feelings came from when I glanced up and saw Harmony standing by the employee door. She must have come out of the office at some point.

She shot a glare at Nic that surely burned holes into the side of him. I could feel the anger dripping off of her. Nic ignored her, but I knew he felt Harmony there.

"Um, well, I'm heading back to the cottage," I announced, nudging Nic's shoulder on the way by. "You should call him."

He nodded as I left.

Chapter Twenty
Long Distance
Whitney

Back at the cottage, Brooke sat on the couch with Rayn as I walked in.

"Hey!" Brooke greeted. "You have good timing. I'm here to tell Ray about some digging I did on Officer Grady. We're long overdue on some dirt."

"I'm listening." I kicked off my shoes and joined them by the fire.

"I found out that Officer Grady has only been on Rifton PD for about a year. He transferred last April." Brooke explained. "He lived in Eugene before."

"That's where Aden said his pack is originally based out of, so that tracks," Rayn replied.

I crossed my legs. "If Grady has been here since April, then that had to be when the protection wards were broken. If I'm understanding them properly, a hunter wouldn't have been able to come to Rifton if they were still up."

"So, that's something I don't understand," Brooke admitted. "Grady must've known the wards were broken. But if the wards could only be broken by witches, why would a witch risk the hunters returning to Rifton when they go after us *and* the Renati?"

"It doesn't make sense to me either." I chewed the inside of my cheek. "Someone is out of their minds breaking those wards."

"That pack leader, Ezekiel? Aden said he's completely lost it. I guess one day he snapped. Started torturing the witches and punished any of the hunters who had anything to say about it. That's why they tried to kill Aden, because he had turned his back on the pack but in reality, he has a fucking heart." Rayn huffed. "Ezekiel wanted to alter the hunter's DNA even further."

"How so?" I dared to ask.

"Aden wasn't sure, but he overheard it right before they caught that missing girl from Falcon Bay. I guess Ezekiel thought the hunters should be stronger to fight the witches to preserve their way of life, that their current alterations weren't enough. He wanted to create a new serum to make super humans."

"That's disturbing," Brooke muttered. "I can't imagine what those hunters would look like."

"Would they even be human at that point? I thought the hunters believed we weren't human because of our powers, but how would they be any different than us if they altered themselves further?" I asked.

Rayn shrugged. "I think the problem is expecting rational actions. Ezekiel clearly isn't a rational person, he's not in that state of mind. Neither is the person who broke the wards."

I tilted my head. "You think Ezekiel had something to do with that?"

Rayn nodded. "He has motives. It would make sense that he wants to target Rifton since there are so many witches living here. And having hunters on the police force to cover up any trace of their presence? That's a smart move."

"But the Renati were the ones trying to kill Abe." I shook my head, still unable to grasp any tangible explanation. "Why would Grady be trying to cover that up for the hunters?"

"Maybe he isn't," Brooke said. "Maybe he tried to pin it on you guys to somehow lock you up and make it easier for the hunters to have access to you? That's a common goal the hunters and the Renati could both get behind, killing us."

"Yeah but Erebus wants to kill us with his bare hands. He wouldn't let the hunters take us out." Rayn shifted in her seat, appearing as confused as me.

Brooke shrugged. "This happened before Erebus came back. Have you noticed Grady has left us alone for the most part?"

I let out a deep breath. "We can't fight them both at the same time, especially if they are low-key using one another to fuck with us."

"I never thought the Renati and the hunters would pull that card, but here we are." Brooke sighed. "It's a theory at least, something to look into."

The back door opened from the porch into the kitchen and heavy footsteps echoed through the house.

"Aden?" Rayn called out.

"It's me," he answered, stepping into the dining room with a water bottle. Sweat beads dripped from his forehead and had soaked the top of his shirt. His shoulder length hair pulled up into a high bun, little strands sticking up from his workout.

"Aden, you know Joseph Grady, yeah?" I asked.

He nodded. "Pretty well actually."

"He's a cop on the Rifton PD."

"Yes, he is." Aden took a drink of water.

"He's been stalking us."

Aden lifted his brow, his eyes wandering to Rayn. "Stalking you?"

"For a while now. He comes into the Corner Cup all the time and he keeps trying to get us in legal trouble," Rayn answered.

"I can take him out," Aden offered with a simple shrug.

"Take him out…Kill him?" I clarified.

Aden crossed his arms. "Why not? He wouldn't hesitate to kill me and if he's bothering you, then I can take care of it."

I scoffed. "Aden we cannot kill people because they bother us."

He brushed me off. "We can if they are a threat."

"I'm trying to be better than that," I pressed.

Aden's face remained emotionless. "War doesn't care about who is trying to be better."

"But we still have to live with ourselves when it's over." Brooke turned to look at him.

Aden set his water down on the table and stepped towards us. "Yes, but doing what is necessary to survive is how most people live through wars."

That made my stomach churn.

Rayn put her hand up to stop him. "No, we don't want you to kill him. Not unless he's actively attacking us or something. But we want to know more about him."

Aden nodded in understanding. "He was the first person in our pack to travel down here. Ezekiel sent him ahead of the rest of us to scope things out."

"April of last year?" I wondered aloud.

"Yeah that sounds about right."

Brooke stood up and paced the living room. "We're trying to figure out who broke the wards that allowed the hunters into Rifon in the first place. I think the Renati are working with Ezekiel, or that he had some kind of inside knowledge since he sent Grady down here. He had to know the wards were broken."

Aden let out a sigh. "I wish I could be more of an asset but Ezekiel didn't trust me. I think he always had his suspicions of me. He and my father did not get along." He glanced out the window with heavy eyes. "I worry about my brother."

"Your brother," I repeated back to him.

"Yes, he's still with them. Not in that same pack that came to your old house looking for me, but he is with another hunting pack. I hope they don't take my actions out on him. He can be such a dumbass, my brother." A sadness washed over Aden's face as his shoulders fell. "I have no idea what they told him about me, or how they explained my absence to him."

My heart broke for him. "I hope he's safe. I had no idea you had a brother."

I imagined being separated from Dmitri and my soul cracked. Wondering if he would be safe amongst the enemy. Wondering if he thought I had betrayed him and our family. Worried they would retaliate against him to punish me. If I were in Aden's position, I wouldn't be able to sleep knowing my brother remained with the hunters.

"He's younger, just turned twenty." Aden slowly nodded. "But he'll be okay as long as he keeps his head down. We have more pressing issues here in Rifton."

That night, I called Bryan as soon as I got into our bedroom. The room felt empty without him, and the best I could do with him in Falcon Bay was to fill the silence with his voice. We talked about our days for a bit, catching up on the mundane. I decided not to tell him about Serenity in the Corner Cup or my conversation with Aden. He filled me in on what he'd done in class, and that he and Emma made burritos when they got home.

Bryan sighed into the phone. I heard him shift, moving around to get comfortable.

"Are you in bed?" I asked, staring at his empty pillow next to mine.

"Mhmmm," he answered. "Though I'd much rather be in *our* bed back in Rifton. Or you could be here, I wish we were together."

"Me too. I have a hard time sleeping with you gone."

"I don't sleep well without you either." Bryan lowered his voice. "Though, if we were together right now, we would not be sleeping."

"Oh?" My voice rose an octave, playfully pretending I didn't understand. "What ever would we be up to?"

"I'd have my head between your legs, licking your clit like a lollipop."

His forwardness caught me off guard and my breath hitched as my pulse accelerated. Excitement pooled between my legs. I rubbed my thighs together but the friction wasn't enough. It never felt like enough without Bryan assisting.

"You okay?" he asked when I didn't reply.

I chortled. "Yeah, I'm good. I just, uh, I..."

"Are you uncomfortable?" A pang of concern echoed in his voice.

"No, not at all. I wish you were here to help me with this *problem*."

He hummed into the phone, his voice low and sultry. "Maybe I still can."

"Yeah?"

"Can we FaceTime?"

My heart leapt into my throat. Bryan had seen me countless times in various states of dress, but I had never been on video chat with anyone before. Ever. I never had a need to. My family was never far enough away that we needed to talk on video. Bryan was the only person I even spoke to on the phone, but I desperately wanted to see his face. And the rest of him too.

"Yes," I paused. "But, are you home alone?"

"No," Bryan answered.

"Um, isn't Emma going to hear us?"

I heard Bryan hop off his bed. The sound of his door opened as he called out, "Em!"

"What's up?" Emma's voice came over the phone.

"Put in headphones, I'm going to FaceTime with Whit."

"Okay!" she answered, not a hint of awkwardness or discomfort at all in her voice.

Bryan's door closed. "You aren't home alone either."

"I have headphones and I'll be quiet."

Bryan laughed. "You are incapable of being quiet when I make you come, but I honestly don't care. Can I see you?"

"Yes," I whispered.

Moments later, the call turned into a FaceTime. After accepting, Bryan's beaming face appeared on my screen. He laid down in bed, his arm under a pillow. He held the phone out far enough that I could see his bare chest. My eyes wandered down to the bottom of the screen, his stomach barely visible.

"Hey, beautiful," he whispered.

I smiled back. "I miss you."

"Mmm, me too. Now, tell me about this problem of yours."

I blushed, looking away from the phone.

"You're never shy in bed," he chuckled. "I know you touch yourself, you do it when I'm behind you."

"I do, but not with an audience...So, do you?"

"I literally got off in the shower thinking about you this morning."

Oh.

"What were you thinking about?" My heart beat accelerated behind my chest.

Bryan readjusted, moving his phone so it propped up against something. He lay back down on the bed and I finally got a full view of his body, down to his knees. He wore my favorite gray sweatpants. "How sweet you taste. Spreading you open until you come on my tongue. I thought about the look on your face when I first enter you, the way your lips part and your eyebrows raise as if you're surprised. As if you feel a fraction of what I feel...How you tighten around my cock."

I stared into his eyes, listening to his words, soaking them in. I sprung up, setting my phone down while I took my shirt off. When I picked my phone up and lay back down, Bryan's eyes wandered across my bare chest.

"Fuck," he whispered. His hand slid down under the waistband of his sweats, gripping his erection.

"I want to see you," I begged, watching his hand under the gray fabric. Everything inside of me tightened and I squeezed my thighs tighter. I wanted to reach down between my legs, but I needed to savor this. I didn't want it to go too quickly.

"Do you now?" He barely moved the waistband down; just enough to tease me but not enough to satisfy the craving.

"You always make me beg," I whined.

Bryan smiled. "It sounds so pretty when you do."

"Please, let me watch you touch yourself."

His breath hitched and he slid his sweats down his thighs. His erection sprung forward as he removed his pants. He spit into his hand and gripped the bottom of his shaft, slowly moving his hand to the tip. Bryan closed his eyes and groaned, his hips moving with the slow, sweet motion of his fingers.

I couldn't look away. My heart pounded in my ears, my face flushed as the heat pooled between my legs turned to a throb. An ache begging for relief. "I want you in my mouth so bad right now." The words fell from my lips.

Bryan's eyes met mine. "You like my cock in your mouth?"

"Yes, but you always pull out before you come."

He lifted his eyebrows. "Should I not?"

"I want to taste you."

He froze, his body rigid as he shuttered. "Keep saying those things and I'm driving back home tonight." He looked down the length of my body. "You aren't touching yourself."

"I'm enjoying the show."

"Take off your panties and show me how you pleasure yourself."

"Is that an order?" I joked.

"Yes," he commanded with authority.

I loved this side of him; comfortable enough to take control and knowing I felt comfortable enough to let him. So, I obliged. I moved my panties down my legs and propped my phone up on the empty pillow. I turned to my side, giving him a full view.

"You," he paused, carefully watching my fingers travel down my stomach. "Are a work of art."

I slid my fingers to my core, soaking wet as I suspected. I let them glide over my entrance and back up to my clit, pressing my fingertips against my most sensitive spot. I breathed out, my body finding only seconds of relief before it demanded more. Bryan moved his hand back down the length of his erection.

"Tell me more," I panted. "When you think about me in the shower."

"I think about you all day long, honestly. But if I was there right next to you, where I belong, I have very specific ideas of what I'd be doing. I'd have one of those perfect nipples in my teeth, the other one between my fingers. I'd kiss my way down your body, in between your breasts and down your soft stomach. I'd lick your inner thighs until your fingers dug into my hair and finally pulled me between your thighs, my favorite place to be."

I moved my finger in a circle, pressing down on my clit. My back arched as a fire burned through my veins. My pace quickened, chasing relief as my body climbed higher and higher, inching closer to the edge. As tortured as my body felt, I never took my eyes off Bryan. The way his hand pumped. The way his chest rose and fell with each pant. How he moaned in between sentences.

"That's it, baby," he said with labored breath. "Are you close?"

I nodded, my moans released in a gasp. I rolled my lips, attempting to keep quiet.

"Me too. Come with me."

Three simple words and I came undone. Everything tensed and shook until I collapsed against the pillow. Absent-mindedly, I reached out for Bryan. I reached for his warmth, to pull him close and feel his chest rise and fall with his labored breaths. The cold sheets next to me served as a sobering reminder that I lay in the bed alone.

"That was fun," Bryan panted. "But nothing compares to the real thing."

I let out a deep breath. "No, but I'll take whatever you can give me. I'll never complain about getting to watch you like that, though. You are a sight for sore eyes."

Bryan chuckled and rolled onto his side, grabbing the phone and bringing it closer to his face. "You're one to talk, you literal goddess." He glanced down the length of his body. "I'm going to get cleaned up. Don't hang up, okay?"

"I'll be back too," I told him.

I got off the bed and walked across the room to the bathroom. I never had a bathroom in my bedroom before moving in with Bryan, and it spoiled me quickly. I may have gone without for all of my life, but I never wanted to give up this master bedroom situation. Getting out of the shower and walking straight into my room was the most convenient thing I'd ever experienced. No more rushing down the hall in a towel or taking clothes into a muggy, damp bathroom.

After I cleaned up and got back into bed, Bryan lay against his pillow. His eyes lit up when he saw me come back onto the screen. I smiled, knowing I could lay in that bed and stare at him for the next three days until he got back home so I could stare at him in person.

"Can we stay on the phone until we fall asleep?" Bryan asked, nuzzling his face into the pillow.

"Of course." I smiled again, watching the exhaustion take over his face as his body came down from the high.

Bryan looked into my eyes and his soft smile vanished. He stared at me for a moment before he whispered, "I hate being here."

"Oh, baby, you're almost done. It'll be over before you know it, and you'll be home every night."

I did my best to encourage him. Only a few months stood between him and graduation. I wanted him to stay focused. Everything in our lives was chaotic and uncertain, making sure Bryan finished his bachelor's degree felt like the least we could do to maintain some level of normalcy.

"Yeah." He looked away from the phone, off to whatever corner of the room caught his attention. Bryan let out a sigh before his gaze returned. "Yeah, you're right. I miss you a lot. It was different when you were at the Hallow, but now that I know you're back in Rifton in my bed...it's harder for me to justify being here."

"You're finishing school. You've worked so hard for this."

"I have, but it feels...trivial with everything else going on."

"Hey, look at me." I brought his attention back to me. "You are going to finish your degree. That is very important to both of us. You're only an hour and a half away. I know it feels like a thousand miles right now, but we are closer than you think. We still look at the same moon every night. Knowing you're out there in the world doing something for yourself makes my life here easier. I take comfort knowing I'm not uprooting everything for you."

Bryan licked his bottom lip and nodded, but the sadness remained in his eyes.

"I love you, so very much. Here, let me read something to you. It's my favorite part." I grabbed *Tides of Time* from the dresser and opened up to the page my bookmark held. "Tristen is about to save Emala from the swamps."

Bryan smiled, a genuine smile. "This is my favorite part too."

"Good." I nestled into the pillow and began to read. I read until the end of the chapter, where the two characters were finally in a safe space, setting up camp for the night. I peeked up from *Tides of Time* to a sleeping Bryan. His eyes were closed and he lightly snored into his pillow. I set the book down and lay there, watching him. He looked so peaceful. His lips slightly parted. His face relaxed; the tension that earlier furrowed his brow vanished. I wanted to reach through the phone and kiss those lips. To wrap my arms around him and ease the stress and sadness he kept locked inside. I wanted to shower him with love and adoration, but maybe for tonight night, I had done enough to ease some of that pain.

I closed my eyes and fell asleep with the call still connected.

Chapter Twenty-One
Suffering in Silence
Whitney

Bryan and I spent the next night on video chat, watching each other strip naked and then falling asleep with our phones close to our faces. It didn't last three nights in a row, and I had the hardest time falling asleep that third night. I knew it couldn't be a nightly thing, but I had looked forward to seeing his face. At least I knew he would be home tomorrow for his birthday.

I lay there for hours. Tossing and turning. Going back and forth between reading and doom scrolling on my phone. I lit a stick of incense and watched the thin line of smoke waft up into the air. I played with my talisman, watching the black ink swirl around the aquamarine. It had been a long time since I'd laid in bed and seen black ink instead of white in the gem. A reminder that I was away from my sister and the other girls.

I didn't realize I'd fallen asleep until someone touched my shoulder. I jolted up and gasped for air. Troy or Dmitri wouldn't be waking me up unless something was wrong.

"Hey," a familiar voice soothed me back down. "It's me, baby, it's me."

"What are you doing here?" I reached out to cup Bryan's cheek. I brought his lips to mine and yanked him into bed.

He laughed, falling on top of me. He wore a thick hoodie and I slid my hands underneath it to feel his warm skin. A rush of excitement but also a pang of anxiety mixed with my own joy. Bryan kissed my neck and my cheeks before he spoke. "I came home a day early."

"You don't have class tomorrow?"

He shook his head. "Nope. Besides, I couldn't wait another day to kiss these lips."

I broke the kiss and pulled him into a hug. "Is it midnight?"

"Half hour past."

"Happy birthday, my love." I clung to him, holding him as close as possible.

"Thank you." I felt his lips smile against my neck. His nerves unraveled as he lay in my arms, his weight pressing me down into our bed. He relaxed and his heart rate slowed. Bryan let out a deep sigh and went back to kissing my neck.

"Twenty-four. You're getting old," I joked, running my fingers through his hair. "Is everything okay?"

"I just wanted to see you," he muttered against my skin in between kisses.

"You just feel kind of anxious-"

He kissed the edge of my mouth and hooked his knee under mine, spreading my leg open. "I'm much better now." He moved his groin in between my thighs and pressed his body against mine. His erection rubbed against me through his sweatpants.

"I haven't even touched you yet." I kissed his soft lips and grabbed a handful of his hair.

"I've had a lot to think about on the drive," he said in between kisses. "Watching you touch yourself has been my undoing."

"I want you to touch me."

He hummed and slid his fingers up my inner thigh. "Anything for you, baby."

Bryan moved my panties to the side, not bothering to unravel us to take them off. He ran his thumb up along my opening and smiled against my mouth. "Always so wet for me."

He slipped a finger inside and pressed this thumb to my bundle of nerves, gently running circles around it. I breathed out, moving my body with his hand motions. He worked me with his fingers, moving painfully slow.

I grabbed the bottom of his hoodie and yanked it up his back, bringing his shirt with it. He removed his fingers, allowing me to take off his shirt. Bryan's eyes met mine as he slipped his finger into his mouth, tasting me.

I watched him carefully before I grabbed the waistband of his sweats. "Today is *your* day and I want you in my mouth."

Bryan looked down at my hands as I slowly slid his pants down his hips. He stood up and finished undressing. I stared at him, never able to get over how perfect his body was.

How much I loved the little freckles that covered his shoulders and the one on his hip bone. How I wouldn't change a single thing about him.

He pulled my shirt over my head and slowly slid my panties down my legs. He lay down on the bed next to me and pulled me into a kiss.

"Sit on my face," he requested.

I turned my back to the headboard and swung my leg over him, hovering.

"I said *sit*." Bryan grabbed my thighs, and pulled me down.

I rested my weight on him. His tongue stroked against me in a long, slow glide before it slid inside of me. A moan escaped my lips in response. I enjoyed him for a moment, feeling his mouth slide to my clit. His lips wrapped around the nub and sucked.

I lay my chest against his stomach and grabbed the base of his erection, licking the tip. He groaned against me, moving his hips and tightening his grip on my ass. Bryan bent his knee out and gently thrust as I took him in my mouth.

The desire coursing through his veins peaked and he moaned into me again as my lips touched his base, taking as much of him as I could. I swirled my tongue around his length.

My body rushed to the edge quickly, overwhelmed with both of our pleasure coursing through me. Bryan moved his hips and his mouth to the same rhythm, digging his fingers into my skin.

I arched my back and attempted to keep my focus on his erection but the pressure in my body built and built until my muscles tightened and I tumbled right over the edge, my orgasm overwhelming every molecule of my body.

I moved my mouth against Bryan's length, slipping my tongue against the little slit on the tip. He fell over the edge right after me. He thrust one last time into my mouth and held himself there as he came. I swallowed every last bit of him.

I collapsed off of him onto my side, both of us lying there panting. He reached for my hand, wrapping his fingers around mine.

"I'm so glad I came back early," he whispered.

"Me too." I smiled, running my free hand along the side of his thigh. "We should take a shower."

"Mmm, we will. Give me a minute." He tightened his grip on my hand. Uncertainty swirled around in his core and he let out a soft sigh. "Whitney, I love you."

I tilted my head to look up at him. "I love you too. What's wrong?"

"Nothing."

I wanted to tell him that I felt something off. Nothing to do with the sex but something that weighed heavy on him before he walked into the house. I didn't want to use my powers to invade his feelings, even though I had no control over feeling them in the first place. Instead, I kissed his outer thigh and flipped around so my head nuzzled under his arm. Bryan held me close and explored my body with a feather-like touch that made my skin tingle.

―――

When I woke up the next morning, the bed sheets beside me were cold. I stretched out my arms and paper crumpled under me. A chill ran through my body as I opened back the paper to see Bryan's handwriting.

Went for a jog with Aden, be back soon. I love you.

A jog with Aden?

I left the note on his pillow and headed to the bathroom, starting the water for the shower. I had been in there only hours before, but I wanted to get back under the water. It poured over my aching muscles, soothing the tension that built in my head. I could've fallen asleep standing up, but I had to get to the Corner Cup for my shift. I didn't want to give Harmony a brain aneurysm by showing up late.

When I came out of the bathroom wrapped in a towel, Bryan stood in our room. His back turned to me as he stripped his sweat soaked shirt from his body.

"Hi," I said, my eyes wandering down his bare back.

He turned around and eyed me up and down. "Hey, there." He smiled and strolled across the room, undoing the towel. He pressed his lips to mine as the towel fell to the floor.

"You're soaking wet." I laughed against his lips.

"In my defense, so are you." He kissed me again before he scooted past me to the bathroom. "Did you save me any hot water?"

"I hope so."

"Don't worry about it." Bryan turned on the water and stripped off the rest of his clothes. "When do you have to be at work?"

"An hour," I answered, picking up the towel to wrap my hair in. I headed to the dresser and dug around for some work clothes. "Are you working today?"

"Nope. I don't remember the last time I had a free day," Bryan answered from the shower.

"You should relax. Do you have anything special planned?"

"Troy wants to get something to eat. My mom wants me to come by sometime this weekend. I don't really want to do anything besides lay in bed with you."

"Me too. I'm sorry I have to work. So, you were out jogging with Aden?"

"Yeah," he paused. "I want to start training with him."

"Why?"

"Why not?"

"I don't know..."

"Give me a second." Bryan finished up his shower and turned off the water. He came back into the bedroom with a towel around his waist. "Listen, at the cottage attack, I was dead weight. There was nothing I could do to help. I didn't know what to do. If Rose hadn't shielded me...I don't know if I would've walked out of there. We all need to be able to defend ourselves in this, Whit."

I sighed. "I know."

His lips curved into a soft smile. "I'm going to meet up with him tomorrow after I get off work and we're going to do another session."

"What does he have planned for you?" I finished getting dressed.

"I don't know. He said he'll teach me some of the tactics he learned from the hunters. You know, it's not a bad idea to learn how they fight. It might actually give us an advantage."

"You're right." I crossed the room to give him a kiss. "Come in later for your birthday drink. Do you want to grab dinner tonight?"

"Yeah, I'll get lunch with Troy. Can we order take out and eat dinner in bed?"

"We will do whatever you want." I kissed him again.

"I want to be alone with you," he replied, an air of anxiety hung over him that I tried to ignore.

"Then that's exactly what we'll do."

The next day at the cottage, Aden threw Bryan over his shoulder for the fourth time. Bryan landed hard on the ground and his back bounced off the dirt. Bryan let out a gasp as the air rushed from his lungs. He gave himself a minute and then jumped back on his feet, coming after Aden again.

I stood on the back porch, watching them spar. Chewing on my bottom lip, I winced at the feeling of Bryan in pain. Every hit against him echoed through my soul. His frustration and determination swam through me as if I were the one attempting to tackle Aden on the lawn. Bryan hit the dirt again and I forced myself to look away.

"It would probably be easier on both of you if you went inside," Dmitri said behind me. "You're distracting him."

"I am?"

Dmitri crossed his arms. "Yes, he keeps looking over here at you instead of paying attention to what Aden is doing."

"Oh." I genuinely hadn't noticed; but now that I realized, I saw Bryan's attention turn to me before Aden knocked him on his ass once more. "Okay, I see it. I'm going, I'm going." I left the back porch and went inside the house with Dmitri on my heels. "You don't feel the need to train with them?"

"I have powers. I don't need to know how to fight like that." Dmitri glanced back over his shoulder. "It's gotta be hard on Byn, being the only one here who's powerless. I know there's something in his blood but he still can't protect himself." He chewed on his bottom lip. "He tried, you know."

"Tried what?" I tilted my head.

"Tapping into whatever he has going on." Dmitri furrowed his brow at me. "He didn't tell you?"

I shook my head and glanced back outside where Aden kicked Bryan's shin, tripping him to the ground. "No, he didn't tell me."

"Oh," Dmitri paused. "Nothing happened so I guess there wasn't anything to tell. He got pretty frustrated. I don't think he likes being the only powerless one in the group."

"Aden is powerless." I opened up the fridge and scanned for any snacks, but quickly closed the door.

"Aden could kill everyone here with his bare hands," Dmitri answered. "This is good for Bryan. The next time something happens, he won't be so defenseless."

I nodded. "That's what he told me."

"We've talked about it a lot, me and him. He doesn't want to be a burden."

"He's never a burden," I snapped back.

"Not to us, because we love him." Dmitri took a step closer to me. "But to the rest of the group? To the other witches out there? Someone is always going to have to divert their energy and attention to protect him. It might get them both killed." He glanced towards the back door. "When the Reanti attacked, Rose got hit pretty hard with an energy wave because she was so focused on Bryan. What if that had been Erebus' poison smoke? They'd both be–"

"I get it," I cut him off, rubbing my throbbing temple. "I get it, Mit. It's good that Aden is training him. I never argued with it."

"Okay, sorry." Dmitri put up his hands in defense. "We weren't sure how you'd react to it."

I raised my eyebrow. "I'm not completely unreasonable, you know."

"No, of course not. You've always been level headed." Dmitri smirked, nudging me with his elbow before he went into the living room where most of the crew dug through info about the key. Amilia sure didn't have much documentation on the key, even though she had kept part of it.

"The hell kind of Archivist doesn't have anything about the key to open the talismans?" Rose closed the book she held. "This can't be everything. Nic, where is her secret stash?"

"These are the books from her secret stash." Nic turned a page in his own book. "I'm missing something." He closed the book and got up from the couch, heading up the stairs. "Whit, I need a hand."

"Okay." I followed Nic up the stairs to Amilia's bedroom. I halted in the entryway of the loft as Nic strolled into her room. Of all the months I'd been around Amilia, all the nights I'd stayed at the cottage, I'd never been inside of her bedroom.

"She's got some journals in here somewhere. I know it. She was a huge journaler." Nic opened up the top drawer of her dresser and started digging, not noticing that I stood frozen in place.

"My mom too," I whispered.

Slowly, I moved into the bedroom, scared to touch anything. It would never be how she left it again. Everything we moved, everything we went through would never look the same. She wouldn't be the last person to touch her things. Her belongings wouldn't be the last place she left them. The more we messed with her room, the less hers it became.

"Start looking in her cedar chest." Nic moved on to the next drawer of the dresser.

I remained frozen in the doorway, looking around at every little detail. Her hairbrush on the bedside table. Next to it was a framed photo of six young witches. I recognized my mom's face immediately, all smiles and no worries. Baby pictures of Abbie, toothless grins and messy curls. A bottle of sweet pear lotion on the dresser. A hamper in the corner of the room with clothes still in it. A jewelry box with necklaces hanging off the sides, rings on her bedside table still sitting where she had taken them off with every intention of putting them back on.

"Whit?" Nic looked over his shoulder and frowned. "Look, I know, okay? I know, but Mia knew more about the Allurements than those books she kept in the living room. It's just stuff. Now that she's gone…this stuff won't bring her back."

I nodded, knowing that if I spoke the lump in my throat would turn to tears. I went to the large cedar chest at the foot of Amilia's bed and opened back the lid, more photos and letters greeted me in unorganized piles. Little baby shoes and old photo albums. Towards the bottom of the stacks were smaller notebooks, a familiar maroon color jumped out at me. The same color as Mom's journal. I picked it up and carefully opened back the cover with trembling fingers. The first chunk of the journal was Amilia's thoughts, words of loneliness yet determination. I'd return to these entries another time. I flipped through the pages, skimming as I went.

A sketch drawing of a key covered the next page.

"Nicky," I breathed, running my fingertips over the drawing. This had to be it.

The ink pen drawing of the key was messy but specific. The perfectly round handle of the key had a skull at the top.

Spirit.

A rain droplet where the handle met the stem.

Water.

Down the stem were flames that turned into swirls resembling a cloud.

Fire and air.

A leaf served as the bit of the key.

Earth.

Nic stood at my side in a flash, the warmth from his body burning down my neck. He reached around me and tapped the page. "Bingo."

"Is this the key?" I looked over my shoulder at him.

He nodded. "That's it."

"Why was the key broken into pieces?" I asked.

"The same reason the Archivists separated the talismans. To keep it safe, keep the Renati from getting their hands on it."

"Little good that did," I muttered and turned to face him."How did Amilia end up being the Archivist the key passed down to?"

Nic shrugged. "She came from a long line of Archivists, her family traced all the way back to the European witch haven, Paradisus. That's why she took her job so seriously, why she worked so hard to keep those books safe."

"I wish she put the same effort into keeping her fragment of the key. We don't even know where her piece is, and the other two pieces are floating around out there." I closed the journal, using my thumb to hold the page. "The Renati already have one and if we don't get to the third piece before they do, we're fucked."

Nic crossed his arms. "Maggie wouldn't hand her piece of the key over to the Renati. She was a member of the coven."

I furrowed my brow. "So was Bonnie Drake."

Nic turned his attention back to the cedar chest. "Go downstairs and show the girls, I'm going to keep digging around here and see what else I can find."

I ran out of Amilia's room and down the stairs, nearly tripping on the bottom one as I rushed into the living room. My voice bounced off the walls. "We found it!"

"Found what?" Rayn jumped up from her seat and met me in the middle of the room.

"Mia's notebook. She has a sketch of the key," I explained, my heart pounding in my throat.

"Holy shit, this is it!" Rayn shrieked, throwing her arms around my neck and pulling me into a hug. "We have the Shepherd's missing pages and Jake's Allurement notes. Now we know what the key looks like. We're going to do this, Sis, we're going to get it done."

I smiled at her and handed the book to Rose as she, Brooke and Lauren circled us, eager to see what I'd discovered hidden in Mia's room.

"Does it say anything about where her piece of the key is?" Lauren asked, reading over Rose's shoulder.

"I don't know, I only got through the first few pages," I replied.

Rose smiled, turning to the next page. "It says here that Margaret Daniels has the tip of the key and Bonnie has the stem. So now at least we know exactly what we're looking for. This isn't some ordinary key, it's us. It's symbolic of our powers, all together in one design."

"It's beautiful," Brooke breathed. "Does that mean Mia had the handle?"

I nodded. "Must be. Nic is insistent we worry about getting the Renati's piece first."

"Easier said than done," Rose said, her eyes glued to the notebook. "We have to take this with us the next time we go to the Hallow. Jake is going to lose it when he sees an actual sketch of the key."

"He's smart," I agreed. "I'm glad he's on our side."

The back door in the kitchen opened and heavy footsteps echoed through the house as Bryan and Aden made their way inside. Aden walked in first, stretching out his arm, rubbing his shoulder as if it were in pain. Bryan came in behind him, his bottom lip swollen and bloody.

"Aden, what the fuck?" I demanded when I saw the blood on Bryan's face. I rushed to his side for a better look at his injury. Anger pooled in my stomach as I gently touched his cheek. His perfect face. I punched Aden in the shoulder. "You asshole."

"He's fine," Aden grunted as I hit him where he hurt. "It was an accident. I didn't punch him in the face." He took a step away from me. "These things happen when you're sparing."

"I got it." Brooke came up behind me and offered her hands, a glowing, golden light leaving her fingertips. Bryan leaned into her touch as Brooke closed her eyes. When she removed her hands, Bryan's face appeared good as new. Brooke smiled up at Bryan, adoration in her gaze. "Handsome as ever."

"Thanks, B." He smiled back and rubbed the once-injured spot. Bryan turned to me and gently stroked my cheek. "I'm fine, baby."

I glared at Aden. He shook his head, refusing Brooke's healing magic on his shoulder.

"I just need some ice, my body will repair itself." Aden strolled into the kitchen and opened up the freezer. "Bryan, when you come back next weekend, I want to see you shoot."

Bryan paused, letting the air slowly leave his lungs. "I don't know how I feel about that."

Aden walked back into the living room with a bag of frozen peas. "You said you've hunted."

"Yeah, pheasants and ducks. Not people."

"You think I enjoy shooting people?" Aden held the peas to his shoulder.

Bryan shook his head. "Of course not, but I don't...I don't know if I could–"

"If the choice is between you or someone who wants to kill you, would you rather die?" Aden took a step towards Bryan.

"No, but–"

"If the choice is between you or one of these girls, would you rather let them be killed than pull the trigger?" Aden took another step until he stood in Bryan's face.

"No," Bryan firmly answered again, glaring up at Aden.

Aden had made his point and moved towards the living room. "Then next weekend, I'd like to see you shoot. You can practice on the bow, too. The bow is a bit more...civilized."

"Killing isn't civilized," Bryan muttered under his breath.

"You okay?" I whispered, linking my arm in his.

He nodded. "I hope it never comes to that."

"Me either," I admitted, pulling him close.

Aden sat down in one of the armchairs by the fire. "Pulling the trigger on a weapon is no different than the magic these witches use. How is shooting a bolt from the crossbow any different than when your girlfriend stabs someone in the chest with an icicle?"

Bryan fell silent.

"There is none," Aden answered for him.

Nic shuffled down the stairs from the loft, holding a stack of papers. He moved slowly, his eyes glazed over with tears as his gaze met mine across the room.

"What's wrong?" I asked, moving to meet him.

Nic cleared his throat and handed the stack of papers to me. I skimmed over the first page, realizing they were medical papers from Rifton Memorial Hospital. Amilia's name and birthdate were printed at the top of the page, listing the results of various tests. I tried to make sense of the blood work, the numbers and codes on the paper but I couldn't wrap my head around any of it.

"What is this?" I glanced back up at my friend, searching his face for answers.

Nic turned to the next page and tapped to the top of the paper.

Biopsy results: positive.

"I don't understand," I admitted.

Rayn stood at my side, reading over my shoulder when she gasped. "Mia had cancer?"

"What?" I nearly dropped the papers on the floor.

Everyone rushed across the room, gathering around me to look at the pages for themselves.

"But the test is dated August third, that's before we moved here," I replied, looking at Nic. "She didn't say anything to you about this?"

He shook his head, a stray tear trickling down his cheek. "I had no idea."

"Do you think Harmony knew?" Rayn asked him.

"I don't see her keeping that to herself, especially after Mia's passing." Nic cleared his throat. "I hope she wouldn't keep this from me, at least."

"Is this..." I paused, the words tasted my poison on my tongue. "Is this why she...jumped in front of me? Because she was already dying?"

"According to these documents, she didn't seek treatment." Nic wiped the tear away with the back of his hand.

I couldn't believe it. Mia's body had been giving out on her. That must have been why she looked so tired around the holidays. Why she insisted on staying behind whenever we went on a mission. I assumed she wanted to hang back to make sure we had the supplies we needed when we returned, but she didn't have the strength. I had noticed her slow down and the dark circles under her eyes, but we were all exhausted. She brushed it off as if nothing happened.

Amilia had spent her final days suffering in silence.

Chapter Twenty-Two
DISAPPOINTMENT
Whitney

That weekend, Bryan and I headed to his mom's house for dinner. I hadn't been over there since the Christmas Eve disaster, and I had begun to wonder if I'd ever be invited back. The girls and I had gone to Nancy and Jack's wedding, but I didn't actually speak to Bryan's mother that night. Nerves rattled my core. Bryan felt stressed too. I couldn't tell if his anxiety came from worrying about me or his mother, but I didn't want to ask.

Bryan opened the front door, letting me in before him. Voices flowed from the living room, hushed and stern. The air hung heavy throughout the house, not at all what I expected for a casual family diner. I expected Rose to greet us at the door, but I didn't sense her presence. I turned around to say something to Bryan but he froze behind me, glaring at the back of the couch.

A man stood up and turned to face us. His short blonde hair was shaved on the sides and familiar green eyes looked past me at Bryan. His mouth a thin line, unimpressed and irritated. I may as well have been looking at Bryan twenty years from now, only no glimmer shone in his eyes and no soft smile curving his lips. He may have resembled the man I loved, but only on the outside.

"I'm leaving." Bryan grabbed my hand and opened the front door when Nancy rushed towards us.

"Byn, we need to talk, preferably alone. You didn't tell me you were bringing a guest." Nancy reached out to stop Bryan from heading out the door.

A guest. An unwelcome addition to this...whatever this was. I shrunk down four sizes, unable to make eye contact with anyone in the room. I didn't understand why Bryan's mother didn't want me here, but clearly her feelings about me hadn't changed since Christmas Eve.

"There isn't anything we need to talk about that involves him." Bryan motioned towards the man across the room.

"Son, send your friend off and come take a seat." The man crossed his arms.

"No," Bryan answered. "If I wanted to speak with you, I would have answered the phone."

"If you'd answered your damn phone, I wouldn't have had to come all the way up here to knock some sense into you," Bryan's father spat back.

I looked up at Bryan for some kind of clue. What he hadn't told me. His pulse accelerated and his fear overwhelmed my system. It made me jittery. Bryan didn't feel fear often. Sadness, anger, admiration...those were all normal emotions I'd gotten used to. But this was overwhelming. The sheer fright that took over him constricted my chest, squeezing my ribs.

"This is low, Mom, even for you." Bryan turned towards his mother.

"You didn't leave me with a lot of options, Byn," Nancy answered with her fists on her hips.

I squeezed Bryan's hand in an attempt to get his attention. His eyes never left his mother's, but he squeezed my fingers back. As if to remind me he hadn't gotten so wrapped up in this situation that he'd forgotten I stood next to him. As if to silently tell me he would explain everything when we were alone.

"You could have talked to me first," Bryan pointed out. "You go straight to calling in Mark? For what, an intervention?"

"You want me to embarrass you?" His father's voice boomed through the living room. "Fine. The hell is wrong with you, boy? You have less than three months left before graduation. You are in your last semester of undergrad, and I get a call from your mother saying you've dropped your classes? Have you lost your damn mind?"

"What?" I finally spoke, catching Bryan's attention. "You dropped out?"

"Wait, you didn't know?" Nancy asked and I realized she spoke to me.

I shook my head, waiting for a response from Bryan.

Nancy looked over at Mark, throwing out her hands in confusion. When she turned back to Bryan, anger rose in her voice. "Are you telling me you made this decision on your own?"

"Hang on, are you insinuating that Whitney made me drop out of college?" Bryan clarified.

"I...What else am I supposed to think, Byn? You've always been so focused on school but once you two started dating, your grades slipped. You move her in with you and then you drop out?" Nancy motioned towards me. Woah. "I'd never think in a million years you'd do this yourself!"

"Mom, I–"

Mark inserted himself into the conversation. "You've always lost your head over girls, Bryan, but this is too far," Mark's demanding voice bounced off the walls. "You moved this girl and her kid in with you when you could barely afford to take care of yourself. You're throwing your entire life away for some ass, which isn't a surprise, but we're extremely disappointed in you."

Bryan moved in front of me, standing between his father and I. "Do not bring her into this. Don't you dare. You aren't allowed to speak about my relationship. Dmitri isn't Whitney's kid, he's her brother. I love them and I *want* to help take care of them. You don't get to stand here and talk about Whitney because you have a false sense of entitlement. You don't get to storm your way in here and control my life. You aren't a father and you never have been."

"Bryan, you don't see it because your head is up your ass but everything I've done is for you and your sister's benefit. Everything." Mark pointed a finger at Bryan's chest. "You may be smart on paper but you have no fucking common sense. If you'd joined the military out of high school like I wanted you to, you would've had the opportunity to grow the fuck up, but–" Mark went off on a tangent.

I looked up at Bryan, who glared at his father. I took his face in my hand and brought his attention to me. "Let's go." I nodded toward the door. "You don't have to stand here and take this."

He opened the front door, gently guiding me out before him.

"You're not walking out in the middle of this conversation, Bryan. You're going to sit down and we're going to figure out a plan for you." Nancy rushed to the door, grabbing his shoulder to stop him.

"You two can do whatever you want, but I won't be a part of it." Bryan grabbed the door handle and firmly shut it behind us.

"Are you okay?" I asked as we walked down the walkway towards his Jeep.

Bryan's hands were visibly shaking as he opened the passenger door and let me into the car. Nancy stood on the front porch with her arms crossed, silently watching Bryan leave. He didn't look back at his mother or answer my question as he got into the driver's seat and pulled away from the curb.

"Are you okay?" I asked again, reaching out to put my hand on his thigh.

Bryan took a deep breath, clenching his jaw. His voice barely a whisper. "No."

"Did you drop out of FBU?" I needed to hear it from him. I needed to hear what the hell he was thinking.

"I dropped my classes but I didn't drop out. They know I'm coming back."

My heart skipped a beat. "When are you going back?"

"Whenever Erebus is dead."

"Bryan, what the fuck?" I turned in my seat to face him.

"I can't keep driving back and forth, going to class pretending like I can pay attention when you're running off to all ends of the forest." Bryan gripped the steering wheel with white knuckles. His emotions were scattered, clashing with mine. "I can't take care of Dmitri if I'm in another city. I tried taking him with me but how is he supposed to work at the Corner Cup and turn in his homework if he's in Falcon Bay?"

I rubbed his thigh. "I thought having Nic and Abe here would make it easier on you. Did they not help?"

"You gravely underestimate how mentally fucked everyone was before you left." Bryan turned to look at me briefly. "Abe finally went to see his parents, Dmitri carried him through that. And Dominic? Are you kidding me, babe? He tried, but you can't pour from an empty cup. No one held themselves together while you were gone, so I swallowed *all* of it and tried to carry the weight but I...It got too heavy. I can't do it alone."

Panic began to course through my veins. "We were only gone a few weeks! I'm back now."

"For how long? Realistically, Whit, for how long?"

"I don't know," I answered honestly.

I hadn't realized we had left so much chaos behind us when we went to the Hallow. I hadn't realized...I thought everyone would band together while we were gone. I didn't think everyone would be falling apart and Bryan would be drowning trying to hold it all together.

But there had been signs since I got home. The dark circles under Harmony's eyes as she drank from the coffee pot. The sadness that hung over Nic, coming and going like the flip of a switch. The exhaustion that hung on Bryan's bones that no amount of rest ever satisfied. Dmitri had Abe to lean on but Abe had spent weeks living in an abandoned hunting cabin, scared to go home and risk his parent's safety.

They were all traumatized, and we left them alone to not deal with their emotions.

"I...I'm so sorry," I whispered.

"It's too much. I'll finish my degree when I have the mental capacity to do so, but until then...I can't do it, Whit. It's too much." His voice broke. He sniffled and swallowed his emotions but they surfaced all the same. Tears welled in the bottom of his eyes as he gripped the steering wheel. "I should've told you sooner. I planned to tell you tonight that I wasn't going back tomorrow morning. I didn't plan on Mark showing up."

"Why did your mom call him?"

Bryan sighed, wiping a tear from his cheek with the ball of his palm. "I didn't get a full ride, and FBU is expensive."

"He pays for it?" I clarified.

"Pays for part of it. I did get scholarships, and I buy all my own books. He covers the difference. That's the only reason I still answer his calls." Bryan came to a red traffic light and finally turned to look at me. "As for my mom...I think she panicked."

"Promise me you'll go back to school, you're so close to graduating."

Bryan got quiet, chewing on his bottom lip. The traffic light turned green and he turned his attention back to the road. "I wasn't going to graduate in June, anyway."

"Why not?" When he didn't answer I asked again. "Why not?"

"I failed a midterm."

I let out a deep sigh and leaned my head back against the seat. "Your dad was right, this is all my fault."

"No, don't let him do that to you." Bryan reached down and grabbed my hand, still resting in his lap. "This is what he does, he throws around blame and makes everyone feel like shit. This isn't on you, this is on me."

"You were distracted with Dmitri and you failed a class because of it. If I'd never gone to the Hallow, you'd be graduating in June."

"It's not on you whether or not I get my shit done, baby. I'm not blaming you for anything. I'm the one responsible for my actions and my choices. This is a choice I'm making for myself." He tightened his grip on my hand. "Something had to give, this is what I chose to take off my plate." His shoulders fell. "I've been going to school nonstop since kindergarten. I'm tired, Whit."

"Your parents blame me."

"Fuck my parents." Bryan brought my hand to his mouth and kissed my knuckles. "I'm sorry they put all the blame on you, and I'm sorry you had to see that."

"No, I'm sorry to put you in this position. I'm sorry your father talks to you like that."

Bryan shook his head. "You didn't do anything wrong, I chose to do this. I'm not mad at you and I don't resent you, not in the least, okay? Keeping you and Rosie alive is more important than a degree. College will still be there when this is all over. My father is a piece of shit and he always will be."

"He sure seems like one," I paused. "You deserve a better dad. You're such an amazing person and you deserved better from him."

"My life would have been a lot simpler if he chose to be a deadbeat. The more he involves himself, the more complicated it's been." His hand tightened around the steering wheel. "I'm grateful he helped pay for school but part of me wishes I'd never accepted the offer. I could've gone to a cheaper college." Bryan shook his head. "I could've gone to community college first. I didn't have to sell my soul to him."

I squeezed his hand, not knowing what to say. I didn't have a father growing up, let alone a complicated one. I had always wondered what it would be like to have a dad, but my mom tried so hard that honestly, I didn't miss having one. Yet, Bryan wished his dad had up and left him. Even though the majority of his teen years were spent with Rose and Nancy, it seemed Mark popped in enough to stir things up and then leave again. My blood boiled for Bryan. How easily Mark talked down to him and belittled him. It should never be that easy for a parent to make their child feel like shit, let alone do it on purpose.

"You never mentioned that Mark wanted you to join the military out of high school."

Bryan shrugged. "Because I never wanted to, so it was moot. He had this grand plan for my life but it never aligned with what I wanted for myself. Even offering to help pay for school was another way he could keep some sort of control over me."

"Does he do it to Rose too?"

Bryan nodded. "She doesn't see it, or doesn't want to. She thinks that he's our dad and he's the only one we're ever going to get so she tries too hard to have a relationship with him, but I can't. I've tried." Bryan tightened his grip on the steering wheel. "He makes me…he makes me so angry I feel violent and that's terrifying. I hate it. It's not healthy and I've always been scared that the more time I spend around him, the more like him I'll become."

"Hey." I leaned across the center console. "You're the best man I know." I reached out with my free hand and grazed his cheek with my fingertips. "You're nothing like him."

"I'm glad you think so." A smile finally hinted on his lips. "My mom doesn't actually think this is your fault...she just, I think it's easier for her to blame someone else than accept that I did this on my own. Me doing something wrong, in her mind, means that she did something wrong raising me. And she has a hard time accepting that."

I leaned back, somehow surprised by his insight. "That's really emotionally mature of you, babe."

"Yeah, well, therapy will do that to you."

Oh. I learned all kinds of new things about Bryan today.

"You went to therapy?"

Bryan stared at the road before he answered. "Ashley's mom is a psychiatrist. She never charged me but we used to have a lot of talks when I was a teenager. It started when she noticed I was stressed but it turned into every Wednesday after school in her home office. She always took really good care of us. Made sure Troy could process his mom walking out on them. Made sure neither of us buried our emotions. She always said the world had enough men who didn't express themselves properly and she wouldn't let us add to the problem."

So that's who I needed to thank for Bryan being so in-tune with his emotions. "That's incredible of her. I've never actually met Ashley's mom."

"She didn't make it to the Christmas Eve party this year, so that's probably why."

"Did your mom know you were talking to Ash's mom about all this?"

"No, never." Bryan shook his head. "But as you could probably guess, my mom would benefit from some therapy herself. She doesn't think she needs it."

I shifted in my seat. "I've been trying to get Dmitri to go but he says it's a waste of time because he wouldn't be able to talk about our powers and fully explain the gravity of everything."

"I tried getting him to go see Ash's mom while you girls were at the Hallow and he gave me the same pushback. I don't think he's ready yet."

"I don't think so either but I'm really worried about him."

"I have been too." Bryan let out a sigh. "He's not as low as he was when you were gone, but it's still concerning."

"Thank you again for taking care of him. I can't say it enough. You are so good to me and I admire you so much, but the way you take care of my siblings..." I cleared my throat, not wanting to get too emotional or make this about me. "I can't thank you enough for loving them too."

"You're all easy to love," he answered.

I smiled at him as red and blue flashing lights caught my attention in the rearview. I turned in my seat to get a better look at the police car riding our bumper.

"The hell?" Bryan asked under his breath as he put his blinker on. He pulled into a parking lot in front of a row of businesses. He rolled down his window and rested his hands on the steering wheel.

I tried to watch as best I could from the side mirror next to my door, but when the officer approached Bryan's window, I recognized his face.

Officer Joseph Grady.

Grady leaned down and peered inside of the car. "License and registration, please."

"Is there a reason you pulled me over, officer?" Bryan asked, gripping the steering wheel.

"Speeding. License and registration," Grady huffed again.

Bryan chewed on the inside of his cheek for a moment before he spoke. "My wallet is in my pocket and my registration is in the glove box."

"Go ahead."

Bryan retrieved the information Grady ordered as I sat frozen in place. I kept my hands on my knees where Grady could see them as I glared daggers into his sunglasses.

"I'll need your passenger's information as well."

"Why?" Bryan asked.

"Are you being noncompliant with an officer?" Grady lowered his sunglasses.

"It's fine." I leaned down and grabbed my wallet from my bag, handing Bryan my license.

Grady took our information and glanced over my card. "Not the first time I'll be searching your name in the system, Miss Dansley." Grady returned to his car.

My heart knocked against my rib cage, causing a pulsing ache in my chest. I grabbed my knees, wrapping my fingers around myself for some stability.

"Hey," Bryan whispered, keeping his eyes forward. "He's only trying to intimidate us. We haven't done anything wrong. Don't let him scare you."

"I'm not scared for me," I answered quietly.

"He won't do anything to me, not in the middle of town in broad daylight," he paused. "And if he does...charm him or something."

I smirked. "Are you asking me to use mind control on an officer of the law?"

"He's a hunter who tried to kill you in the woods, baby. He's not some innocent bystander."

Grady came back to the window with a small metal clipboard and a filled out ticket. He handed Bryan our information and slid the ticket in front of his face.

Bryan blinked down at the ticket, refusing to take it. "I was not going 55."

"That's what I clocked you at."

"I'm driving down Main Street, there's too many cars for me to be going that fast," Bryan argued.

"We can go debate this down at the station, or you can sign your ticket," Grady offered simply. "The decision is yours."

Bryan let out a harsh sigh and scribbled his name on the bottom of the ticket. "This is harassment."

"Drive safe." Grady tore off the ticket and dropped it in Bryan's lap before he headed back to his squad car.

"I fucking hate that man," I said through my teeth as heat swelled in my chest, climbing up my throat.

I wanted to scream. I refrained from jumping out of the passenger's seat and throwing an icicle straight at Grady's face. I wanted to end this once and for all. The harassment. The stalking. The meeting in the woods with his skull mask as we tried to kill one another, then suffering through these interactions where he abused his power just to fuck with us.

Bryan reached across the center counsel and grabbed my hand. "Let's go home where those douchebags can't get to us."

I nodded, attempting a smile but my hands trembled with rage. I took a few deep breaths, attempting to calm myself. I had no control over other people's actions, I could only manage my own reaction.

Bryan's phone began to ring, and I thought for certain it would be another catastrophe waiting to strike. I let out a sigh of relief when Rose's name popped up on his screen.

"Hey," Bryan answered, putting the call on speaker.

"Uh, hi. I got home and Dad's here? What the fuck happened?" Rose asked, her voice dripping with concern.

"I know Mom already told you," Bryan answered in a flat tone.

"I want to hear it from you, not Mom's version of what happened."

His eyes softened. "I failed a class, so I dropped the semester. I'm taking a break from FBU. Mom called Dad so he could cuss at me in person instead of over the phone for not following his plan."

"Oh, Byn," Rose let out a sigh. "I'm so sorry. Are you okay? Is this because of us?"

"I will be fine, don't stress," Bryan answered. "I'm sure Mom is having a full-force melt down right now?"

"Oh yeah, she's losing her shit. Dad is staying for dinner so they can talk behind your back."

"Good. Go take care of Mom. I don't need to be taken care of." Bryan's words broke my heart in half. He was lying. I could feel the insincerity of his words swim through my chest like any other emotion of his. Of course he needed to be taken care of. He literally told me how heavy this had all been on him.

"I wanted to make sure you're okay. I know you hate Dad, and when I saw he showed up unannounced, I knew something bad happened. Is Whit there?"

"She is."

"She's got you then." Rose paused. "I'll go...Call me if you want to talk."

"Love you." Bryan hung up the phone before Rose could reply.

I debated whether to say anything, but I hated the way that conversation had gone. "Babe, you know Rose was trying to–"

"Make sure I'm okay, I heard her." He cut me off.

"You were very dismissive of her."

He let out a deep sigh. "I'm wound really tight right now. I don't mean to be."

As we pulled into the driveway of our house, I cupped his cheek in my hand and turned his face towards me. "Hey, I love you with every ounce of my being, you know that right?"

He nodded, a gentle smile on his lips. "I love you too."

"After we defeat Erebus, I will be sitting in the front row at your graduation. I'm going to be the loudest person in the crowd. Everything is going to be okay. Your dad is an asshole but you, my love, are everything. You are the moon and all the stars."

Bryan moved a strand of hair out of my face. "The moon doesn't shine without the sun."

I leaned in and kissed him. "You should have been nicer to your sister."

He sighed. "You're right. I'll call her later."

"We didn't get to eat, why don't I make us something?"

"You hate cooking." He furrowed his brow.

"Yeah, but I still know how to," I opened the door and waved for him to follow. "Come on, I'll make you some comfort food."

"What do you have in mind?"

I smiled. "Grilled cheese."

Chapter Twenty-Three
SURPRISING RELATIONS
Whitney

"Been busy today?" Nic asked the next morning at the Corner Cup as he tied a black apron behind his back.

Harmony walked out of the employee-only area, her nose buried in a stack of files. I watched the exhaustion hanging off of her, feeling my own grief deep in my bones. I didn't want to stay behind this counter and make small talk. I wanted to fall apart.

"How are you coping with all this so well?" I asked Nic, setting my coffee down on the counter. "How are you not falling apart after losing Mia and Warren the way that we did?"

He took a step back and looked at me like I'd slapped him. "Did you fall apart when Audri died?"

"Yeah, kind of," I answered, the muscle memory of that time washed over me as my chest constricted and my knees turned to jelly. "I had Ray and Mit to take care of though, so I had to get out of bed in the morning but it destroyed me."

"And what gives you the impression that there's anything left of me to destroy in the first place?"

"I–" I didn't know how to respond to that. "I'm sorry."

Nic reached out and put a warm hand on my shoulder. "Everyone grieves differently. Lauren lost both of her parents, in a way, she took that sadness and turned it into anger.

She wants revenge. I'm numb. It's the feeling I'm most comfortable with. Harmony kills herself with stress and takes it out on everyone else. You bury it. Everyone's different."

"I'm not–" Harmony put the files down to fire back at Nic when the bell above the front door jingled. A tall man with light brown hair and an expensive-looking jacket walked in, holding a little girl's hand. Her brunette ringlets were pulled up in a messy ponytail that swayed behind her as she walked. Harmony dropped the files all over the floor at the sight of them.

"Mommy!" The little girl squealed and ran across the dining area to Harmony. She kneeled and caught the little girl, wrapping her arms tightly around her.

Harmony had a child? I glanced over at Nic, his eyes glued to Harmony on the floor holding her daughter, barely noticing that the little girl didn't walk in here by herself.

"What are you guys doing here?" Harmony asked, looking up at the man who accompanied the little girl.

"She missed you. Plus, it sounded like you needed some emotional support." The man held out his hand and helped Harmony to her feet. She turned away as he pressed a small kiss to the side of her mouth.

Her husband, then? Harmony never wore a wedding ring.

"You should have called first," Harmony said under her breath. She kissed her daughter's head and repositioned the girl on her hip.

He took a step back. "You don't want to see us?"

"No, no, of course I do." Harmony scrambled, her emotions seemed to fly all over the room. She smiled at her daughter. "I missed you so much." Harmony glanced over at Nic and I, realizing she had an audience. "Oh, um, this is Whitney. She is Amilia's best friend's daughter, one of the supervisors here at the coffee shop."

"Nice to meet you, I'm Jerry," The man introduced himself with a smile.

I waved and smiled back. "Hi."

Harmony motioned to Nic standing next to me. "And, uh, this is Dominic. He's…an old friend from when I grew up here. He's been helping run the place while I figure things out."

"How's it going, man?" Jerry approached the counter and held out his hand.

Nic looked down at it before he blinked out of a daze and remembered his manners, shaking Jerry's hand. "You can call me Nic."

"Um, did you just get in?" Harmony asked Jerry, her voice trembling as she spoke.

"Yeah, we came straight here. I'm sorry if we surprised you, it didn't make sense for us to be sitting in Seattle when you're here going through all this." Jerry put his hand on Harmony's shoulder.

"It's fine. I'm happy to see you. Uh, I'm kind of busy right now, but let's grab some dinner this evening? There's a good Italian place a few doors down," Harmony suggested.

"Sounds perfect." Jerry smiled.

"Give the cute blonde a good tip," I told them. Harmony gave a half smile over her shoulder as she walked them to the door. I turned to Nic, who had moved back to his coffee. "Harmony is married with a kid?"

He shrugged a shoulder. "Guess so."

I watched Harmony usher the man and their daughter out the front door. "Wow, I never really pictured her as a mother. Her daughter is super cute."

"Yeah, she is." Nic left the counter and went into the break room without another word.

I began to follow him when Harmony came back inside. "Whitney, I need you to do something for me." She put her ink pen in between her teeth and handed me a form. "This needs to be filed with the business bureau."

"What is it?" I asked, taking the paper from Harmony.

She took the pen out of her mouth and sighed. "I hate it here, stupid small town politics. We have to get permission before we can have events."

I furrowed my brow. "Did Amilia have to do this for Acoustic Nights?"

"Only the first one, but now that there is new ownership the council is requesting we resubmit the request." Harmony rolled her eyes.

I glanced over the paper she'd given me. "And if they say no?"

"They have no legal reason to, it should be fine."

"This seems kind of trivial doesn't it?" I lowered my voice. "They have attacked us and killed our own and we have to file paperwork to save the CC like it's an average Tuesday?"

Harmony blinked back at me with tired eyes. "Yes, in the grand scheme in things, this is fucking ridiculous. We should close the Corner Cup and find the key, but we are sentimental human beings and this building means something to us, doesn't it?"

My shoulders fell at her words. "I will file this paper."

"Thank you." She sighed in relief.

"What if...what if *he* is there?"

Harmony mouthed Erebus' name with wide eyes.

I shook my head. "No, Drake."

"Oh, that old douche." Harmony dismissed me with a wave of her hands. "I don't know, I don't care. Do whatever you want."

I began to walk towards the door but I stopped myself, turning back around to face Harmony. "I'm sorry, but I have to be nosey. Are you married?"

Harmony stared back at me for a moment before she spoke. "We're separated."

"Oh, I'm sorry."

"I'm not." She shook her head. "Go file those papers."

) ·) · ● · (· (

In front of the elaborate town hall building stood big pillars and large, glass doors. I walked up the concrete steps, eying the private security who strolled back and forth out front. Inside, beautiful marblesque tiles covered the floor and a chandelier hung above the reception desk. Smaller circular lights hung down from the ceiling around the chandelier attached to wooden beams.

Photos of Rifton throughout the years hung up on the walls. I paused and examined each one, dating back to 1843. The founding of Rifton was the biggest photo, framed in dark walnut. Horse-drawn carriages trotted down the dirt roads where the town square now stood. All the buildings must have been rebuilt because I didn't recognize any of them. I bet the Renati who founded Rifton would have lost their minds knowing the Allurement called out to the Elementals and our followers. That one day we would return and show up on their descendant's doorsteps, ready to reclaim what had been stolen from us. They could kill us, but they could not stop the elemental magic from reincarnating.

"Excuse me?" I walked up to the front desk. "I have some paperwork to file with the business bureau?"

"Oh, yes, down this hallway to your right and follow the city council signs." The woman smiled warmly, pointing me in the right direction.

"City council?" I clarified as a chill ran up my spine.

The woman nodded. "Yes, the council has to approve all the requests that come from the local businesses in town, but there usually isn't any problem getting things passed. Down the hall and follow the signs."

"Oookay…" I drug out the syllables. "Thank you."

My knees trembled as I went down the hall, staring at the sign at the end of the hallway that said 'City Council Offices' with an arrow pointing to the right. Did I personally have to gather the signatures from each council member? Would I leave the papers with a secretary? Questions I should have asked the receptionist but the mention of the council caught me off guard. I hadn't planned on coming face to face with Henry Drake when the day began. Surely, he would deny Harmony's request purely out of spite.

The city council offices had their own hallway in the back of Town Hall. Leading down the hall were the five offices, with each member's last name on their own plaque. Drake's sign hung at the end of the hall. Luckily, someone sat at a desk before I had to walk down to the offices.

"Hi, I have some papers to file for the business bureau," I said to the man sitting at the desk.

"Oh, hi, I can take those." He took the file from me and opened it up, scanning through the papers. "Okay, so you want to get an event approved?"

"Yes, we are hosting a weekend-long fundraiser for the Corner Cup." I put my hands on my hips and took a step back. "What about that needs to be approved exactly?"

"A formality the council established, nothing to worry about. The council is very involved in the inner workings of the town, especially the small businesses," the man explained. "I'll take this to the council meeting this afternoon and add it to the agenda. There are a few other small business matters the council will be addressing today so it's perfect timing."

"Okay, thanks. Will someone give us a call?"

"Yes, once this is voted on, I'll contact the number on the form." He offered me a warm smile. "It's very routine, I promise."

"Thanks for your time." I glared at the council names on the plaques one more time before I turned to leave.

"Miss Dansley, what a pleasant surprise."

A chilling voice spoke behind my back, turning my blood to ice.

I huffed, turning to face that piece of shit. "Mr. Drake. I was just leaving."

"You have something for the council, I see?" Henry Drake leaned against his cane and took the paper from the council's secretary. He skimmed it over with a furrowed brow. "A town event to save the Corner Cup. How inspirational."

"Renewing our permit to continue hosting Acoustic Nights, nothing fancy." I gritted my teeth to keep myself from punching him in the face.

"Such a shame to hear about Amilia Burnett's passing," Drake dared speak her name. "I do hope she had her affairs in order."

"Respectfully, my family affairs are none of your business, councilman." I took a step away from him as the other council members came out of their offices. The five of them stood together, watching me.

I turned to leave as Henry Drake's voice stopped me in my tracks again. "We do require those requesting special permits to attend the hearing in which they are discussed."

"I wasn't aware of that." I spun back around to face him.

"Remind Ms. Vasquez many things have changed in this town since she lived here. Take care of yourself, Miss Dansley. You never know what dangers may be lurking around the next corner," Drake purred.

"Nice cane, Drake, looks like karma is already catching up to you.'" I dared say aloud.

"We don't take threats to council members lightly, young lady." The female council member took a step towards me.

"Not a threat, an observation." I flashed a smile and left the hallway with adrenaline coursing through my veins.

When I got back to the Corner Cup, I headed straight to the manager's office, hoping Harmony still sat behind the desk. Thankfully, she did.

"Yes, I remember," Harmony said into her cell phone when I walked in. She put up a finger when she saw me, asking for a moment to wrap up her call. "Look, I have to stay in Rifton longer than I planned. I know and I'm sorry, but if it wasn't important, I wouldn't be here. Thank you, I'll call you back tomorrow." Harmony hung up the phone and groaned. "How did it go?"

"We have to attend the council meeting when they vote on it," I relayed the message.

"What?" Harmony's voice bounced off the walls of the small office. "Since when?"

I leaned against the door frame and crossed my arms. "Henry Drake said to remind you that things have changed since you lived here."

"That mother fucker." Harmony rubbed her tired eyes with the balls of her hands. "When is the hearing?"

"This afternoon."

"Okay, um, I'll be there."

"Let me come with you," I offered.

"No, I need you here."

"Robby isn't on the schedule today, I could call and have him cover me for an hour or two. He owes me for covering his last shift." I stepped into the office. "Let me help."

"Whitney, we literally sit there and listen to them blab on about bullshit." Harmony waved her hand.

I offered her a soft smile. "Yeah, but you have been doing all this by yourself. Wouldn't the bullshit be easier to listen to if you had someone to roll their eyes with you?"

Harmony sighed. "Okay, yeah, come with me."

As we prepared to leave for the meeting that afternoon, Dmitri stood in the breakroom clocking out for the day.

"Where are you guys going?" he asked.

"Some stupid ass town council meeting for the fundraiser," Harmony answered, slipping into her coat.

"Can I come?"

"You want to?" I asked my brother.

He tilted his head. "Why would I ask if I didn't want to? Besides, we have to make sure the event still happens. I finished the poster." Dmitri handed me a sheet of paper.

"Mit, it's perfect." I took a closer look at the flier he had made for the Acoustic Weekend. Bright and colorful designs with attractive handwriting covered the page. A beautiful, yet fun border trimmed the edges. "Save the Corner Cup Acoustic Weekend, in memory of our beloved Amilia Burnett." I read the top of the flier.

"If you guys give the thumbs up on it, I'm going to take it down to the print shop today and make copies. I already talked to them, and they'll donate the copies of the flier and something for the silent raffle too," Dmitri explained as I handed the flier back to him.

"You did an amazing job."

Harmony waved the two of us along. "It looks amazing, Dmitri, now hurry up or we'll be late."

Harmony, Dmitri and I took empty seats towards the back of the room. The council members had yet to arrive but there were several over citizens waiting for the meeting. I assumed most of them were there for their own permits.

"We should have brought coffee," Harmony said as she smoothed her skirt over her thighs.

"To throw at them?" I smirked.

She chuckled. "That would be a waste of coffee."

Finally, the five council members took their seats and began the meeting. With plenty on the agenda, we waited impatiently as they took their sweet time going through each item. Naturally, our permit request was the last on the agenda.

"The Corner Cup is requesting a permit to host events. The last permit expired with the death of the previous owner. The new owner, Harmony Vasquez, is submitting to renew the permit," One of the council members whose name I couldn't remember read from the notes. "All in favor?"

Not a single member of the council raised their hands.

Harmony muttered under her breath, "You have to be fucking kidding me."

"All opposed?" They all raised their blood-stained hands. "Motion p–"

Harmony jumped up before the gavel could be rapped and marched to the front of the room. "On what legal grounds are you denying my permit? I want code numbers and specific laws that this is against. Otherwise, I'd say this is discriminatory and I will be taking legal action."

"Oooh, shit," Dmitri leaned over to whisper.

"Now, Ms. Vasquez, there is no need for threats," Councilman Sean Glover replied, crossing his hands on the table. I glared at Tom Campbell's uncle, wishing him nothing but harm for all the damage his nephew did.

Harmony stood tall and proud. "That isn't a threat, Councilman, it's a fact."

The councilwoman, Alice Mullins, sitting next to Henry Drake turned to him. She widened her eyes as if waiting to see how he would respond.

"It's a fire issue," Henry Drake finally spoke. "We received several complaints under the last permit that these Acoustic Nights constantly broke the capacity limits."

"I'd like to see the formal complaints." Harmony rested a fist on her hip. "Proof that these violations actually took place."

"That can be done, but it will be timely," Sean Glover replied. "There is no guarantee that the request can be resubmitted and approved by the date of your event."

This was infuriating to watch. The way they all but forced us to beg to host a damn event at our own business. The council members smirked as Harmony argued, as if they were determined for her efforts to be in vain.

Harmony crossed her arms. "This cannot be legal."

"You are welcome to attend the next session with any concerns you have, Ms. Vasquez. That concludes the meeting." William Ward, the oldest of the council members, rapped the gavel.

The council rose from their seats and the crowd of people began to disperse.

Harmony turned to look at us with an icy gaze. "This is outrageous!" She followed the council members as they left the platform.

Dmitri and I pushed our way to the front of the room where Harmony argued with the council.

"I know what this is really about, and I'll be damned if you think your bullshit politics will stop me from doing whatever I please," Harmony pressed.

"We will have law enforcement shut down the event," Drake replied simply.

Harmony grit her teeth. "I dare you to send your corrupt cops to my place of business. They'll find us rather...charming."

I stepped up next to Harmony. "You forget who you're messing with."

The older councilman standing behind Drake, William Ward, scoffed as I spoke. He met my gaze with a hardened look that told me he would attack me right then and there if he could. He looked past me and froze. His eyes widened and the blood rushed from his face as if he had seen a ghost. I looked over my shoulder to where my brother stood. Dmitri stared back at the councilman, his brow furrowed in confusion.

"Dmitri?" The councilman took a small step forward.

"Who..." Dmitri leaned back as I stepped in front of him. "How do you know my name?"

"It is you...I can't believe it," the councilman whispered, clearing his throat. "I am Will Ward, your grandfather."

"N-no you aren't," Dmitri stammered, moving further away from the Renati members.

The councilman turned to Henry Drake with fire in his eyes. "Did you know Kyle's son was back in town? Did you know he's being held by *them*?"

"I know nothing about the company those people keep," Drake answered, matter of fact.

Ward darkened his gaze. "I have a hard time believing that, Henry."

I squared my shoulders and glared at Drake. "You knew damn well who Dmitri was when your daughter held a knife to his throat," I hissed.

"She *what?*" Will Ward demanded.

"So you're Kyle's father then?" I remained in front of Dmitri. It did little since he towered over me, but at least something stood in between my brother and the Renati.

"I am, though I'm sure you don't know anything about your father, Dmitri. Your mother would have made sure of that." Ward spoke to Mit as if he had been the one to ask.

Dmitri scoffed. "I know he was evil, just like you. I know he abandoned my mom and I."

Will Ward's shoulders fell. "Abandoned you? Dmitri, Kyle loved you. He wanted to be part of your life but your mother kidnapped you. Kyle never stopped looking. When he finally found you, she killed him."

"Shut up!" Dmitri snapped. "You don't know what you're talking about."

Ward shook his head. "No, son, I'm afraid I speak the truth. You have been lied to your entire life about your father. He never abandoned you."

Ward had to be lying, trying to lure Dmitri to the other side. They would do anything to turn our supporters against us, even my own brother. This man probably wasn't even related to Dmitri. Sure he also had brown eyes, but so did I. Brown eyes were too common of a trait for that to be a deciding factor in this revelation.

"Dmitri, your mother–"

Mit cut Ward off. "How dare you talk about my mother. She gave me everything." Dmitri leaned over me and pointed his finger. "I don't know who you are or what you think about us, but I have no interest in knowing anything about my sperm donor. I know all I need to."

Harmony put a hand on his shoulder. "Come on, Mit. Let's get out of here."

I linked my arm in Dmitri's and led him away from the scene.

All this time we had spent in Rifton and Kyle's father had only now discovered Dmitri lived here? It didn't make any sense. Serenity tried to kill Dmitri. She knew he had been here since August, and so did Henry Drake. If Kyle's father was a member of the council and part of the founding families, then of course he knew Dmitri returned to Rifton. He didn't give a shit about the DNA they shared when Serenity had her blade to my brother's neck.

They didn't care about him all the years that we spent in Kansas. All the years that Mom stretched her pennies to provide for all of us. No one came out of the shadows when Mom died and Dmitri needed someone to care for him. Not a single person related to Kyle or Mom stepped forward. The court signed him over to me without a word of contention from anyone outside of a judge asking if I would be able to handle the responsibility. I had a hard time believing any of them would give a shit about Dmitri now.

No, this had to be calculated. They were trying to manipulate him, and thankfully he didn't take the bait.

"Are you okay?" I asked as we left the building and stepped out into the sunlight.

Dmitri blinked at me. "Do you think that man is really my grandfather?"

"I don't know," I answered, honestly. "Mia did say that Kyle was a member of the founding families, so I guess it's plausible. What doesn't make sense is him acting like he didn't know you've been in Rifton all this time."

"Yeah," Dmitri whispered. "That doesn't add up to me either. Him accusing Mom of killing Kyle? You would think we'd remember that."

Harmony cleared her throat awkwardly. "Will Ward is your grandfather. I'm sorry I never said anything, but I assumed you already knew and I have been preoccupied." She crossed her arms. "I don't know anything about his accusation that Audri killed him, but Mia told me Kyle died about ten years ago."

Dmitri let out a shaky breath. "She couldn't have."

Harmony put her hands on Dmitri's shoulders. "Mit, whatever happened between your parents, I want you to know that your mom did what she did to protect you. If she let Kyle have any access to you at all, they would've tried to convert you. They would have hurt your mom if she resisted." She hardened her tone. "That's why Audri left Rifton, to keep you the hell away from those people."

I blinked as memories of childhood washed over me. Mom had kept all the lights off, but she had been out of breath and in a rush to get us back to bed. Her hair had been a mess and the blood on her cheek glistened in the glow of the nightlight. She had locked the door behind her when she left our room. I knew because I had gotten up and tried to open it after I heard her footsteps down the hall. She wanted us to stay in our rooms. She had pretended nothing happened the next morning, claiming it had all been a bad dream. A delusion our sleepy little minds created.

Who is that man, Mommy?

Oh...

Oh shit.

I remembered.

Chills shot through my body as I halted in my tracks. My stomach tied into a knot as my chest constricted, squeezing against my lungs.

"What's wrong?" Harmony asked, scanning my face.

"N-nothing." I stammered. "Just tripped up by the whole thing."

Harmony put a comforting hand on Dmitri and my shoulders. "Don't let them get under your skin. They'll say anything to shake you up."

The truth in their words rattled me to my core.

Chapter Twenty-Four
PEONIES AND PIRATES
Lauren

I stood in the kitchen in front of the open fridge. I had already opened it twice before, but I couldn't decide what I wanted to eat. Maybe if I closed it and opened it once more, something new would catch my eye. I grabbed a small cup of yogurt and a spoon from the drawer. I leaned against the counter and sighed, taking a bite of the creamy peach yogurt.

Dominic walked into the kitchen, drying his dark hair off with a towel.

"Where have you been?" I asked.

"I went for a jog."

I raised an eyebrow. "You run?"

"You think my metabolism does this on its own?" He motioned down his body. "Not in your thirties, Lauren, remember that."

I chortled. "Tell me next time, I'll come with you. I miss running."

"I will." Nic smiled. He dropped his towel into the washer off the dining room and reached into his pocket, pulling out a wrist watch.

"What's that?" I nodded towards Nic's hand.

"Uh, so Honey and I were going through the things Warren left here, and I thought maybe you'd like to have something of his?" Nic ran his thumb over the band of the watch and handed it to me. "He thought highly of you and I hoped those feelings were mutual."

I pushed off the counter and set my snack down. "They were, and I'd love to. Thank you."

I took the watch from Nic and smiled, the bottom of my eyes welling with tears. I slipped the watch around my wrist and secured it in place. I had seen Warren wear it before. I had noticed this very watch around his wrist the first day we had trained together.

I hadn't been back in Rifton long. I'd already spent a drunken night with the girls in Pines Row. The girls were all preoccupied with Bryan showing back up in the picture but I wanted to see these Magisters.

Meeting someone like me had been a pipe dream. Someone who could control the wind and move with the breeze. Someone who could hear whispers in the air and glide across a room. Warren had been everything I imagined and more.

When I first met Warren, he hugged me. Not to say hello or because we controlled the same element. He wrapped his long arms around me and gave his condolences.

I lost my mom when I was young too, and I'm so sorry this is a heartache we share, he had whispered during our embrace.

I cried against his chest until I drained myself of tears. Warren got me a drink of water, allowed me a few deep breaths and then he took me outside and taught me how to float. He taught me how to focus when multiple whispers carried through the breeze. He taught me how to magnify my energy waves with the wind. Warren had taught me to embrace my powers; they made me unique and strong. He had been born into a powerless family too, and he understood why I feared my powers, why I hated them.

Why I hated myself.

Warren had put a warm hand on my shoulder and smiled. *You have so much to offer your generation, Lauren. You are the strongest of them all, and I don't mean your magic. I mean your determination, your inner strength.*

The memory moved through my mind as easily as breathing. I brought myself back to the present. "He was a good one."

"The best of us," Nic replied. "The best of the three of us. Abbie definitely took first place for our generation, but Warren was a very close second."

I nodded and admired the thick, silver watch. It took me a while to process how losing Warren affected me. I didn't know him well enough to mourn him the way Harmony and Nic did, but I did feel an instant connection to him. Probably because we were both Air Elementals, the same soul in two different bodies. He'd been more patient with me than anyone else in my life and I would always picture his face with a smile on it.

"Thank you so much for this." I wiped a tear from my cheek. "So, what was your Soul Elemental like? No one ever talks about him."

Nic let out a short sigh. "Finn had a rough life. Quiet, always off somewhere else in his head. He and Harmony were in the same grade, two years ahead of me. He, uh, he was nice though. Obsessed with music. I still listen to a lot of the songs he introduced me to. Honestly, I think he liked music so much because it drowned everything else out."

"Everything else?" I asked for clarification.

"The voices in his head. The spirits. I know they weren't actually in his head, but being the only one that could hear them drove him crazy," Nic explained.

My eyes widened as my heart plummeted into my stomach. "Is that going to happen to B?"

Nic shook his head. "No, Brooke is going to be okay. By the time Finn was Brooke's age, he already started to crumble. His parents medicated him."

A cold chill coursed through my veins. "Brooke's parents have tried to do that to her. You know they institutionalized her the night the cottage was attacked?"

Nic put a hand on my shoulder. "What I'm saying is, Brooke's parents are paranoid but Finn actually needed help balancing back out. There's no shame in it, I should probably be medicated too. Does Brooke actually need that kind of help or does she need her parents to listen?"

"She needs her parents to listen," I whispered.

Nic nodded. "There's a difference. I think Finn had preexisting conditions we didn't watch out for because back then, mental health wasn't paid much attention to. We failed him."

"You were a kid, Nic, you guys had too much on your shoulders."

He gave me a soft smile. "Sounds familiar, huh?"

The front door opened and little feet ran into the living room, giggles echoing through the house. Harmony and her little family walked in through the front door. She stopped in her tracks, surprised to see us.

"Why aren't you two at the CC?" she asked, looking back and forth between Nic and I.

"I don't start until noon," I answered, picking my yogurt back up.

"I'm off today," Nic replied.

"Oh. Sorry. I got my days switched around." Harmony cleared her throat and gestured towards the empty china hutch in the dining room. "This is the one."

Jerry, or whoever, moved towards the oak display case. "Got it." Harmony's husband...ex-husband?

Whitney told me and the other girls about him dropping into the Corner Cup unannounced, but this was my first time seeing him in person.

"Are you getting rid of that?" Nic asked, stepping into the dining room.

"Yeah, I'm selling it. Unless you want it?" Harmony asked, watching Jerry remove the top piece of the cabinet.

"No, I don't want it," Nic answered, his shoulders falling. "We should sell the stuff we don't need."

"I'm sorry, I should have said something first." Harmony's attention diverted as a second man walked into the room. "Oh, thank you. That's the hutch right over here." She gestured towards Jerry and the china hutch. Harmony turned her attention back to Nic. "I'm trying to make extra cash."

"As long as the kids are okay with it, that's all that matters. It is their house after all."

Harmony nodded. "I spoke with all three of them first, I promise."

"Sounds good." Nic gazed over at the little girl, who folded herself over the arm of the couch. Her feet up in the air and her arms stretched out at her sides, making airplane noises. Nic smiled at the little girl. I joined his side, finishing up my snack. She was a cute little thing, full of innocence and wonder. I tried to imagine myself young and unscathed by the outside world. Having an addict as a biological mother, I wondered if I had ever been so carefree.

"There's another piece out in the garden shed that is going with it. Um." Harmony looked over at Emery and then up at me. "Can you keep an eye on her? She should entertain herself and we'll only be a short while. We're dropping these off and then coming right back."

"We got her, take your time," I answered, smiling over at the little girl.

"Thank you. Right this way." Harmony led Jerry and the other man outside as they carried away the empty china hutch, leaving her daughter with Nic and I.

"Hi! I'm Emery." The little girl smiled up at us with her two front teeth missing.

I chortled. "Hi. I'm Lauren."

"What's your name?" Emery asked, turning to Nic.

"You can call me Nicky," he answered. "That's what my friends call me."

Emery jumped up from the couch and trotted into the kitchen. "Do you have any snacks?"

"Uh, do you like yogurt?" I opened up the fridge.

"Strawberry?"

"It's your lucky day." I took the last strawberry yogurt and set Emery up at the table with a spoon.

"Thanks!" Emery took a giant bite.

A silence fell over us as I tried to remember how to talk to little kids. "So, how old are you, Emery?"

"Four! I'll be five June 8th." Emery smiled. I had very little experience with children, but Emery seemed well spoken for a preschooler. She turned her attention to Nic. "Ooh wow!" She jumped up from her seat and ran to Nic's side, grabbing his wrist in her little hands. "Someone drew all over you!"

Nic laughed. "They're tattoos."

Emery looked up at him with eyes full of surprise. "With needles?"

Nic nodded. "Lots of needles."

"Did it hurt?"

He shrugged. "Yeah, at the time but they don't hurt anymore."

"Wow!" Emery flipped his arm over. "Ooh, a bird!"

"Sparrows." Nic got down on his knee and pulled his short sleeve up to his shoulder, showing Emery the rest of his artwork. "This one is my favorite, it's a pirate ship."

Emery looked up at Nic with wide eyes. "Are you a pirate?"

He laughed again. "In some ways, yeah."

"That's a peony!" Emery pointed to a pink flower tattooed underneath the ship. "That's my mommy's favorite flower."

"Oh yeah?" Nic didn't seem surprised at the coincidence. "What's *your* favorite flower?"

"Hmmmm." Emery tapped her chin. "The white ones with the yellow middle."

"Daisies?" I offered.

"Yes!" Emery jumped up, going back to her yogurt. "I like those a lot." She turned to look back at Nic. "Nicky, are you friends with my mommy?"

Nic chortled. "Some days."

Emery laughed, turning to me. "Are you?"

"Uh, yeah, I would say your mom and I are friendly," I answered. "She's nice."

"She's the greatest mommy ever, she seems kind of sad." Emery took another bite. "She goes swimming when she's sad. My daddy has a pool at his apartment. I love it."

Nic and I met each other's gaze. I didn't want to press Emery further on what she meant, feeling it wasn't my business, but Nic didn't seem to share my intention.

"Your daddy's apartment?" he clarified.

Emery nodded. "Daddy used to live with us but he moved out before my birthday. He gets mad sometimes. That's why he doesn't live with us."

"Oh, well...everyone gets mad sometimes." Nic leaned against the counter.

"Do your mom and dad live here?" Emery asked Nic.

"Oh, um, no." He shifted awkwardly. "Not anymore."

Emery gasped. "Did they die?"

"Uh, yeah, they did," Nic answered.

"My grandma died last Christmas. My daddy cried."

Nic let out a short sigh. "That's what people do when they're sad, honey."

"That's what my other grandma calls my mommy! Do you call her that too?"

"On the days we're friends, I do." Nic smiled. "I remember your Grandma Susan."

Emery's eyes widened. "You know my mommy's mom?"

A hint of sadness panged Nic's voice. "I used to, yeah."

Harmony's voice called out from the living room as she entered the kitchen. "Hi! Sorry. I sent those two to deliver the furniture and I decided to stay back. Oh, are you getting some lunch?"

"Strawberry!" Emery held up her spoon.

Harmony smiled at me. "Thank you."

"She's a sweet kid," I answered. "I can't believe she's only four."

"She's smarter than I am," Harmony smirked.

Emery pointed to Nic with her yogurt-covered spoon. "Mommy! Nicky has your favorite flower tattooed on his arm!"

Harmony glanced at Nic sideways. "Has Nicky been showing you all his artwork?"

"Just my arms," Nic answered.

"How many tattoos do you have?" I glanced down the length of his body.

Nic winked at me and turned to Emery. "It was so nice to meet you, sweet girl."

Emery waved at Nic as he left the kitchen. Silence fell over Harmony and I as Emery finished her food.

"Uh." I cleared my throat. "So, how long will your family be in Rifton?"

Harmony let out a sigh that bordered irritation. "I don't know. Until the memorial, I guess."

"That's nice that they came to be with you."

Harmony stared at the floor, blinking slowly. "I'm happy my girl is here." She glanced at Emery and smiled. "I've missed her a lot these past few months. I hated leaving her behind, but there was no way I could bring her and expose her to..." She waved around the kitchen. "All this."

"It has been chaotic, so I understand," I replied.

"She deserves a normal childhood. I can't imagine if she'd been here when Mia and Warren..." Harmony glanced down at my wrist. "Oh, good, he gave you the watch."

I smiled at it. "Thank you for thinking of me when you were going through his things."

"Warren liked you a lot. You have a lot of his temperament buried under all that anger. I know it's easy to get lost in it, I do all the time. Warren always brought me back down. He and I clung to one another for over a decade and now..." Harmony got a far away look in her eyes. "Anyway, when you find those people who bring you back down, you have to hold onto them. You never know how long you have left with them."

I stared at Harmony and blinked, overwhelmed with realization of who brought me back down. "Thanks. I'll, uh, see you at work?"

Harmony nodded. "I'll be in this evening to take care of some paperwork."

I drove to the Corner Cup in a daze. I stopped at the red lights, vague awareness of my surroundings but I only had one thing on my mind. Warren's watch hung heavy on my wrist, a reminder of the ticking clock. The seconds passed by regardless of whether people were ready for them or not, and we had no control over when someone's watch would stop abruptly.

When I walked in through the front door, the bell jingled and alerted the shop to my arrival. Luckily, I appeared to have shown up in between the crowds, and only a few customers lingered from the lunch rush. Ashley wasn't out on the floor nor did she stand behind the counter.

I interrupted Robby while he messed with the espresso machine. "Where's Ash?"

"On her break." He glanced up and furrowed his brow. "Are you okay?"

I smiled. "I think so?"

I left the counter and stormed into the break room, my breath coming out in short pants as if I'd run a marathon. Ashley took a bite from a burrito before she looked up to see me in the doorway.

Ashley covered her mouth and chewed. "Hi."

"Don't worry, you don't need to talk, you only have to listen. Keep eating." I crossed the room and stood at the other side of the table. Ashley looked up at me with wide eyes as I continued. "I played along when you said we were being drunk and stupid at the wedding, but I wasn't. I don't want to be friends. I don't want to be someone you're drunk and stupid with and then we move on. I don't want to pretend like my heart doesn't skip a beat when you walk into the room." I held my hands over my chest. "I don't want to be another person in your life, I want to be *the* person in your life. I want to bring you food when you've had long days, and I want to hold your hand and buy you flowers. I think if I keep pretending that I'm not stupid in love with you, I'm going to explode."

Ashley had stopped eating, setting her burrito down on the table. She quickly wiped her mouth with a napkin and cleared her throat.

"Nothing?" I asked when the silence had become more than I could bear.

"I wish I didn't ask for extra onions on this burrito because what shitty timing," Ashley muttered, standing up from the table.

"Onions?" My shoulders fell. "Are you serious?"

"Lauren, of course I'm in love with you!" Ashley threw her arms out. "I didn't want to rush you into anything or make you feel weird."

I closed the gap between us and kissed her. Ashley's hand cupped my cheek, gently brushing my skin with her thumb. I broke the kiss and whispered against Ashley's lips. "I want to be with you."

Ashley smiled. "You already have me, Lo."

We kissed again but Ashley stepped back, her hand slid down my arm to grab my hand. "This is fantastic and I want more of it, but since we're clocked in…I'm a supervisor and you aren't. I don't want to make things weird here."

"Oh, yeah." I stepped back, remembering I needed to clock myself in for the day. "I agree."

Ashley squeezed my hand before she let go.

I let out a deep breath, feeling like I could've floated from the room. "I needed to get that all sorted. Um, finish eating, I'm already supposed to be out there."

Ashley nodded and sat back down.

I felt her eyes on me as I set my bag in the locker and put my apron on. "I'll see you out there?"

Ashley gave the widest smile I had ever seen, wrinkling the skin around her eyes and scrunching her nose. "I love you."

My heart exploded. "I love you too."

Chapter Twenty-Five
Little Secrets
Whitney

The day of Amilia's memorial came sooner than I had mentally prepared for. I leaned against the counter of the Corner Cup, watching the guests shuffle in.

Dmitri and Abe were tucked in the corner on the other side of the room, their fingers intertwined as they leaned in to whisper to one another. I smiled at how relaxed Dmitri rested against the wall. The genuine smile on his face when he looked into Abe's eyes. Dmitri had never been able to be this open in public. He never had any romantic interests in Kansas, not that I knew of anyway, but seeing him like this was truly freeing. Seeing him able to be himself unapologetically and have someone look at him with light in their eyes made my heart swell.

Rayn tended to the food table with Aden and Rose, setting up a tray of apple pastries she had made. Rose poured punch into a glass beverage dispenser that I recognized from her mother's Christmas Eve party. Aden laid out small paper plates and arranged plastic cutlery in cups at the end of the table. He had followed Rayn around all afternoon, doing whatever little odds and ends she needed to get the food taken care of.

"Where's Brooke?" Lauren asked, coming up next to me.

"She's on the way, according to her last text," I answered, checking my phone again for any updates.

Harmony chatted with another business owner by the register. I didn't know where Nic hid, I hadn't seen him since we showed up. He had given me a subtle wave and disappeared into the back employee hallway.

The front door jingled once more and Harmony stiffened as Jerry and Emery walked in. Jerry was dressed in a simple black suit and tie, freshly dry cleaned without a wrinkle in sight. Emery's black dress had ruffles on the sleeves. When the little girl saw Harmony, she ran across the dining area.

"Mommy!" Her little voice echoed through the coffee shop.

Harmony picked up her daughter and planted a kiss on her cheek. "Hello my sweet girl. You look beautiful today."

"So do you." Emery put her hands on Harmony's cheeks and smiled.

Jerry walked over and leaned in to give Harmony a quick kiss on her cheek.

"Thank you." Harmony flashed a smile that did not reflect in her eyes. Her body visibly tensed as Jerry squeezed her shoulder and took Emery into his arms.

"Come on, would you like a snack?" Jerry carried the little girl off to the refreshment table.

"You always seem tense when your husband is around." I approached Harmony, watching the discomfort spread across her face. "Or, sorry, ex-husband, right?"

"It's...it's complicated." Harmony turned to look at me. "He's powerless. He doesn't know about any of this, and I've worked damn hard to keep it that way. Now he's here in Rifton and I don't know when all this is going to blow up in my face."

"You don't think he'd react well if he knew the truth?"

"No, I don't think he would." Harmony shook her head.

"Then why..." I began to ask a question but half way through I realized it sounded insensitive.

Harmony took a deep breath. "Then why did I marry him in the first place?"

"You don't have to answer, it was a rude question. I can't judge your marriage from the five minutes I've seen of it."

"I'd deserve it. I judged your relationship with Bryan without seeing any of it." Harmony paused. "Things, uh, things between us hadn't been good for a while. He's a good father, but he isn't a good husband. Before I came back here we had talked about trying again for Emery's sake. I thought I could stomach staying in a loveless marriage to keep her from having to be shuffled back and forth. She doesn't deserve a broken home."

"A loveless marriage?" I turned to face her. "Harmony...that's not fair to you. You deserve better than that. You should be with someone who looks at you like you're the center of the solar system."

Harmony sighed and squeezed her eyes shut for a moment. "I do care for Jerry. He's a good dad but he's old fashioned and I don't see him being as accepting of my secrets as Bryan is with yours. I've always...watered myself down for him."

"Watered yourself down?" I tilted my head.

"Jerry cares too much about appearances and it didn't stop when there was no one around to impress." Harmony blinked the sadness from her eyes. "Bryan lets you be yourself, no matter what anyone thinks of it."

"I mean, it isn't all me." I glanced at Rose across the room. "I think if Rose wasn't in the middle of everything he may have reacted differently."

"I don't think it matters." Harmony smiled at me. "He's here for Rose too, and you can tell he's as protective over her, but he would still be here for you."

"Well, Jerry may not know about our powers but he's still here. He knew you were going through a hard time and he came to support you," I offered as if it would make any difference.

"You're right. He is trying...which is something he hasn't done in five years. You know..." Harmony took my hand in hers, catching me by surprise. "The more I get to know you, Whitney, the more I see it. I see so much of my younger self in you. I only ever knew my own generation for so long but after spending time with you and the girls, I truly believe our powers are reincarnated. It's like getting to know a younger me all over again."

"Maybe that's why we bang heads so much." I smiled.

"And I'm sure there's plenty more of that to come." Harmony leaned her shoulder against mine. "But I respect you, and I hope I've earned your respect as well."

"You have." I gave her hand a gentle squeeze. "You've done so much work after we lost Mia. You're trying so hard to keep CC open and I really admire it."

"It's what she would have wanted." Harmony glanced around the dining area. "Mia loved this place, it was a lifelong dream that finally came true. To be honest, I don't think I can keep it going forever." Harmony let go of my hand and started playing with her hair. "I won't always be here to keep the doors open. I don't know what the future holds for this place."

"Because you can't stay in Rifton?"

"No." Harmony shook her head. "I won't be staying in Rifton. I don't know who else loves this place enough to keep it afloat."

I chewed on the inside of my cheek, looking around at everyone who had come to Amilia's celebration of life. It wasn't even the scheduled start time and the dining room appeared close to capacity. Owners from the other shops on the street were all there. My former coworker, Olivia, grazed the refreshment table, pouring herself a small cup of punch. So many people I didn't recognize but Amilia had touched their lives in one way or another. They all respected her enough to come show their support. Tears welled in my eyes as the gravity of losing her sank in.

"I do," I answered softly. "I love this place enough."

Harmony sighed. "I hope someday that back office is yours, I really do. The future..."

"I know, I know. The future is uncertain, but you know...I like it here. I love Rifton. I love this coffee shop. If I come out of this–"

"You will," Harmony cut me off. "There's too many of us fighting to keep you alive. I know we all have different methods and I know Dominic is your favorite, but I only have your generation's best interest at heart. We genuinely want to protect you, and the talismans. The fucking world is over if we don't." Harmony looked over at her daughter. "And I have something worth preserving this world for."

"Do you think she'll have powers?"

"Nothing has manifested yet, so who knows...but I hope not. I hope it ends with me." Harmony peered deep into my gaze. "Would you want your kids to live like this?"

I shrugged. "Bryan and I don't want kids."

"Then I suppose that simplifies things."

The next jingle of the bell above the front door brought in Bryan and Ashley. He did a quick scan of the room, finally seeing Harmony and I against the back wall. He made his way through the dining area and kissed my cheek before he settled against the wall next to me.

"Hi," Harmony greeted.

"Hey, Harmony. Do you guys need anything?" Bryan asked.

Harmony shook her head, pushing off the wall. "So far so good. I'm going to check on a few things."

Bryan wrapped his arm around my waist as Harmony walked away. He rubbed his thumb along the fabric of my dress, leaning down to whisper in my ear. "Are you doing okay?"

"Yeah," I answered honestly. "It's nice to see how many people cared about Mia."

"She was a good person."

Ashley came up on my other side and put her head on my shoulder, sniffling into a tissue. "What's going to happen to this place?"

"Harmony wants to keep it open but she doesn't live here. She has a life out there she wants to get back to," I answered.

"So she'll probably sell. It won't be the same either way." Ashley wrapped her arm around mine.

"Harmony doesn't want to sell, but it probably won't be the same, unfortunately." I tightened my arm around Ashley's.

"Maybe we got all we needed out of it," Bryan answered, moving his hand from my waist and placing it on Ashley's shoulder. "Maybe it's time to move on to something else."

"Ugh, I don't want a new job," Ashley whined.

"Nothing is certain yet, let's take it a day at a time," I said.

I watched Harmony from across the room, holding her daughter in her arms, gently rocking her from side to side. Jerry came up to her, holding a red and black flannel in his hands. He smiled as he took Emery from Harmony and handed her the flannel.

"I brought your lucky jacket," he answered as Harmony took the flannel and quickly tucked it under her arm.

"Thank you, um, I'll be right back." She rushed off to the back office, rolling the flannel up tight as she hid it in her arms.

Every interaction I saw from Harmony since Jerry had arrived appeared awkward and messy, the exact opposite of the Harmony I'd witnessed over the past four months. Harmony was usually a solid block of ice, cold but sturdy. Jerry was a sledgehammer. She didn't seem herself around him. I always thought your spouse should be the one who brought out the best in you, the one you could be your true self around without having to hide or pretend. This is what my mom always talked about when she said witches have two choices when it comes to love. Live a double life or tell the truth and risk being left. Harmony had been living a double life.

"Hey, Angela," Bryan greeted a red-headed woman who crossed the dining room towards us.

"Have they started yet?" Angela asked, taking the empty spot on the other side of Bryan.

"Not yet," he answered. "Whit, this is my boss, Angela. Her parents own Giani's."

"Hi, Whitney." Angela smiled and offered her hand. "I wish we were meeting under different circumstances."

"Me too." I shook her hand.

"I keep telling Bryan we all want to meet you." Angela nudged him with her elbow.

"I'm sorry, I already live there." Bryan shook his head.

"I know, but my mother wants to meet her." Angela leaned around Bryan to look at me. "She adores him. Likes him more than me and I'm her only child."

Bryan chortled as Harmony took to the center of the room, her heels clacking against the floor with every step.

Harmony glanced around at those who gathered in the dining room. The CC was filled with familiar faces as well as strangers. Regular customers who came in almost daily gathered for a cup of coffee in Amilia's name. Nic finally came out of hiding, keeping himself tucked against the back wall.

Harmony cleared her throat and addressed the crowd. "Thank you everyone for coming today. It means a lot to see the impact Amilia made on the community. She loved Rifton, and she loved this coffee shop. Mia was not a traditional woman, so we didn't want to host a traditional memorial. Instead, we wanted to gather everyone who loved her, have something to drink and share stories. Amilia loved stories and she understood the importance of preserving them. As long as we share our stories and say their names, those who have left us are never truly gone."

Everyone clapped as Harmony held her composure better than the rest of us. Ashley tightened her grip on Lauren and nuzzled into her as Lauren wrapped her arm around Ash's shoulders.

Harmony stepped back and chatter took over the Corner Cup as everyone began talking amongst themselves. The building filled with warmth, laughter and tears. I smiled, blinking back my own tears, knowing this is exactly what Amilia would have wanted.

Where are the photos of Mom and Mia? Rayn's voice asked in my head.

If they aren't out here, they're in the back office. I'll go get them. I answered her, excusing myself from the group.

The back office was an absolute mess. I had a hard time referring to it as Amilia's office, yet calling it anything else felt too painful. Papers covered the desk, delivery times and schedules for the upcoming work weeks. All of our employees stretched too thin without enough time off yet none of us had the heart to complain.

I surpassed all the business papers and went to the back shelves where I assumed the photos would be. They hadn't been brought down here that long ago, but they probably sat under a stack of papers. Harmony was such a chaotic presence in the office. Everything scattered and strewn like her thought process. I imagined how she presented herself in the courtroom, if she always had this mess following her around or if our situation drove her to the edge of insanity.

I opened the bottom drawer of the desk, thinking maybe they'd be tucked away in there for safe keeping. Red and black plaid stared up at me. So this is where Harmony shoved the jacket Jerry had brought her. I ran my fingers along the worn fabric, well loved and faded in certain areas. Something about it compelled me. Why had Harmony suddenly left the room when Jerry handed it to her and hid it in here? He said it was her lucky jacket but she didn't want to wear it. Instead, it lay balled up in the desk, hidden from sight.

I picked it up and took a closer look. The collar had a missing button and the pocket on the breast had clearly been sewed back on a time or two. I analyzed every stitch, every little worn spot that had been mended by a needle and thread. Harmony obviously cherished it if she had worn it until it fell apart and then put it back together again. Flannels like these were a dime a dozen. Harmony could have gone to the store and replaced it a hundred times over, yet she kept putting this one back together.

The tag on the back of the collar was ripped in half but the thread of initials stitched into the tag remained. Worn but legible.

D.G.

I ran my thumb over the stitching.

Whit? Did you find them? Rayn asked, causing a chill to run up my spine. I wadded the flannel back up and tucked it into its hiding place.

I dug through the shelves and found the photos Rayn had been looking for under more papers.

I have them. I answered my sister and walked back into the dining area.

Rayn and I added the framed photos to the table of pictures we'd brought from the cottage. Pictures of Amilia and her family, photos of her as a teenager. The day she married Jackson Burnett. I focused on the memories before me, barely hearing the chime of the bell over the front door. The chill that took over the dining room didn't come from the thawing winter cold outside. A darkness slithered into the Corner Cup, an unwelcome face amongst those who gathered to remember Amilia.

Harmony saw him too, moving quickly to meet him halfway across the dining room. I squeezed Bryan's hand, silently telling him to stay as I joined Harmony's side

"Ms. Vasquez," Henry Drake said, waltzing up to Harmony. "I've heard that this beloved coffee shop seems to be in a bit of financial trouble."

"Where did you hear such a thing?" Harmony crossed her arms. "Whispers from the shadows?"

"Hmm." He smiled. "I'm here to offer assistance, a proposition."

"I have no interest in anything you have to offer," Harmony stated. "You shouldn't even be here."

"I mean no disrespect. I've been interested in investing back into the community. I am a businessman and I wouldn't be a very good one if I didn't take advantage of opportunities when they presented themselves." Drake tucked a hand into his pocket.

Nic made his way across the room and stood next to me, glaring at Drake with fire in his eyes.

"Get to the point," Harmony snapped at Drake.

"I could take this place off your hands," Drake offered.

"Get fucked," Harmony hissed. "I'd rather this place burn to the ground than sell it to you."

"No surprise there." Drake's eyes wandered over to Dominic. "Your affiliates seem to have a history with such events, burning down buildings and all."

Nic stiffened next to me and I wrapped a hand around his forearm, keeping him in place. We were in a very public place and brawling on the floor with the enemy would be unwise. Today was about honoring Amilia's memory.

"You've made your offer and we have declined. You're welcome to show yourself the door, Councilman." I hardened my gaze at Drake. "This is a private event, family and friends only."

"Oh, I see. Forgive the intrusion." Henry Drake gave a coy smile.

I glared at Henry Drake as he smirked at us. With a wave of my hand, my powers bubbled under my skin and a conspicuous wet spot appeared on the front of Drake's khaki pants. Those around us began to murmur amongst themselves as they noticed the stain, some of them giggling. Harmony looked down and covered her mouth, allowing a loud laugh to escape before she composed herself. Drake glanced down at his pants and gasped, quickly pushing his way through the guests to the front door. His cane tapped against the floor with every step.

Harmony looked back at me with wide eyes, still covering her mouth. Those standing around us began to whisper about the famed council member pissing his pants.

"Whitney," Harmony giggled, grabbing my shoulders. "You know better than to use in public."

"Whatever are you referring to?" I asked innocently.

Harmony laughed, glancing around the room. "He'll have to approve our permit now, or else he'll never be seen in public again without his uncontrollable bladder."

Nic growled over my shoulder, unamused by my prank. "I should have fucking killed him when I had the chance."

I wanted to agree, but knew it would only make Nic feel like a failure and I didn't want to add insult to injury. Instead I gently rubbed his bicep.

"Excuse me?" A quiet voice came up next to us.

A younger woman with fidgety hands approached. She wore a simple black dress with her hair up in a claw clip. Her eyes traveled back to the front door, as if making sure Henry Drake had truly left the building.

"Hello Miss…" Harmony greeted, dragging out the last syllable as if waiting for the woman to introduce herself.

"Oh, yeah, um…my name is Jane Worthing. My aunt Lacey was friends with Amilia. I remember you two from years ago, but I'm sure you don't remember me." The woman waved her finger between Harmony and Dominic. "It was so long ago, I'm not offended."

"Oh, yes, of course we know Lacey. We actually went to see her not long ago at her place on the beach." Harmony nodded.

"I remember you," Nic said to Jane. "You were a year behind me. We had Spanish together."

Jane smiled. "I can't believe you remember that. Rifton, uh, became a less than ideal place for my aunt but my parents stayed behind. They didn't have the same issues, if you get what I'm saying."

"I might," Harmony hesitated. "Powerless?"

Jane nodded. "Only, I could have had the same problem as my Aunt Lacey if I didn't stay, um, undetected?"

Holy shit.

I finally spoke. "But you're coming to us now because…?"

"I know Amilia Burnett didn't have a heart attack. A car crash taking out Audrianna Dansley? No, I don't believe it. I hope you're gearing up for a fight, because I'm here to fight with you."

"Hang on, wait." I stepped forward, my entire train of thought taken over by the mention of my mother. "My mother did die in a car crash, that wasn't the Renati."

Jane's eyes grew. "Your *mother?*"

Harmony put her hand on my shoulder. "Audri adopted after she left Rifton. Whitney is her daughter."

"Wow," Jane whispered. "My condolences all the same."

"Who else is still in town that can help us?" Nic asked eagerly, taking a step towards Jane.

Jane leaned in to whisper. "No one in my family, but I do know of a few others who remain under the radar."

"How is that possible?" I asked.

"The Renati pay more attention to the children of those they already track. They forget that our…abilities go to whoever it pleases and genetics play a role, but not *the* role. Fools." Jane laughed to herself. "There are two others. I wanted to reach out sooner but it never felt safe. Even now, Rifton is the worst it's ever been, but this is the time to step up and do something. So, what can I do?"

Harmony lowered her voice and pulled Jane in closer. "Come to the cottage with the others and we will discuss this further. We are doing a private ritual on Ostara to say goodbye and would love for you to join us. Do you remember where Amilia's house is?"

Jane nodded. "On Maple Drive, with all the flowers?"

"Yes," Harmony whispered with a soft smile. She reached into her purse and pulled out a business card. "Here is my card with my information."

"We will be there." Jane took Harmony's card and left the Corner Cup.

I looked at Harmony and Nic with wide eyes. "Is this real? Are they finally showing up?"

Nic smirked. "We'll find out."

Chapter Twenty-Six
CONFESSIONS
Whitney

Our crew gathered at the cottage after the memorial. No one spoke a word and the exhaustion hung heavy in the air. It weighed me down as I slumped into the corner of the couch.

Burying my mom had been a surreal, out of body experience. I remembered every detail, but not as myself, not as her daughter. I watched it unfold as a bystander, disassociating to keep myself from imploding. And then Rayn did implode and burned her ex-boyfriend, and that took over my attention. It gave me something else to focus on.

But burying Amilia? I was stuck in my head, unable to escape. We had been allowed to publicly mourn my mother for what killed her; that fucking truck crashing into the side of her car. We couldn't do the same for Amilia.

To anyone outside the cottage, I had to pretend a heart attack ended her life. Amilia's death was no one's fault, nothing that could've been prevented. These kinds of things happen to everyone. Illness doesn't discriminate, like the sickness growing in Amilia's body. Only it wasn't the cancer or her heart failing that ended her life. It was avoidable.

Surprisingly, Harmony had brought Jerry and Emery to the cottage after the memorial. The couches and chairs were already full with all of our people, so Jerry pulled out a chair at the dining room table and sat down. Emery settled herself in between Dmitri and Abe on the couch.

"Sorry, it gets a bit crowded here," Harmony said to Jerry.

"Then quit bringing everyone over," Nic muttered.

"Dominic Grant, I swear if you don't shut up," Harmony snapped.

Nic put his hands up in defense and plopped down on the floor in front of the couch.

I glanced down at him as his shoulder rested against my knee. I gave him a comforting pat on the head. We'd all had a rough day. We had all buried someone we loved. Amilia meant something to all of us, especially Nic and Harmony.

I looked back and forth between the two of them, unable to move past their bickering. Dominic Grant.

D.G.

A chill ran up my spine as I glanced sideways at Harmony.

"What?" she asked, confused.

Jerry cleared his throat. "I'm amazed at how remarkably well you've all been dealing with this loss." He put his arm around Harmony's shoulders. "I'm sure that memorial service was difficult for all of you but you've all been holding it together and I think that needs to be acknowledged."

"Thank you." Rayn gave him a soft smile.

Nic's voice startled me as his tone completely changed. "I want to hang myself from the Willow River bridge."

"Dominic!" Harmony's eyes wide with surprise.

I turned to look at him expecting to see playfulness, but no sarcastic tone dripped from his voice and no mischievous smile brightened his eyes. His shoulders tensed and his gaze hardened, his head low as he stared across the room at nothing.

He continued on. "I'm not handling things remarkably well and I have to physically restrain myself from ending it. The only thing keeping me going is pure spite."

I glanced over at Emery's face for only a second before I jumped up from the couch and grabbed Nic's warm hand in mine. Whatever breakdown he was on the verge of would not be happening in front of this little girl. "Okay, come on."

He didn't fight me. He didn't grab my hand back. He simply kept his fingers limp as he followed me to the back porch and onto the grass. He wouldn't look me in the eyes. Instead he stared down at the ground, not at anything in particular.

My pulse accelerated with panic.

"Dominic." I snapped my fingers in front of his face, desperate for him to look at me. "If you hurt yourself, I swear to the generations, I will hunt you down in the next life and kill you again myself." I grabbed his shoulder with my free hand. "Nicky, look at me!"

"I want to be alone," he whispered, pulling his hand out of my grip.

"Well too damn bad because I'm not leaving you alone after you just announced to the group you want to hang yourself from a bridge. What is going on?"

"I..." His voice trailed off, catching in his throat.

I grabbed his shoulders again. "It's me. Your only friend in the fucking world, remember? You can talk to me, or we can not talk and stand here but either way, I'm not going anywhere."

Nic plopped down on the grass, pulling his knees close to his chest. Finally, he glanced up and his eyes met mine, lined in tears. "I don't want to talk, but I'll show you."

"Okay." I got down on my trembling knees in front of him, patiently waiting for his mental walls to drop.

When I entered Nic's mind, flashes of memories happened before me. He never stayed on one for long. My head spun and my stomach churned from the dizziness, but I found my footing and focused on the first one I could mentally grasp.

Teenage Nic stood at the edge of the massive rocks that surrounded the lake. A cloudless sky hung above him and the sun beat down on his tan skin. Freckles covered his bare shoulders as he peeked over the edge. He turned around and smiled, offering out his hand to Harmony.

"Jump," he said.

A young Harmony took a step back, shaking her head. "It's too high."

"You scaredy cat. I wouldn't let anything happen to you."

Harmony smirked and put a hand on her hip. "Considering we're jumping into the water, wouldn't it be me who kept us safe?"

"Honey." Nic took a step closer, a look of seriousness washed over his face. His smile faded and his brows relaxed. "I love you. Jump off the cliff with me."

"What?" she whispered.

"I'm in love with you. Jump with me." Without another word, Nic lept from the edge off the rocks.

Harmony froze, watching where Nic once stood. A smile swept across her face before she jumped. Harmony plunged into the water behind him with a scream. Nic laughed, waiting for her to surface. Harmony wiped her hair back out of her face and swam to him, pulling his lips to hers. He closed his eyes and kissed her, holding the back of her neck.

"I love you too," she confessed.

The memories began to flash again. Nic and Harmony singing in the car together, their fingers intertwined on the center counsel. The two of them lying in the tall grass of the meadow. Them sneaking longing glances across the living room at the cottage when no one paid attention. Sitting on the roof of a car with Abbie in the middle, watching fireworks explode in the night sky. Harmony stared up at the show but Nic's eyes were on her. Nic and Harmony wrapped in bed sheets. Talking on the phone after the sun had long set.

This time, Nic was the one who focused on a single memory.

A roaring bonfire illuminated the scene. Nic stood in the trees, leaning his back against the bark. He tapped his foot impatiently until he heard someone approach. Nic turned and flashed the happiest smile I'd ever seen from him. Harmony came into view and attempted to smile back, but she kept her distance.

"What's wrong?" Nic moved closer to her but Harmony took a step away.

"I, um...I don't know what we're doing. I'm leaving for college in Seattle and you're still in high school."

"But that's all temporary...Honey, the way I feel about you, it's not a temporary thing. This is the real deal, me and you. You said so yourself." Nic stammered as a tear fell down his cheek. He reached for her hand. "Don't spiral...don't do this."

Harmony pulled away again. "Dominic, I care about you but this isn't going to work. Maybe if we were closer in age or maybe if we didn't have to hide, but I can't keep this secret and if we're doing something we have to keep secret then maybe we shouldn't be doing it in the first place."

"You said it's only until I turn eighteen. We have less than a year!" He stood frozen, staring at her. "You're only worried about Mia finding out, but I could care less if she doesn't approve."

She turned away from him, staying silent.

"That's it? You're ending us just like that? Like we're nothing. I love you, Honey. I love you so much it hurts."

Harmony balled her fists in frustration. "It's not supposed to hurt, Nicky! I'm sorry, but...right now, it's for the best."

"I-I can't believe this." He ran his fingers through his hair and choked on his words. "Is this real? Are you serious?"

Harmony stood firm. "We can't be together, Dominic."

Nic turned and ran without another word. He disappeared into the trees and as quickly as he ran from Harmony, I was kicked out of his head.

I stared back at thirty-year-old Nic, sitting in the grass. He stared at me, as if he waited for me to speak first.

"Holy shit, Nicky," I whispered.

"I'm still in love with her, and I'm not handling it very maturely. I thought I could, but...Mia and Warren both died and I'm falling apart." He sniffled, wiping his nose on his sleeve. "I'll be fine, Whitney, I'm not going to kill myself. I had a moment."

"No, you aren't having a moment. You're having a whole episode. Stop burying it or it'll eat you alive. We–"

"Burying it," he laughed, repeating my words. "I'm consumed by it."

"I swear I thought you two hated each other, but then I found her flannel with D.G. on the tag and...I don't know what I thought but I didn't think it was like this."

Nic narrowed his eyes. "What flannel?"

Oh.

I cleared my throat and shifted my weight between my knees. "Um, Jerry brought Harmony a flannel to the memorial and called it her lucky jacket. I found it hidden in the office at CC and I snooped. It took me an embarrassingly long moment to realize it was yours." I studied his face, unsure if I should even tell him this. "I'm not trying to complicate things. I don't know why I'm talking so much. You should be the one talking."

He stared at me and I watched as the wheels in his head turned. We looked into each other's eyes for an eternity before he spoke again. "She still has it."

"The flannel, yes."

"She's a fucking liar," he hissed through his teeth.

I chewed on my bottom lip, panicked and confused. I wanted to talk. I wanted to reach out and pull him into a hug but I froze, not wanting to make things worse. I didn't know how to comfort him or what I even truly comforted him about. "I don't know what to say," I admitted.

"I'm so fucking mad at her, for a lot of things." Nic grabbed at the roots of his hair. He thrilled his lips, flopping onto his back with his arms up around his head. "Lay down with me?"

"Okay." I lay down on the grass next to him. We lay there in silence for a moment, nothing but my heartbeat filling the space between us. "So, being around one another has stirred up old memories? Why did it take so long?"

I turned on my side to face him, tucking my arm under my head. I waited for him to go at his pace, to take his time. When he seemed to realize I waited for him to continue, he turned his head to look at me.

He let out a deep sigh. "I had turned seventeen right when we got together, but she's a couple years older and we decided to keep it quiet for a year. Honey was worried what people would think, even though she was only nineteen. I didn't see the big deal, but she ended things out of the blue at that bonfire and...I ran. I had to get away from everyone and I wanted to go hang myself from the bridge but Abbie followed and..." Nic cleared his throat. "While you were at the Hallow, we were here alone. I guess old feelings that I didn't know she still had surfaced. She crawled into my bed and now...now I'm seventeen again."

"Wait...wait, hang on." I propped myself up on my elbow. "The night you and Abbie were captured by the Renati...you were out in the woods because Harmony broke up with you?"

He nodded.

"And you two slept together while we were at the Hallow?"

"Glad to know you listen when I speak." His gaze met mine. "She broke things off the day you guys got back, but that barely lasted a week."

"Nicky, her husband is here."

"*Ex-husband*," he corrected me with a scoff. "You think I am not painfully aware of that fact?"

"So, you and Harmony..." I paused, remembering something Harmony had once said to me.

We are two versions of the same person.

"Is that why you and I," I caught myself before the words left my lips.

I had already said too much, and Nic seemed to know what I planned to say. "Why we connect? I think so."

"That's why you only spoke to me and not the other girls when you first came into town. Because I reminded you of Harmony?"

Nic furrowed his brow. "I was very upfront about you reminding me of Harmony."

"Before I knew the whole picture." I sat up. "I don't know how I feel about that, Nic. It feels kind of gross."

Nic rubbed his face and let out a frustrated groan. "Whitney, I love you very much, but stop making this about you. Not everything is about you, kiddo. Not many people have the balls to tell you that, but reel it in a bit, 'kay? I'm having a fucking existential crisis here. This is about *me*."

I chortled, relieved to see the old Nic shine through the crack in his shell. "I'm sorry."

"You don't remind me of Honey in *that* way, for the record. She used to be my best friend, and with you...it's like having a best friend again." Nic pulled headphones from his pocket and handed it to me, connecting the cord to his phone.

I took the earbud and watched his fingers tap on the screen until a song began to play. "You're my best friend too, Nicky."

"I don't want to talk anymore." He put the earbud in and rested his head against the grass.

"Okay." I put the earbud in my ear and lay next to him, listening to the song he'd chosen.

A person standing on the back porch caught my peripheral vision and I lifted my head to look at them. Nic had his eyes closed and didn't see me move. I squinted to get a better view of the silhouette in the darkness, but as they turned to leave, unmistakably flowing curls flipped over a shoulder.

Harmony.

No doubt she had come out to make sure Nic lay in the grass instead of dangling from a rope.

"I wish triggering these memories of the past generations were as easy as getting into your head," I said, unsure if Nic even listened.

Nic shifted his weight and turned to look at me, the music still playing in both of our ears. "You haven't tried to reach the past generations since the Hallow?"

I shook my head.

"You should try again," he encouraged. "Everything is connected with the Elementals. The past creates the present and the present determines the future. If we're going to figure out how to get the advantage, maybe looking back is the answer."

"Maybe." I reached out and linked our arms together, closing my eyes. "Are you going to be okay?"

Nic lowered his voice. "Please don't worry about me."

"I'll stop breathing while I'm at it. It'll be as easy."

Nic huffed. "I don't know if I've ever been okay, but I'm trying. Harmony and I were alone in this house and...I got distracted. I've been distracted, but we're going to get that key from Bonnie Drake. I feel it in my bones. In the meantime, keep triggering those past memories."

"Brooke is hellbent that I see the Spirit Elemental from the Martyrs but I think trying to see the Shepherd's memories would be more helpful. I mean, the talismans hold their powers after all."

"Follow your gut." Nic tightened his arm around mine. "You're more powerful than you give yourself credit for."

"So I keep hearing," I muttered.

"What did you do the first time you triggered the memories?"

"I lit a candle and manifested."

He smirked. "Fire, huh?"

"It felt right...Fire feels like home," I admitted.

"Twin flames," he whispered. "The lake was always my favorite place in Rifton. I'd live up there all summer. Water feels like home, too."

"Twin flames," I repeated. "Rayn mentioned something about that. She said our magical connection was stronger than the other Elementals. That's why she and I found each other first."

Nic nodded. "It's always been that way. Sometimes I wonder...I wonder if Harmony ever really cared about me, or if it was only her powers connecting to mine."

I nuzzled my head against his shoulder. "I wish I had an answer for you."

"Me too."

The next day, the girls and I went up to the meadow with Bryan and Aden. Being back in the meadow felt like coming home. We hadn't been there since we practiced charming with Nic and Warren. So much had happened since we listened to the two of them laugh together. Warren had been such a calming presence amidst all the chaos. I often wondered how different things would be if he were still here.

Aden remained at the tree line, watching the rest of us carefully. He froze in place, as if stepping foot in the meadow would cause him to spontaneously combust.

"Aren't there charms here to keep hunters out?" Aden asked Rayn.

She stopped to turn around a few steps ahead of him. "It's charmed to keep unwanted guests out. You aren't unwanted."

Aden stared at the ground before he slowly stepped onto the grass. When nothing happened, he let out a sigh of relief and followed us the rest of the way. I followed behind Bryan and the girls as the chilly air blew through the clearing. Signs that spring was on the way surrounded the meadow. The blades of wild grass and weeds grew back bright green. The sky had gone from wintery gray to a robin egg blue. While the chill in the air remained, the bright sun hanging in the sky promised of warmer days.

Rayn wasted no time, closing her eyes and drawing in a deep breath to steady herself. When she opened them, she created a fireball in her hands. She poured all of her focus into the fire, growing the flames as she pulled her hands apart and decreasing it as she moved her hands closer together.

Aden watched her carefully, his face emotionless, but fear reflected in his eyes. He tilted his head. "What are you doing?"

Rayn kept her eyes on the fireball as she spoke. "When we were under the shield, it felt like I was surrounded by gasoline. I need to control my powers better."

He nodded and turned to Bryan. "Are you ready?"

Bryan pulled his hoodie over his head and I shamelessly stared at the exposed skin before he pulled his shirt back into place. "Ready."

They came at one another quicker than I had mentally prepared for. Aden flipped Bryan up over his shoulder and slammed his back on the dirt. Bryan jumped up quicker than he had the last time I'd seen them spar at the cottage. Aden went for Bryan's shoulder again, but Bryan kicked the side of Aden's ankle, a blow that Aden didn't seem to be suspecting.

Aden fell to his knee and Bryan wrapped his arm around Aden's neck, trapping him in a headlock.

Aden smiled wide and looked up at Bryan with pride. "You're learning."

I tried to give them space to practice where I wasn't a distraction. We had our own training to do. Harmony had admitted a while back that I'd learned everything she had to teach me. While she had shared many pointers that had already saved my life, I doubt she faced much combat while practicing law in Seattle. If the last few months were any indication, we had to be prepared for an altercation with the Renati and their shadows at any moment.

Across the clearing, Brooke, Rose and Lauren practiced their energy waves. In the past, Brooke had struggled getting the push behind the energy waves but with Rose's help, she quickly caught up to the rest of us.

Lauren held her hands out with her palms facing the ground. Her powers tingled under my skin as she used the wind to lift herself into the air. Lauren's feet left the ground as she floated up so high I had to bend my neck back to look at her. She levitated before she lowered herself back down.

"I will never get over how cool that is," I told her with a smile.

Lauren returned the gesture, then glanced over my shoulder, shock taking over her face. "Oh, shit! Look at you, Byn!"

I turned around to see Aden pinned to the ground with Bryan's knee in the middle of his chest. Aden patted Bryan's side, accepting defeat. Bryan got off Aden, offering out his hand to help him up.

"You've come much farther than I anticipated," Aden clapped his hand on Bryan's shoulder. "You should be proud of yourself."

I looked around at everyone, in awe of how far we'd come since we first ventured into the meadow together. When the girls and I first came here, we barely knew one another. We didn't trust each other. We didn't trust ourselves. We were five separate entities who happened to have matching jewelry, with no idea of what the floating ink inside of the gems held.

Now, we were a complete generation. We had gone through so much; life and death. We had battled Shadows and the Renati. We had faced down Erebus together and come out the other side stronger.

Even Aden and Bryan had changed. When we first met Aden, he wanted to kill us. Now he stood on the very ground his pack had first ambushed us, teaching Bryan how to protect himself. Aden had gone from hunting down those with the ability to use magic, to sleeping under the same roof. He protected us against those who used to be his people.

Bryan had grown so much as a person too. The first time I watched Aden throw Bryan over his shoulder, I couldn't bear to watch. Now, not only could he hold his own against Aden in a spar, but he had given his entire self to our cause. Though, that last part still didn't sit well in my stomach. I hated that Bryan had dropped out of FBU. I know he referred to it as a break, but he dropped out. I hated seeing how he had been negatively affected by all this. By me. I wanted to hate that he practiced fighting with Aden, but the look on his face melted the anger I carried.

Bryan held himself with pride. He held his head high and his shoulders back. He smiled as Aden talked to him. I didn't want to drag him down with us, but if he insisted on being here, at least he learned to hold his own.

That night in bed, I turned on my side to face Bryan. "I'm really proud of you."

"Oh, thank you." He smiled, reaching out to touch my face.

"You've been working really hard training with Aden and you kicked his ass today. I'm really impressed."

"I'm trying to keep up with everyone," he admitted. "It's hard being the only powerless person in the group. I don't want to be a burden, and this seems to be the only way I can protect myself."

"You will never be a burden, not to me or anyone else in our group. We all have our own problems and baggage, but we all play our part. We all bring something to the table and we make the crew stronger."

"Even me?" he asked, clearly still unconvinced.

I leaned in and pecked a kiss to his lips. "Especially you." I paused for a moment, wondering if I should change the subject but I couldn't keep the information to myself any longer. "So, Nic and Harmony are a thing. Like, romantically."

Bryan lifted his eyebrows in surprise but his demeanor remained relatively calm. His pulse remained the same. "Whaaaat?"

"You already knew!" My eyes widened as I playfully smacked him in the shoulder. "How did you know?"

His gaze left mine. "Um, I walked in on them at the cottage."

"What?" My voice echoed off our bedroom walls.

"Kissing," he clarified. "I walked in on them kissing."

"Why didn't you tell me?"

Bryan shrugged. "They asked me not to, and it wasn't mine to tell. I figured Nic would fill you in eventually. I'm honestly surprised he waited so long."

"Me too," I admitted. "He's not doing well. This is all a big distraction and he's scattered."

Bryan looked into my eyes and tucked a strand of hair behind my ear. "Love can be consuming."

I remembered how panicked I had been when we first got back into town. How desperate I was to see Bryan. I would have walked to Falcon Bay if I had to. Not knowing where we stood, if he even wanted to see me...Hearing how angry he felt.

I sighed, knowing I would quite possibly want to hang myself from the bridge too if I had to watch Bryan be with someone else. "It's crazy how there is a real life and death situation happening in town, and we are all still driven by hormones."

Bryan chortled. "Humanity at its finest."

"Do you think he's going to be okay?" I asked. "I'm really worried about him."

"I think..." Bryan paused. "Yeah, I think he's trying to be okay. He has his moments, but nobody wants to see this through more than Nic."

"I'm glad you two are getting along."

Bryan offered a soft smile. "Yeah, me too."

Chapter Twenty-Seven
Walking Memories
Whitney

I sat on my bedroom floor with a tealight candle in front of me the next afternoon. The house was silent. Dmitri and Abe were having lunch with Janice and Jeff. Bryan and Troy were at work. I had the house to myself and I could hear a pin drop. Since I wasn't in the middle of the woods, I had more materials to set the ambiance. I lit a stick of cedarwood incense that smelled like Bryan. I played with my mom's moonstone ring, twirling it around my thumb.

Letting myself unwind, I took my time relaxing. I had nowhere to be and didn't want to rush this process. I allowed my mind to fade into nothing; no worries and no stress. I hummed to myself as I closed my eyes, focusing on the balance within my body.

Once I entered the right headspace, I flicked the lighter and lit a candle. The flame danced around as it caught to the wick, and a small pool of melted wax gathered at its base. I watched the flame, allowing it to fill me with the warmth of my loved ones and our purpose. With a deep breath, I closed my eyes and called out to the Shepherds.

I pictured their spellbook and the talismans that held their power. I felt the weight of my aquamarine around my neck; how the gem pressed against my skin. I reached out into the abyss, feeling for any indication that I could reach them. The slightest little tether that I could grasp onto.

Nothing.

Trilling my lips, I wasn't ready to accept defeat. I slipped the talisman from around my neck and held it in my hands, running my thumb over the smooth gem. I closed my eyes and pushed further into the ether. I called, begged, for the Shepherds.

No one answered.

"Okay," I muttered, slipping my talisman back around my neck. I closed my eyes once more and settled back into the zone, resting my limp hands in my lap. Brooke had been so insistent that I try to reconnect with the Elemental she had created such a connection with. If the Shepherd's wouldn't answer, maybe he would.

"Gabriel," I whispered his name, calling out for him. "Gabriel."

My stomach dropped and everything in my body shifted; suspended like I had gone down a drop in a roller coaster. A sharp, sudden pain pierced through my temple before it dulled into a steady throb.

I stood in a large, open room. My vision no longer blurred like it had been the first time. The wooden panel walls were decorated elaborately with swirling designs. The windows went from floor to ceiling and curved at the top, filling the room with sunlight. Delicate pieces of furniture were scattered through the room. Two men sat on padded arm chairs, one with his back to me while the other faced me. A third man paced the room with his arms crossed. They spoke in hushed tones, their voices stern as they argued.

"Thomas, you clearly do not understand the urgency of this matter," the man with his back to me pleaded.

"You two of all people know we can only do so much," Thomas replied.

The man who paced the room halted and turned towards the one called Thomas. When his face came into view, I nearly screamed. His face haunted my dreams. Those dark eyes had glared at me as those hands choked the air from my throat. The man who killed Amilia before my eyes.

Erebus snarled. "If not us, then who? Are we not the ones responsible for the safety of Paradisus?"

Thomas hardened his gaze. "*You* are not responsible for anyone but yourself."

"How are we to call ourselves their leaders and live in this lavish building if we are not to do everything in our power to protect them?" the man with his back to me asked.

"Gabriel, our main focus must be locating the youngest generation. Now that we are Magisters, our responsibility is finding the young ones." Thomas rubbed his temple and scooted to the edge of his seat.

Erebus let out a deep sigh. "Finding the newest generation may be a priority to the Elementals but to the rest of us, there are more important matters at hand."

"Garreth, mind your place," Thomas snapped.

Garreth. Erebus' real name?

Gabriel turned so I could see his face. "Brother, please."

Brother.

Gabriel and Garreth were surely twins. They shared so many facial features, the strong nose and the thick eyebrows. The only difference was the hatred in Garreth's eyes. I'd seen that hatred directed at me too many times to ever forget it.

"I called you here, Gabriel, to inform you that I had a vision." Thomas changed the subject. "I suppose since you are never without Garreth, I will tell you both."

"Oh?" Gabriel leaned back, tilting his head to the side.

Thomas nodded. "An Allurement in the new land."

"The Americas." Garreth crossed his arms. "How can you be certain?"

"I did not recognize the rock formation to be anywhere in our part of the world, it appeared to be an eagle with expanded wings. It is the gateway to an Allurement, there were energy waves radiating off the rocks near a coast line." Thomas stood and moved to a small table across the room. He picked up our spellbook and brought it back to Gabriel. "I drew it out as best as memory allowed."

Gabriel took the book and held it in his hands. "This is a significant discovery."

Garreth moved to read over his brother's shoulder.

Thomas watched them both carefully. "Yes, for the future generation we have yet to find. If we are to preserve whatever future this new land holds, we must find them."

"It may take years for the Allurement to call them here." Gabriel closed the spellbook. "I do not disagree with the urgency, but my brother is right. Feeding our people must take priority, Thomas."

"Our legacy is all that matters!" Thomas raised his voice, anger dripping from his words.

"Your legacy is nothing if we do not care for the present!" Garreth argued back.

"Care for the present? The magic from our Allurement is draining. We have tapped into the magic too many times to care for the leeches who reside here." Thomas pointed to the window with a shaky finger. "We must take the strongest of our clan and find the next generation. We must move to the new Allurement."

"Leeches? How are they leeches when you are the ones who encouraged them to come to Paradisus? The new Allurement is promising but we must repair the one here first. At least try!" Garreth shouted. "We cannot abandon these people or our home!"

"Would you choose those lesser witches over your own generation, Gabriel?" Thomas asked with a stern voice.

"I do not see why there is not room for both." Gabriel turned away from Thomas.

"Your inability to see what is truly important will be the end of us, Gabriel," Thomas scoffed. "Locked up in your apothecary with your potions and remedies, only sticking your head up for air when absolutely necessary. Allowing your brother to speak for you when you are the Elemental and he a common witch."

"I did not come to argue. We came to understand why you have not put an end to the drought," Gabriel stated. "You're the only one who can."

"There have been whispers of insubordination," Thomas answered simply. "If I must deprive them of luxuries to teach respect, so be it."

"Water is not a luxury," Garreth pointed out. "We cannot be so focused on the needs of Elemental succession that we ruin Paradisus."

Thomas wandered towards the window. "It is not the Elementals who will ruin Paradisus. These witches have grown too comfortable, too reliant. They were once self-sufficient, and now they rely on us for every basic need, unwilling to lift a finger."

"It is not that bad," Gabriel brushed him off.

Thomas clenched his jaw. "I will repeat myself only once. If I must deprive them of luxuries to teach respect, so be it."

The memory faded as quickly as it came and my vision went dark. It speckled back as my bedroom appeared before me. The tealight candle in front of me had completely burned, only an empty aluminum cup remaining.

How long was I gone for?

My stomach churned seeing Erebus' mortal face, who he had been before his darkness twisted and ruined his soul. Before he rose up as something else and killed the Martyrs, his own brother's generation. One of the last generations before we showed up.

I rubbed my forehead, attempting to dull the aching throb as I dissected what I'd seen. I recognized Thomas and Gabriel's names from our spellbook. The Spirit and Water Elementals – Brooke and I in another life.

It made sense why I had felt so drawn to the map of the Hallow; if Thomas had been the Seer and he had been the one to draw it into the book. The map always seemed a distant memory calling out to me, pulling me in as if trying to get me to remember why it had been so important in the first place. That part of the memory I could make sense of.

I had a hard time understanding the cruelty Thomas displayed when speaking about the citizens of Paradisus. How could they be deprived of water when he literally controlled the element? How could the city possibly be in a drought when the rains would return with a wave of Thomas' hand? I rattled my brain, trying to understand how anyone could justify that kind of cruelty...How *I* could justify it.

Thomas may have used my magic centuries ago, but he and I were not the same person. That I refused to believe.

I let out a deep sigh and rubbed my eyes, letting the vision sink into my bones. The sound of pages rustled from across the room. I glanced across the way to where the Martyr's spellbook rattled on top of my dresser. I jumped to my feet and dashed across the room as the pages flipped, finally settling towards the middle of the book. I stared down at the parchment, eager to see what the book had decided to share with me.

The book lay open to a spell that I didn't recognize.

How was there a spell in this book I hadn't already seen?

"Walking Memories," I read aloud, running my finger down the words. "Storm vine and littiory oil mixed together and inhaled will give the Seer the ability to physically enter memories. The Seer could move within the memory, seeing more than the memory holder allows. What?"

I sat down on the edge of the bed as the information I'd received spun around in my head. I squeezed my eyes shut, still seeing Garreth...*Erebus'* face. Even if I were able to pull this spell off and walk amongst the memories, being that close to Erebus again made my skin crawl.

☽ · ☽ · ● · ☾ · ☾

That evening, I gathered the girls at the cottage. The five of us crammed into Lauren and Rayn's bedroom. I sat on my sister's bed with my legs crossed under me, drumming my thigh with my thumb. We chatted about the mundane day to day until Lauren returned with a big bowl full of popcorn. She closed the door behind her and waved her hand, activating the charm that sound proofed the room.

"So, what's going on?" Rayn turned to face me.

"I triggered another vision," I began. "I haven't tried since the Hallow and this time I actually saw what happened, it wasn't fuzzy at all."

"What did you see?" Brooke scooted to the edge of Lauren's bed.

"Three men were having a conversation. Their apparel and the decorations in the room were old. They were talking about a vision one of them had of Falcon Ridge. Talking about how they wanted to move their people out of Europe into the new world and find the Allurement. Something about the magic draining from their Allurement in Paradisus."

"Wow," Rose breathed, a smile widening on her face. "And here we are all these years later. So that safe haven for witches in Europe was already failing before Erebus rose to power."

"It appears that way. They used names too. Thomas and Gabriel." I swallowed, attempting to keep my heart in my chest. "And Garreth."

"Gabriel? *My* Gabriel?" Brooke's voice echoed off the walls of the cabin.

"I called out to him right before I had the vision, so I'm pretty sure. The third man, Garreth...I recognized his face." My chest tightened as his dark eyes flashed in my mind. "It was Erebus."

The room fell silent.

"Before he was Erebus?" Rose finally asked, her face draining of color.

I nodded. "I think so." I paused as another memory crept through my brain, making my skin crawl. "Erebus called me Thomas at the cottage."

"I remember," Rayn replied. "Thomas must've been the one who fucked everything up."

I cleared my throat. "In the memory, they argued. Paradisus was in the middle of a drought and Thomas did nothing to help. He called water a luxury. Sounds like Thomas made a few different enemies." I shook my head.

"No wonder Erebus killed the entire generation. If the rest of them were anything like this Thomas guy." Lauren took a bite of popcorn.

I swallowed the lump in my throat. "Gabriel definitely seemed bothered by Thomas' behavior, but he also didn't seem like the type to actually do anything to change it. Thomas made a comment about Gabriel losing himself in his remedies and letting Garreth speak for him," I explained.

Brooke nodded. "That makes sense. From what I've read, he spent most of his time researching and experimenting."

"He must have kept his head down and let his generation run Paradisus into the ground," I agreed. "Then his brother killed them all."

"Okay, this is good." Rose ate some popcorn. "We are understanding Erebus' motives, and you can't defeat an enemy unless you understand them."

"Still doesn't explain how he has our magic," Rayn pointed out.

"Didn't he absorb the Martyr's magic when he killed them? Isn't that why the Shepherd's locked their souls in the talismans?" Lauren asked.

"That's how I understand it too." Rose chewed on her bottom lip. "This Garreth guy must have been one hell of a strong witch to hold all that magic inside of his body."

"I'll keep triggering memories and see what I can figure out," I told the girls. "Has anyone else seen him around town? I know Nic and Bryan saw Erebus while we were at the Hallow, but he hasn't been out and about since we've been home."

Lauren shook her head. "I haven't seen him."

"Me either," Rose said. "I can't imagine walking past him down the street."

"I haven't seen much of Serenity either," Rayn pointed out. "She's only been into CC once. Something is up."

I ignored the knot forming in my stomach and turned to Rose. "Hey, I found a spell in the Martyr's book that may help with these memories I'm triggering. Have you heard of storm vine or littiory oil?"

Rose chewed on her bottom lip. "Littiory oil?"

"Yeah, I wrote them down so I wouldn't forget. I have no idea what those herbs are. They are herbs right?"

"I don't know." Rose shrugged. "But I will find out. I'll look them up in Mia's books."

"Thank you." I gave her a soft smile. "Bryan and I are going to Falcon Bay tomorrow to get his things that he left at Emma's apartment. I'm going to search for the key while Emma is at work."

Rose sat up. "I want to come with you. You need someone else with powers to use the powder and help you look. Plus, if Emma comes home and sees us both with Byn, it'll be easy to play off. Less suspicious."

"Okay," I agreed.

"Emma just started her last class of the day so we have a few hours," Bryan told Rose and I as we walked into the apartment in Falcon Bay the next day. "I'll get my stuff together while you look."

Rose glanced around the living room. "We should look in Emma's bedroom first."

I agreed and led the way down the hall. Emma's bedroom was decorated much like the rest of the apartment. Soft pinks and mint greens. Neon signs on the walls and a framed photo of her and Troy on the bedside table.

Rose took out the small pouch of enchanted dust and grabbed a handful.

"Does that stuff leave any trace?" I asked before Rose began. "I don't want Emma to know we were snooping around in her bedroom. She barely tolerates me after everything with the ledger and her dad."

"Oh." Rose looked down at the dust in her hand. "Honestly, I don't know. But we'll do a cleaning spell before we go. We'll leave everything the way we found it."

I nodded as Rose held the dust in her open hand and gently blew. Little particles flew from her hand and floated around the room, sparkling in the daylight like a cloud of glitter. The dust swam through the air, spreading across Emma's bedroom. The tiny particles spread to every surface in the room and settled slowly.

"Sooo," I drug out the syllables. "I've never actually used this stuff before. What's it supposed to do?"

"Reveal hidden things. It counters against cloaking spells, but nothing in here seems to be cloaked." Rose walked over to the closet and slid the door back. The dust had gone in through the cracks and settled on the clothes hanging up.

I barely opened the first drawer of Emma's dresser to see socks covered in the glittering powder. After looking around a bit more, the dust didn't seem to sense anything. "We can cross her bedroom off the list."

"Clean this up? I'm going to check the living room."

"Check Byn's room too," I told Rose as she left the room.

With a wave of my hand, all the magic dust swirled up from its resting places and formed a cloud that hovered over Emma's bedroom. The dust floated in place before I sent it back to the pouch Rose held in the living room. The dust answered my call and returned to its home. For good measure, I waved my hand again, making sure we left everything in its proper place.

An internal conflict I'd been struggling with stirred in my stomach. I genuinely liked Emma. Prior to Lauren and I exposing our powers to her, Emma and I were friends. I wanted to go back to that, but I didn't think we ever could. I hated it. She was one of Bryan's closest friends. He had lived with her for years as they attended university together. What Bryan and I consider to be our first date took place at her bonfire. Dmitri and I lived with her boyfriend. She and Ashley were best friends.

I was smack in the middle of her circle. Yes, I hated her sister and her father. Her mother crept towards the top of my list, but I didn't hate *her*.

With a sigh, I left Emma's bedroom and closed the door behind me. Meeting Rose in the living room, I glanced around at the settled dust on all the furniture. "How's it going in here?"

"Nothing yet," Rose answered. "I don't think it's here."

"I don't either, but we had to make sure before we crossed it off the list."

Bryan came out from the bedroom with a duffle bag hanging from his shoulder. "We can check that house Henry is renting out here too."

"Hopefully no one is living in it," Rose muttered.

"I doubt he'd be spending money on an empty house." Bryan glanced around the room. "Nothing here?"

"No, it doesn't look like it." Rose used her power to gather up all the dust she'd scattered around and secured it in the bag. She tied the string around the opening and put the dust in her pocket. "Do you have everything?"

Bryan nodded. "Yeah, I'm ready to go."

His feelings had been conflicting all day. Bryan had been nervous on the drive over, he gripped the steering wheel and answered with short sentences when Rose and I spoke to him. He had been anxious when we pulled into the apartment complex, staying in his seat for a few moments longer than usual. I couldn't tell if he had been worried we'd find Emma hiding something or if he had been sad about leaving FBU. His sadness coursed through me while he packed up his things, but now standing in the living room with his bag, a wave of relief washed over him. Bryan let out a deep breath and led the way to the front door.

We got back into Bryan's Jeep and followed the directions on my phone to Henry Drake's rental house. We drove out of the city, along a road that followed the coastline. Pine trees towered over the road as a fog rolled in from the sea.

A small house with a big tree in the middle of the yard stood before us. Brand new wood created a fence around the perimeter and the paint on the house looked new. The rental had been maintained with a gray sedan parked in the driveway. Someone obviously lived there. We parked down the street and snuck up to the other side of the fence.

Rose pulled out the bag of magic dust and blew it towards the house.

Nothing.

With a defeated sigh, Rose called the dust back and shoved the bag into her pocket. "There's nothing here. We need to head back if we're going to get to the cottage in time for Ostara."

I nodded. "At least now we know."

"So what exactly do you guys do on these holidays?" Bryan asked curiously, beginning the walk back to the car.

"It's the first day of Spring," I answered. "Rayn is making dinner and we are hosting those witches from Mia's services."

"I'm going to do some work in the garden. It's been in such sad shape since Mia passed, and someone needs to keep it alive," Rose replied. "It's to celebrate the sun coming back after the darkness of winter. Harmony wants to do something special to honor Mia and Warren."

"That sounds nice." Bryan opened the car door. He barely sat in the seat before he stopped. Bryan leaned over the steering wheel and squinted his eyes. "Do you see that?"

"No?" I searched the side of the road, but nothing stood out to me.

He got out of the car in a rush. Rose and I followed him around the side of the fence where trees grew along the property line. The closer we got, I finally saw it.

A diamond and circle with a crooked cross carved into the tree.

The Renati symbol.

"How did you see that?" Rose reached out her hand to touch the tree but stopped herself.

"I don't know..." Bryan answered. "To be honest, something in my head told me to pay attention to the trees over here."

"That's your intuition, baby." I smiled at him and moved closer to the symbol.

"Don't touch it," Rose warned.

I turned to look at Rose. "Do you sense anything buried in the dirt here?"

Rose closed her eyes and nodded. "It's not very strong...but something is here."

She waved her hand, and the dirt scooped away, neatly piling itself at the base of the tree. A small metal box lay in the dirt, worn and rusted, probably buried for years. I got down on my knees to take a better look but there were no markings or words on the box. No indication of who it might belong to other than the symbol on the tree it had been buried under.

"Do you think the key stem is in there?" Bryan asked behind me.

"Could it be that easy?" I dared to reach out towards the box. My heartbeat pounded in my ears as my trembling fingers neared the box.

"Be careful," Rose warned over my shoulder.

I reached out with my magic, feeling for any energy to react against mine, but nothing stood out. My hand stopped inches from the box. "Rose, do you feel anything from the box?"

"No," she answered. "Only that something unnatural was in the dirt."

"Okay," I whispered, mustering all the courage I had.

I reached out and touched the box with my fingertips. No electric shocks or dark cruses appeared, only cold metal. I pulled the box from the hole and flipped the lid open.

Empty.

Bryan cussed under his breath. "All that for nothing."

I stared at the empty box before I dropped it back into the hole. I hopped up and wiped the dirt from my jeans. "Come on, let's get home before someone realizes we were here."

Chapter Twenty-Eight
Hellos and Goodbyes
Whitney

The cottage sat eerily silent as we waited for Jane and her friends to show up for Ostara. Harmony hadn't heard anything from them, but that didn't mean they wouldn't show up. They would. I had to remain hopeful. Jane would not have exposed herself if she wasn't serious about helping us.

I had been convinced that there were no Elemental supporters left in Rifton, that they all packed up and ran to the Hallow. Knowing that even a few witches on our side remained in town gave me hope.

I got up from the couch and went into the kitchen.

Rayn moved around the kitchen, clanging dishes and closing cupboards. She stood in front of the stove, stirring a saucepan filled with lemon curd, a pot of potatoes boiling next to it. A cooked tart shell cooled in the corner. Various herbs from the garden were scattered across the counter. Thyme and sage for the pork loin in the oven. Dill and chives for the cheeses on the charcuterie board. Lavender for the shortbread cookies Rayn had baked that morning. She had been buzzing around the kitchen for hours, not accepting help from anyone, of course.

Rose stayed in the backyard, getting her hands dirty out in the garden. Everything grew back lush and green, as if part of Amilia stayed with us.

Raindrops began to patter against the windows as Rose came in through the side door, kicking off her shoes. "Are they here yet?"

I shook my head.

"Okay, that's good, though. I have time to get cleaned up." Rose headed down the hall to the bathroom.

"Ray, everything smells amazing." I leaned against the counter. "Are you sure you don't want help with anything?"

"I'm okay for now. I'm not doing dishes though." Rayn grabbed the handles of the boiling pot with her bare hands and poured the cooked potatoes into a colander in the sink.

I smiled. "You never do. We'll make the boys clean up."

"Speaking of boys." Rayn leaned forward to look out the garden window above the sink where Aden stood outside with Bryan and Dmitri. The three of them were busy getting the wood together for our bonfire. "Aden said he won't be joining us for dinner."

"Why not?" I tilted my head.

"After how the Hallow witches reacted to him, he doesn't want to mess up this dinner with Jane and her friends," Rayn explained with a sigh.

"The Hallow witches knew he was a hunter because he showed up in full gear. If he's just a guy sitting at the dinner table, they won't know. You can't tell Grady is a hunter by looking at him."

Rayn poured the lemon curd into the tart crust and set the empty pot in the sink. "Keep an eye on the pork. I'm going to talk to him again." She went outside without waiting for my reply.

I stared at the dishes beginning to pile in the sink and turned on the faucet. I dumped the drained potatoes back into the pot and set them aside. Adding some soap to a wet sponge, I began scrubbing. Half of the dishes were clean when Bryan and Dmitri came up behind me.

"Harmony finally got a text. They're almost here," Mit replied. "We'll finish cleaning up."

I nodded and dried my hands off on a dish towel as a knock on the door echoed through the living room. I bolted from the kitchen to answer. Out of my periphery, I saw Harmony stand to do the same, but once she saw me move, she sat back down with a small smile. Finally, she had decided to let me take the lead and not fight over it.

"Byn, go get our sisters," I called over my shoulder before I opened the door. I smiled at Jane and the two friends she brought with her. Stepping back, I invited them inside. "Come in, please."

"Thank you." Jane returned the smile and stepped over the threshold. Her two friends followed close behind. Harmony motioned for the three of them to sit on the couch.

"Oh! Hi!" Rayn came into the living room and waved at the tall brunette Jane had brought with her. "You own the florist shop! I stopped in a while back."

The woman smiled at Rayn. "You bought the orchid. I'm Rebecca."

Rayn moved towards the woman. "I did! It's nice to see you again! Something about you stood out to me. I felt the pull. But your shop was on a list of potential Renati hideouts...?"

"My grandmother was a member, but she did not tell them about me for a reason." Rebecca cleared her throat. "After a while, she agreed less and less with their practices. She remained a member until she died, but I believe she did so not to bring attention to herself." Rebecca wrung her trembling hands together. "When my powers manifested, she taught me to keep them hidden. She taught me about Erebus and the Elementals and their talismans, but she had been skeptical that the Renati had their own version of history. I met Jane in school and felt drawn to her, but I kept my distance."

Rayn's smile beamed. "I'm glad you're here."

The third member of the group, a short blonde woman with bright blue eyes, seemed overwhelmed by everyone. Even though only my generation and the Magisters sat in the living room with them. I felt it would be too overwhelming for the entire crew to greet them, but even with the surviving Elementals in the living room, there were still seven of us and only three of them.

"Welcome," Rose said to them as she walked into the room. "Can I get any of you something to drink?"

"No, thank you," the blonde answered.

Jane let out a soft sigh. "We're nervous." She gestured to the blonde at her right. "This is Kim."

"I understand the nerves, this whole situation can be overwhelming at times, especially when you think you're alone in the fight," I reassured them as I sat on the arm of the couch opposite them. "My sister, Rayn, and I used to think we were the only Elementals until we met the rest of our generation. That was mind-blowing enough for us, and then we met the Magisters. While our magical world keeps getting bigger, it means we have more people to support us. It makes it easier for us to keep each other safe."

Jane agreed with a nod. "Yes, that's why we decided to finally approach you. We've been watching... Not in a stalker way, but I knew them already." Jane motioned towards the Magisters. "And when I saw they were back in town, I knew something had changed. Especially Dominic since, you know, he has a headstone."

Nic didn't say a word.

The blonde finally spoke. "We can see the dark cloud over Rifton, we can feel those shadow gargoyles keeping tabs on everyone. The town is changing and we don't want to run and hide."

"We appreciate that, more than you know," Lauren replied. "It will make a world of difference having more support in this fight."

"We're stronger together," Brooke added. "Tell us about yourselves, if you're comfortable. We'd love to hear from you before we talk your ears off."

I smiled at the girls, seeing them bloom into leaders. How each of them knew the right things to say and offer something new to our supporters. The parts of our souls where the previous generations lived shone brightly. We didn't need to become leaders, but remember we already were.

Jane went first. "Well, I grew up here, like I said at the memorial. My Aunt Lacey recognized my abilities quickly and taught me everything I know. She said it would be best if I did not share the truth of my powers with many people, she always said Rifton was a safe place for witches as long as they kept it to themselves. I don't think anyone expected me to have powers since neither of my parents did."

"I didn't actually reach out to Jane until Rayn came into my shop. I always knew there were witches in Rifton, a few who weren't Renati. But when I met Rayn, I saw her ring and suspected it was a talisman. I knew the Elementals were back," Rebecca replied.

"Wait, really?" Rayn asked.

Rebecca nodded. "My grandmother may have been Renati but she knew all about the talismans and told me stories about the Elementals, both good and bad. Kim is from out of town, though. So we have been catching her up on all the lore."

"I met Kim in college and we quickly realized we were the same," Jane told us.

"My parents thought I was crazy for leaving Portland for the community college here in town, but I always found the Dark Star Forest beautiful. My family would come here for holidays sometimes, to go camping and see the bay. I could never forget about it," Kim explained.

"The pull," Rayn smiled. "Do you guys know about the Allurement?"

Kim shook her head.

While Rayn explained what the Allurements were and how the powerhouses of magic drew witches to the forest, I excused myself and went into the kitchen. Our guests may not have accepted any refreshments, but I needed coffee. I poured myself a cup and opened up the fridge, searching for the container of oak milk. When I closed the fridge door, Abe stood in the kitchen with me.

"Hi," I said to him, going back to my coffee.

He smiled. "I had a feeling you were in here caffeinating. Mind if I get some too?"

"Of course not." I pulled another coffee mug from the cupboard and poured him a cup. "How are you feeling?"

"I'm okay," he answered and poured some milk into his coffee. "Wanted to check on you."

"I am...I am here," I answered. "I'm not great but I'm not falling apart, just...existing."

Abe nodded and took a drink. "I'm kind of surprised we have guests, I didn't think there was any support left in town."

"I know, me too."

He glanced over his shoulder. "We should, um, be mindful though. In case this is a trap."

"Oh, I don't think it is."

"Probably not, but I wouldn't put it past the Renati to send fake supporters into this house and have them gain our trust only to turn on us."

"You have a good point." I leaned against the counter. "Tom Campbell did that very thing."

"I worry, that's all." Abe traced the rim of his coffee mug. "I have a hard time trusting anyone, and we have to take care of our own. If those three are our people, then that's great but we have to make sure first."

I tilted my head. "How do we vet that?"

"The brand. They all have it." Abe rubbed his wrist where the brand remained on his skin.

"So we force them to show us their wrists?"

"Not all Renati wear the brand on their wrists," Abe lowered his voice.

"Wait." I set down my coffee cup. "They don't?"

He shook his head. "Most of them do, but they get to choose where the mark goes. Some of the higher ups choose to put it in a more discrete location. I know for a fact Henry Drake doesn't have it on his wrist."

"That complicates things slightly, doesn't it?"

Abe nodded. "I don't recognize any of them as Renati members, so that's something. I also don't know all the members." Abe tapped his thumb on the side of his coffee cup. "This could potentially be one of their trials to get in, so they wouldn't have a mark yet."

"What trial?"

Abe cleared his throat. "Everyone who joins the Renati has to go through some sort of trial. It's different for everyone though, they customize the tasks based on the person, since everyone has different things that matter to them."

"Oh," I paused for a moment. "What about your trial?"

"I, uh." Abe turned his head away. "Let's just say I was friends with someone a while ago and now I'm not."

I nodded, accepting his desire for privacy. "I understand." I reached out and put my hand on his shoulder. "Thanks for looking out for us. We need to make sure the Elemental support left in Rifton feels safe and, well, supported."

"You converted me, that's gotta look good for your cause."

"You left the Renati before we met," I pointed out.

"Yeah, but I didn't believe the Elementals were true leaders until you." Abe took his coffee to the back porch.

After dinner, we all gathered in the backyard and circled around the firepit. A bundle of wood had been arranged in a cone shape, decorated at the top with various flowers. I had never been around this many witches before, let alone preparing to perform a ritual with them. Bryan and Aden remained on the back porch, talking amongst themselves. Aden had requested to stay inside but Bryan wanted to watch.

"Dominic, put out that cigarette so we can start," Harmony snapped, glaring across the yard.

"Shit, are you waiting on me?" Nic put his cigarette out on the bottom of his shoe and joined us around the firepit. "I'm sorry."

He stood next to me and smiled at Rayn. The two of them held out their hands and lit the fire pit. Flames danced up around the logs, illuminating everyone's faces. The new witches across the way from us lit up with awe seeing the Flame Elementals perform their magic.

"Everyone, please join hands and close your eyes," Harmony instructed.

All the witches in the circle did as she asked. I grabbed Rayn and Nic's hands in each of mine, their heat radiating into my skin. I initiated my second ice skin to cool myself down. Rayn didn't seem to care but Nic flinched at the cold.

"Too hot for you?" he whispered with a smirk, gently rubbing my hand with his thumb.

Harmony cleared her throat uncomfortably, looking down at Nic's empty hand. She hesitated, staring down at his fingers. Nic reached out, offering his hand to her. Harmony grabbed his hand and turned her attention back to the flames. Nic's eyes stayed on her, the fire lit up his face but his eyes sparkled looking at her. His brows were relaxed and his soft gaze admired Harmony. None of us in that circle existed except for her.

Harmony closed her eyes and let out a deep breath.

"Tonight, we say goodbye to Amilia Burnett." The tone in Nic's voice changed from when he teased me only moments ago. "One of the greatest witches and women of our time. We are honored to have met and known her. Mia was…a good mother, and a good friend. She dedicated her life to serving the Elementals, and her faith in the generations never waivered."

Harmony took over. "Amilia served as an Archivist, caring for the sacred texts. She kept them safe and protected from those who wished to end our kind and our history. She spent many years of her life searching for lost spellbooks, though some were passed down from her mother, who served as an Archivist before her. Dmitri now holds the title, as Amilia passed it onto him when she passed."

Harmony looked to Dmitri and nodded, encouraging him to take over.

"Oh," Dmitri paused as he gathered himself. I saw his fingers tighten around Abe's hand before he began to speak. "Amilia was my mother's best friend. When my sisters and I moved to town she took us under her wing and watched out for us. Amilia had her own way of doing things, but at the end of the day, she always had our best interest at heart."

Jane spoke next. "Amilia was a beloved member of the community. She welcomed everyone into the Corner Cup with a smile and warm heart. Amilia provided a place in this town where we could go to relax or re-energize, whatever we needed. She saw the darkness that lurked in Rifton for those of us living in hiding and gave us a space to feel at ease."

Harmony smiled at them but any sliver of joy on her face disappeared. "Tonight we say goodbye to Warren Edwards," she sniffled as a tear fell down her cheek. "Warren was my…mine and Dominic's brother, a beloved member of his Elemental generation. He cared for us deeply. He did not hesitate to return to Rifton with me when we received news of the new generation and the talismans."

Nic cleared his throat. "Warren was kind and patient with an infectious laugh. He cared for his loved ones and protected them fiercely. I…I wish we had more time, but I'm grateful for the time we did spend. And I take comfort knowing that I will see him on the other side."

"See you on the other side," Harmony whispered, staring into the flames.

"Warren was the only other person like me in this world," Lauren spoke next. "He taught me so much more than how to take full control and potential of my powers. He taught me, tried to teach me at least, that holding onto the past will only suffocate you. He told me I needed to move forward and honor the memories of the people I've lost, so I will honor his memory by trying to live by those words."

Silence fell over us and no one dared to break it. The energy of the circle felt warm and comforting, blending with the roaring fire before us. A lightness hung in the air; content and at ease as if Amilia and Warren both stood with us. They were at peace and without anger. They held no regrets for the way their lives ended and I felt lighter. The tension in my shoulders faded and I squeezed Nic and Rayn's hands.

Harmony let go of Nic's hand and reached down to grab a handful of dirt. She motioned for the rest of us to join her. After everyone had their dirt in hand, Harmony threw hers into the fire. The flames danced as the dirt hit the wood. As the rest of us unleashed our handfuls of dirt, the fire dimmed and the flames died briefly. The dirt did not extinguish the flames and it quickly caught back up.

Lauren wiped a tear from her cheek and sniffled. I knew losing Warren hit her harder than the rest of our generation. He was a good man and I mourned him in my own way, but he and Lauren…Well, they were the same person in different bodies. Rose turned to Lauren and pulled her into a hug, gently rubbing her back. Saying goodbye to Warren and Amilia weighed heavily on us all, but seeing Lauren and Rose reconnect and get to know one another for who they truly were warmed my core.

Harmony wiped her own tears, taking in a deep breath as the circle broke apart into little groups. I reached out and took her hand in mine, attempting to bring her some comfort. She squeezed my fingers and gave me a soft smile.

Bryan and Aden came from the back porch steps, joining us by the fire.

"That was beautiful." Bryan kissed the top of my head.

Aden added, "We...the hunters do a similar ceremony for the fallen, joined around the fire."

"It's, uh, it's been a while since we've done one of those." Harmony offered me a soft smile through her tears. "We did one for your mom last July and Finn died six years ago," Harmony sniffled as she glanced at Nic with heavy eyes. "Before that, we um..."

"I figured you'd do this for Abbie, but..." Nic whispered.

Harmony scoffed, snapping out of her sorrow as she hardened her gaze. "Why wouldn't we mourn you? Asshole." She let go of my hand and shoved past Nic as she retreated up the back porch.

Nic stood frozen in place, waiting until Harmony reached the top step before he went after her.

Bryan watched them both retreat before he sighed and turned to me. "How are you holding up?"

"I'm okay," I answered. "I think. I wish everyone would stop asking me that."

"Oh, I'm sorry." His heart sank into his stomach.

I pulled him into a hug and nestled against his chest. "Don't be. I want to be okay but the more I'm asked, the less I am. If that makes any sense."

"It does," he answered. "Speaking of feeling better, you didn't eat earlier. I noticed. Come inside and get some food."

At the mention, my stomach growled at me. I nodded, giving in. Bryan led the way up the stairs and into the kitchen. I sat down at the dining room table and watched him make me a plate of the leftovers. I fell back and let him take care of me.

I took a quick scan of the living room, but Harmony and Nic were nowhere in sight. I silently wondered where they were and if they were okay. I almost got up to go look for them when Jane and her friends walked into the kitchen.

"I hope we aren't interrupting," Jane said, wringing her hands together.

"Not at all. Come sit." I motioned towards the seat next to me.

The witches joined me at the table as Bryan set a plate down in front of me. I glanced up at him. "Can you please go check on Harmony and Nic? I want to make sure everything is okay."

"Um," Bryan glanced over his shoulder. "I'm sure they're fine."

"Please?"

"Okay." He gave a slight nod and left the kitchen.

I turned my attention back to the witches at the table. "Thank you so much for coming tonight, and for approaching us at the memorial. You have no idea how much it means to know our supporters are still out there. I know the Elementals have not always deserved the dedication, but you are all appreciated."

Jane smiled. "Thank you, that means more than you know. I cannot thank *you* enough. We feel the shift in Rifton, but we can also feel the tides turning."

"I think the Renati are scared," Rebecca said.

I turned to face her. "Even with the return of Erebus?"

"As the return of Erebus has fueled the Renati's hope, your return has fueled ours," Kim explained. "Renati aren't the only ones in this town with something to believe in."

"Wow, thank you." My heart swelled in my chest.

This was such a drastic difference from when we went to the Hallow. The witches in the compound were afraid of us, but the three witches sitting at the table with me were proud to be there. Their eyes smiled back when I looked at them and they sat taller than before. Taking part in the ritual with us must have helped our cause.

"We should get going." Jane stood up from her seat. "But we will be close by. If you need anything, please don't hesitate to reach out."

"We won't, and the same goes for you." I walked them to the door. "Please be safe getting home. Goodnight."

I bid them farewell and closed the door behind them, securing all four of the locks. I let out a deep sigh, feeling lighter than I had that morning. When I turned around, Bryan stood in the living room next to the fireplace.

"Did you find them?" I asked, taking my place next to him.

Bryan shifted awkwardly. "They're fine, Whit."

"But did you actually check? I–"

He cut me off. "Baby, they're in Nic's room with the door closed. I'm not inserting myself in that." He took my hand in his and softened his gaze. "Everyone's okay. Funerals are emotional, regardless of how they're done."

"You're right." I wrapped my arm around his waist and stared into the low burning flames.

Chapter Twenty-Nine
Headstones
Whitney

A few mornings later, I tiptoed on dew-covered grass past a row of headstones. The sun hid far behind the clouds on that muggy spring morning; the twisted tree branches finally getting their leaves back. Small buds of new life covered the branches and a thin layer of fog hung above the ground. I hadn't been to the cemetery since the girls and I found the Martyr's spellbook in one of the crypts. Something about the memorial on Ostara stuck with me, and I had been deep in my thoughts about those who had passed before us.

I stopped in front of a granite headstone, the engraving fairly new.

Grace Marie Dansley

May 6, 1949 - March 17, 2015

So my "grandmother" had been gone for a few years. I stared at her name; the middle name Mom had given to Rayn when she adopted us and changed our names. Whitney Anne and Rayn Grace. I wondered where Anne came from, and why she named my sister after her mother who she never saw again after running away to Kansas. Even more answers that died with my mom.

I felt the need to say something, anything. I wondered what my mom would have said if she stood here instead of me. What her final words to her mother would have been. If she mourned her mother silently or if she felt any level of relief when she heard the news of her passing. I would've given anything to talk to my mom again, but part of me felt like she didn't share that same sentiment with her own mother.

The very thought shattered my heart. I swallowed my tears and shook my head. "My mother deserved better. You should have been better to her."

I sniffled and turned my back when I saw a figure in a leather jacket across the way. I wasn't alone in the cemetery. I approached the figure casually, not worried about hiding the emotion I wore on my face or wiping away the tear that streaked down my cheek. I'd recognize those shoulders anywhere.

"Hi, Whitney," Nic answered with his back towards me.

I joined his side and looked down at the grave he stared at.

Dominic Aaron Grant

April 7, 1987 - August 30, 2004

"That must be surreal." I glanced over at him.

His face was unreadable with his brows slightly furrowed, but his eyes were soft. He had his lips curled back into a thin line with his hands shoved into his pockets. The two other names on the headstone bore the same surname.

Aaron Samuel Grant

December 3, 1965 - August 19, 2011

Katherine Josephine Grant

June 29, 1997 - October 6, 2000

"You okay?" I asked, staring down at his father and sister's graves.

"I haven't been out here since I came back. The other night at the ritual...I didn't know they had done that for me. I figured I should see this for myself." His voice was soft as he finally turned to look at me. "Why are you here?"

"The memorial has been weighing heavily on me too. And after Kyle's father approached Dmitri at the town hall, it got me wondering about my mom's family. What were they like? Why did my mom leave and never look back?" I glanced over my shoulder at my grandmother's grave.

Nic nodded slowly. "It's hard being born into the wrong family."

"Yeah," I whispered. "You know, I genuinely think Harmony meant well when she told your mother–"

Nic cut me off. "I don't care what her intentions were, she knew how her scheme would end."

I shrugged. "Maybe, but if I had the chance to see my mom again, even for a second..."

Fire burned in Nic's eyes as he snapped. "I don't know why everyone is projecting their own experiences onto *my* life. I don't like my mother. I didn't want to see her. My mother is cruel and cold. Harmony isn't looking at this from my perspective." He pointed to his chest. "She's looking at this as a mother, like it's her and Emery. It's not. Why can't any of you respect my fucking boundaries?"

I looked at the heat in his hazel eyes before I admitted, "You're right. I'm sorry."

Nic let out a hard sigh and his lips trilled. "Don't be. I'm not mad at you, just...mad." His shoulders fell as he looked up at the sky. "I wonder if she's going to leave this headstone here, now that she knows I'm alive. Maybe once I do finally kick the bucket, they'll change the dates."

"Do you even want to be buried in Rifton?"

"I'll be dead. What do I care?" He paused, turning to look at me. "I'm sorry I snapped at you."

"We're all so stressed, Nicky, I don't hold it against you." I linked my arm in his. "I wish we could find something to give us an edge. If only we could be a fly on the wall listening in to Erebus and his plans."

Nic muttered, "Things are never that simple."

"Maybe not." I glanced across the way at the columbarium filled with cremated remains. My eyes wandered to the crypt where we'd found our spellbook. Where Abbie had led us right to it. "But Brooke can see spirits, and we've received help from a certain spirit before. Maybe Brooke can find Abbie again and–"

"No," Nic cut me off, his voice sharp as a knife. He pulled his arm away from mine.

"Nicky, I know it's hard for you, but the girls and I could–"

"No," he said through his teeth, sterner this time.

"But we could–"

"Are you deaf? I said no!"

"I don't need your permission," I snapped back.

His eyes glazed over with fear. "Whitney, don't do this to me."

"You don't have to be there. She hasn't moved on yet if Brooke has seen her before." I motioned towards the crypt. "Do you know what kind of intel she could gather for us?"

"How is telling me she hadn't moved on supposed to land any better?" Nic backed away from me. "I...I can't handle it."

"Okay." I sighed, knowing I fought a losing battle.

Nic could put his foot down all day long, but that didn't mean I couldn't take my idea to Brooke. I couldn't begin to wrap my head around how painful that night had been for Nic, but maybe this could give him some closure. Maybe this could give us an edge.

"So, what do you think?" I asked after taking my idea to the girls.

Brooke sat quietly and I watched the wheels slowly turning in her head. "I haven't seen her since we found the book in the crypt. I don't know if she's still around."

"Is there a way to summon her?" Lauren asked, crossing her long arms.

"There is, but..." Brooke paused. "There is. I found a spell from Gabriel where a Soul Elemental could summon a spirit and they could be temporarily seen by those in the summoning circle."

"A seance," Rose replied. "Call it what it is."

"Which is why I've never brought it up, and why I'm so hesitant to perform it," Brooke said. "It's risky pushing Nic's emotions like that or we could end up summoning something else. It could go wrong, like, really wrong."

Rayn shifted in her seat. "But it's Amilia's daughter and she's already helped us. We know who we're summoning, we aren't going in without any idea of who she is."

"The Magisters would shit themselves if they knew we were considering this," Lauren pointed out.

"Nic yelled at me when I mentioned the idea to him," I told the girls. "He's in a delicate place. If we involve them in this, I'm worried it'll push him over the edge. But on the other hand, I think he needs closure and if I can give him that, I want to try."

Brooke sighed, giving me a side eye. "I question your intentions, but fine. We can try if we all agree to it."

Lauren nodded. "Yeah, I'm down. Why not?"

"I think contacting Abbie is a good idea, but I'm not sure about involving the Magisters." Rose chewed on her bottom lip. "That part of the plan could backfire."

"If it does, I'll take care of it. I'll handle Dominic," I attempted to put my generation at ease.

"You're sure about this?" Rayn asked, not hiding her concern.

I nodded. "Yes, I'm sure."

I became less and less sure about my decision as we led the way through the cemetery with Harmony and Nic dragging their feet behind us. Harmony didn't explode like Nic had, but the spell we wanted to perform required a personal item of Abbie's and we needed the Magisters to confirm what all in the cottage had belonged to her.

Nic had not spoken to or looked at me all night.

Brooke took charge of the spell, putting Abbie's scarf in the middle of our circle. We formed it in front of her grave, buried in the same plot as her father, Jackson. The same plot where Amilia's remains would be placed. I stood in between Rose and Rayn, glancing over to see Nic standing a yard away from us.

"Nicky, you have to be part of the circle in order to see her." I held out my hand to him.

"I don't want to see her," he snapped back through clenched teeth.

Harmony sighed and stepped out of the circle, moving into Nic's personal space. "Hey," she whispered to him. "It'll be okay. However this goes, and I doubt it will go poorly, I'm right here. Whit's over there too. We're here and we've got you."

Nic turned his head away from her and closed his eyes.

"I'm right here." Harmony reached out and touched his elbow. "I've got you."

"Okay," he muttered.

Nic joined the circle in between Harmony and Rayn.

"I don't want to risk losing the connection, so continue holding hands the entire time." Brooke looked at Nic from across the circle. "And keep yourself together. Everyone stay focused."

Rayn lit the stick of incense we'd brought, the smoke leaving the tip in a chaotic, swirling string. Brooke walked around the outside of the circle, cleansing the area. After she stood back in her original spot, Brooke placed a large chunk of jade on top of Abbie's scarf. She offered out her hands and we all closed the circle, joining hands with one another.

Brooke closed her eyes. "We call on you, Abigail Burnett. Show yourself to our circle and hear our words. We call on you."

Fog rolled in around our ankles, rising to our knees. I looked around nervously, sure that something would reach out of the fog and pull us into the earth. The fog pooled into the middle of our circle and rose higher until it blocked our vision. I coughed on the rich earthy scent as the fog lifted above us.

When my vision became clear again, a young woman stood in the middle of our circle on top of the scarf with her back to me. Her translucent form floated and her feet never touched the ground, but she was there.

Harmony gasped, pulling Abbie's attention to her.

"Honey," Abbie's voice had a slight echo to it. "Nicky."

Nic fell to his knees, staring up at her. His sudden movement jerked on Rayn and Harmony's hands and nearly pulled them down with him. His breath caught in his throat and his eyes glazed over in tears. Harmony kept a tight grip on Nic's hand, her knuckles turning white. The two of them stood frozen in time. They needed a moment to process and we could not waste our opportunity to speak with her.

"Abbie, can you hear us?" Brooke asked, stepping into the ghost's line of sight.

Abbie turned to Brooke and nodded.

"We called you because we need your help. Erebus is back and we have to know what the Renati are planning, if they've made any moves. Surely you've seen something," I began, jumping right into it.

Abbie smirked at me. "Calling in the reinforcements, I see."

"Have you seen anything?" Brooke repeated my question.

"I see many things," Abbie replied, spinning around slowly to look at us. "Erebus does not rest, he plots and plans. He waits for the perfect moment to pounce. He is calculating and patient."

"Oh, good. Riddles. She is Mia's daughter," Rose leaned in to mutter to me.

Abbie whipped around to Rose. "Do you want my help or not?"

Rose stared back at her with wide eyes.

"Abbie," Harmony said her name, soft and uncertain. Her voice quivered as she spoke. "What is he planning?"

"He seeks the palace. He's already sent spies into Maggie's home. She is none the wiser, unsuspecting. You will delay going there yourselves and pay a price," Abbie answered. "Erebus plans the blood sacrifice. Many of the Renati have offered themselves, and their children, in place. They feel it is a great honor to do so."

"Their children?" Lauren asked, horrified. "You can't be serious!"

"He is a god to them, resurrected and reborn." Abbie turned to look at me. "The twins are not all one-sided. As sisters they have many things in common, and they both have weaknesses to be exploited. Take advantage."

I nodded, trying to keep up with her riddles. The twins, Emma and Serenity. Got it.

Abbie looked to Rayn next. "The hunters are working with members of the Renati. Erebus does not know. The rogue Renati broke the shield and let them in. You must snuff the hunters out and do it quickly, or they'll steal from you."

"Wait, wait, wait." Rayn shook her head. "Working *with* the hunters?"

"That is all. I am fading and I need a moment alone with my own." Abbie turned to face Harmony. "You have been made small and weak for too long. Break free and admit your heart's desire, Honey, before it's too late. You cannot spend this life denying your truth."

Harmony took a step back, quickly looking away from Abbie.

Abbie finally looked down at Nic. "Nicky, do you like your present?"

"What?" The word barely left his lips.

"I sent your gift in a dream. Have you not enjoyed her company?"

Nic furrowed his brow, but stayed silent.

I dared speak. "You showed Nic the dream of Rayn and I in the meadow?"

Abbie spoke only to Nic. "Too long, your wounds have been gaping. You deserve to heal, and she is healing you, putting you back together. You needed a true friend. Home is here in the water, and it has always been. Your gift, for carrying too much for too long. Let the guilt go, Nicky. Let me go."

"I can't," he whispered, hanging his head.

Abbie bent down before him tilting her head to see his face. "You will. The clock ticks and you must not waste the minutes. Two sides of the same coin. One to heal and one to love. My gift to my dearest friend."

Nic turned his head up slightly to look at her. He nodded with tears streaming down his face. My heart ached watching him crumble at her feet, finally facing the demons that he had buried for so long. Finally allowing himself to try and let go, to move forward from the night that had haunted him for over a decade, shaping his entire core.

"I am fading." Abbie straightened and looked to Rayn and I once more, gazing back and forth between us. "Your mother is very proud of you."

All the air left my lungs from the suckerpunch her words delivered. The fog descended down to the earth and as it settled into the ground, Abbie's spirit vanished.

Nic broke the circle and collapsed forward onto his hands, hyperventilating. Rose looked at me with wide eyes.

This is what the girls were afraid of; that it would be too much to handle and backfire. But we received valuable information from Abbie, now I needed to take care of the rest.

I fell to my knees next to Nic and wrapped him in my arms. He turned to me without hesitation, burying his face into my neck. I held him close, gently rubbing his back. Nic cried deeply, his chest heaving as he held onto me for dear life. His weight pushed against me, but I kept him upright, tightening my grip around him.

"It's okay. You're going to be okay," I whispered into his dark hair over and over again.

Harmony stood over us, staring down at Nic falling apart in my arms. She watched my hands comfort him and finally her eyes met mine, lined with tears. "One to heal," she whispered, the words catching in her throat.

"One to love," I said back to her.

Both of us knew who we were.

Chapter Thirty

Incapable

Whitney

The next few nights were spent in recovery mode. I left Nic and Harmony alone, after ensuring they were both okay. I went to work then straight home, lying in bed with Bryan and enjoying the silence. There were many things Abbie said that bothered me, but so many other conversations I'd heard recently hung heavy on my heart.

Bryan rolled over to face me. "Talk to me."

I let out a deep sigh. "Remember when I told you one of the council members approached Dmitri and said they were his grandfather?"

Bryan nodded, waiting for me to continue.

"Will Ward. Are you familiar with the family at all?"

"Only by name," Bryan answered. "I know he's been on the council forever. He's the guy?"

"Yeah." I chewed on my bottom lip. "He, uh, he told Dmitri that his father came looking for them and when he finally found them, my mom killed him."

Bryan's eyes widened. "That your mom killed Dmitri's father? That's quite the accusation."

The words sat on the tip of my tongue, knowing once I spoke them aloud, they were no longer a thought in my head. I could no longer pretend it wasn't real. "I remember it."

He stared back at me. "Remember what, exactly?"

I relayed the memory to Bryan as best I could. How I thought I had repressed the memory because my mom insisted it had all been a bad dream. We weren't remembering the night clearly. She told us enough times that I began to believe her. I hadn't asked Rayn yet, worried that if I did and she remembered too and then it would be real.

"What did Dmitri say?" Bryan finally asked.

I shook my head. "I haven't told him...that's something I wanted to get your opinion on." I blinked back the tears that threatened to blur my vision. "How do I tell him something like that?"

Bryan stared at me for a moment. "I don't think we should. Not right now at least."

I tilted my head. "We should keep this from him?"

"You do whatever you feel is best, but if you're asking for my input, yes. I don't think now is a good time to drop this kind of information on him. I think it'll do more harm than good." Bryan reached out and pulled me close to him. "It'll change the way he feels about your mom, it'll over take every memory he has of her. Everything he's been clinging to since she died. I don't know if the truth is worth it."

I knew Bryan had a valid point. This wasn't as simple as telling Dmitri that he didn't remember an event properly. This would change his entire world. Like Harmony had said, if Kyle got his hands on Dmitri, he would've done everything he could to convert my brother.

"Is there ever a right time to tell him something like this?" I rested my head against Bryan's chest. The steady rhythm of his heartbeat echoed against my cheek.

"Probably not." Bryan rubbed my back as he pulled me in closer. "Are *you* okay? This is a lot to process and it happened when you were so young."

"I don't know, honestly." Tears stung my eyes as my heart constricted in my chest. "I've been sitting with it. I'm afraid to bring it up to Rayn. I don't know what to think. I mean...if Kyle posed a threat, I know my mom would do anything she could to protect us. She left Rifton to keep Dmitri safe. She must've been so scared, defending us all alone. I'm heartbroken thinking about it, not because I think less of her, but it must've destroyed her. She had to have loved him at some point, don't you think?"

Bryan nodded. "Maybe, yeah. They did have a baby together."

I wiped a tear away. "Right? I worry that my mom carried too much by herself. That's what makes me look at her differently, knowing that she didn't have anyone to carry that burden with her." My breath caught in my throat. "I wish I could tell her that I see her, that I appreciate everything she did for us."

Bryan kissed the top of my head and tightened his arms around me. "She knows, baby. She's still with you."

I grabbed a handful of his shirt, attempting to ground myself. "I won't tell Dmitri."

"If that's what you want to do, I support whatever decision you make." He kissed me again. "But I agree that you're making the right choice."

"Mit is finally finding some solid ground, you know? He has Abe, and it seems like things are going well between them."

Bryan shifted his weight. "Seventeen is such a hard age. Everything felt like the end of the world when I was that age." He ran his fingers up my back. "I also want to keep things as good as possible for Mit. Life hasn't been easy on him, on any of you."

"I know." I lifted my head and pressed a soft kiss to his lips. "Thank you for talking this out with me."

"Thank you for trusting me with it," he whispered against my lips.

) ·) · ● · (· (

When I got to the cottage the following night, Rose and Dmitri were in front of the fire splitting a package of Pop-Tarts.

"What are you guys up to?" I asked, noticing Amilia's journal open on the couch between them.

"I wanted to see if Mia had written much about Abbie in here," Rose replied. "Especially after the other night. She's like me, you know? I finally got to meet my Magister and she snapped at me."

I sat down next to her on the couch. "I'm sorry, Rosie."

"You have Harmony and Rayn has Nic. I know he's gone but Lauren had some time with Warren to at least get to know him." Rose's shoulders fell. "Brooke may not have met Finn, but she feels so connected to Gabriel. I am shit out of luck and it sucks."

"I understand." I reached out and covered her hand with mine. "I wish you could have had time to talk with her. I didn't realize the conversation would be so short."

She shrugged. "It was a hectic night, but I still want to learn more. I think Abbie has been in the spirit world for so long without crossing over, that she's losing herself a bit."

"But witches don't believe in the afterlife? They believe in reincarnation, right?" Dmitri asked. "What is she waiting for?"

I chewed on the inside of my cheek. "Generations used to all die together so that the Elemental magic could pass on to the newest generation."

Rose's eyes grew. "Does that mean she can't move on until the entire generation is dead?"

"I don't know, honestly." My heart skipped a beat at the realization. "If it is, she's going to be waiting a long time. Nic's only thirty."

"That's sad." Rose's shoulders fell.

"Hey, maybe we can contact her again? Just for you and her to talk. We won't bring the Magisters," I offered.

"I'd like that." Rose gave a soft nod. "By the way, I found those herbs you were asking about. The littiory and storm vine."

My back straightened. "And?"

"Mia had some dried storm vine here in her supply, it's in the pantry. Littiory oil was a little harder to track down, but I got in touch with Rebecca and she had some seeds," Rose explained. "So they're ready whenever you need them."

I sighed in relief. "You are a miracle worker, you know that?"

Rose waved me off. "Aw, shucks. It's nothing really, if it'll help you do what you need to do, I'm happy to help."

"You're the best. I know Ray and Lauren are closing CC, but where is everyone else?" I glanced around the quiet cottage. Usually there were so many people here it made processing thoughts difficult. Laughter typically flowed from one of the bedrooms and dishes would clang in the kitchen. The cottage was silent enough to hear a pin drop.

"Harmony is out somewhere with Jerry. Emery is asleep up in the loft. Nic and Byn are outside," Rose replied.

"Outside? What are they doing?" I asked, tilting my head.

"Hanging out, I think? Nic went outside to smoke and Byn went with him," Dmitri explained.

I knew they had gotten friendlier than their first interactions but picturing Bryan and Nic outside hanging out warmed my entire soul. Our crew wouldn't be able to survive if we didn't stick together. Everyone didn't click at first, but we had finally reached a point where my loved ones seemed to feel as close as I hoped they would.

"I'll go talk to them, see how Nicky is feeling." I got up from the couch and headed to the back porch.

The guys weren't anywhere in sight, but I heard their giggles echo through the night towards the back of the property. As I got closer to where they'd hidden themselves, I could smell that Nic hadn't lit a cigarette.

"What are you two stoners doing back here?" I laughed, finding them sitting in the grass by the back fence.

"I was going to seduce him, but here you are, foiling my plans." Nic offered the joint back to Bryan.

"In another life, man." Bryan laughed and put his arm out, welcoming me against his side. "Did you have a good day, baby?"

"Good enough. How are you feeling, Nicky?"

He brushed me off. "I'm fine."

"Are you sure?"

Nic let out a deep sigh. "I will be."

I accepted that would be the most anyone could ask of him, so I decided to change the subject. "We need to talk about Mia's part of the key."

"Do we?" Nic lifted a brow.

"Nicky, come on. You're way too nonchalant about it, and it's stressing me out."

Nic turned to Bryan. "She doesn't trust me."

Bryan shrugged and took a hit. "We have to worry about it eventually, don't we? The key won't work without all three pieces."

"I'd be a lot more trusting if you were honest with me," I added.

Nic leaned forward, resting his elbows on his knees. "I've never lied to you about anything. After we get the stem from Bonnie Drake, our next focus needs to be Maggie Daniels and the palace, that's the truth. We need to leave the second we get the stem."

I lifted a brow. "So you two are back here getting high as you plan our next big adventure? Because the whole plan to the Hallow fell apart real quick."

Nic tilted his head. "Well, lucky for us, I won't let that happen again."

"Nic, I can never tell if your confidence is trustworthy or if you talk out of your ass." Bryan handed the joint to me.

I stared at it for a moment, the smoke wafting up into the air.

Why not?

I took the joint from Bryan and inhaled. My lungs immediately rejected the smoke and I coughed into his shoulder. Bryan patted my back and kissed the top of my head. My eyes blurred over in tears but my throat finally cleared after another few good coughs. It had been a long time since I'd partaken in such activities, and my body seemed to have forgotten it had ever touched this stuff before.

"Don't hurt yourself." Nic leaned against the fence and laughed. "Kiddo, you know me. You know I'm all in, right?"

I nodded.

"Trust me. After we get the Renati's piece, the palace is next."

"And you've never been there? The palace?" Bryan asked. He took the joint from my fingers and handed it back to Nic.

Nic shook his head and took the joint. "Nah. Maggie did not leave Rifton on good terms with the other coven members. They broke up, and ending friendships between women like that? I'm honestly not sure how we'll be received."

Footsteps and two voices came through the backyard with the creak of the garden gate. Harmony's harsh tone cut through the breeze. The chill of her anger froze the grass all the way up to where we sat against the fence. I glanced over at Nic and Bryan, both still as statues.

Harmony hissed, "I didn't ask for this! *You* made the executive decision to show up here unannounced and insert yourself. I let you back in for Emery's sake, but you lost all right to me last year."

"You would rather live the rest of your life miserable and alone than admit you made a mistake," Jerry's voice shot back.

"*I* made a mistake? You don't get to dictate the narrative in your favor because you decided to try after I'd already called it quits."

Oh this was ugly.

I wished I could mentally reach out to Harmony and let her know she had a hidden audience. Instead, I stood up on my tingling legs and called out to her. "Harmony?"

Harmony snapped around to face me. "What the fuck are you doing back here?"

"Uh, just...you know, smoking weed," I stammered.

"Dominic, you're a terrible influence." Harmony crossed her arms, looking right at where Nic sat under the darkness of the trees. She seemed to hide it well, but the blush of embarrassment on her cheeks reflected off the porch lights.

Jerry waltzed over to us, brushing past Harmony with a stiff shoulder. The mood changed as he approached, like all the air had been sucked out of the room. Considering we were outside, that was an impressive feat. "So, Nic, did you used to have a red and black flannel with your initials stitched on the tag?"

Harmony's lips parted in a silent gasp and my heart dropped into my stomach.

Nic stared back at Jerry, his face unreadable. "That's oddly specific."

"I'm trying to wrap my head around when all this started," Jerry said.

Nic didn't dare glance at Harmony, but he did look sideways at me. Casually, Nic lifted the joint back to his lips and took a drag. "I'm not sure I follow."

"Don't play dumb with me," Jerry snapped, turning back to Harmony. "Unless there is something *you* want to tell me."

Harmony sucked in a breath. "If you want to talk, we can go talk in private but I'm not doing this with an audience."

"Why not? You're embarrassed for everyone to know you've been having an affair?" Jerry crossed his arms.

Bryan shifted uncomfortably and got up on his feet, offering me his hand. "We should probably go."

"Don't," Nic whispered under his breath. "I need witnesses."

"We are separated, Jerry." Harmony crossed her arms, that icy glare washing over her face as she turned to Jerry. "You don't know what you're talking about. Nic has moved on and I'm trying to do the same."

"Moved on?" Nic asked, leaning forward. "What?"

Harmony shot daggers at him with her eyes. "I saw that interaction at the Corner Cup. That guy slipped you his number, you took it."

Nic shook his head. "I never called him. I never wanted to call him, Honey."

Harmony's shoulders fell. "Oh."

Jerry's face turned a deep shade of angry red. "Is this your way of admitting you're sleeping with someone?"

"Oh, fuck you, Jerry." Harmony whipped back to face him. "You want to talk about affairs?"

"That was years ago and we got past it." Jerry took a step towards her.

Harmony shook her head. "No, *you* got to pretend it never happened. *I*, on the other hand, don't forget anything."

"So, this is all to get back at me for my mistake. That's not fair to me, Harmony. It's not fair for you to let me walk around this town like a fool when the other man is right there in front of me." Jerry pointed his finger where Nic sat.

Frost covered the grass where Harmony stood as she snapped, "Nic isn't the other man, Jerry, *you* are."

Jerry scoffed. "How can I be the other man when we are still legally married with a child?"

Her shoulders fell as she admitted, "Because if I knew Nic was out there somewhere, you and I would not be married with a child."

All the air left Nic's lungs as he gasped, sitting back like the wind had been knocked out of him. This felt too personal. This shouldn't be a conversation I witnessed. I hadn't agreed with the way Harmony had behaved, but part of me understood it. If I thought something horrible had happened to Bryan…if I thought he was gone, who knows where grief would have taken me. Who knows what kind of decisions I would have made.

One thing I knew for sure, Jerry never looked at Harmony the way Dominic did. That meant something to me.

Harmony continued on. "You and I were never supposed to happen and I'm sorry for the part I played in this. But we were over a long time ago. The separation trial, the therapy…none of it worked. For Emery's sake, I held on even though it already died. But it's not fair to her, and it's not fair to either of us. Nic isn't the reason you and I are done, Jerry, but if you need someone to blame because accepting your own faults is too hard for you, then do whatever you need to. You make sure you can sleep well at night and I will try to do the same."

Jerry didn't say a word to Harmony. He turned and charged at Nic, who remained seated on the dirt. Nic barely moved, putting his hands up as Jerry froze in place. Jerry struggled to move, straining as he tried to break free from the spell holding him in place.

Nic tilted his head and took another drag from the joint. "I don't want to hurt you, Jerry."

"W-what is this?" Jerry stammered, wincing as he tried to move again. "What the fuck is this?"

"Ugh," Harmony groaned, rubbing her face. "We're going to have to charm him now."

"Charm?" Jerry shrieked. "What is that?"

"I can't deal with this. Someone charm him and get him to go back to Seattle. Emery is staying here in Rifton with me." Harmony turned and headed back to the house.

"Wait." I jogged after her as Nic held Jerry firmly in place. "Are you sure it's safe here for Emery? With everything going on?"

"I've missed out on enough time with her, I'm not giving up another second. She's staying with me."

I nodded slowly, not wanting to push her over the edge. "Okay…okay. I'll take care of Jerry."

"Thank you. I-I'm sorry about all this," Harmony whispered. She wiped a stray tear off her cheek before she marched up the back porch steps and into the cottage.

"Nic, let him go," I ordered, heading back over to the men.

Bryan remained frozen in place as if he was the one behind held down by a spell. He looked at me with raised brows as secondhand embarrassment coursed through his body. I felt it too, for all three of the people involved in this mess.

"Jerry," I said his name, waiting for his attention. "Jerry, look at me."

His hateful eyes remained locked on Dominic. A snarl curled his lips and I was certain that Jerry would swing at Nic if he let go. I said his name again but he ignored me.

"I could fucking kill you both," Jerry muttered, his eyes daggers as he stared Nic down.

"Keep threatening my woman and see how that goes over for you." Nic grit his teeth.

"Fine, I'll do it. Since you're already gazing longingly into my eyes." Nic hopped up. The joint held loose in his fingers, his free hand out towards Jerry so the spell wouldn't break. Nic looked deep into Jerry's eyes and slowly, his face relaxed. The hatred melted off Jerry as Nic spoke. "You and Harmony are done. Your marriage is over. The therapy didn't work, but you're going to stay civil for Emery's sake. She will be staying here with Harmony and you will return back to Seattle and give them both space. You won't call and you will wait until she is ready to speak to you. You will tell your friends and family that things ended amicably and you wish Harmony nothing but the best. You will not remember this conversation."

Jerry nodded calmly and Nic finally dared to drop the spell. Jerry stood there for a moment, he and Nic still locked in a staring contest before Jerry slowly left the backyard. He left through the side gate and got into his car. None of us said a word until his car disappeared from sight.

"That didn't feel right," Bryan finally spoke. "You shouldn't have charmed him."

Nic turned to look at Bryan, throwing his hands into the air. "What do you suggest, then? I should have let him swing on me? Should I have let him swing on Harmony?"

"No, of course not, but you can't go around charming everyone to get your way, either. It's not right to get into people's heads," Bryan argued. "You do it way too much, Nic."

Nic's frustrated sigh turned into a growl. "There's more important things going on right now than Harmony's sham marriage to some powerless asshole. Do you have any idea how him being here fucked me up?"

Bryan shook his head. "That's always your excuse. That there are more important things, bigger things happening, but you can't lose your humanity in the process." Bryan motioned back and forth between him and Nic. "We have to maintain some level of integrity if we're going to be able to still look in the mirror. Our choices still matter."

Nic's shoulders fell and his voice sobered. "Mine don't."

"Nic–"

"Your integrity matters, Bryan, but not mine." Nic put the joint between his lips and headed back to the house.

"I don't even know what to say," I admitted, watching Nic's back.

Bryan trilled his lips. "Promise me we'll never get that far gone. If you ever want to end things, please end them before we become that."

"Baby." I took a step towards him and grabbed the side of his face. "You know in your heart that'll never happen."

"No one gets married thinking they're going to get divorced."

The rest of the night passed quietly. Harmony stayed in the loft with Emery and Nic's door remained closed for the night. Not wanting to let their internal conflict hold up our progress, those of us left at the cottage began planning our next step.

Bryan, Rose, Dmitri and I sat in the living room making the best plan we could to ambush Bonnie Drake. Even after Lauren and Rayn got home, we continued planning. Aden stepped out of his room once Rayn had gotten home and joined the conversation. Brooke was at her house, though and I missed her presence.

Rose leaned her back against the couch, glancing up at the loft. "When we do go to the palace, do you think we should go alone? Like we did for the Hallow?"

"It would probably be for the best. They can figure their shit out while we're gone," Lauren replied, waving towards the bedrooms. "It's an unnecessary distraction." Lauren glanced over at Aden. "You're coming either way, of course."

He nodded in acknowledgment, his eyes wandering over to meet Rayn's gaze. "I go where you go."

I chewed on my lip, waiting to see how the rest of them felt. I didn't think leaving Nic and Harmony alone would be the best option and I didn't want to go to the palace without them. But this generation was a democracy.

"I'm on the fence," Rayn replied. "They are helpful and their preexisting relationship, no matter how strained, to Maggie Daniels will probably come in handy. Especially with how Roberta spoke about them. But I don't know if they're in the headspace to deal with everything."

"Listen," Harmony's voice made me jump. I hadn't heard a single footstep down the stairs from the loft, but she stood at the bottom of the staircase. She looked around at all of us before she spoke again. "I should have sent Jerry packing the moment he got into town and I apologize. This was embarrassing enough that I will not allow anything like it to happen again. My business is taken care of. I am here. I am focused. All right?"

Rose and Lauren glanced at each other across the living room. Everyone shifted or moved their bodies in some way but nobody spoke a word out loud.

Rayn's voice said in my head, *I think she wants to mean it.*

But...? I responded.

But I don't know if they're capable of keeping it together.

I cleared my throat and spoke aloud. "You all know how I feel, I don't want to exclude them. So the rest of you decide how you feel and majority rules. Does that sound fair?"

"Make your plans and act quick." Harmony crossed her arms. "We can't sit around waiting for the Renati to attack. Not again."

Chapter Thirty-One
No Boundaries
Lauren

Nerves riddled my body thinking about meeting Ashley's mom for the first time. I shouldn't be this nervous. Everything I had heard about the woman gave the impression that she would be easy to get along with. I wondered if I'd mess it up anyway.

It had been a few nights since we gathered at the cottage and we still only had half of a plan to get the key stem from Bonnie Drake. Whitney had been hyper focused on the Harmony and Nic of it all, but the other girls and I hung onto the intel Abbie had given.

The hunters were working with the Renati. Erebus was close to getting the key fragment from Maggie Daniels. He plotted in the shadows while we…whatever the hell we had been doing. Burying our loved ones and slaving away to keep a coffee shop open. I hated feeling the resentment build in my chest. I loved the Corner Cup and I wanted to honor Amilia by keeping it open, but it often felt like a waste of time. We were distracted, and I didn't know how to get my friends back on track.

I shook my head clear and focused on what stood before me; meeting my girlfriend's mother.

My *girlfriend*.

Ashley led the way up the walkway to the house, opening the front door before she paused to look over her shoulder. "You okay?"

I nodded. "Kind of nervous."

"No, *I* am kind of nervous." Ashley let out a sigh. "My mom is embarrassing."

"Embarrassing? Me?" a voice called from the other side of the open door. "I'm sorry, lamb, I think you've gotten me confused with someone else's mother."

"Lamb?" I giggled. That had to be the cutest thing I'd ever heard.

"Mom, please don't call me that," Ashley begged. "I brought Lauren over to meet you. And Whitney and Bryan will be here soon too. So, behave."

"Lauren! How nice to finally meet you!" Ashley's mother had the same red curls as her daughter with freckles and bright hazel eyes. They could've been twins, with the same slender limbs and wide smiles.

I smiled and shook the extended hand offered to me.

"Please, call me Polly. Ash has told me *so* much about you." Polly gave Ashley a playful nudge with her elbow. "She's smitten, this one."

"Mom," Ashley groaned.

"She's always been so touchy. So, Lauren, please come in. Have a seat! Tell me everything, all about you." Polly led the way into the living room and plopped down on an armchair.

Ashey and I sat side by side on the couch, our hands almost touching. I decided to reach out and close the gap between us, lacing our fingers. As nervous as I had been, Ashley was already flustered and we'd barely walked through the front door.

"Uh, what do you want to know?" I tilted my head.

"Oh, whatever you're comfortable with sharing, of course. That could be nothing at all. Ashley told me you two work at the Corner Cup together?" Polly's shoulders fell. "I'm so sorry about the loss of your boss. Amilia was a kind woman."

"Thank you, she really stepped up and helped me out when my mom died. We're doing everything we can to keep the doors open," I explained.

Polly nodded. "Yes, Ash filled me in on all that too. I love the idea for the Acoustic Weekend. What a beautiful way to honor her memory."

Another knock came at the door and Ashley lept from her seat, dashing across the room. She flung the door open.

"You're alone," Ashley pointed out, letting Whitney inside.

"Bryan wanted to stop by the house and change. I came straight over from the cottage." Whitney smiled at me as she entered the living room.

"Whitney! Darling, meeting you has been a long time coming." Polly lept from her chair and shook Whitney's hand. "I cannot tell you how excited I was when Ash told me she found someone to hook Byn up with. He is such a good man. I only have daughters so I snatched him right up, he is like a sweet son to me."

Whitney smiled back and sat down on the couch next to me. "He's a good one, I think I'll keep him."

"You better. Now, before he gets here, I have to ask." Polly leaned forward, resting her elbows on her knees. "How is your sex life?"

"Mom!" Ashley called out, horrified.

I raised my brows and glanced over at Whitney, who also had surprise written all over her wide eyes.

"What? Is that too forward? You aren't teenagers anymore and a healthy sex life is very important to young relationships! You don't have to answer if you're uncomfortable, Whitney." Polly leaned back in her chair, sipping at her glass of iced tea.

Whitney giggled, covering her mouth with her hand. "Um, it's good. It's very good."

"Oh, what a relief. I am also not surprised, our Byn is a giver. He's always had so much love in his heart, looking for the right person to give it all too." Polly shifted in her seat. "You three women are at such a pivotal time in your lives. This is the time where you get to not only discover who you are, but decide who you want to be. There's such a big world out there and to have a moment in time for fun and self discovery? I wish I could go back and relive those days."

I silently disagreed. If I was an average twenty-year-old girl, I would be making my way through college and figuring out who I wanted to be. I would be making mistakes and having fun. I'd be learning to be an adult and deciding what I wanted my future to look like, but I was not average. I did not get to decide my fate, that had been decided for me centuries ago.

The day these magical powers manifested, I felt like I lost all control over my life. Even the decision to stifle and hide my magic backfired the day the rest of my generation dragged me to the meadow.

The front door opened again without a knock and Bryan strolled into the living room.

"My boy!" Polly lept from her seat and pulled Bryan into a bear hug. They held each other for a moment. "Why are you in town and not heading back to the bay?"

"Oh." Bryan pulled away and rubbed the back of his neck. "Um, I'm taking a break from FBU."

"A break?" Ashley straightened her posture. "You're graduating in June."

Bryan huffed, looking across the room to Whitney, who didn't seem surprised by the news. "I'm not."

Ashley nearly fell over. "You're not graduating? Byn, what the fuck?"

"I failed a midterm, okay?" Bryan held out his arms. "I failed a midterm and I couldn't get my grade up in time, so I'm not graduating in June. I'm taking a break and I'll go back later down the road."

"There has to be something you can do! Talk to your professor or do extra credit. Something," Ashley urged.

Bryan shrugged. "I dropped two weeks ago, Ash."

My heart sank knowing the truth behind Bryan dropping out. I knew the stress going on behind the scenes that Ashley and her mother were oblivious to. I saw how tense he stood, how he stressed over Whitney and Rose. How Bryan worked as tirelessly as the rest of us in a joint effort to save the sinking ship we were all on.

"*You* failed a class? Mr. 3.8 GPA and scholarships up the ass failed a class?" Ashley crossed her arms in disbelief. "You didn't tell anyone?"

"Knock it off, Ash, he feels bad enough as it is," Whitney spoke up.

Polly reached out and took Bryan's hand in hers. "Are you okay?"

Bryan sighed. "Mark showed up to the house and ambushed me. My mom called him when she found out."

I turned to Whitney and silently mouthed my question. *Mark?*

"His father," Whitney answered in a whisper.

Oh. I didn't know anything about Rose and Bryan's family dynamic, but I had gone to their mother's wedding so I knew their parents were not together.

"How did that go?" Polly asked Bryan.

"Oh, you know...he yelled. I yelled. My mom watched me leave from the porch." Bryan sat down on the arm of the couch next to Whitney. She leaned into him and put a comforting hand on his thigh.

"I'm sorry, Byn, I know how triggering Mark is for you," Polly said.

Bryan shrugged. "I'll be okay." He turned to me and forced a smile. "We aren't here to talk about me, anyway."

"Okay, so do you guys want to head upstairs? Before Mom turns this into a therapy session?" Ashley asked, pushing off the wall she had leaned on.

Whitney and I followed Ashley up the stairs to her bedroom. Polly grabbed Bryan's arm at the base of the stairs and leaned in, keeping her voice low.

"You should come by this week and talk to me, hm?" Polly squeezed Bryan's hand.

"I will," he promised as he nodded and followed us up the stairs.

I walked into Ashley's room first. The walls were painted mint green with lights strung up. Sheer gray curtains hung in the windows and around her headboard. The walls were covered in photos, some polaroids and others all different sizes. An entire wall covered in a massive collage of photographs. I took a step towards the photos to get a closer look and a smile swept across my face.

Pictures of Ashley and Emma at the beach, bikinis and wind blown hair. A photo of Ashley in a prom dress with Bryan standing next to her. Ash and her friends all piled into a car together. Graduations and birthdays. She had even added photos from her New Year's birthday in Falcon Bay, one of the entire group. And another of Ashley and I from the same night, our faces close together and bright eyes.

My heart exploded in her chest knowing Ashley had photos of us on her bedroom wall.

Ashley closed her bedroom door behind us and grabbed Bryan's arm. "Hey, I'm sorry. I shouldn't have jumped your shit, it caught me off guard. Two weeks, Byn? Why didn't you tell me? Why didn't Em tell me?"

"Because of that look you have on your face right now." He frowned and let out a sigh. "Everyone is so disappointed in me. I told Emma to let me tell people on my own."

Ashley's shoulders fell and she pulled Bryan into a hug. "Are you okay?"

"Yeah, I'm good." He hugged her back and cleared his throat. Stepping back from Ash, he lay down on her bed. "I don't want to talk about it."

"I didn't mean to come off as judgmental, Byn, you know I'm here to support you in all these big life changes. I'm here for you, but I'm confused. It feels out of nowhere," Ashley didn't drop the topic.

Bryan let out a deep sigh. "It's not out of nowhere. I've been struggling for a while and I can't hide it anymore."

"Please come talk things out with my mom," Ashley urged.

Bryan nodded. "I already told her I would."

Ashley laughed, covering her mouth. "Okay, well, speaking of my mom. I have to tell you...Mom asked Whit about your guys' sex life."

"She what?" Bryan shot up, his eyes wide, looking over at Whitney. "What did you say?"

Whitney chortled. "I told her it was good."

"No, you said *very* good," I laughed.

Bryan smiled. "She has no boundaries."

"She's awful." Ashley plopped down on her bed, motioning for Whitney and I to join them. "I told you she is embarrassing. This is why I never have people over. I've been putting off her meeting you for a while, Lo. Only a matter of time before she scares you off."

"Nah." I waved my hand. "I don't scare that easily."

"Your mom isn't that bad." Whitney sat down next to Bryan. "She seems really nice. My mom was weird about that stuff too, talked about orgasms very openly."

I laughed again. "My mother would have clutched her pearls hearing women talk to their kids that way."

The thought of my mother no longer existing on this earth wiped the smile right off my face. Would this feeling ever fade? Would I ever be able to go a full day without thinking about my mother being ripped away from me?

Whitney hopped off the bed to take a closer look at Ashley's photo wall. She pointed to one in the corner. "Did you two go to prom together?"

Ashley smiled. "We had a blast."

"Aw, Byn, look at your suit! You guys look so cute." Whitney stopped at a photo with five faces instead of the usual four that Whitney and I had spent so much time with. Whitney's demeanor changed. I saw the tension build visibly in her shoulders.

I hated seeing Serenity's face too, especially in a safe place such as Ashley's bedroom. I wished we could explain to Ashley that Serenity couldn't be redeemed, that she needed to rip her out of all those photos and burn them.

Ashley noticed Whitney pause at the group picture. "That's from the music festival in Seattle we all went to. It was the last thing we did together as a group."

"The last thing? How come?" I asked casually as Whitney slowly turned to listen. Maybe Ashley had something to say that could help us fill in the blanks.

"Serenity got super weird afterwards, she stopped talking to us. I had fun that weekend. It ended on a sour note with Byn breaking his arm," Ashley explained.

Bryan didn't comment.

"That's kind of weird for her to up and stop talking to you guys," I pushed.

Ash shrugged. "All I know is she and Emma got in a *huge* fight at the festival, literally hitting each other. We had to break them apart. And Emma never spoke about it again, so I haven't pushed. She'll talk when she's ready."

"Four years later? I don't think so," Bryan finally spoke. "Anyway, I haven't eaten so we should order some food." He pulled out his phone, changing the subject.

"Oh, yeah, I'm hungry too." Ashley leaned in to see Bryan's phone, talking amongst themselves on what they wanted to eat.

I glanced back at Whitney, both of us suspecting his intentions. Bryan probably thought he protected Ashley. I wanted to keep her safe too, but he also had the same protests involving Emma. When we finally enlisted her help, we were able to burn the ledger that kept tabs on all the witches in Rifton. So, as far as I was concerned, it wouldn't hurt to poke around and ask questions.

I wished I had the same telepathic abilities Whitney had with Rayn. I would tell Whit to say something, to bring the subject back to Serenity and that weekend their friend group fell apart. When Whitney glanced over and met my gaze I widened my eyes, inconspicuously darting my eyes in between her and the photos on the wall.

Whit looked at the photo from the music festival and then back to me. I waited for her to press the conversation, but she didn't. Bryan and Ashley moved on to choosing between pizza or burritos.

I pulled out my phone and sent Whitney a text. **We need to find out what happened at that festival. Exploit the twin's weaknesses.**

She read my text but never said a word.

After we finished eating, Bryan stacked the paper plates into a pile and smiled across the bed at Whitney. "We should probably get home."

"Oh, yeah, we have that thing." She hopped off the bed and smiled at me. "I'll text you."

Ashley furrowed her brow as Whit and Bryan scurried from the room. "Bye." The door closed behind them and Ashley turned to me. "Byn thinks he's so sly, but he isn't as sneaky as he thinks."

I smiled at her. "I appreciate what they're trying to do."

Ashley nodded and slowly scooted closer, filling the space between us. "Not that I'm complaining about privacy."

I attempted to swallow my nerves as Ashley came closer, but the heat pooling in my stomach overpowered any other emotion swimming through me. A smile swept across Ashley's cherry red lips and I melted into the blanket, unable to think of anything other than the freckles across her nose. I brushed a curl from her face and brought her lips to mine.

Ashley deepened the kiss with her tongue, not wasting a moment before she pulled me on top of her. I pressed my thigh between her legs and rested my weight against her. Ashley's cold hands traveled up my back, flirting with the clasp of my bra.

Chills shot through my body, causing every little hair on my arms to stand at attention. I had imagined what this moment would feel like since I laid eyes on Ashley in the Corner Cup, even before I had met my generation and my life had been turned upside down. It had always been a fantasy, a secret desire I had kept to myself. I couldn't imagine someone as confident and bright as Ashley would ever look twice in my direction, let alone touch my bare back with her fingertips.

Ashley nibbled on my bottom lip, bringing me back into the moment. I cupped the side of her face and deepened the kiss, sweeping my tongue against hers. She moaned into my mouth, setting my entire body ablaze. How could someone make me come undone simply by existing?

I slid her shirt over her head and unclasped her bra while she sat up. As she laid back down, the sight of her knocked the air from my lungs.

"You are so beautiful," I muttered, bringing her mouth to mine. A fire swam through my veins. I had never wanted someone this badly; never *needed* someone. "I've never done this with a girl before, but I really want to," I whispered against her lips and Ashley winked. I laid her back down and kissed her cheek and her neck, working my way down in between her breasts and down her stomach. With every kiss I peppered on her soft skin, my heartbeat pounded louder in my ears.

I unbuttoned her jeans and Ashley lifted her hips as I took them off. With trembling fingers, I slowly slid her panties down her legs. Ashley's eyes locked onto me. Even after I looked away from her glowing hazel eyes, I still felt their gaze burn into me.

With one long swipe of my tongue, I licked up her core. Ashley shuddered around me, grabbing my fingers wrapped around her smooth thigh. Hearing how her breath quickened, I gained some confidence and moved up to her clit.

She arched her back and muffled her moans with the back of her arm. I wrapped my lips around her most sensitive spot and worked her with my tongue.

Suddenly, she grabbed the bottom of my shirt. I pulled away from her as Ashley slid my shirt over my head. I leaned back down to continue between her thighs, but she gripped my shoulders and flipped me onto my back. Ashley's lips crashed onto mine as she unbuttoned my jeans and slid her hand under the waistband.

My muscles clenched as she grazed her fingers down my slick center and into my core. Ashley curled her fingers and hit a spot inside of me that had never been touched before. I shuddered and every inch of me melted into her bed. A rogue moan escaped my lips but Ashley seemed to have seen it coming because she swallowed my noises as her mouth covered mine.

She worked me with her fingers, pressing her thumb against my clit in a circular motion that made me want to live in that moment for the rest of my life. My body climbed higher until my hips buckled and I came crashing down, gripping onto the bed sheets for dear life as Ashley rode out the high with me.

Once my labored breaths eased and my pounding heart returned to a steady beat, I turned to Ashley, reaching out to touch her. Ashley grabbed my hand and laced our fingers, bringing the back of my hand to her lips.

"You don't want me to…" I wasn't sure how to finish the question.

Ashley smiled, her eyes bright. "When we are home alone, yes."

"Did…" I paused, building up the courage to ask my question out loud. "Did I do okay?"

Ashley gave a sly smile. "Of course you did."

"It's just…you stopped me."

Ashley reached out and ran her thumb across my bottom lip. "Because my mom is downstairs and she would've heard me shatter."

"Shatter?" I asked, attempting to hide the smile that swept across my face.

"Can you stay the night?" Ashley's eyes gazed into mine, begging me not to leave.

I nodded and she smiled back, kissing the corner of my mouth before she trailed down my neck. She slid my bra strap down and gently bit my shoulder, sending a shock through my body. I rubbed my thighs together and gently wrapped my arm around her back. "I thought you wanted to wait until we were home alone."

"Hmm," Ashley hummed. "I did say that, didn't I?" She kissed down to where the cup of my bra met my breast. "I changed my mind." She reached behind my back and undid the clasp of my bra. Putting a gentle hand on my shoulder, she laid me back on her bed. "Hopefully my mom won't hear you shatter."

Ashley kissed her way down my body and I stared at her bedroom door. Discreetly, I waved my hand and cast a silencing spell on her room.

Chapter Thirty-Two
Irreparable Damage
Whitney

After we left Ashley's house, I followed Bryan back to our place. I parked along the curb and sat still in the driver's seat, drumming against the steering wheel with my thumb. I went over Lauren's text in my mind, knowing she was onto something.

Bryan parked in the driveway and walked over to me, opening the door. He bent down to look at me, resting his arm on the body of the car. "You okay?"

I nodded and followed him into the house in a daze. I couldn't let go of seeing Serenity's face on Ashley's photo wall. Even though years had passed since they'd been friends, Ashley never took the pictures down. Lauren had been paying attention to all the right things.

Abbie's spirit had said that the twins were not as different as I assumed, and they shared the same weakness.

"Exploit her weakness," I whispered to myself as I sat down on the couch.

Bryan watched the wheels in my head turn before he spoke. "What are you talking about?"

"Whatever happened at that music festival is important." I looked up at him. "Abbie told me to exploit Serenity's weakness, and I think it's you. She cut you off for some reason, but I don't understand why. I saw the way she looked at you in your memories, she still cares about you."

"You don't think it was all an act?" Bryan asked.

I shook my head. "She let the location of the old hospital slip, I don't think she'd do that intentionally. I need to see what happened at the music festival."

Bryan lowered his voice as embarrassment swam through him. "I don't have a lot of memories for you to see, Whit."

I hummed. "That doesn't make any sense though, because you drink but never enough that you black out."

Bryan crossed his arms. "I try not to make the same mistakes twice."

I patted the spot next to me. "Can I at least try?"

He hesitated but eventually sat down next to me. "So, what exactly are you wanting to do?" Nerves took over Bryan's core as he bounced his heel against the floor. "You want to get into my head and search for a memory I don't have?"

"Maybe if you focus on what you do remember from that night, I can use my powers to unlock the memory. You lived it, but you don't remember it so maybe I can still see things from your perspective." I reached out and took his hands in mine, attempting to ease his concern. "Open your mind."

"How do I open my mind?" His hands trembled slightly.

I gave him a gentle smile. "It'll be like when I saw your conversation with Serenity. Think about the weekend the best you can and I will do the rest."

Bryan chewed on the inside of his cheek nervously.

I squeezed his fingers. "I love you very much, and I'd never do anything that would harm you. You know that right?"

Bryan nodded and watched intently as my body relaxed. I narrowed in on his gaze and let my magic wash over him. No mental wall kept me out, nothing pushed against me as I settled into his head. Bryan sat completely still, as if moving an inch would disturb the process.

Flashes of Bryan and his friends at the festival appeared in my mind. They all shared one large tent and pushed their way through crowds to get as close to the stages as possible. Bryan wore a blank tank top with a bandana wrapped around his head. The hot summer sun beat down on their skin and I could almost feel the heat.

Bryan left the crowd as the sun set behind him, searching for something, someone. He caught a glimpse of Serenity's back leaving the festival, heading towards a hill off in the distance. Bryan furrowed his brow and tilted his head, watching her for a moment before he followed. I attempted to go with him, to follow the memory but everything began to blur.

The closer Bryan got to Serenity, the fuzzier it all became. I searched, but none of the images were clear enough to grasp onto.

I blinked and let out a heavy sigh, coming back into my own mind. "It all gets fuzzy after you follow Serenity away from the festival."

"It's fuzzy for me too...so I'm not surprised," Bryan paused, licking his bottom lip. "Baby, I don't know what to tell you. That weekend was a big wake up call for me. I never drink that much anymore and it's not something I enjoy dissecting."

I laced our fingers together. "Did you see Serenity at all after the festival? After she and Emma got into their argument?"

Bryan nodded. "Yeah, she came to the hospital when I got my arm casted."

"Can I see that?"

"She came to say sorry that I got hurt, and that is when she told me about her powers." Bryan shifted in his seat. "I didn't believe her at first so she showed me a glowing light in her hands. I told her I didn't remember what happened but I would stay out of it. I didn't want to pick sides." He let out a deep sigh and looked away from me. "Serenity said that not picking her was siding with Emma, and she left. We didn't really see each other after that."

I stared at him for a moment. "And you won't show me that?"

He shook his head. "I already told you exactly how it went."

I collapsed against the back of the couch, burying my face in my hands. "I don't know what I'm going to do."

"Bryan doesn't remember most of that weekend, but I do." The sound of Emma's voice made me lift my head. Emma walked into the living room from Troy's bedroom, her arms crossed tightly against her chest.

"Have you been here the entire time?" Bryan turned to face her.

Emma nodded. "Troy is at work, so I'm back there reading. Anyway, how does this memory thing work?"

I sat up. "Are you sure?"

Emma moved across the room to sit on the couch next to me. "I want to know why my sister turned her back on me. Explain the process."

I paused, knowing that simply viewing Emma's memories wouldn't cut it. I wouldn't be able to see anything she couldn't remember and she obviously didn't know what happened to change Serenity that weekend. The spell I had found from Thomas was my last resort. Luckily, I had the herbs Rose hunted down in my bag.

I turned to face Emma. "Usually I can only see what you remember but I found this spell from a previous Seer and maybe…I'm thinking maybe I can use your memories to transport myself to the location and see things you guys didn't, or don't remember. I don't know though, I've never done this before."

Emma blinked at me. "Don't turn me into a vegetable, okay?"

Bryan leaned forward to look at her. "Emma, you don't have to do this. If your dad ever found out you were helping us–"

"I've already helped you." Emma cut him off. "I'm already in it, whether either of us want to admit it or not."

I nodded. "She's right, you know. So, it's not much different than when I've seen memories before," I explained as Emma stared into my eyes intently. "Are you familiar with a Seer?"

She shook her head.

"Okay, a Seer is an Elemental who has visions of the future and can access people's memories of the past. I can't see Bryan's memories of the weekend because they're too fuzzy. This spell I found isn't much different, just more involved. All you have to do is think about the event and I can do the rest, but try to be specific. Try to think about the exact time when things fell apart with Serenity. The fight you two had and the events that led to it."

"I didn't see what she did though…" Emma paused. "I found her and Byn afterwards."

"Wait, what?" Bryan leaned around me to look at Emma. "After what?"

"I don't know!" Emma threw her hands up. "That's the problem! It was only the two of you. You don't remember any of it and Serenity would never tell me what she did to you!"

"She did something to him?" The words left my mouth in a hiss. My blood boiled as my pulse accelerated. I had to take a deep breath to refrain from leaving the house and hunting Serenity down.

"I'm fine, baby," Bryan urged, grabbing my hand.

"Nothing is fine when the Drakes are involved," I told him over my shoulder.

"Hey." Emma furrowed her brow. "I am a Drake, in case you've forgotten."

I turned back to Emma. "I know they're your family, but you have literally no idea, Emma. Do you?"

Emma leaned back. "About what?"

"That your sister has tried to kill me more than once, and I don't mean she and I have fought. I mean she gave me this." I pulled the sleeve of my shirt up to show Emma the scar from Halloween night. Her eyes widened but she didn't say a word. "Serenity held a knife to my brother's throat and tried to drown his boyfriend. Your father kidnapped my best friend and tried to murder him thirteen years ago. Even our moms have ugly history."

"Our *moms?*" Emma asked softly, confused.

I nodded. "My mom grew up in Rifton, she was a witch too."

"But not Renati."

"No, but your mom wasn't always Renati either. Our mothers used to belong to the same coven, they were friends. There is this key that is required to unlock the trials that allows us to get the magic out of our jewelry. Their coven had the key long before they ever knew about us or that we'd end up with the talismans." I balled my fists in my lap. "They broke the key to protect it, and your mom took a piece. She betrayed her friends and gave her piece to the Renarti when she converted."

Emma sat in silence.

"Ring any bells?"

"No," she whispered. "But I'm not surprised, my parents have this story about always being in love. My dad has always been about appearances. It never mattered what went on behind closed doors as long as it looked pretty on the outside."

"I don't know the details. All I know is a piece of the key went with your mom, but we need it. We're dead in the water without it."

"Who told you all this?" Emma crossed her arms. "Your mom?"

I shook my head. "No, another member of the coven. The Renati drove her from town when she refused to convert. They burned down her house."

"Oh…wow." Emma cleared her throat. "Help me figure out what happened with my sister and maybe I can help you out too. I don't know how, but a favor for a favor."

I nodded in agreement. "Deal." I grabbed my bag and pulled the small vial of storm vine mixed to littory oil. I uncorked the concoction and a pungent, earthy scent overwhelmed my senses.

Bryan stared at the vial in my hand. "What is that?"

"Rose got them for me, it's safe," I reassured him, taking a deep breath to inhale the mixture. My sinuses burned and tears welled in my eyes. I quickly blinked them away as the scent settled in my taste buds. A deep throb took over my frontal lobe and I clenched my jaw, trying to keep a look of pain off my face.

"You two do not have to do this," Bryan reminded us one last time.

"Be quiet, Byn, you're distracting us." Emma glared at him over my shoulder.

Within seconds, I was inside Emma's head and back at the music festival.

Emma stood at the back of the crowd with Troy and Ashley. Troy's arms wrapped around Emma, holding her close to his chest as they all watched the band together.

I scanned the crowd for the other two members of their group when I caught a glimpse of Bryan following Serenity up that damn hill. I followed him, amazed that I could move around within the memory. It was difficult, like moving through the mud, but with persistence I walked away from Emma.

I felt a tug against my subconscious as I moved further away from Emma but I pushed, forcing myself away from her. The pounding in my temple took over my focus for a moment but I leaned into the pain. I knew Emma would follow Bryan and Serenity up the hill eventually, but I had to see what happened before she showed up.

When I got to the top of the hill, Bryan and Serenity were surrounded by trees and large boulders. The side of the hill opposite of where they had climbed was a straight drop down to the bottom.

"What are you doing, Ren?" Bryan asked, approaching Serenity on the top of the steep hill.

Serenity kept her back to him. "I'm trying to clear my head. You should go back to the festival."

He took another step towards her. "But I want to make sure you're okay. You've been off all weekend."

"Just because we hooked up doesn't mean you're responsible for me now," Serenity snapped over her shoulder.

Bryan halted in his tracks. "I never assumed that. What is going on with you?"

"Byn, please leave," she pleaded, her shoulders falling in defeat. "Please?"

Bryan crossed his arms. "This is so fucking stupid, Ren. You never keep stuff from us, and lately you've been a completely different person." He moved around her until he stood in her face. "Talk to me!"

"No!" Serenity put her palms against his chest and shoved.

Bryan stumbled backwards, his heel caught on one of the large rocks. He tumbled back and went right over the edge of the steep cliff.

Panic washed over Serenity's face as her eyes widened and she scrambled towards him. She fell forward onto her knees at the edge and threw her hand out. Bryan floated in mid air, frozen in place by Serenity's powers. He looked down at the ground far below him and back into Serenity's dilated pupils.

"Wh-what is this?" *he stammered.*

"Fuck," *Serenity cussed under her breath.* "Fuck, fuck, fuck." *She waved her hand and brought Bryan back to solid ground, only lifting the spell once his feet were planted on the dirt.*

A quivered breath left Bryan's lips and he looked down at his body once more. "I didn't actually take that ecstasy, did I?"

"Ugh!" *Serenity groaned, running her fingers through her hair. She furrowed her brow and let out a deep breath.* "Hopefully this is enough for him."

Serenity threw out her hand once more and Bryan fell onto his back. He grunted as the air left his lungs, in shock from the attack. "What the fuck?"

Serenity got on top of his chest, digging her knee into his sternum. Bryan tried to fight against her but she held him in place with her extended hand, magic pouring from her body.

"I'm sorry, Byn, but you don't understand. You have no idea what it's like being his daughter." *Serenity blinked away tears.* "I have to do this, it's the only way I can prove myself to them."

Serenity levitated one of the rocks over to them and Bryan's eyes widened as it came closer. "Ren, I don't know what's going on, but please don't. Please."

"Trust me, this is child's play compared to what he first demanded of me. Hopefully it's a clean break." *Serenity closed her fist and the rock landed in the crook of Bryan's elbow.*

He cried out in pain and squirmed to get away from Serenity but she held him in place. "Look at me, Byn."

The moment Bryan's eyes locked into Serenity's, he stopped fighting. His body relaxed and his head rested back against the dirt.

"Bryan, you've had a lot to drink today. You tripped on a rock on the way up here and broke your arm. Nothing else happened. You don't remember anything else. It's all fuzzy."

"Yeah, it's fuzzy," *he whispered as the charm took over.*

"What the actual fuck is going on?" *Another voice cried out and the throbbing in my head eased. Emma.*

Serenity rolled off of Bryan, jumping to her feet. "He...he fell."

Emma looked down at Bryan and rushed to his side, shoving the boulder off his arm with her foot. "The rock fell on top of him? Ren, what the fuck were you doing?"

"N-nothing," *Serenity stammered, taking a step back.* "I didn't do anything."

"Byn, what happened?" Emma asked him, pulling on his good arm to help him to his feet. Bryan looked at her and blinked. "I...I fell on the way up here. Everything is fuzzy."

Emma's head snapped towards her sister. "You charmed him, didn't you?"

"Of course not!" Serenity lied.

"I can tell, Ren."

Serenity crossed her arms. "Oh, can you? Powerless you with no ability at all can tell when someone has been charmed? You can't even tell when you've been charmed."

Emma tightened her grip on Bryan. "You haven't."

"What makes you so sure? You think Mom and Dad never charmed you to get you to shut up?"

Tears welled in Emma's eyes as she left Bryan's side and moved closer to Serenity. "You did this, Serenity. I don't believe this bullshit story for a minute." Emma squared herself up in her sister's face. "Is this it? Was this your big test to get into Mom and Dad's stupid, secret club? You want to kiss their asses that badly?"

"Fuck off, Emma!" Serenity yelled with fire in her eyes. "You have no idea what it's like! The kind of pressure they put on me!"

"This had nothing to do with them!" Emma glared at her sister. "This is your choice, and you can sleep in the bed you've made."

Serenity scoffed. "You act like you're above it all but you're jealous."

Emma chortled and crossed her arms. "Jealous of what? Mom and Dad may have convinced you that you're special, but outside of their exclusive circle, no one thinks anything of you. Byn was the person you had to betray to prove yourself? He only looked twice at you because I'm taken and Ash is gay."

"Hey, that's not–" Bryan began to say but stopped as Serenity's hands met Emma's chest. Serenity shoved Emma over the side of the hill.

Emma flailed her arms, grasping for anything to keep her from tumbling to the bottom. Emma's hand wrapped around a low hanging tree branch as Bryan rushed to her side. Serenity took a step back and watched as Bryan pulled Emma back onto solid ground with his unbroken arm.

Emma scrambled to her feet and threw her fist into the side of Serenity's face. "You tried to kill us for a father that doesn't love me or you. I hope this was worth it, because you don't have a sister anymore. Come near any of my friends again, and you'll regret it."

Serenity stepped back and watched Emma and Bryan walk down the hill together. Her lip curled and her eyes narrowed before she took off after them. Emma and Bryan had made it to the bottom of the hill. Emma waved to Troy and Ashley, who were heading towards them when Serenity got within reach and tackled her sister to the ground.

"Hey!" Troy bellowed and ran the rest of the way to them. Troy wrapped his arms around Serenity's waist and pulled her off Emma. "Get off of her!"

"Byn, are you okay?" Ashley asked, noticing Bryan cradled one arm in the other.

He winced in pain. "I think it's broken."

Troy finally broke Emma and Serenity up, holding Serenity out at arm's length as he stood in front of Emma like a shield. "What the fuck is your problem, Ren?"

Serenity ripped herself out of Troy's grasp and left their group without another word. Troy turned back to Emma and pulled her into his arms. "Are you okay?" he asked.

"We need to take Byn to the med tent." Emma left Troy's embrace and put her hand on Bryan's back, leading the way.

I blinked back into the present, staring into Emma's tear-filled eyes. She jumped up from the couch and paced across the living room.

"Please tell me you saw all of that with me?" I asked, watching Emma's hands tremble.

She nodded, clearing her throat but the tears continued to fall. "I fucking knew it."

Bryan scooted to the edge of his seat. "Are you going to fill me in?"

Emma faced him, wiping a tear away with the back of her hand. "Serenity broke your arm, she dropped a boulder on you."

His eyes widened. "What?"

"At the festival, she broke your arm on top of that hill with a rock. You didn't fall. That was her way to prove herself to get into the Renati, hurting you," Emma's voice cracked as she explained to Bryan.

He turned to look at me. "Is that what you saw?"

I nodded, unable to speak. My blood boiled under my skin and I saw red as my chest constricted. I attempted to take a deep breath but my throat burned with anger. Serenity had hurt Bryan without hesitation, without a second thought. *My* Bryan. A broken bone would be the last of her worries once I got my hands on her again. Now that I knew the truth of her fallout with Bryan and his friends, that she had intentionally hurt him...

"I need to get some air." Emma opened the sliding glass door and stepped outside.

Bryan's heart sank as he watched her disappear into the back yard. With a deep sigh, he put his hand on the small of my back. "I healed without any issues."

"It doesn't matter." I turned to face him. "She made her choice. She broke your arm and then charmed you into thinking you drank too much and acted like an idiot. You weren't too drunk, you were attacked. She shoved Emma off a cliff."

"That I remember," Bryan whispered. "I didn't realize Emma had been so mad because Serenity hurt me. I never understood what they were fighting over."

"They were fighting about their dirtbag father." I stood up from the couch and ran my fingers through my hair. I turned to face him and let out a short breath. "Before she charmed you, Serenity said breaking your arm was child's play compared to what her father first demanded of her."

Bryan raised his brow. "Did she say what the first demand was?"

I shook my head. "Probably to kill you, but Abe told me that every trial is different for each member. They personalize it so that each member proves themself in a special way."

Bryan stood up from the couch and peered out the window to where Emma sat in the backyard. I took my place at his side and waited for him to speak. "I was in the wrong place at the wrong time. I don't believe I'm the person Serenity had to hurt to prove herself."

I stared at Emma through the window. "Their own daughter?" I asked in disbelief. "Why would the Drake's ask that of Serenity?"

Bryan shrugged. "I don't know, but my arm getting broken is not what has Emma so shaken up."

Chapter Thirty-Three
CLASS C FELONY
Whitney

A few days later, I left the Corner Cup after an unsettling normal day. I hated when I finally made some headway only for my discoveries to not reflect in the rest of my life. I made it down the street when my phone rang. I knew Dmitri called before I pulled over and dug my phone from my purse.

"What's wrong?" I answered, gripping the steering wheel with trembling fingers.

"I, uh...I need you to come down to the police station." Dmitri's voice shook with fear.

"What happened?"

"They came by the house and told me that Abe and I had to come down to the station for questioning. I told them no but they threatened to cuff me and...I'm scared." He cleared his throat as if attempting to compose himself. "I told them I won't talk unless you're here. They have Abe in a different room."

"Grady?"

"Uh, yeah he's here."

"Son of a...I'm on my way. I will get Harmony down there too."

"Okay," Dmitri's voice cracked. He cleared his throat again in an attempt to cover it, but I felt it in my soul.

"Hey, I'm on my way. Everything will be fine. You didn't do anything wrong, they're trying to–"

He cut me off. "They're telling me I have to hang up. They want to take my phone. I only got one call."

"I'll be there soon. Don't say a single word to them until Harmony and I get there. Tell them to get a warrant if they want your phone. Don't give–"

The line went dead.

I could kill Officer Joseph Grady with my bare hands.

I peeled away from the curb, driving faster than I ever had before. I barely stopped at the next stop sign, tapping my breaks long enough to make sure no one came before I sped back up. My entire body trembled. My bones rattled until my skin and my muscles constricted. My brain ran over what they could possibly be trying to pin on Dmitri. No possible way Mit had found himself in legitimate legal trouble. What could they have brought him in for? Not getting enough Vitamin D? Reading too much?

This was personal, no way around it.

The only question was were the Renati or the hunters responsible?

At the next red light, I called Harmony and filled her in.

"Are you fucking kidding me," she grumbled. "I'll meet you there."

When I pulled into the police station, I barely had the engine shut off before I bolted towards the front door. I jogged to the first officer I saw. "I'm looking for my brother, Dmitri Dansley. He was brought in for some ridiculous questioning."

The officer glanced around the room and stood up. "Uh, hang on, let me see what I can figure out for you."

Clearly, the officer didn't know what I referred to.

"I'll take this, Smith." Office Joseph Grady rested against the wall across the room, as if waiting for my arrival. I glared at him and squeezed my hand into a fist, wishing I could punch his smug face. Grady nodded his head down the hall. "Follow me."

"I know what you really are and you don't scare me," I hissed, following behind Grady.

He peeked over his shoulder at me. "I could say the same to you, Miss Dansley."

"My brother hasn't done anything wrong."

He ignored me and continued down the hall. He stopped in front of a closed door and I could see Dmitri sitting at a wooden table across from Officer Higgins through the window. I shoved past Grady and opened the door, rushing to Dmitri's side. I gave him a once over to make sure he hadn't been harmed. The cops would be stupid to hurt him but I wouldn't put it past them to bring Dmitri in heavy-handed.

I glared at Officer Higgins. Witch hunter, Renati, douchebag. Whatever the hell he was.

"Has he been arrested?" I asked.

"No," the cop answered. "But we do need to question him on some recent accusations. It won't take long. He'd already be out of here by now if he'd cooperate."

"Questioning a minor without their guardian or legal representation? There has to be some kind of law against that." I crossed my arms, standing tall behind the chair Dmitri sat in.

"He seems nervous," Grady remarked from behind us.

I glared at him over my shoulder. "No shit he's nervous, he's a seventeen year old boy sitting in a police station. He's just a kid."

The door to the office flew open as Harmony burst into the room. She panted, out of breath but still held her head high. She straightened out her blouse and fixed her hair.

"Who are you?" Grady demanded.

"I'm Harmony Vasquez, their lawyer," she replied, standing behind Dmitri and resting her hand on his shoulder. "What is the meaning of this interrogation?" She didn't look at me but I could sense the anger dripping from her like a leaking faucet moments away from exploding.

Higgins sat back in his chair and chuckled. "Holy shit, I heard you were back in town."

Harmony looked Higgins in up down. "Rory Higgins. Of course you became a cop."

I should have been surprised, but considering that Harmony grew up in Rifton, of course she knew one of these douchebags.

"Couldn't handle all those big shot cases in Seattle? It's okay, Harmony, not everyone can make it outside their hometown," Higgins replied.

Harmony looked like she could kill him. "Are you going to tell me why my underage client is in your office or not, Rory?"

"We have footage of your *client* breaking and entering into the Drake estate," Higgins answered, looking up at Harmony with a clenched jaw.

"That is ridiculous!" I shouted. "I don't believe a word of it without seeing this footage for myself."

"Whitney, stop talking," Harmony snapped. She finally looked at me, but behind her icy stare hid the tiniest sliver of fear.

This wasn't Harmony coming in and trying to control the situation, she genuinely wanted to take care of Dmitri. I took a step back and let her do her thing.

Higgins pulled a printed picture from the file in front of him and slid it across the table. The black and white photo appeared blurry because it had been zoomed in, but the content was clear enough. Dmitri climbed into the back window of Drake's living room; half of his body already through the window, his worn sneakers dangled behind him. Abe stood at his side, his head turned as if he had been keeping watch. His unmistakable curly hair and flannel I'd seen him wear a dozen times caught on camera.

I glanced over at Harmony, waiting for her to speak.

She cleared her throat, analyzing the photo. "This isn't concrete proof that the photo is of Dmitri."

"There are several stills taken from the security camera footage that Mr. Drake turned in," Higgins informed us.

"Ms. Vasquez, your client is looking at burglary in the second degree, which is a Class C felony in the state of Oregon," Grady said behind us.

Felony.

My blood turned to ice as I held my breath. I didn't want to give away how my knees trembled or my heart skipped a beat. I couldn't give Grady the satisfaction of seeing how shaken I felt under my skin.

Harmony shook her head. "There's no proof either of the boys had intent."

"Why else would they be climbing in through the window?" Higgins questioned.

Harmony paused. "I suppose that is something for a judge to decide, not a couple of small town beat cops. Last I checked, trespassing is a misdemeanor at best."

"His court date has been set. I recommend taking these charges seriously." Higgins slid another piece of paper across the table.

Harmony snatched up the paper and tapped Dmitri's shoulder for him to stand up. "Good day, Officers."

Dmitri and I followed Harmony out of the police station and into the parking lot.

"Thank you," I turned to Harmony. "I...I don't know what to do."

Harmony sighed, running her fingers through her long brown hair. "Dmitri, be honest with me, what the fuck were you doing at the Drake's?"

Dmitri's shoulders fell and he looked away from us. "Looking for the key."

"Are you fucking–" Harmony's voice began to raise but with a deep breath, she brought herself back down. "I'll take care of this, okay?"

Dmitri nodded, his eyes still wide. "Abe is still in there, we can't leave him."

"I'm not Abe's parent, I can't get him out." I turned to Harmony. "Can't we charm them out of this?"

"You're talking to the wrong Magister, Whitney. I do not charm people to get my way," Harmony snapped back.

"But this isn't to get our way, this is to get out of trouble," Dmitri pointed out.

Harmony pinched the bridge of her nose. "That isn't how I operate."

I crossed my arms. "I wouldn't hesitate to charm all of them to keep Dmitri from going to jail."

"Stop escalating things," Harmony hissed. "He isn't going to jail. He'll have community service and may have to pay a fine. He doesn't have a record. He's a good kid who made a mistake and the system will go easy on him."

Anger rose in my blood listening to Harmony. "The system never goes easy on anyone. I lived in it for years."

Harmony blinked at me. "I'm sorry, but I promise that is how this situation will go. Those cops are trying to make things seem bigger and scarier than they are to intimidate Dmitri into admitting something. We have to be one step ahead of them."

"He's been following us," I replied, looking over my shoulder at the station.

"The witch hunter?" Harmony inquired.

"He's always coming into the Corner Cup to sit and stare at us."

"Does he ever say anything?"

I shook my head. "No, but he knows. He tried to pin Abe's disappearance on us. He saw Rayn light a candle with…you know."

"I'll do some digging. This is the last thing we fucking need." Harmony turned to my brother. "Mit, are you okay?"

He nodded but didn't reply.

"Okay," Harmony sighed again. "If either of those clowns come near you again, call me immediately. Don't speak to them without me present. That goes for all of you, the other girls included. Stay the fuck away from the Drakes and out of trouble." Harmony put a hand on Dmitri's shoulder. "Listen to me carefully, Dmitri, don't give someone ammo when they already have a gun pointed at you."

"Whitney?" Janice's voice called out from the parking lot as she and Jeff rushed towards us. "We got a call that the police brought Dmitri and Abraham in? What is going on?"

"Uh." I motioned towards Harmony. "This is my lawyer, Harmony Vasquez. She's a family friend. She's going to get them out of trouble."

"Hello, Mr. and Mrs. Roberts, um…the boys seem to have gotten caught up in a trespassing charge, but it's not nearly as serious as the police are making it out to be. The police in this town have turned into a crew of bullies," Harmony explained.

"Trespassing? I don't understand." Janice's hands shook visibly.

"Abe is still inside," Dmitri told them. "They separated us when we got here."

"Let me come inside with you and talk to him. He shouldn't be speaking to the police without legal representation," Harmony offered.

"We, uh, I'm not sure if we can afford your services," Jeff admitted.

"Pro bono. Dmitri and the girls are family," Harmony explained with a soft smile. "Let's go get Abe out of there and we can figure out what to do next, okay?"

Janice nodded as she and Jeff followed Harmony back inside.

"Whit, I–"

"Get in the car, Dmitri," I cut him off. The last thing we needed was me yelling at him in front of the police station. That would only incriminate him further.

"Whit, I'm sorry," Dmitri said as we got into the car. He closed and locked the door behind him. "We were trying to help! You've been so stressed, I thought if I took matters into my own hands, maybe we could find the key on our own. You and Brooke got the ledger without any issues. I didn't think they'd turn us into the police."

"Brooke successfully stole the ledger because she can walk through walls, Mit, she didn't go in through the window," I pointed out. "You did something incredibly reckless. You and Abe both could have gotten hurt, or worse. Why didn't you tell me?"

Dmitri chortled. "Is that a serious question? You never tell me anything, either."

I let out a deep sigh. I knew for him it was a realistic comparison. I disappeared into the woods without telling him and he went into the Drake's house without telling me. We were even. I hardly thought the two were even remotely the same, not with the police involved. When the girls and I went to the Hallow, we had planned and I left him with people who would keep him safe. He and Abe decided to go off on their own and got caught.

"Point made," I muttered. "I see you, I hear you. Please, don't ever do anything like that again."

Dmitri leaned back in his seat. "Do you think Harmony is going to be able to help us? The cops seemed pretty serious about getting real charges."

"If anyone can, it's Harmony. You and Abe lay low in the meantime and wait to see what she comes up with, okay?"

Dmitri nodded and checked his phone. "Nothing from Abe."

"He'll be fine," I promised. "Can you call Brooke for me?"

"And say what?" Dmitri asked, bringing Brooke up in his contacts.

"She looked up dirt on Grady. I want to see what she can find on Higgins."

"This Higgins guy had been in Rifton his whole life," Brooke announced, setting her bag down next to my bed.

The girls, Dmitri and Abe all sat in my bedroom the next day. Luckily, Harmony had gotten Abe out of the cop's grip but the boys still had court dates scheduled in a few weeks and we had no idea how to get them out of their predicament. Harmony promised she would figure something out, but I knew she was already stretched too thin.

"He and Harmony recognized one another from high school," I told the group.

"He went to Rifton High, graduated and joined the police force after getting an AA at the community college. All pretty basic stuff," Brook explained. "I did, however, find out that he also has a cousin on the force. Kevin Abrams."

"And why does that matter?" Rayn asked.

"Because he's Chief Abrams' son. The Chief of Police," Brooke said.

"Isn't the Chief of Police a member of the Renati?" Rose asked.

Abe nodded. "He is. I had no idea Higgins was related to Abrams."

"They probably keep it on the down low, to avoid nepotism and all that," Dmitri suggested.

Rayn sat down on the edge of my bed. "That makes sense why Grady and Higgins are always the ones trying to get us in trouble. They were there when B's parents first found out she'd snuck out. They came to our house trying to get us in trouble for Abe disappearing. They called Mit and Abe in about breaking into the Drake's house. Are we supposed to believe it's a coincidence?"

I nodded as the pieces fell into place. "Higgins being Renati is pretty obvious at this point. What confuses me is that his partner is a hunter. Do they know about one another or is that why they are partners?"

"You'd think as a hunter, Grady wouldn't trust Higgins if he's a witch." Rose crossed her legs underneath her, getting comfortable.

"Unless that's part of them working together? Abbie said they were helping each other behind Erebus' back. Do you think Drake is involved?" I asked.

Brooke shrugged. "He's the one pressing charges. If Higgins is Renati, then Drake should know what is going on behind closed doors."

"He'd have to," Lauren agreed. "Okay, so let's look at the timeline. Grady got here in April of last year, right? That would have to be around the time the wards broke. These three," Lauren motioned towards Rayn, Dmitri and I. "Didn't get here until August. We didn't open the Shadow Realm portal until Halloween. So, whoever broke the wards did it long before any of our shit happened. I don't know if breaking the wards had anything to do with us."

"I see that too, but why else would they want to break the wards and let witch hunters into the forest? It's dangerous for them as well," I pointed out.

Abe shook his head. "Not if they have an agreement. The hunters aren't attacking and killing Renati. They attacked you, they killed that girl in the bay, but none of the Renati witches in Rifton have been threatened, that we know of."

Rose leaned back. "Is this their final attempt to get the witches who aren't Renati out of Rifton? To bring in the hunters to take them out?"

My stomach churned at the thought. "The wards have been down for almost a year, but they didn't come at us until a few months ago. Have they been watching us the entire time?" I turned to Abe. "You were in the woods for a while, did you see much of them?"

"Oh, yeah, they knew I was out there. They'd always find me whenever I'd leave the hunting cabin, like they were waiting for me. If they're working with the Renati, then they probably were looking for me."

"But they never found you in the hunting cabin?" Rayn asked Abe.

He shook his head. "I'm very good at cloaking spells."

"In the meantime, stay the hell away from them," Lauren said. "Let Harmony figure out how to get you out of legal trouble and hope they don't show up to the Acoustic Weekend."

Brooke nodded. "I agree. Also..." She shifted her weight. "I think I figured out what I did when we were fighting the Shadows at the Hallow."

"When you disappeared?" I clarified.

"I always do this stuff unintentionally," Brooke laughed nervously. "But yes, I think I astral projected."

"Astral projection? What is that?" Dmitri asked.

"When your conscience leaves your body and goes somewhere else. I tried it again and it's actually pretty easy." Brooke shifted her weight. "Nic asked me a while back if I could, that their Soul Elemental, Finn, used to. Finn would pass out when he astral projected, but I don't seem to have that problem."

Lauren leaned forward. "From what I've been told, Finn was nowhere near as strong as you are."

"Of course you would find something like that easy, B." Rose shook her head with a smile. "Show us!"

"Okay, uh, hang on." Brooke left the bedroom and closed the door behind her.

The room fell silent as we waited for, well, I didn't know what we waited for. Brooke's Elemental powers had always been a bit of a mystery. Yes, Brooke had remarkable healing powers, but the rest of it seemed to be trial and error. Her ability to go through walls didn't manifest until she tried. And now her astral projection happened by accident as well.

"What is–" Rose began to ask when Brooke appeared in the middle of my bedroom. Only, she didn't quite look like herself.

Brooke was almost translucent, like she had become a spirit herself. Light waves of energy emitted from her as she held out her arms, showing off her party trick. "Ta da."

"Where is the rest of you?" Lauren asked, looking around the room.

"In the living room. My body kinda goes to sleep when I leave, I think," Brooke answered.

I smiled at her, truly impressed with how her powers had grown and developed. "That is incredible, B, but you should get back in your body before Bryan or Troy get home and you scare the shit out of them."

"Good idea," she agreed and disappeared. When Brooke came back into the room, she appeared solid again. "I'm still working out the kinks."

"What happens to your body while you're out of it? Like, what if someone messes with it?" Dmitri asked.

Brooke shook her head. "I don't want to find out."

Abe shot up and gasped. "I have something!"

"About Brooke's body?" Dmtiri asked, confused.

"No." Abe waved him off. "About knowing whether people are actually Renati members or not. Whenever I'd help my parents clean up at the mini mart, they always cleaned with Windex and it would irritate the hell out of my brand." Abe pulled up his sleeve to expose the mark in his skin. "I don't know why, but it got super itchy."

"Could you be allergic to Windex?" Rose tilted her head.

Abe shook his head. "No, because *only* the brand would itch, it wouldn't bother the rest of my skin."

Lauren chortled. "So we go around spraying people with Windex and see if they scratch their wrists?"

Abe's shoulders fell as he turned to her. "Don't make fun of me. I'm serious about this. Higgins? Sure, spray him down. But these three witches who have come out to help us? Invite them over to help clean up the Corner Cup for the Acoustic Weekend and ask them to clean the windows."

"The three witches?" Rayn asked. "Do you think Rebecca and them are Renati?"

"I think we should be cautious," Abe replied.

"And I agree with him," I spoke up. "Can we really be too cautious? Rebecca's florist shop was on the list of potential Renati hideouts. I'm not saying she's trying to pull something, but it's good to know for sure."

"I think we should," Rose agreed. "If nothing comes of it, then things continue as they are. And if we find out one of them is lying, we'll be glad we did it."

I glanced down at Abe's wrist where his Renati mark permanently marked his skin. I wouldn't put it past the Renati to send someone into our circle like a Trojan horse, but how many of the witches under Erebus's spell were good people? How many of them believed we were evil because that's all they knew? They had no reason to question their beliefs.

Whether the past generations of Elementals deserved their downfall or not, Erebus would not be the better option. Hopefully in time, those good people stuck in the Renati would see that.

Chapter Thirty-Four
Acoustic Weekend
Whitney

H armony took the stage the last night of Acoustic Weekend, holding the mic in shaky fingers as she scanned the crowd, waiting for the noise to die down.

"Hello, um, hi, everyone." Harmony cleared her throat. "Thank you for coming to our Acoustic Weekend. It means so much to see how many of you came out the last few nights in support of this amazing place. And in memory of our darling Amilia Burnett, who built this place into what it is today. My name is Harmony Vasquez and Amilia was one of my dearest friends," Harmony paused, placing her fingers over her lips. She blinked a few times before she continued. "I know she would have done anything to keep these doors open. Acoustic Night was one of her absolute favorite events to host. We're honored you're all a part of this with us." The crowd clapped and cheered as a smile broke out across Harmony's face. "Now without further ado, our first guest of the night, Addison Lee."

Harmony clipped the microphone back into the stand and clapped as she backed off the makeshift stage. She took her spot in the corner where Amilia used to stand, waiting to announce each guest after the previous performer finished.

We had all hands on deck that weekend, except for Aden, who stayed behind to "guard the cottage," as he had said. Rayn, Ashley, Lauren, Dmitri, Robby, Luke and I worked all three nights. The last night was more crowded than the first night of the event. Good thing we decided to sell tickets because we would have violated fire code for max capacity. Luke and Dmitri buzzed around the dining room bringing customers their orders, while Rayn manned the toaster oven, keeping the endless supply of bagels going. Lauren handled the cash register like a pro, hitting buttons and putting in drink orders without thinking twice. Ashley, Robby and I made drinks while Nic managed the raffle table. The atmosphere was hectic, but that meant we were making money.

The donations for the raffles were more than I could have hoped for. Bryan got Giani's to donate a romantic dinner for two including a bottle of the house wine, cork fees included. The ice cream parlor between CC and Giani's donated a seat at one of their decorate your own ice cream cake classes. The boutique down the street provided a bunch of coupons as well as a gift basket. Rebecca donated a gift basket with gardening tools, seeds and a gift card to the florist.

So many businesses in the area were glad to reach out and lend a helping hand, though not all of them. It made me wonder if the ones that didn't reach out were Renati businesses, or if the ones who did were but in disguise to throw us off.

The trio of witches had come to help us set up earlier that day. I had asked them to wash down the big windows that took up the front corner of the building and they gladly agreed. I had watched the three of them closely, none of them seemed bothered by the cleaning chemicals in the least. Either Abe had a Windex allergy or Jane, Rebecca and Kelly were genuine in their desire to help us.

"This is incredible." Ashley smiled, watching the line of people at the raffle table grow longer. "So many people love this place as much as we do."

"My life definitely wouldn't be the same if I didn't wander in here looking for a job last year," I added.

"Same." Ashley glanced back at Lauren as she started more coffee brewing.

In my peripheral vision, I noticed Nic wave me over to the table. I turned back to Ashley. "Hey, I'll be right back. Two seconds." I joined Nic behind the raffle table. "Everything okay?"

He nodded. "Just checking in on you."

I raised an eyebrow at him. "I'm fine. Do I not look fine?"

"You look like you haven't slept in two nights." He glanced across the room at Harmony. "Both of you."

"Tonight is the last night of the event."

Nic didn't seem convinced. "Sure, but is this all going to be enough?"

Rebecca approached the raffle table next and held up her phone. "We should take some photos for the newspaper. We can drum up extra publicity by doing a follow up article on the event."

"Sure." I threw my arm around Nic's shoulders and pulled him close.

Nic wrapped his arm around my waist and smiled. Rebecca clicked the picture and winked before she crossed the room to take a photo of the performer currently on the stage.

The bell jingled above the door and I turned towards the sound. Abe walked in with his parents, Janice and Jeff.

I waved them over with a smile and met them at the register. "Hi, guys! Thanks for coming in."

Janice reached out and put her hand atop mine. "It's wonderful to see you, dear. How are things going? Are you still living with that blonde number who moved your things?"

I laughed. "Bryan, yes. Dmitri and I are living with him and his best friend."

"Good for you. He's a looker." Janice winked at me and Abe groaned in disgust.

"Ugh, Mom, please stop," he begged.

Jeff handed me his debit card. "I'll take a black coffee and whatever they'd like. I'm going to our table."

I took the Roberts' order and handed Jeff's card back to Janice. Abe's parents took seats at a table Dmitri had reserved for them, but Abe made his way across the dining area to where Dmitri stood. Busy taking the next customer's order, I barely heard Ashley speak behind me.

"Oh, Em's parents are here."

"What?" My head shot towards the front as Henry and Bonnie Drake walked into the dining area. They were dressed up like they were strolling into a campaigning event. Panic flooded my core and an icy chill ran through my veins. I swallowed, trying to bring air back into my lungs but I choked on my own spit.

Ashley took a step towards me. "You okay?"

I nodded, gathering my composure. "I'm good."

I wish Ashley understood what it meant to see the Drakes here; that they were so much more than Emma and Serenity's parents or popular faces in the community. I wish she knew them for the snakes they were; that she needed to stay far away from them. That they would kill her without a second thought to get under Lauren's skin. As the Drake's made their way to a small reserved table in the corner, I realized they had planned to be here all along.

Harmony glared at them with every step they took across the crowded dining area. Harmony's gaze met mine, her jaw clenched tightly as she raised her eyebrows. Silently telling me to watch them without having to say a word. Whoever had reserved the table for the Drakes must not have told Harmony who the special guests were.

Lauren and Rayn both froze behind the counter. Lauren's nails dug into the side of the cash register as Rayn stood with wide eyes, the door to the toaster oven left open.

Ashley went into the back room for more milk and I took the opportunity to talk with Lauren and Rayn alone. "Keep it together."

Lauren turned to face me. "Every Elemental in existence is under this roof. It would be so easy for them to blow this place up and end it once and for all."

"There are a lot of innocent people in this building."

Rayn scoffed behind me, reaching in the toaster oven to pull out a hot bagel with her bare hands. "Like that would stop them."

"This has to be some kind of distraction," Lauren suggested, clenching her hands into fists. "We are here trying to do something good, and they're out there one step ahead of us. I want to save the CC as much as anyone but we are wasting valuable time."

"Lo has a point," Rayn said. "What if those moles they sent to the palace already have the last piece of the key? What if they have Amilia's piece and are heading to the Allurement as we speak?"

"You guys are spiraling." I shook my head.

Lauren put a fist on her hip. "Are we? Or are you distracted by your emotions?"

I huffed, knowing nothing I said would calm either of them down. The Drakes had done exactly what they had intended to do. We were rattled. They knew their presence would throw us off of our game and they'd walk out of here one step ahead for that simple act. I took a closer look at the Drakes, analyzing every little detail I could in hopes that something would stick out to me.

"Excuse me," a man said at the register. "Can I place an order for two cappuccinos? For the councilman and his wife."

"Oh, of course, we live to serve the Drakes." Lauren punched the buttons on the screen as the man swiped his card.

"Lauren, chill," I muttered under my breath.

Robby came up to the counter, waiting to take the order out but I waved him off. "I've got this one, why don't you go take a break? You haven't had one since you got here."

"Thanks, Whit." Robby smiled and left the dining area.

I made the drinks myself and carried the small cups across the dining area to the Drakes. I gently set the drinks on the table and smiled. "Two cappuccinos for our guests of honor."

"Why thank you, Miss Dansley." Henry Drake took a sip, humming his satisfaction. "You know, this place always had the best coffee in town. I forgot where everyone went before Burnett opened this place."

"Someone had to shine some light on this town. Generations know the management is subpar." I crossed my arms.

Bonnie Drake looked up at me wide eyed, shocked at how I offended her husband without a care.

"You're welcome to fill out a formal complaint," Henry Drake offered.

"Enjoy the show." I gave them both another glance over, hoping the key stem would be dangling from the chain around Bonnie's neck. That would have been too simple, wouldn't it? I went back to the counter, where Rose and Brooke now sat on the barstools off to the side of the counter.

"What did you say?" Brooke asked as I took my place behind the counter next to my sister. "Bonnie Drake is fuming."

"Nothing. I wanted to show them that they don't scare me," I answered.

The front door opened again but this time it was Bryan and Troy. I let out a deep sigh of relief as they shuffled through the crowd. Bryan leaned across the counter with a smile, pecking a kiss on my cheek. Troy gave us a wave before he headed to the restrooms.

"The Drake's are here," I told Bryan in a whisper.

"Which ones?" He discreetly scanned the dining area.

"Bonnie and Henry." Rayn crossed her arms.

"They have literally never come in here before," Bryan pointed out.

Dmitri came up to the counter at Bryan's side and slipped a twenty in the tip jar. "I'll give you one guess who this is from."

"They came here to distract us from whatever the rest of the minions are up to," Lauren muttered.

"Maybe." Dmitri scanned the room. "Or this is our chance while *they're* distracted to find that damn key stem."

"What are you thinking?" I watched the wheels in his head turn.

Dmitri turned to Brooke and whispered, "Let's go check his downtown office, the one at town hall. You can go in through the walls and I'll keep watch."

"I'll come with you." Rose jumped up from her seat.

"Wait, Dmitri you're clocked in." I stopped the three of them as they rushed towards the door. "And you're kind of awaiting trial for breaking into their house."

"Like that matters?" Dmitri hardened his gaze with determination.

"Mit, no." I shook my head.

Lauren leaned over the counter. "Go out the back, that way no one sees you leave. And be careful, please."

"No, I'm not okay with this," I protested once more, raising my voice.

"We got this." Dmitri nodded and followed Rose and Brooke through the employee only doors.

"That doesn't make me nervous at all." Bryan sat down on the empty bar stool, still looking at the door swinging back and forth where our siblings had rushed out.

"Nobody listens to me." I glanced across the dining room at the Drakes. "At least Henry is here and it's late at night. I doubt anyone is at town hall."

"Yeah, well, they better keep an eye out for Big Boy," Rayn pointed out. "That Shadow is always popping up when the Drakes are near."

Lauren rested her back against the counter. "I doubt any of us will forget Big Boy is lurking around out there."

My gaze returned to Henry and Bonnie Drake, sitting at the little table sipping on cappuccinos. It didn't make sense for something as precious as the key stem to be hidden in the bottom of a desk drawer. I would have never taken my talisman off and hid it in my dresser under my socks. I kept it on my person. I always had eyes on it. I could reach up and stroke the gem with my fingers, easing the tension that built in my muscles, releasing the gravity of what would happen if any of them got their dirty fingers on it.

Lauren had tried taking her talisman off and she lost everything, nearly losing the bracelet itself. We had to fight tooth and nail to get it back.

Bonnie Drake was not stupid enough to let the piece of the key out of her sight.

"She has it on her person," I announced, unsure if I'd even said the words aloud until my sister replied.

"What?" Rayn furrowed her brow.

"Bonnie Drake," I whispered, staring at the back of her perfectly-styled black hair. "She keeps it on her person."

"How do you know?" Lauren turned around to glare at them.

"Because that's what we do with the talismans. It's the easiest way to ensure it's safe." I pulled my phone from my pocket and sent a text in our group chat.

Come back, it's not in the office.

I sent a silent wish that one of them would see the text before they got too far into the building, but none of them responded.

Rayn tapped the counter as Harmony took the stage and announced the next performer. "I don't like this, someone has to go get them."

"Agreed, but we're slammed here." Lauren looked around the dining room. "It would draw the Drake's attention if the three of us disappeared."

"Then I'll go alone." I untied my apron.

"Baby, please don't," Bryan protested but I shook my head.

"I'm going." I scanned the room to make sure no one paid attention as I slipped around the counter. "Get Nicky to cover for me. I'll be right back."

I crept through the employee only doors before anyone could argue another word. I snuck around the side of the building and rushed two streets over to the town square. The street lamps weren't brighter than usual, but they felt like spotlights, following my every step. I checked my phone again; still no messages from Rose or Dmitri. When I got to town hall, there was no immediate sign of them. I rushed around the side of the building where two figures crouched in the bushes.

"Mit, Rose," I hissed as loudly as I could without giving away their location. I let water drip down my fingers, exposing my powers knowing Rose would feel my magic before she heard my voice.

"Whitney?" Rose popped her head up from the bush, looking in my direction.

I rushed to their side and knelt down next to them. "Get Brooke out of there, the key stem isn't in Drake's office."

"What do you mean?" Dmitri asked.

"I don't know for certain, but I'm almost positive Bonnie has it on her. It's not there. Please trust my gut and get Brooke out."

Rose grabbed Brooke's arm and shook her but she didn't come to.

"How long has she been in there?" I questioned.

"A while," Dmitri answered. "No one has gone in though, we've been watching every direction."

"Unless someone's already in there." Panic coursed through my veins. "Mit, stay with her body. Rose, we gotta go in there and get her."

"I can see a back entrance on this side." Rose jumped up from the bushes and rushed towards the building with me hot on her heels. She waved her hand over the lock and pushed the door open.

Rose and I crept inside, looking both ways down the hall before we tiptoed to Drake's office. Half of the lights were turned off but enough were left on to keep the halls lit, maybe to deter people from sneaking in.

"There's a guard on duty, but he's sitting at the front reception desk eating cheetos," Rose whispered, turning the next corner to the city council offices.

When we got to the offices, a man stood outside of Drake's door, peeking in through the window. He motioned down the hall and a woman joined his side. Both of them moved as stealthy as lions. One of them opened the door and they crept inside.

Rose and I snuck down the hallway and peeked into the window. Neither of them had touched Brooke's astral projection yet. They kept their distance but we couldn't assume they wouldn't strike at any moment.

"This was a trap," I whispered to Rose, watching the Renati stalk Brooke like prey. "The Drakes knew showing up tonight would rattle us."

"If they trap her in here, will she be able to return to her body?" Rose's eyes grew wide with worry.

I motioned towards the Renati members. "Don't let them touch her."

Rose waved her hand and vines crept into Drake's office, wrapping around the two Renati's ankles. Rose closed her fist, getting a tight grip on the Renati's legs before she yanked her arm back, pulling their feet out from underneath them. Both of the witches fell flat on their faces.

The commotion startled Brooke's subconscious, and her translucent figure turned sharply to look over her shoulder.

"Brooke! Go back!" I shouted across the room, drawing the attention of the Renati to me. "Go back!"

Brooke's figure nodded and disappeared. I let out a sigh of relief.

"Hey! Who's back there?" A voice bellowed down the hall.

The security guard.

"Shit, we gotta go." Rose wiggled her fingers and the vines around the Renati members slithered up their bodies. "That should hold them."

We sprinted down the hallway back the way we came but the security guard waited for us, his thick orange-stained fingers wrapped around a flashlight. He pointed it in our faces, blinding us as he shouted, "You're not supposed to be in here!"

With a wave of my hand, the guard levitated into the air. He lost grip on his flashlight and it floated away from him. He flailed around in the air, struggling to get his balance.

Rose and I dashed past as he yelled, "Stop! Get back here!"

We bolted through the door and Brooke and Dmitri waited for us outside. By the time we got back to the Corner Cup, the event neared the end. The last scheduled performer stood on the stage and a line wrapped around the counter of everyone grabbing last minute drinks and bagels before we closed. Harmony stood by the front door arguing with two police officers.

Grady and Higgins.

I grabbed Nic's arm as I rushed behind the counter. "What's going on over there?"

"The fuck? Where did you come from?" He startled like I had appeared out of thin air.

"The cops, Nicky, why are the cops here?" I asked again.

"Noise complaints, apparently. They are also verifying that we have not gone above capacity, I guess there was a complaint that we had let too many people in," he explained.

"Are they going to shut down the event?"

"Let them, it's almost over." He shrugged and slid another bagel into the toaster.

Higgins stepped away from Harmony and coned his hands over his mouth to magnify his voice. "Show's over! Everyone out!"

Grady marched over to the sound equipment and unplugged it from the wall with a hard yank. The customers began to murmur amongst themselves as everyone stood frozen in surprise.

"I said everyone out! This event is shut down!" Higgins yelled again.

"My permits got approved! We've been doing this for two nights. Why are you doing this, Rory?" Harmony asked Higgins but he brushed past her and opened both of the glass doors. Higgins waved his hand in the air, directing customers to exit the Corner Cup immediately.

Nic let out a harsh sigh and crossed his arms. "They'll probably write us tickets."

"Why?" I asked.

"Anything to get this place closed down."

"This is a gross abuse of power. I'm coming for your job, Rory, so kiss that stupid badge goodbye," Harmony threatened the cops with a middle finger before she marched over to the counter and grabbed my arm. "Where the hell have you been?"

"Um, we, uh…I stepped out for a second." I glanced over her shoulder to see if the Drake's were still there.

"You're being shady, Whitney," Harmony spat out my name like it was venom. "You've been spending too much time with Dominic."

"What did I do?" Nic crossed his arms.

"I'm not…" I looked back into her eyes. "I'm not being shady." I lowered my voice. "We…we're trying to get the key stem. We figured the Drakes were distracted here, but we didn't find it. I think Bonnie is keeping it on her person."

Harmony ran her tongue across her teeth and let out a sigh. "Yeah, I think she is too. Next time, say something to me before you run off and leave me short staffed."

"I didn't plan to go, but B and Rose went with Mit and they…I went to get them out of a mess before they got caught," I explained. "You've been really stressed with everything. I'm trying to let you focus on this place."

Harmony's shoulders fell. "I am losing sight of what's important, aren't I?"

Nic put a hand on her shoulder and gave a gentle squeeze.

I leaned against the counter. "I know this place was important to Mia, and it's important to me too. But if the Renati burns the town, CC is going with it. That's a hard realization I still struggle to accept."

"I know that," she spoke in a soft voice, almost defeated. She put her hand on top of Nic's. "It's been hard thinking about letting go, like it's all I have left of Mia. Warren is gone and he always kept me grounded. Without him I'm just…lost. And everything with Jerry threw a wrench in my gears."

"I can imagine." I nodded.

"The Drakes left about ten minutes ago." Harmony changed the subject. "We'll have to get Bonnie alone, away from Henry. It's the only way to find out for sure."

"How the hell are we going to pull that off?"

"Get her while her guard is down."

Chapter Thirty-Five

Switching Sides

Whitney

The few days after the Acoustic Weekend fundraiser were easy shifts. The chaos at the Corner Cup died down to only a few customers in the dining room. I sighed in relief, knowing it would be a relaxing Tuesday. My feet still ached from all the running around I had done. Harmony still crunched numbers, but it looked like we had raised enough money to keep us afloat. For now.

The bell above the front door jingled, and to my surprise, Emma walked in. Her purse hung low on the crook of her elbow and her feet shuffled across the floor. She gave me a subtle wave and climbed up on a barstool where Bryan normally sat. She leaned against the counter and rested her head on an open hand.

"Hi," I greeted, a bit uneasy at her unannounced arrival.

"I wanted to come see how you were…after the memory stuff," Emma replied.

"Oh, thank you. I appreciate that. I'm okay…still processing all of it, to be honest." I paused. "Are *you* okay? That must've been really hard to relive."

"I'm not, honestly." Emma blinked away tears. "Everything has been a lie. All my family has done is lie to me. I feel like I don't even know them anymore. I don't know what to believe."

"I'm sorry…I can't imagine how hard it's been on you." I wanted to reach across the counter and cover her hand with mine, but I refrained, unsure of how it would be received.

"I'm the one Serenity needed to hurt to prove herself."

I shifted awkwardly. "Bryan and I suspected."

Emma wiped a tear from her cheek. "My own family...They go around fucking with everyone's lives, not caring who they take down with them."

"Like my brother," I muttered.

"Your brother?" Emma tilted her head.

Of course no one told her. Why would they?

I let out a deep sigh. "Dmitri and his boyfriend were looking for the key stem and they kind of broke into your parent's house."

Her eyes widened. "What?"

"Your dad is pressing charges. There's a court date and everything."

"Shit," Emma whispered. "I'm sorry."

"You aren't mad that they broke into your house?"

She shook her head. "My mom stole that piece of the key in the first place. I always tried to understand my parent's devotion to the Renati, but I don't agree with what they've done."

"I'm sure you feel stuck in the middle."

"Yes and no." Emma tapped her fingers against the counter. "I think I can get your brother out of trouble with the police."

I jumped to alert. "You do?"

"I still have a bedroom and half of my stuff in the house. I can tell them I gave Dmitri permission to go inside. It wouldn't be a break in if they had permission."

"He went in through the window."

"Hmm..." Emma thought for a moment. "I can work with that." She stood up from the barstool and grabbed her bag. "I'll go talk to the cops. See if I can get the charges dropped."

"Are you serious?"

"My parents have done enough, don't you think?"

I heard Bryan's voice inside my head telling me to keep Emma out of this, but if she offered assistance that could actually get Dmitri out of a serious situation...How could I say no to that?

"I'll come with you," I offered. "But we should bring my lawyer with us. She was very adamant that we don't speak to the police without her."

When Emma nodded, I went to the breakroom to grab Lauren. "Hey, when your break is over, can you hold down the fort? Emma is going to tell the police she gave Dmitri permission to go into the Drake house."

Lauren perked up. "Are you serious? I'll come back now. Go!"

I left Lauren with a smile and knocked on the closed office door. I leaned towards the crack in the door and raised my voice. "It's me."

"Hi, Whitney," Harmony said from the other side.

I opened the door and stepped into the office. The temperature of the room felt freezing; so cold I glanced up expecting to see icicles forming from the ceiling.

"You okay?"

Harmony nodded. "Are *you* okay?"

I waved for Emma to join me. She hesitated, standing in the doorframe of the swinging door that led to the employee only area. "Emma has a plan."

"Emma *Drake?*"

"That's me." Emma walked into the office to stand next to me.

"Elaborate, please," Harmony requested.

"My father is an asshole and I want to get these charges against Dmitri dropped," Emma explained. "I'll go talk to the police and tell them that I gave Dmitri and his boyfriend permission to enter the house even though it was locked."

Harmony tilted her head, deep in thought. "What exactly would he be breaking into your house to get? What would be so important that it couldn't wait until you got to the house yourself?"

"Uh," Emma thought. "Well, I did leave for Falcon Bay early in the morning and I could have also potentially left my inhaler at my parent's house."

"Good." Harmony rested her elbows on the desk. "Why wouldn't you call your boyfriend or one of your friends? Why Whitney's brother?"

"I mean, everyone has jobs, right? Everyone else could have been busy," I offered.

"Now where is the proof that you asked him?" Harmony questioned.

"See, that's where we will have to get creative because I don't have an answer," Emma admitted.

"Harmony, fucking charm them," I complained. "I will do it if it makes you uncomfortable, but we are going to have to use some kind of magic to pull this off."

Harmony leaned against the desk and chewed on the inside of her cheek. "Fine, type up some text messages and we will charm them into seeing a different date and time stamp on it. Now the final question, why didn't Dmitri tell them this story when they first arrested him?"

Emma froze, glancing over to me. "You know him better than I do."

I nodded. "Dmitri was terrified when the cops first pulled him in. He could have been worried about getting Emma in trouble?"

"Hmmmm. It's a stretch, but it's something." Harmony stood up from the desk. "I will meet you at the police station. Do not go in without me."

I dropped my apron on the desk and followed Emma out of the Corner Cup. On the way to the police station, Emma asked for details about the situation as I typed out text messages between Emma and Dmitri on her phone. Emma wanted to know who the cops were that pulled Dmitri in. What kind of evidence they had. If I knew whether the cops were Renati.

"One is a witch hunter. I don't know about the other one," I told her.

Emma froze in her seat and turned to me. "Hunter?"

"Do you know about them?"

"Uh, no, that is not information they shared with me. There are witch hunters?"

"There didn't used to be. There were wards up protecting our part of the forest, but someone broke them. We got some insider information that members of the Renati are working with the hunters behind Erebus' back. They are the ones who broke the wards," I explained.

"Which Renati members?"

"We weren't given names."

"Who is your insider?"

"Uh, a ghost." I smiled awkwardly.

Emma furrowed her brow. "I'm not even going to ask because at this point, sure, I accept that answer. Renati members working with witch hunters feels kind of counter-productive, though. Because they are also witches?"

"I can't make sense of it either," I answered. "Unless they are desperate to take us out."

Emma nodded. "They are desperate. They're scared shitless of you, my father especially."

"He acts pretty cocky whenever I see him."

"*Act* is the key word there. Trust me, he's terrified."

I had a hard time believing that. Even after Nic nearly killed him when we closed the Shadow Realm portal, Henry Drake appeared to be as confident as ever. The way he strolled into the Corner Cup at Mia's memorial and our fundraiser weekend as if he owned the place, even trying to buy it. He certainly wouldn't have kept it as a coffee shop out of pure spite. Just like he tried to get my brother and Abe in serious legal trouble.

We waited in the car until Harmony pulled up next to us. She sat in her car, fixing her hair in the mirror of the visor before she got out.

"Do you have the texts?" Harmony asked.

Emma nodded. "Whit typed up Dmitri's responses too."

"Good. Keep your fingers crossed and be confident in your story." Harmony led the way up the stairs into the station.

My knees trembled as we walked into the building together. This would work, it had to.

We had to get the police off our backs so we could dedicate all of our attention towards the Renati and the damn key stem. It had already taken too long. We simply did not have time to deal with court and legal battles on top of everything else.

Emma marched up to the desk, not waiting for the police officer to acknowledge her.

"I'm here to speak with Officers Grady and Higgins, thank you." Emma stood tall, clasping her hands in front of her casually.

"In regards to?" The cop at the desk lifted a brow.

"Tell them it's Emma Drake in regards to the charges my father has pressed against Dmitri Dansley and Abraham Roberts."

The cop looked back and forth between the three of us before he left the desk and disappeared down the hallway. I glanced sideways at Emma but she didn't appear nervous at all. She rolled her shoulders back and lifted her chin, waiting for the officer to return.

Grady appeared around the corner with the other cop and froze when he saw Emma and I standing there together.

"Yes?" he asked, crossing his arms.

Emma stepped forward. "We have proof that these breaking and entering charges my father has pressed are all a big misunderstanding. If you'd so kindly lead us back to your office we will provide the evidence."

Grady huffed, unconvinced. "Sure."

Emma and I let Harmony lead the way down the hall behind Officer Grady. He waved for his partner, Officer Higgins, to join us in the same office they had attempted to interrogate Dmitri in.

"They apparently have evidence that the Drake case against the Dansley kid is a big misunderstanding," Grady informed his partner.

"Is that so?" Higgins turned to Harmony. "Nice to see you again, Harmony."

Harmony's glare told him to go to hell. "Emma, explain to the officer's what happened."

Higgins clicked on a recorder and crossed his arms.

Emma cleared her throat. "I attend Falcon Bay University during the week and on the weekends I return home to my parent's house in Diamond Gate. I left for school early that morning and forgot my inhaler. As someone who suffers from asthma, you can understand why it's imperative for me to have that on my person." Emma put her hand over her heart. "I would have been late if I drove all the way back to my house. Attendance at FBU is taken seriously and we are only allowed so many absences and tardies throughout the semester.

Fortunately, Dmitri was available, unlike the others I called to retrieve my medication. Dmitri and Abe graciously agreed to drive to my parent's house and grab my inhaler." Emma held her head high as she continued her tale. "We planned to meet in town at the Corner Cup where I could quickly grab it and head back to Falcon Bay in time for my class. Unfortunately, my parents removed the spare key from its usual hiding place on the front porch. They had it locked up tighter than a fortress. As you will see in our messages, I told Dmitri and his boyfriend to go through the window in the back because I knew it would be unlocked. Dmitri didn't break into my parent's house, he actually did me a huge favor. If I had an attack without my inhaler, I could have died."

I bit my lip to hide the smile that threatened to form on my lips. Emma's attention to detail made her story believable without a second thought. The thin lips and heavy brows from Grady and Higgins indicated that they didn't find her story as convincing.

"How convenient that neither boy mentioned a single detail about this conversation when we spoke to them," Grady huffed.

"Maybe you should reevaluate your approach of attempting to scare the memories out of teenagers instead of giving them a chance to explain themselves," Harmony offered. "You had them both so rattled thinking they had committed a felony while helping a friend, I'm surprised they remembered their own names."

"I didn't realize you were friends with the Dansleys, Miss Drake," Higgins replied.

His statement threw me off. Why would a police officer care who the local college kids were friends with? Unless, he knew why Henry Drake would be so against his daughter making friends with me and my generation.

"Dmitri is Whitney's brother, and Whitney is in a relationship with my best friend. Whitney and Dmitri live in my boyfriend's father's house. Of course I am friends with them." Emma scrunched her forehead. "How strange of you to assume you keep up with the social lives of all the locals. Or did you make that statement because I happen to belong to a founding family and therefore, the townspeople feel entitled to my personal life?"

Neither Grady nor Higgins replied.

"Emma, please show these dedicated officers the text conversation between you and Dmitri," Harmony replied.

Emma took her phone from her bag. As she moved to place it on the table, Harmony's fingers discreetly waved at her side. I barely caught a glimpse of the text conversation altering when Emma set her phone down.

Higgins slipped a glove on before he picked up Emma's phone. Grady read over his shoulder as the two of them analyzed the altered text messages. They looked at one another before Higgins turned back to Harmony.

"Why are you here presenting this information without your parents?" Grady asked Emma. "Why not explain things and have them drop the charges themselves if this is all one big misunderstanding?"

"My father is in Portland on business," Emma answered. "This urgent matter couldn't wait until he got home."

"I see," Higgins paused. "We will have to contact the Drakes and their lawyers."

"Please do." Emma took her phone back. "I'm sure my parents will be eager to get this whole thing sorted out."

"This doesn't mean the charges are dropped, but this does change things significantly. We'll be in touch." Higgins held his hand out, showing us the door. I guess he figured we knew the way out of the building.

I pulled Emma into a hug as we stood on the sidewalk. "I cannot thank you enough for doing this. Seriously, Dmitri means the world to me, and I don't know how to repay you for keeping him and Abe safe."

"You can repay me by keeping Bryan safe," Emma replied against my arm. "*He* means the world to *me*."

"We can agree on that." I released Emma from the hug.

"We'll celebrate when the charges are officially dropped, but I'm feeling optimistic about this," Harmony replied. "This won't stop them from coming at us again."

"Grady already gave Bryan an expensive speeding ticket he didn't deserve and tried to shut down our fundraiser, so that doesn't surprise me," I said.

"The police in general or those two hooligans?" Emma nodded towards the station.

"It's always those two." I turned to Harmony. "Do you think Higgins could be Renati?"

Harmony glanced back at the building. "I'm starting to wonder about that myself."

"He's Chief Abram's nephew," I pointed out.

"I know," Harmony answered.

Emma glanced back at the police station. "My parents have Chief Abrams and his wife over for dinner all the time." She huffed and turned back to me. "We know for sure Grady is a witch hunter?"

"Yes, that I am absolutely positive about." I nodded.

"Well, if they are partners, and Higgins is actually Renati...that makes sense doesn't it? Higgins could be the liaison between the two, for lack of a better word," Emma said.

Harmony crossed her arms and looked at Emma. "Have you switched sides?"

"I'm not a witch," Emma answered.

"But you'll go against your entire family? For what?"

Emma sighed. "I'm not the one who turned their back. My family has turned their back on *me*. I've always had less worth than my sister because she was born with magic. My loyalty is with my family, but you misunderstand who my family actually is." She put her hand over her heart. "The ones I chose myself."

"Byn." I smiled.

Emma nodded. "My friends are my family, and they are all wrapped up in this one way or another. I can't stand on the sidelines knowing the ones who mean the most to me are in danger. Especially when that danger comes from my own fucking father."

"Okay. I believe you, for now." Harmony said. "Excuse my skepticism, but trust has to be earned. Though, today you earned quite a bit."

"Well," Emma paused. "My dad is going to be pissed when he hears about this. I mean, like, he'll contemplate strangling me with his bare hands."

"We won't let him lay a finger on you," I promised.

Emma gave a half smile as if she didn't believe me.

"Either way," Harmony said. "We have to get the key fragment before they retaliate for real. Everything they've pulled since the cottage attack has been annoying, but now is the time to act before things get worse."

"Any idea where your mom could possibly be keeping it?" I asked Emma.

She shook her head. "I've never seen anything like it in the house."

We had wasted enough time searching for clues on this goose chase. Time to go directly to the source.

Chapter Thirty-Six

Hostage

Whitney

Are you sure this is going to work? Rayn asked mentally. The two of us hid behind a row of bushes in the parking lot of Drake Real Estate office. *Won't the Shadows warn her?*

I honestly don't know, I answered.

Cool. So a typical plan, then.

An ambush isn't exactly what I originally had in mind, but I thought in the beginning we would be able to snoop around and steal the stem of the key like we did the ledger. But the Renati knew we were coming and they wouldn't leave anything valuable lying around again.

If we stood any chance of getting the pieces of the key before the Renati, we had to act now. Kidnapping Bonnie Drake sat pretty low on the list of war crimes that would keep me up at night.

Only one car remained in the dimly lit parking lot – a black Cadillac I'd seen Bonnie drive around town. My knees trembled as I crouched down out of sight. This could go terribly wrong. Bonnie was not a defenseless woman. She had powers and practiced her craft with Mia and my mother, two of the most skilled witches I'd ever known. I anticipated Bonnie to be on the same level of expertise.

We did have one advantage over whatever power Bonnie Drake did possess.

A witch hunter with a dart gun.

Bonnie came into my line of sight out the back door of the office. She locked up and strolled to her car, texting away on her phone. She didn't look up to make sure nothing waited for her. She didn't stop to question her safety. Bonnie had grown too comfortable around Rifton.

From across the parking lot, Aden lifted his pistol and shot with impressive precision. The black feathered dart struck Bonnie directly in the side of her neck.

Bonnie froze in place, searching the parking lot before she pulled the dart from her neck. She looked down at it in horror before she dropped it and put up her hand, maybe trying to put up a shield.

Nothing.

Lauren released a gust of wind that blew through the pine trees with such velocity the thick branches snapped off at the base. The wind roared across the parking lot and knocked Bonnie Drake flat on her back. Her head hit the pavement and she remained motionless.

Rayn and I quickly bolted from our hiding places to Bonnie's side. I checked her pulse and waited for the faint beating of her heart to throb against my fingertips. After I confirmed her pulse, I checked the back of her head to make sure she wasn't bleeding out.

She lived.

Good.

Lauren rushed out of the bushes and joined our side. Once we knew we hadn't killed Bonnie, the three of us waved our hands over her car, using a cloaking spell Abe had taught us.

Harmony pulled into the parking lot, her car skidding to a stop as the back doors flung open. Rayn and I levitated Bonnie to the back seat and climbed into the car. Rayn ran around to the empty front passenger seat while I sat at Bonnie's feet.

Harmony peeled out of the parking lot and drove straight back to the cottage where the rest of the crew waited. Lauren and Aden followed close behind in Lauren's car. We didn't want to take everyone with us. Herding a dozen people around was usually disorganized and would have caught the attention of anyone who happened to be nearby.

I pulled a vial of sleeping drought from my pocket that Rose had brewed and opened Bonnie's mouth, pouring only a few drops in. The bumps and sways of the car threatened to shake my hands and accidentally overdose her, but I kept my fingers steady. I wanted Bonnie to sleep until we got her secured and ready for interrogation, but I did eventually want her to wake up.

As Harmony pulled into the cottage driveway, Bonnie remained unconscious. Nic, Dmitri and Abe met us in the front yard as we levitated Bonnie from the car and into the cleared out garden shed in the backyard.

Nausea rose in my stomach as they sat Bonnie in a chair and restrained her. Her head fell forward as Aden tied her hands behind her back. She may have been unconscious now but she wouldn't stay that way. Aden ran low on magic numbing darts, and who knew how long it would take to wear her down, to get her to admit where the damn key fragment hid.

I swallowed my nerves and stood tall, not wanting anyone else to see me second guessing my own plan when they all agreed to follow my lead.

"What now?" Dmitri asked after they had Bonnie secured to the chair. The vines that grew up around her body reminded me of when we did this to Aden. So much had changed since then.

"We wait for her to wake up," I answered.

"Where is it, Bonnie?" I attempted to hide the shake in my voice.

She sat with her shoulders squared and her hands tied behind her back. Bonnie looked me up and down, unimpressed. She pulled against the restraints but they didn't budge. "What are you talking about?"

"You know exactly what we're looking for. Where is the stem of the key?"

"What key?" Bonnie tilted her head.

"You know what I don't understand?" Rayn took a step towards Bonnie. "I don't understand how someone could betray their friends for a grease ball like Henry Drake. You knew the damage the Renati did to this town and you joined them anyway."

"We saved this town." Bonnie grit her teeth. "We are the only reason there is still a Rifton, so watch your tone when you speak to me."

My lip curled as I spat back. "You turned your back on your coven, on our mom and Amilia. I will speak to you however I damn well please."

"You speak as if you know the truth, but you only know what you've been told." Bonnie straightened her back and held her head high. "I don't have to prove myself or justify my actions to a group of girls no older than my own daughters. Once you gain some maturity, you'll learn how complicated real life is."

"I didn't ask for a lecture, Mrs. Drake, I asked for the key stem," I said through my teeth.

"You'll never find it. We have been planning this longer than you've been alive, you'll always be one step behind." Bonnie stared daggers at me, sending a chill up my spine. "You never deserved to be in power. The Elementals never took care of their people, they only took advantage and abused their followers."

I blinked, staring into her dark gaze. Serenity and Emma had her eyes. I scoffed and turned to Rose. "Lock the door, keep the vines on her." I waved my hand in Bonnie's direction as I spoke to Aden. "Give her another dose from the darts. Keep her down here until she talks."

"They'll come looking for me," Bonnie threatened. "Henry will come for me."

I smiled. "I'm counting on it."

We left Bonnie in the tool shed with a charm over the lock and one of Aden's darts in her neck. Back in the living room of the cottage, we warmed ourselves by the fire and contemplated our next move.

"What if she doesn't give us the key? The Renai broke through the wards around the cottage once before, who is to say they can't do it again?" Dmitri paced in front of the dining room table. "We won't give her a choice," I answered.

The front door opened and Bryan walked in, his hands balled into fists at his sides.

"Dmitri called to tell me that you locked Emma's mom up in the tool shed?" he snapped, raising his voice at us. "What the hell is wrong with you?"

I turned to face him, a mixture of his anger and fear swirled alongside my own uncertainty. "She's also a member of the Renati and she has the stem of the key. We need that key."

"Whit, we can't–"

I put my hand up to cut him off. "Mia and my mother trusted her with the stem of the key because she was supposed to be their friend, a member of their coven. She turned her back on them!" My voice erupted from my lungs. "I'm not showing her restraint because she happens to be related to someone. Everyone is important to someone."

Bryan's shoulders fell. "Please don't kill Emma's mom."

"They had no problem killing mine." Lauren shoved off the wall where she had been leaning.

Rose shook her head, turning to her brother. "It's only a matter of time before the rest of the Renati find us. They're going to be looking for her." Rose glanced over her shoulder at me. "We have to do something now before we're ambushed."

"It won't be an ambush if we know they're coming." Lauren paced the room. "But we are wasting time. She's never going to tell us where the key stem is. Let's knock her out and search her for it."

"Better than killing her," Brooke muttered.

"Why not kill her? Why should we let her walk out of here so she can come back and end us herself?" Lauren crossed her arms. "If the roles were reversed, she wouldn't think twice about ending our lives."

"She's Emma's mother," Rose echoed Bryan's words. "What happened to being better than them? If we're going to start murdering people then why are we even bothering with the labyrinth? At that point, do the blood sacrifice and end it."

"Rose is right," I let out a sigh of frustration. "As much as I hate the Drakes, we aren't murderers. The Renati killed Mia and Warren in cold blood, we won't stoop to their level."

"Then knock her out and search her for the key," Lauren repeated herself.

I turned towards the kitchen and stared at the door leading to the backyard. "I'll get into her head," I announced to the crew. "I charmed Serenity, I'll be able to get into Bonnie's mind. I'll look into her memories if she won't tell us where it is."

Nic stepped towards me, lowering his voice. "You sure?"

I nodded. "I'll be fine."

Aden, the Magisters and the girls all followed me to the tool shed. Bryan, Dmitri and Abe stayed behind in the house. I caught a glimpse of Dmitri moving across the room towards Bryan as we left, lowering his voice and reaching out for his shoulder. I pretended I didn't feel Bryan's distress with the situation and led the way through the backyard.

When I opened the toolshed, Bonnie barely lifted her head to look at us. Her eyes widened when she saw Harmony and Nic enter behind us.

Bonnie hardened her gaze at Nic. "I always knew you'd be the one to destroy us all."

Nic raised a brow. "Oh yeah?"

"The moment Amilia's daughter brought you home...I saw the fire in your eyes. You and that temper. I knew you were a demon the moment I laid eyes on you. And here we are all these years later. Look who is dead because of you."

"Don't listen to her." Harmony took a step towards Nic. "Don't let her get under your skin."

"I don't have to try, because he knows it's true. You all see it. The Elementals have always been their own worst enemy. The reason for your own downfall." Bonnie smirked. "I wonder how many more he will kill before all is said and done."

I glared at Bonnie, my heart pounding in my ears. "Nicky will be the one to kill your husband, but your daughter is mine."

Bonnie did as I hoped and slowly turned her head back to me. Her lip curled in hatred as her gaze narrowed. She opened her mouth to speak but I paid no attention to the words slipping from her lips. Instead, my powers washed against her mental wall like the sea in a storm.

I continued speaking, unsure of what Bonnie's reply had been. I had to keep her eyes on me, keep her glaring all that hate into me so I could break down those walls and see her memory of where she hid the damn key fragment. "I've thought about the best way to kill Serenity. Should I end her quickly to get it over with, to make sure she doesn't have a chance to fight back and get away? Or should I take my time and make her feel every ounce of pain she's forced on the rest of us?" I tilted my head. "I think I'll drop a boulder on her arm first."

Bonnie furrowed her brow as my powers shoved against the weak spot I found in her mental wall. I pushed harder this time, throwing everything I had at her blockade in what would probably be the only attempt I got. The barricade of magic in my way shattered and my powers seeped into her memories.

They came like a flip book – much like Nic's mind had been when he thought about a number of different events. Bonnie thought about her girls, but I didn't see them as they are now. Emma and Serenity were younger, toddlers maybe. Pigtails and matching dresses as they played at the park. Bonnie thought about Henry on their wedding day, everything surrounded with white lace and blush flower petals.

The next memory I found myself in knocked the wind out of my chest as I stared at the face of someone I'd only ever seen in a photo. The only picture Amilia had of my mother and Dmitri's father.

Bonnie sat across from Kyle at a dining room table. The table had a crystal fruit bowl in the center filled with various citrus fruits and a wine-colored runner down the middle. The way Bonnie lounged in the chair, they must have been sitting in her kitchen. Kyle didn't look nearly as relaxed as Bonnie. He sat hunched over in his seat, nursing a glass of whiskey.

There were bags under his eyes as if he hadn't slept in days and a dark bruise covered the side of his face.

Kyle took a sip of the amber liquid. A large ice cube in the glass clunked against the side as he set it back down on the table. "It wasn't supposed to happen this way," he whispered.

Bonnie leaned forward, resting her elbows on the cherry wood table. "And what exactly did you think would happen?"

Kyle shook his head.

"This wasn't supposed to happen because you got too deep, you know that right?" Bonnie tapped the side of her hand against the table. "You were supposed to get information and spellbooks, maybe the rest of the key? But you lost sight of the objective. I figured you'd lure her into bed to gain her trust but I didn't expect you to impregnate her."

Kyle shot a dirty glare across the table at Bonnie. "You left everything you knew behind for Henry. You gave up everything *for him*."

"That's because I love him, Kyle. Henry is my everything."

Kyle blinked at her. "And what do you think Audri is to me?"

Bonnie shifted in her chair. "I assumed you cared to some extent since you shared the boy together, but I didn't realize you–"

Kyle cut her off. "She was supposed to pick me. We have a family together. She was supposed to join us. She was supposed to trust me. She said she loved me." Kyle covered his eyes with his hand and slumped forward. His back bobbed as a silent sob left his body.

Bonnie tilted her head; sadness hung heavy in her gaze. She left her chair and knelt down next to Kyke's seat.

Bonnie let out a short sigh. "Kyle..."

"What do I do?" Kyle wept, covering his face with both of his hands. "I know it wasn't all me, I know she loves me too. I know she does. She didn't give me a chance to explain, to tell her all the ways she's been lied to. Now she's gone and I'll never see my son again."

Bonnie put her hand on Kyle's knee and whispered, "I'm sorry."

Kyle's hands drug down his face in a long sweep before they landed on the table. "I'm not giving up on her."

Bonnie's eyes grew as she scooted closer to him. "I know Audri pretty well and I know you do too. We are never going to change how she feels about the Renati, not after we burned Roberta's house down. Kyle, we got Jackson killed. Did you think she'd ever forgive losing Amilia's husband? They were so close."

"But she loves me," Kyle whispered, as a tear streamed down his cheek. "I'm Dmitri's father."

Bonnie shook her head. "It's not enough." She licked her lip and rose up to his level, pulling Kyle into a hug. "I'm sure the decision to leave hung heavy on Audrianna, but staying obviously wasn't an option for her."

"I'm not enough," he breathed, leaning into her.

Bonnie's shoulders fell. "Audri was never going to betray Amilia. Not even for you."

I slipped into another memory before my head could fully wrap around what I had seen between Bonnie and Kyle.

Henry Drake gazed at Bonnie from across the room, stepping closer to her desk. Her eyes widened with every movement he made as she sat behind a receptionist desk.

"Have you given much thought to our conversation from last night?" Henry asked, leaning against the desk.

Bonnie looked away from him and swallowed. "I have to admit, I'm a bit confused."

Henry smiled at her. "I know you only came to work here to spy, and I know you've been delivering information to your little coven of Elemental supporters."

Bonnie leaned back in her seat and dared make eye contact. "If you knew, then why did you let me in?"

"Because I find you intriguing, and as these months have gone by, I've grown to care for you, as foolish as that may sound. I hope you heard me last night, I only spoke the truth. I don't want to see you trapped in a web of lies."

Bonnie licked her bottom lip. "Considering you have evidence and the others only have stories...but they're my friends. I've known them since we were little girls."

Henry nodded. "I don't want to push you into anything that makes you uncomfortable. Take your time, Bonnie. For you, I will wait a lifetime."

Without warning, the memory faded. This time, I didn't let Bonnie control the narrative. I searched her mind, shoving my powers into her subconscious. My mind fully focused on the key when finally, I felt a pull.

Bonnie Drake parked her black Cadillac on the street and retrieved a shovel from the trunk. She walked alongside a row of trees. I recognized the house the trees grew next to – the Drake's rental property in Falcon Bay. Bonnie paused at the tree with the Renati symbol carved into it and began to dig. Finally, the shovel hit something hard.

With a subtle smile on her face, Bonnie retrieved the box that Rose, Bryan and I had found. When she opened back the lid, a thin piece of metal with a water droplet and flames blending into a swirling design sat inside.

Bonnie retrieved the stem of the key and held it tightly in her hand as she left the shovel against the tree and walked back to her car.

Bonnie's mental wall crashed down around me, pushing me out of her memories. When my vision came to, she glared at me with hate still sparking in her eyes.

"How dare you–" she hissed but I didn't let her finish.

I slammed into her mental blockade again and again until I felt a trickle of blood run down from my nose. I ignored it. If Bonnie Drake wouldn't let me see where she took the key after she retrieved it from the box, I'd wear her down until she caved.

My powers scratched down the walls she had put up, pushing like a persistent ocean wave. Eventually, the ocean could erode away anything; it could break down whatever stood in its path. I only had to stay patient.

Bonnie Drake hissed in pain, gritting her teeth. She squeezed her eyes shut and winced. Surprisingly, she never once screamed out. Her pain tolerance impressed me but I secretly wondered how much it would take to actually break this woman. I was willing to find out.

I heard someone say my name, but I didn't respond. I didn't turn to see who the voice belonged to. The only person who mattered sat in the middle of the room, burning holes into me with her eyes.

My vision began to blur, but I planted my feet, determined to keep myself conscious long enough to finish this. I gave one final shove; a tidal wave of magic left my body and washed over Bonnie Drake.

"Okay, okay," Bonnie panted. "It's tattooed on my leg."

Lauren blinked at her, not quite understanding what she meant. She looked at the other girls in confusion. "Tattooed?"

Bonnie let out a deep breath. "It's disguised as a tattoo on my thigh."

"So it is on your person," I muttered, taking a step towards Bonnie. "Show us."

"I do not have use of my hands to show you," Bonnie snarled.

Rayn glanced over her shoulder. "Aden, numb her powers."

"She's already numbed." Brooke pointed out.

"We have to make sure," I replied. "Hit her again."

Aden blinked at me and lowered his voice. "I only have so many of these darts, little witch."

"I need my powers to get the key," Bonnie replied, looking back and forth between Aden and I. "If you keep drugging me, I'll never be able to reverse the spell. I am the only one who can."

"Show us the tattoo," I demanded. "We aren't going to take your word for it."

Rose met my gaze before she stepped forward and united Bonnie's hands. Bonnie lifted her skirt to her upper thigh.

Tattooed on her skin was the stem of the key. The droplet of water blended into flames and swirls of the wind, almost identical to the drawing from Amilia's journal.

"No fucking way," Lauren muttered, taking a step towards Bonnie for a closer look.

"Get away from me." Bonnie pointed a powerless finger at Lauren.

"How do we get it out?" I asked.

Bonnie scoffed. "It's a spell. You are supposed to be these great witches, but you will always be miles behind us."

Harmony stepped up behind me. "Oh, shut up, you insufferable traitor. Reverse the spell before I cut it out of your skin. The choice is yours."

Nic side-eyed Harmony, a glimmer of heat sparked in his gaze.

"We can't let the darts wear off, I don't trust her to have her powers," I whispered to Harmony, leaning in close to her.

Harmony hardened a glare at Bonnie Drake. "Then we cut it out."

Bonnie's eyes widened, looking around the room at everyone staring her down. Her shoulders fell as she turned to me with heavy eyes. "I will give you the key fragment under two conditions."

I crossed my arms. "You aren't in any position to be making demands."

"First, you let me leave this place alive." Bonnie ignored me. "Second, you will not harm my daughter."

I shook my head. "Absolutely not. Serenity does not get protection from us under any circumstances."

"Deal." Rose stepped forward. "I accept the terms."

Brooke nodded, glancing over at me. "So do I. I don't care about Serenity Drake. I care about completing the key and getting to the labyrinth."

I turned to them in disbelief. After everything Serenity Drake had put us through, how could they possibly want to exchange her safety for anything? This would only set Serenity off, she would be able to taunt and attack with no repercussions. "But–"

My sister cut me off. "I'm with Rose and Brooke, we have to look at the bigger picture."

Lauren shook her head. "I want Serenity Drake dead."

Brooke shrugged her shoulders. "Three to two. You've outvoted. I'm sorry, but it's safer this way. We can't risk the Renati descending on the cottage again."

We couldn't make deals with the devil. How could we ensure that Bonnie Drake would hold up her end of the bargain?

We waited in silence for Bonnie's powers to return. I didn't want to talk to anyone. I didn't have anything productive to say, and fighting in front of one of the highest-ranked Renati members was not on my to-do list. She didn't need to see any weak moments between my generation.

Aden's dart finally wore off and Bonnie held her hand out in front of her face, moving her fingers as if she felt her magic swirl beneath her skin. Bonnie turned to me, her face washed over in hatred. I could see the wheels turning in her mind, weighing if attacking us was worth it.

Considering she had seven Elementals and a witch hunter surrounding her, she made the wise decision and waved her hand over her thigh. She winced in pain as the skin covering the tattoo rose. She squeezed her eyes closed, tears dripped down from the corners as the metal stem of the key ripped through her skin. Blood trickled down her thigh as a cry escaped her lips. The key fell to the concrete floor with a clang.

I dashed to the key, kneeling down before Bonnie Drake. The moment I wrapped my fingers around the key, Bonnie lunged for me. I hit the ground, her weight on top of me before I saw her move.

In a flash, Aden darted across the room and drug Bonnie off of me, grabbing handfuls of her hair and yanking. Bonnie let out a yelp and grabbed for her hair as Aden hauled her across the small shed.

Everyone jumped to attention, ready to strike against Bonnie if need be, but she didn't fight back. Her shoulders fell and she seemed to give up quickly.

I turned to face her and snarled. "If you want us to uphold our end of the bargain, you'll watch your temper, Mrs. Drake."

Bonnie let out a sigh as Aden looked to Rayn for instructions.

"Take her out to the street, outside of the perimeter," Rayn told Aden, nodding her head towards the door. "Let her go. She gave us the key, we will let her live."

Bonnie glared at me. "And Serenity?"

I rolled my eyes, biting my tongue. "A deal is a deal."

Aden dragged Bonnie though the door, barely looking back to see if she kept up with the strides of his long legs.

I clenched the bloody key in my hands and let out a deep sigh. "One down, two to go."

Chapter Thirty-Seven
BROKEN SHIELDS
Whitney

When I walked into work the next day, I simultaneously felt heavier and lighter. Now that we had Bonnie's key fragment, we had to get the other two pieces before Erebus did. I hoped that Erebus had yet to get the fragment hidden at the palace with Maggie Daniels. Either way, he stayed one step ahead of us. Not knowing where Amilia's piece hid wore me to the bones. I couldn't decide what was worse, that the girls and I were left clueless as to where Mia had hidden it, or that Nic and Harmony didn't seem the least bit phased by it.

The dining room of the Corner Cup was empty and I double checked we had the sign flipped to open. Lauren and Rayn were already behind the counter, Amilia's journal lay open before them.

"Hey, Whit." Lauren smiled.

"Finding anything useful?" I joined them.

"Kind of," Rayn answered. "Now that we have the key stem, we are seeing what all Amilia wrote in here. Hoping for some kind of clue to where she hid her piece."

Lauren chewed on her bottom lip, turning to face us. "You don't think she had it on her person like Bonnie Drake did, do you?"

"Shit, I hope not." I struggled to get the words out. "Is that...is that something they would have found when they...you know, cremated her?"

The color drained from Rayn's face. "That is not a mental image that sits well in my stomach."

"Mine either," Lauren whispered. "They would have found it."

I nodded in agreement. "Nicky keeps telling me not to worry about it."

"Well, I'm worried," Rayn replied.

I glanced around the empty dining room of the Corner Cup and crossed my arms. We certainly had slow periods like any other business, but someone usually sat at a table. There were always a handful of regulars who came here to work or catch up. All the months I'd worked here, I never remember it feeling so empty.

I left the counter and moved to the massive windows overlooking the street. No one walked down the sidewalk. No one shopped at the other stores. There weren't any cars driving down the road.

As if everyone in Rifton had disappeared.

A dark cloud formed over the square in the middle of town. Normally, I wouldn't have looked twice at overcast weather, but this wasn't a normal cloud. Waves of magical energy permeated off of it, emitting out as if it intended to signal every witch living in Rifton. Hell, energy that strong probably pulled on the powerless too.

I glanced over at Lauren and Rayn, who had already noticed the dark cloud too.

"What...what the fuck is that?" Lauren joined me at the window.

I opened the front door, still wearing my apron with Rayn and Lauren close behind. "Something is wrong," I muttered, scanning the empty street.

My phone began to ring. And so did Rayn's. And Lauren's.

We all looked at each other with wide eyes as we frantically dug our phones from our pockets.

"It's Aden," Rayn said.

"Rose?" Lauren answered her phone.

"Nicky, what the hell is that cloud over town?" I answered the phone.

"Get down to town square now," he ordered. "Fucking now, Whitney. Hurry."

I turned and ran. I didn't have time to go back inside for my car keys or worry about leaving the Corner Cup unattended. The contents of my work apron bounced off my thighs and I untied it as I jogged towards town square.

Ripping the apron over my head, I threw it on the sidewalk, not caring if I ever saw it again. Rayn and Lauren's feet echoed off the sidewalk behind me, and they soon passed me; both of their long legs carrying them further than my shorter ones could manage. Lauren passed Rayn, sprinting faster than I'd ever seen her go.

Adrenaline shook my entire body. The energy of town had shifted, and not like before; not a subtle shift that slipped through town like a warm breeze during the cold winter. My magic felt different, reacting to the cloud like a cancerous cell that my body desperately wanted to fight off.

We didn't pass a single person on the streets as we ran to town square.

Finally, I caught up to Rayn and Lauren at the edge of the square where a crowd had already gathered near town hall. I scanned the crowd, looking for any member of our crew but all I saw were worried faces of witches and powerless alike.

"Ashley!" Lauren shouted, shoving her way through the crowd. Rayn and I followed close behind as Lauren flung her arms around Ash and pulled her close. "What's going on? Why is everyone here?"

"I don't know...I was at the bakery and next thing I knew I started walking here. It's the weirdest thing." Ashley looked up at the steps leading up to town hall. "Who is that man?"

I turned towards the direction she pointed and nearly passed out.

Erebus stood at the top of the stairs with Henry Drake and the rest of the city council at his side. Out in the open for everyone to see. He wasn't plotting any more, whatever he had planned would come to fruition.

"Where is Bryan?" I grabbed Ashley, panic coursing through every molecule of my body.

She furrowed her brow. "I don't know. Is something wrong?"

"Jesus Christ," I muttered, ripping my phone from my pocket and nearly dropping it as I dialed him.

It rang a few times and then went to voicemail. I tried again, but he still didn't answer. I called Nic instead.

"Where are you?" I demanded when he answered.

"By the Snack Shack. He's with me, I have them both."

"Bryan and Mit?"

"Who else would I be talking about? Get over here."

I breathed out in relief. "Bryan and Mit are with Nicky." I motioned for the girls to follow.

Lauren laced her fingers with Ashley's and led her through the crowd.

"Aden said he is with Harmony, Rose and B over by the bakery. He said they want us to stay in two groups," Rayn told us.

"What the fuck is happening? No one is telling us anything," Lauren said through her teeth, pushing past a bystander.

"I don't think they know either." Rayn scanned the crowd with worried eyes. "Can we protect all of these people?"

"We have to," Lauren answered with a shaky voice.

I spotted the guys and nearly knocked over an old woman getting to them. I flung myself into Bryan's arms as he nuzzled his face into my neck.

"I tried calling you." I pulled away only to grab my brother's shoulder.

"I think I left my phone in the Jeep," Bryan answered. "We kind of panicked getting here."

"What is all this?" I asked Dominic, who took a puff from a cigarette.

"I don't–"

Erebus' voice boomed from the cloud above us, amplified like a massive microphone. "Citizens of Rifton, for too long this land has been allowed to fester with the powerless like a plague. We are taking back what we built many years ago. The witches will no longer hide in the shadows, for we have always been here and we will never deny our existence again for your comfort."

Thunder cracked in the sky as Erebus yanked someone forward by their arm.

Emma came into view, trying to pull away from the dark witch's grasp. Bryan immediately took a step forward but I stopped him. Whatever Erebus had planned, I didn't want Bryan throwing himself in the middle of it.

Erebus held Emma's arm in the air as she struggled against him. "We are not the only witches hiding amongst you in plain sight. An ancient evil has resurrected itself from the depths of darkness, and we must eradicate it. We cannot protect you against it while there are people in this town who aid them in their quest to steal back power. They use elemental magic, and they will do whatever means necessary to take back control. Even if it means burning this town to the ground and all those who defy them." Erebus tightened his grip on Emma. "This girl has turned her soul black. May she be an example of what happens when you aid the enemy against our righteous cause."

"Whit." Bryan turned to me, eyes wide with panic.

"We will take care of it, okay? Stay back," I told him, but my words fell on deaf ears. I tightened my grip on his wrist as Bryan took another few steps forward.

Nic put out his cigarette and got in front of us. "Why is her father allowing this?"

Henry Drake stood off to the side, watching Erebus dangle his daughter in front of the crowd. He stood still, proud almost, showing no intention of intervening.

Serenity flinched, her eyes wide as if she didn't know this would be part of the presentation. She turned to her father, muttering something to him. He dismissed her with a wave of his hand.

"Whitney, don't you dare," Nic warned over his shoulder, as if knowing what I thought without having to look at me.

Emma was innocent. She was Bryan's best friend. *My* friend, despite everything. I wouldn't stand by and idly watch her get hurt.

"Keep them back." I brushed past Nic, making my way towards the front of the gathering crowd.

Footsteps behind me caught my attention as Lauren's magic swirled through me, making me feel weightless. Rayn's magic warmed my core and I felt braver having them with me. They stayed close as we crept towards the front. Moments later, Rose and Brooke's energies showed themselves.

My generation's magic tingled under my skin as the five of us prepared our attack.

I unleashed first, striking Erebus in the chest with a thick icicle.

Erebus froze in place, glancing down at the ice sticking from his chest. Erebus shook his head and tsked, finding me easily in the crowd. He smiled as if he knew the girls and I would show up.

Luckily, I distracted him.

Rose and Brooke struck from one side. Lauren and Rayn from the other, hitting him with two massive energy waves. The combination of all four of their powers caused Erebus to stumble and his grip loosened on Emma's arm.

Emma ripped from Erebus' grasp and scrambled backwards. We distracted him long enough for Emma to jump to her feet and run. Henry Drake bolted towards his daughter. I threw an ice spell at him, freezing him in place. Serenity no longer stood at her father's side, but I couldn't spot her amongst the other Renati.

I struck again, throwing everything I had at Erebus. We attacked from all angles, beating down on him with all we had. The different elements crashed around him in chaos. Erebus didn't seem to know which to counteract before the next attack came.

I kept my water frozen, knowing ice would hurt the worst. Rose hurled chunks of solid rock as Brooke's energy waves produced a stronger impact, while Rayn's flames were fueled by Lauren's wind, pushing the Renati council members away from him, leaving Erebus alone.

Erebus shot back at us, his powers rippling through the air.

I immediately put up a shield, expanding my magic out as far as I could to cover as many people as possible. If Erebus wanted to kill a single powerless person in this event, he'd have to get through me.

The bystanders screamed and ran in all different directions but none of them seemed to be able to leave the town square. The powerless crowd ran into invisible walls, bouncing off the cage as they tried to escape.

We were all trapped.

Erebus' first attack bounced off my shield. His magic pushed against mine, like someone beating on the other side of a door I desperately held closed. I pushed all my energy and focused on the shield, but Erebus unleashed a stronger second attack.

The shield cracked down the middle. My eyes widened and my pulse quickened in my throat.

I had never seen an energy shield crack before.

I scrambled to mend the crack but the next attack came quicker than I had prepared for and my shield shattered into a million pieces. The energy scattered throughout the square, knocking people down and shoving them like a massive wave. They screamed as they hit the ground, scrambling to get back to their feet. Those behind them trampled over the others in an attempt to get to safety.

"Help!" I shouted to the girls and put up another shield.

The girls quickly added to the shield, our magic melding together with ease. Nic's magic pushed against mine and I let him in, hoping it wouldn't crash the shield to have an Elemental that wasn't part of our generation join, but he jumped in with no issue. Something I didn't recognize pushed into the shield. An icy chill that rose all the little hairs on my arms.

Harmony.

People began to scream and disperse. I screamed out for them to stay under the shield but no one heard me in the chaos.

I glanced over my shoulder. Bryan grabbed Ashley and kept her close. Dmitri ran to my side and put up his hands, his magic fusing into ours.

Rebecca and Kim appeared in the crowd with their hands up, combining their magic into our shield. We held strong and worked together as a team.

An ear-piercing scream erupted from the crowd as a massive pair of stone wings appeared. The wings spread wide as Big Boy pounced into the crowd, snapping at the nearest person. Cries of terror filled my ears as everyone ran for their lives from the Shadows that stalked around baring their fangs. They appeared to be enjoying their game of cat and mouse as they moved at a fraction of their potential speed.

Thunder boomed above us and a thick bolt of lightning crackled against the darkening sky. The thick clouds that hovered above the square began to tremble and shout. Thick raindrops poured down as the clouds unleashed. Another massive bolt of lightning struck the dome of the shield, sending electric shocks through our magic. The energy singed my hands but I grit my teeth and pushed through the pain. The wind shoved hard against our shield as it whipped through the square.

Even with all of us pushing against the impending storm, the shield weighed heavy above us. The physical weight of the energy pushed down on my palms like I held up a boulder. Atlas with the weight of the world on my shoulders. My knees buckled and I fell, catching myself with one hand. My concentration wavered but I kept my magic pouring into the shield.

"Guys!" Dmitri's panicked voice rang in my ears.

A massive crack in our shield began to splinter and spread like a spider web reaching the length of the entire town square.

"Drop it before it shatters," I ordered, lowering my hands.

"No! We can hold them off!" Lauren shouted. A gust of wind whipped through the cracks in the shield, blowing our hair around with it. Debris and leaves caught up in the wind. A paper cup slapped me across the face.

"Lauren, the energy is going to shatter!" Rayn pulled her magic back.

Lauren let out a groan that turned into a scream as she pulled back. The shield began to fall as I felt my generation pull their magic back. We had to protect the innocent bystanders who had no hand in this war.

Even though we had put up the shield to protect the crowd against Erebus and his followers, the powerless still ran. They ran from those who were trying to help them because they had no way of differentiating between a good witch and a bad witch. All these people knew is that magic had been exposed to most of them for the first time and they were terrified.

They should be.

Erebus and his Shadows showed no intention of slowing down.

The wind picked up and my sneakers began to slide across the sidewalk. I reached out, grabbing Dmitri's arm for stability.

"We need to get to cover!" Dmitri's voice rang in my ears.

"What about everyone else?" I answered.

"If they're smart, they'll go too." He tightened his grip on me.

The dark clouds began to swirl, coming together in a funnel that quickly reached towards the ground. The spout started off small, but by the time it reached ground, it had doubled in size. The whirlwind touched down across the town square, snatching up everything in its path.

Chapter Thirty-Eight
GENEROSITY
Whitney

"Oh, shit!" Lauren's muffled voice screamed out as she put her hands up into the air, desperate to take control of the cyclone before it grew stronger. Her powers tingled through my body as I stood helpless. None of us could control the air and we had no way to help her.

Something snarled behind me and the sound of talons tapped against the pavement. I knew Big Boy inched closer. His presence sent chills down my spine but the winged Shadow was the least of my concerns.

Dmitri yanked on my arm, pulling me towards the nearest building. People rushed inside but I wouldn't leave Lauren.

I broke free from Dmitri's grasp and stumbled towards her, grabbing Lauren's shoulder. "We need to go!" I shouted over the wind.

"I can do this!" she yelled back. "I can fix this!"

"Lauren, please!" I begged as a droplet of water splashed against my cheek.

Thunder rumbled above us and the dark cloud opened up, dumping water to the ground. Thick rain droplets pelted towards us. I threw my magic into the air and tried to take control of the storm but it pushed back, rebelling against my powers. It felt wrong; dirty and polluted. The water in the sky too heavy as it rushed to the ground.

This was not nature. It didn't even act like Elemental magic. Whatever Erebus had done with our powers, he'd contaminated them with the darkness he brought back from the Shadow Realm.

A pea sized piece of hail crashed against the pavement next to my feet. The chunks of ice bounced against the sidewalk as more fell from the sky. The hail hit my face, irritating my skin.

"Lauren." I grabbed her again as we both slid forward. I threw out my powers, trying to keep us stable as Lauren's magic swirled around my bones. A large chunk of hail crashed inches away from us. I covered my head with one arm as another piece came hurtling down, smashing into my shoulder.

"Fuck!" I winced in pain.

Lauren and I skidded again towards the whirlwind when a force behind us yanked, pulling us back towards the buildings.

I looked behind me, squinting through the thick rain at Rayn, Dmitri and Nic all with their hands out using their powers to fight against the winds of the cyclone. I reached my magic out to them and pulled.

Finally, I managed to take a step towards them as Lauren and I both struggled to get back to the building. Thunder crashed and I glanced up as lightning shot across the sky, sending a brief streak of light behind the clouds. A bolt crashed towards the ground, striking a small tree near us in the courtyard.

Rayn grabbed the sleeve of my sweater and yanked me inside the nearest shop as Dmitri grabbed Lauren. Once we were all inside the building, Nic slammed the door closed and barred it with his powers.

"Everyone to the back! As far as you can go!" My voice rang through the shop as those who had made it inside shoved against each other to get as far away from the windows as possible.

I pushed out my magic, sending metal shelving units full of goods towards the windows, giving us some kind of barrier between us and the storm. I jumped behind the counter and found Ashley and Bryan. Ash pressed into Bryan's side gripping onto his sleeve for dear life. Bryan wrapped his other arm around me, pulling me close to his chest. He pinned us against the wall, stretching himself out to shield both of us. I burrowed in, grabbing a fistful of his shirt and Ashley grabbed my hand, holding on tight as we hunkered down.

A loud boom echoed through the shop as the windows blew out, sending glass everywhere. I put up a shield around the three of us as the metal shelving units slid away from the windows and rolled over each other. Everything around us went flying, bags of chips and canned goods flew off the shelves as the tornado passed by us. It only lasted a matter of seconds, but that short time felt like it took five years off my life.

Once I didn't feel the pressure of the wind whipping against my face, I lifted my head from Bryan's chest and took inventory of the damage. The shop had been destroyed but no one seemed to be seriously hurt, no one who made it inside anyway.

Rayn popped her head out over Nic's shoulder. He had flung himself over her to protect her and my heart swelled with gratitude. Lauren and Dmitri had kept each other safe behind a sturdy metal shelving unit.

As Lauren looked across the way, she left his side and sprinted towards us, pulling Ashley into a hug. "Are you okay?" She looked Ash over for any injuries.

"I...What is happening? I don't understand," Ashley stumped over her words, clinging to Lauren for dear life.

"Baby? Are you hurt?" Bryan pulled my attention back to him.

"No," I answered, watching everyone else who had hidden inside the store. "We need to find the others."

I led my group through the blown-out window. The town square had been destroyed; trees pulled up by the roots and thrown across the way. Metal stop signs were bent or ripped from the ground all together. A handful of bodies lay scattered in the grass like discarded trash.

Dead bodies.

"Oh shit," Bryan whispered next to me, taking in the scene. "This is horrific."

I closed my eyes, pretending I didn't see as my stomach churned. I turned away and ran to where Harmony, Rose, Brooke and Aden had been, where I assumed they were based on where I had sensed their magic.

"Honey!" Nic's desperate voice came from behind me as he sprinted past. "Harmony!"

"Here!" Harmony's voice answered from inside the post office. She stepped out from behind the debris and onto the sidewalk. A cut on her forehead bled down her face.

Nic collided into her, pulling her close. She wrapped her arms around him, grabbing fistfuls of his t-shirt.

"You're hurt." He pushed her hair back from her cut.

"I'm okay, everyone else is fine," she answered, out of breath.

Nic shook his head and pulled her into a kiss, not seeming to care who saw. She cupped his cheek and kissed him back.

Pain constricted in my chest as I took another scan of the wreckage. "Nothing about this is okay." My heart pulsed through my entire being.

Bryan rushed past me as Rose and Brooke emerged from the post office. He helped Rose over a blue mail drop box that had been ripped from the sidewalk and gave his sister a hug. Brooke reached behind her and offered her hand, helping Rebecca over the rubble. Kim followed close behind. Rayn brushed past me and threw herself into Aden's arms, he caught her and lifted her from the ground.

All of us reunited with our people.

"Where is Jane?" I glanced around at the group.

Harmony cleared her throat as Nic tightened his arm around her. "She's at the cottage with Emery."

"This is your doing." A deep voice growled behind us. Erebus stood across the square. His voice carried across the way as if he stood right next to me.

"*Our* doing?" I spat back. "You did this!"

"You are the ones who fight. The more you resist, the more people will die." His voice dripped with hatred. "Their blood is on your hands, it always has been."

"You cowardice piece of shit!" Nic stormed towards him. I grabbed his arm before he could pass me. "How dare you kill innocent people and put the blame on us! You started this war!"

"How wrong you are." Erebus shook his head, unbothered by the death and destruction that surrounded us. "Heed this warning. Our next interaction, I will not be as generous."

"*Generous*? You–"

Erebus disappeared before I could finish.

"We are dealing with a genuine psychopath." Brooke stepped up to my side.

A male voice echoed through the town square, desperate and shaky. "Dmitri!"

I turned towards the direction of the voice to see Councilman Will Ward rushing through the debris, frantically calling out my brother's name.

Mit stepped forward and watched the older man for a moment before he waved his arm and shouted. "Here!"

Will Ward spun around and put a hand over his chest when he laid eyes on Dmitri. He rushed across the way but paused as he saw Dmitri back away from him. Ward panted, holding his chest. "Are you all right?"

Dmitri blinked and glanced around the town square. "Absolutely not."

Ward caught a glimpse of the bodies and squeezed his eyes shut. "This...this wasn't supposed to happen. I had eyes on you and then..." He paused. "I thought...Dmitri, I know you don't want anything to do with us, but you're all we have left of him." Tears lined the bottom of Ward's eyes. "You're all that's left of my boy."

"Why would I want anything to do with the Renati after all this?" Dmitri held his arms out and motioned to the destruction around us.

"Not them. Us, your grandmother and I." Ward's words caught in his throat. "Dmitri, we had no idea this would happen."

Bryan brushed past me and glared Ward down, his hands balled into fists. "None of us give a flying fuck about your remorse." He glanced over his shoulder at me. "We need to find Emma."

I nodded and reached for my brother's arm. "Are you—"

Dmitri cut me off. "Go."

"It looked like she ran around the back of town hall." I joined Bryan's side as we headed towards the large buildings on the other side of town square. Wherever Emma had run off to after she escaped Erebus' grip, I hoped she found cover from the tornado. And her father.

Rayn's voice called out behind us. "Find Emma and we'll start accessing the damage!"

Bryan jogged down the sidewalk, avoiding the lawn where the majority of the damage had been done. Where the majority of the bodies lay.

I stopped and took it all in. The blood splattered across the pavement from blunt impact. The fearful screams echoed in my head when the tornado had touched down; how terrified everyone had been. How could Erebus commit such a horrendous crime and call himself generous? How would this convince the people of Rifton that we were the enemy and the Renati were the ones wanting to protect them? We weren't the ones out here scaring people into submission or murdering them in the middle of town.

"Em!" Bryan's voice echoed through the air, reeling me back in. I realized I had lost him. I took off towards town hall again, following his voice as he called out for Emma.

"Emma?" I called, jogging up the stairs of town hall. The glass doors had been blown out, and the people who had hidden inside slowly made their way out. I looked at their terrified faces and trembling hands, reaching out to the first woman I saw. "Are you all right?"

"What happened? Witches? I don't understand?" The woman rambled out question after question, clinging onto me with an iron grip as her eyes welled with tears.

"A tornado," I answered. "Um, everyone should go back to their homes and check on your loved ones."

A scream erupted from the lawn where the people trickling out from hiding had discovered the bodies. I turned towards the noise and saw my sister wrap her arm around a woman's shoulders in comfort. My crew would take care of the survivors. I needed to help Bryan find Emma.

I left the people who had come out of town hall and stepped through the shattered door frames. Glass crunched under me and I stepped carefully, mindful not to let any of the shards stab through my rubber soles.

"Emma!" I called out again, venturing further into the building. When I got to the bathroom at the end of the hall, two arguing voices carried from behind the door. I stepped closer, recognizing them immediately.

"He was going to let them kill me!" Emma cried. "How can you justify that? How can you stand by him after that?"

"I told you not to get in the middle of it. I told you this would happen! You don't listen, you never fucking listen. Being powerless isn't going to protect you like it used to," Serenity argued back with her twin.

"Protect me? Dad has never protected me. If Mom would've let him get rid of me, he would have."

"No, that's not true."

"He hates me and you do too. You stood there and watched."

"He would have killed me too."

"I hate you!" Emma snapped. "I hope they kill you. I will let the Elementals kill you. I might actually help them do it."

"Emma, you have no idea what they are. They're dangerous."

"The Elementals aren't the ones who blew up town square. Byn was right, there's nothing left of you worth saving."

Neither of them spoke for a moment.

"He said that?"

I pushed the bathroom door open and they both startled towards me.

"Emma, are you okay?" I stepped into the bathroom. "We came looking for you."

"Whit, oh my god." Emma rushed past her sister and threw her arms around me. "If you hadn't...I'm sorry."

I rubbed her back, glaring at Serenity over her shoulder. "Let's get out of here. Bryan is looking for you."

"Is everyone okay?"

"Byn and Ash are. I don't know where Troy is, but I didn't see him so I don't think he was here."

Emma wiped a tear from her face and turned back to her sister. She flipped Serenity the middle finger as we left the bathroom together. We exited town hall through the broken glass doors. Bryan ran up the steps towards us and pulled Emma against his chest. She cried, gripping his hoodie.

"Where's Troy?" I asked Bryan in a whisper.

He shrugged and shook his head, silently answered that he didn't know. I pulled out my phone and called him. He answered on the third ring.

I let out a deep sigh of relief. "Are you home?"

"Yeah," he paused. "Was that a fucking tornado? Is Em with you? She isn't answering her phone."

"Yes, Em is okay. Don't leave the house, please stay inside. I have the house protected, but if you leave I can't do anything," I begged.

Troy paused. "Protected from what?"

"Please stay home. We'll be there soon, all of us. Everyone's okay but you have to stay inside."

"Okay, okay. I hear you."

I hung up and put a hand on Emma's shoulder before I headed down the steps where the rest of my group spoke with paramedics. Firetrucks and ambulances had shown up in hoards, flashing red and blue lights everywhere I looked. White sheets now covered the bodies. The survivors who needed medical assistance sat on the curb with blankets around their shoulders, getting their cuts bandaged.

Not a single cop could be seen through the wreckage.

Knowing the chief of police was Renti and Grady was a hunter, I wondered how many members of the force were against us. And why those who didn't belong to either group left the calls for help unanswered.

"Byn, take Emma and Ash home," I said. "You need to be somewhere safe."

Bryan shook his head. "I don't want to leave you."

"I know." I grabbed his hand and laced our fingers. "But I need to be here right now. I don't think they'll come back so soon. Em needs to be somewhere the Renati can't touch her and so do you."

"Please come home soon," he begged with heavy eyes.

I forced a smile even though my vision blurred with tears. "I promise." I glanced over at Ashley shivering from shock against Lauren's side.

Bryan looked at them over his shoulder. He wrapped an arm around Emma and led her towards Ashley and Lauren. Ashley gave them both hugs and nodded as Bryan spoke to her. Lauren smiled and spoke encouragingly to her before Ashley left with Bryan and Emma. I let out another breath of relief watching the three of them leave the scene and return to safety.

Chapter Thirty-Nine
Left Behind
Lauren

After the paramedics cleared our crew and the coroner vans had taken the bodies, Whitney turned to me. "You have a decision to make."

I glanced at her. "About?"

"Ashley saw everything. She's terrified and confused. I have no idea what Byn and Emma have said to comfort her, but if she's going to hear the truth, it should come from you." Whit took a step towards me. "Or, if you want, we could help her forget."

I chewed on my bottom lip, my heart heavy with indecision. "She's already been charmed and I hated knowing her mind's been manipulated. But the truth isn't easy to hear."

"I know," Whitney agreed. "It's your call either way."

"Can I think about it on the drive?"

"Sure." Whitney nodded and turned to Rose. "Do you guys want to come with us?"

"I think the less people around for that conversation the better," Rose answered. "I'm not sure how Troy is going to take all this either."

"You think Emma will finally tell him everything?" I chewed on my thumbnail. I didn't know Troy well enough to guess how he'd react to the discovery of witches in Rifton.

"I don't think she has a choice." Rose ran her fingers through her messy hair.

Whitney shrugged. "Troy might be kind of pleased with himself that he knew the truth this whole time, don't you think?"

Rose shook her head. "This is the most fucked up thing I've ever seen." She paused. "I'm going to check on my mom and then head to the cottage."

Whitney closed her eyes for a moment and let out a deep sigh. "Okay. We should stay in pairs, that way none of us are alone right now."

"Yeah, we need to stick together," I agreed.

Crossing her arms, Brooke walked over. "My dad isn't here. None of the cops are here. Something isn't right."

Rose grabbed Brooke's hand. "Let's find our parents, even if it's a phone call, and then we will investigate the cop situation."

With a deep sigh, Whitney nodded. "Good idea. Lauren and I are heading back to my place to talk with Ash and check on Emma."

"Rayn?" Rose called over her shoulder. "Are you going back to the cottage?"

Rayn walked over to us. "I honestly don't know what to do. Stay out of sight? Regroup?"

"Go somewhere safe," Whitney told her sister.

Whitney and I left the girls and walked over to where Nic and Harmony stood, deep in their own conversation.

"Nicky," Whitney interrupted.

He turned to her. "You okay, kiddo?"

She nodded. "Could you take Ray and Dmitri back to the cottage, please? Make sure Abe is okay too. We're going to split up and take care of some things."

"Okay." He rubbed his eyes with the balls of his palms. "Don't do anything reckless."

"We're going to Whit's place to check on those guys, make sure Emma is okay," I explained, taking another look around the destroyed town square.

"I can't believe Henry Drake would sacrifice his own child like that." Harmony wrapped her arms around herself. "I just...I can't fathom."

Nic put his hand on the small of her back. "Come on, let's go home and get Emery."

"We'll meet you back there soon," Whitney told them and linked her arm in mine as we left the scene.

When we pulled up to the house, Bryan's Jeep was parked out front. All the windows were blown out and his windshield had cracked down the middle.

"Oh, fuck," Whitney muttered, taking in the damage to his vehicle. Luckily, Troy's truck and the house seemed untouched. The tornado hadn't left town square. Whitney turned to me as we stared at the house from the sidewalk. "Have you decided?"

I slowly nodded. "I'll tell her the truth."

As we walked into the house, I realized the conversation we intended to have already took place without us.

"Hang on, hang on. Stop. This is a prank, right?" Troy asked as I closed the front door.

Bryan looked at us and widened his eyes before turning back to where Emma and Troy were deep into their discussion.

Emma scoffed, though tears lined her eyes. "Why the fuck would this be a prank? Do you think my father trying to kill me in front of the entire town is funny?"

Troy raised his voice. "Of course not! This is all just…I'm confused, okay?"

Ashley jumped up from the couch and pulled me into a hug. I slid my hands down her arms, lacing our fingers together. "Can we go talk in private?"

Ashley nodded.

"You can use our room," Whitney offered.

I pulled Ashley's hand to follow me and we disappeared down the hallway. I let Ashley go first into the bedroom and gently closed the door behind us.

"Are you okay?" I asked. This would be the hardest conversation I had ever anticipated. Never in a million years had I ever planned what to say when telling someone I loved about my powers. I never thought I'd need to have this discussion, let alone experience the fear of what would happen if the conversation didn't go well.

Last year, I hadn't stayed at the cottage long enough to see how Bryan reacted when Whitney and Rose told him about their powers. I knew they hadn't talked while I was gone, but I knew how it ended, how Bryan stayed despite all of it.

I couldn't imagine anyone wanting to risk themselves to jump into the middle of a war that wasn't theirs. Yet, here I stood in front of someone I cared about, preparing to tell them a truth that I wouldn't be able to take back.

"Not really," Ashley answered, sitting down on the edge of the bed. "I'm…confused. Like, I know what I saw, but I don't know *what* I saw? If that makes any sense…?"

"I understand." I sat down next to her, forcing myself to keep my hands in my own lap. "It's been a really confusing journey."

"Emma said the stories about the witches are true? That everyone in her family has powers except for her…" Ashley's voice trailed off. "How can that be true?"

"I guess all stories have some layer of truth to them," I answered, letting Ashley have control of the conversation for now.

Ashley's eyes were lined with tears. "Yeah, but this is hard to swallow. If I hadn't seen what happened downtown I would never have believed it. Why are they now revealing themselves? Have they been hiding this entire time?"

"Um, because their leader is back in power and he wants control over Rifton. He wants to make it the new magical haven that he had before he was locked up. There are these magical power houses called Allurements and the Dark Star Forest is one of them," I simplified as best I could. The reality of our situation weighed heavy on my shoulders. "Things are going south really quick, and I don't know if we can fix it in time."

"That's what I'm most confused about." Ashley turned to look at me. "Your role in all this. You...you're smack in the middle and I had no idea."

I let out a sigh. "I wanted to keep you safe from it. I thought if you didn't know, it would be for the best. I didn't want to lie to you, but this is a lot to digest."

"You...you have them too?" Ashley swallowed. "Powers?"

I took a deep breath before I dared speak the words I'd been denying my entire life. "I am a witch, yes."

"A real one?"

I nodded, picking my next words carefully. "I'm an Air Elemental. My generation is the last complete group of Elementals. We're the only ones who can stop the Renati and Erebus from destroying our world."

Ashley didn't appear to be breathing as she stared off into the corner of the room. Finally, she blinked a few times and tilted her head. "It's like a bad dream."

Oh.

"Yeah, I feel like that sometimes too." I stared down at my hands.

Ashley kept her eyes fixated on whatever pulled her focus across the room. "This isn't all one bad joke?"

"I wish." I squeezed my eyes shut, wishing I could erase the memories from my mind. "I wish Erebus hadn't attacked downtown and killed all those people. I wish he hadn't used *my* magic to do it. I wish they didn't kill my mom. I hate every fucking second of this."

Ashley's voice caught in her throat. "Your mom...it was part of this?"

I nodded.

"Oh my god. I'm so sorry." Ashley grabbed my hand. "I...I don't know how you're so strong."

"I don't have a choice." I fought to hold back tears. "If I don't hold it together, a lot more people will die and it'll actually be my fault because I can do something to prevent it."

"Whitney too?"

"Whit and Ray, yeah. Rose, too. And our friend, Brooke. The five of us make up our generation."

"Rose too," Ashley repeated. "Jesus, no wonder Bryan is in so deep. Who else?"

"Who else has powers that you know?" I stared down at my feet. "Um, Dmitri is a witch and so is his boyfriend. Uh, Harmony and Nic are Elementals…the rest of their generation has been…they're the last of theirs. Amilia."

Ashley straightened her back. "*Our* Amilia?"

I nodded. "Amilia was best friends with Whit, Rayn and Dmitri's mom."

"I'm the last person to know." Ash's shoulders fell. "I've been kept in the dark by *everyone*."

"You and Troy both it sounds like, but it's not because we didn't trust you." I tightened my grip on her hand. "I didn't want to put you in any danger."

"I was in danger today." Ashley wiped a tear away with the back of her hand. "I've never been so scared in my life."

"I know." I placed my other hand on her thigh. "I'm so sorry."

"You're a witch…like, a real witch," Ashley spoke the words out loud as if she still attempted to accept it.

"I'm a real witch," I repeated.

"I, uh, I need some time to process. I need to go home and make sure my parents are okay." Ashley let go of my hand and stood up. She ran her fingers through her thick curls and grabbed for the door knob. Ash glanced at me over her shoulder. "I'll call you."

I nodded, watching Ashley leave, wondering if she had any intention of calling. I sat there for a moment in silence, listening to the voices from the living room trail down the hallway. I didn't want to go out there and explain that Ashley finally knew the truth and chose to leave. I knew in my heart this is how things would go, but I had hoped she would accept me without needing time to think about it. Hope was supposed to be this powerful thing that kept a person moving through life; that gave them purpose and motivation to move forward. But I never regretted having hope more in my entire life.

My phone rang in my pocket but I ignored it, letting the call go to voicemail. Ashley had already left and I didn't want to speak to whoever reached out. I clenched my teeth and fought back tears. I tried to convince myself that the swelling pain in my chest resulted from the tornado downtown and not watching Ashley walk away. That the stabbing sensation spreading through my entire body wasn't really there. I willed it away and buried my emotions deep below the surface.

My phone rang again.

I pulled the phone from my pocket, ready to scream at whoever called until I saw the called ID.

Rifton Memorial Hospital.

"Hello?" I answered in a rush, nearly dropping the phone as I lifted it to her ear.

"Lauren Thaner?" the voice on the other end asked.

"Is my dad okay?"

I couldn't lose him too, not after everything I'd been through that day. Not after everything I'd already lost, after everything my generation and the town itself had lost. The doctors warned me that my father may never wake up, but then that stupid hope bubbled in my chest and I waited.

"Your father is awake."

I raced to the hospital. I didn't remember the drive or walking in through the doors. One moment I sat on Whitney and Bryan's bed, and the next I followed a nurse down the hallway.

Full panic mode overwhelmed the hospital. Everything felt scattered in a chaotic panic with staff running past, yelling to one another as they tended to those injured in the attack. A gurney wheeled past me, pushed by three running nurses all talking over one another. The patient on the gurney had a bandage covering half of their face, groaning in pain.

I looked away from the chaos and shuddered, letting my thoughts wander. Images of people trapped under debris and crumbled structures filled my mind. People screaming for help. People who woke up covered in wreckage, scared and alone.

I pushed away the thoughts and followed the nurse into an open doorway.

When I walked into my dad's room, he no longer lay motionless connection to monitors and tubes. He sat up. His eyes were open. He spoke to the nurse, real words that I could hear. I could hear my father's voice.

A sob escaped my lips as I dashed across the room and flung myself onto the hospital bed. One of the nurses tried to stop me, but I wouldn't hear it.

"Oh...uh." Dad pulled away from my embrace. "Who is this?"

I slid off the bed and took a step back, staring into my father's eyes. "You don't know who I am?"

He shook his head and looked nervously to the nurse for answers.

"I...wait, is this real?" I turned to the nurse.

The nurse let out a sigh. "Temporary memory loss is common in patients who were in a coma as long as your father. There is no neurological damage in his scans, so we're hopeful that his memory returns in time."

"Father?" Dad looked me up and down. "I don't...I have children?"

I nodded, fighting the tears that threatened to fall down my face. Fighting to force my emotions down deep into my stomach where they wouldn't surface and shatter across the room.

The nurse tucked her clipboard under her arm. "I can give you two some privacy. Try to be patient, okay? And let me know if you need anything. I'll be back to check his vitals in a few hours."

I waited until the nurse left the room before I dared take a step towards my dad. "What's the last thing you remember?"

"I..." he paused. "It's all blurry."

"Your name?"

"Ted." He answered without hesitation. "Everyone calls me TJ."

I let out a soft sigh of relief. At least he remembered something.

Dad looked me in the eyes again and squinted, as if he studied me. "You look like my mother."

I forced a smile but I couldn't hide the first tear that trickled down my cheek. My heart constricted in my chest, sending a shooting pain through my body that would consume me if I let it. On the drive over, I had been so frantic to get here. Overwhelmed with thoughts that I'd jump into my dad's arms and he'd hold me close. He'd kiss the top of my head like he did when a storm brewed outside and tell me that I was always safe with him. He'd call me princess and we'd mourn the loss of my mom together.

My mother…

"Did the doctors tell you about the break in?" I dared to ask.

Dad looked away, blinking tears from his eyes. "She's gone."

I sniffled. "I'm so sorry, Dad."

"Debbie couldn't have children." He turned back to me and paused. "The doctors told us before we got married. How…how are you ours?"

I cleared my throat as the pain swelled in my chest. I swallowed but it wouldn't go away. I couldn't bury it anymore. I had been ignoring it for too long and it had grown into a monster that lived inside of me. I let the tears fall. Even if my dad didn't remember, he was still my dad.

"You remember Diana?" I asked.

Dad thought for a moment. "My sister?"

"She has problems…"

Dad nodded. "Always has."

"So, uh, she got pregnant with me. I couldn't tell you anything about the guy. But she had me for a short amount of time, until CPS got involved. They sent me to Grandma's for a while but you and Mom…you've taken care of me for as long as I can remember."

"Oh, so you're Diana's."

"No," I snapped, tears streaming down my face. "I haven't been for a long time. You and Mom adopted me when I was four."

Dad paused, a tear sliding down his cheek. "I'm so sorry. What's your name?"

"Lauren," I choked. "Lauren Bethany Thaner."

"Bethany. My mother's name…your grandmother?"

I nodded. "She's been here to see you, but Grandma lives in Idaho now."

"Okay," Dad nodded softly. "I think, uh, I think I need some time to process all this."

He asked me to leave. The second time in the span of an hour I'd been left.

I took a step backwards. "Okay, uh, can I come back?" When he didn't answer, I spoke again. "I'll call first."

I barely made it to the door. I scrambled into the hallway and pulled the door closed behind me, narrowly missing a nurse. She reached for me as I collapsed onto the floor. The weight of the day pressed down on me, crushing every little molecule.

Squeezing my eyes shut, I covered my ears, but I still heard the screams of the townspeople as the tornado ripped through the square. I still felt the powerful wind whip my hair and slap across my face. The sound of Erebus' voice as he pointed his finger at us.

The sights of the dead bodies littered across the square. The sound of my father, the only parent I had left, asking who I was. Calling me Diana's, not his.

Holding my legs close to my chest, I curled up into the tightest ball. Ignoring the concerned voices of staff that asked if I was okay, I lay there on the hospital floor allowing the grief to consume me, to pull me down into the darkness. I let every wound split open, tearing my soul in half.

Erebus had attacked Rifton, killing innocent people.

My mother died.

My father didn't remember me.

Ashley finally knew the truth and ran away.

I lay here, drowning in loneliness and pain until I became numb.

The next morning, I slept through my alarm. It wasn't until pounding on my bedroom door grew louder that I lifted my head from the pillow.

"Go away!" I called out and threw the blanket over my head.

"Lauren, your alarm has been going off for an hour," Nic's voice called through the door. "Are you okay?"

"No. Now go away, I don't want to talk to you." I turned off the alarm and tossed my phone across the bed.

Silence. Finally.

I fell back into a dreamless sleep until my phone rang. I groaned, contemplating throwing it across the room.

Why wouldn't anyone leave me the fuck alone?

I went to yell at whoever disturbed me, but it was my grandmother.

"Hi, Grandma." I rubbed sleep from my eyes.

"Hi, darling. Did I wake you?" she asked. A noise in the background muffled the call.

"No, it's fine. Are you driving?"

"I am," Grandma paused. "Lo, baby, the hospital is discharging your dad."

I sat up straight in bed, throwing the blankets off of me. "Already?"

"He's clearing all of his tests. The only thing is his memory and the doctors are convinced that will return in time." She cleared her throat. "Um, he wants to come back to Idaho with me, so I'm driving down to get him. He's going to stay for a while until he's more like himself again."

Tears caught in my throat as the words slipped from my lips. "Makes sense. I'm a stranger. Why would he stay here for someone he doesn't know?"

"Oh, honey, I'm so sorry. He's still your dad. He loves you so much. He's been through something traumatic and his brain is still catching up. It won't be like this forever. Why don't you come home with us?"

"I can't." I flopped back into bed, staring up at the texture on the ceiling.

"Lauren, there isn't anything left for you in Rifton. Come be with your family," Grandma urged.

"I have to stay here, I have a job and...I can't." I cleared my throat, hiding the tears as best as I could. "Can I at least come down to the hospital and say goodbye? I want to see you and I want to see Dad before you guys go."

"Babe, you don't need permission to come see your own family," She paused. "I'll be there this evening."

"Bye." I hung up the phone, not wanting to hear another word.

The look on my dad's face when I jumped in for a hug the day before flashed through my head. The confusion. The furrowed brow. He didn't recognize me and didn't want me anywhere near him. My grandmother was the only family he had left, of course he would want to be with her. He'd want to go home and heal from the absence of my mother, while I sat here in Rifton mourning both of them.

When evening finally rolled around, I almost didn't show up at the hospital. Why should I? My dad didn't know me. I didn't know if my heart could take his looks of confusion or my grandma's sympathetic glances. I dragged myself out of bed and drove to the hospital anyway.

My dad and grandma sat on the edge of his hospital bed together when I shuffled into the room. Their hushed voices abruptly halted when they glanced up at me. I stayed in the doorframe, unsure if I'd be welcome.

"Hi, Lauren." My dad smiled. "Uh, we were just talking about you."

"Yeah?" I asked, unsure of what else to say.

"Your...your grandmother has been catching me up on the past twenty years," he replied.

I leaned against the doorframe. "Still no memory?"

My grandma shook her head. She stood up from the edge of the bed and pulled me into a hug. Even in my grandma's embrace, my heart constricted inside of my chest. I didn't want to stay and make awkward small talk. I couldn't handle it.

I stared at the ground and muttered, "I came to say goodbye."

"Lo, darling." My grandma rubbed my back. "Please, come back with us."

I shook my head. I couldn't explain to them why I needed to be here, that there were countless people relying on me and the others. How could I put into words the severity of our situation?

Instead, I kissed my grandma's cheek and turned to my dad. "Stay safe, okay?"

He stood up and took a step towards me. "Will you be okay here? Do you have someone you're staying with?"

I gave a quick nod. "I have friends and roommates. I'm fine." I looked him in the eyes as a quivering breath left my lips. "I have a girlfriend."

My grandma tensed at my side and my dad raised his eyebrows. He stayed quiet for a moment before he offered me a soft smile. "Good. I'm glad you have a support system here."

"I'll be fine." I took a deep breath of courage and turned to see my grandma's reaction.

She smiled at me with tear-lined eyes. Grandma wrapped me in her arms and squeezed me so tightly that my breath caught in my lungs. "I am so happy for you, my sweet girl," she whispered into my neck. "I love you, Lo."

"I love you too." I blinked away tears but one still fell onto her sweater.

Chapter Forty
Dangerous Territory
Whitney

When I got to the cottage, a heaviness in the air slapped me the moment I walked in. The incident at town square the day before weighed on all of us. We may not have been the ones who created the storm, but I still felt responsible for Erebus' actions. He wouldn't have been able to hurt all of those people if we had ended him by now.

Nic emerged from the kitchen as I secured the front door behind me, his arms crossed firmly against his chest. "We need to discuss the palace, but you should go check on Lauren first."

"Oh." I glanced towards her closed bedroom door down the hall. "The talk with Ashley didn't go as she'd hoped." I moved past him.

Nic shrugged. "This seemed deeper than a lover's quarrel. She locked herself in the bedroom and won't talk to us."

I let out a deep sigh and nodded, patting his shoulder as I went down the hall to Lauren and Rayn's bedroom. I knocked on the door twice before I heard any noise. "Lo, it's me." I muttered into the crack between the door and its frame.

The door unlocked and swung open by itself. Lauren's hand returned to her legs, pulling her knees close to her chest. Her eyes were red and puffy, surrounded by smeared eyeliner. Lauren wouldn't look me in the eyes, even after I closed the door and sat on the edge of her bed. I reached out and put my hand on her knee.

"Do you want to talk about it?" I asked.

Lauren let out a huff and wiped her nose on her sleeve. "My dad is awake."

My posture straightened and I nearly lept at the news. "That's great!" I studied her face, not a spark of joy in her eyes. She stared into the void, barely blinking. "Isn't it?"

Lauren's voice quivered as she spoke. "His memory is shot. He doesn't remember the last twenty years." She sniffled, another tear falling down her cheek. "He doesn't remember that I'm his."

"Oh...I'm so sorry," I grabbed her hand in mine, at a loss for any other words.

"My grandma called this morning. They discharged him, but he's going to stay with her in Idaho. He doesn't want to stay here now that my mom is gone, and he doesn't want to stay for a stranger."

I tightened my grip on her hand. "You aren't a stranger, you're his daughter."

Lauren shook her head. "Not anymore."

I slumped down, feeling the weight of Lauren's sadness on my shoulders. "Is there any chance his memory will return in time?"

"The nurses said there is a possibility, but nothing is guaranteed."

"Hey, look at me," I requested, waiting for her to meet my gaze. "There was no guarantee he would wake in the first place. There is still a chance his memory will return."

Lauren finally met my gaze. "And what am I supposed to do in the meantime?"

I let out a deep sigh, unsure of what words I could string together to comfort Lauren. She had probably been so hopeful when she found out her dad woke up, only to be met like a stranger. Even if TJ Thaner did regain his memory, would it be enough to overshadow the trauma she already experienced?

"At least he'll be out of Rifton and away from the Renati. He'll be safe with your grandma and he will remember you." I put my hand over hers. "You are too amazing to ever forget, Lauren."

The sound of the front door echoed through the house and Lauren and I sat up with alert. Lauren wiped the tears and make up from her eyes and followed behind me as we rushed into the living room.

Brooke leaned forward, out of breath with her hands on her knees.

"What is it?" I demanded, coming to a stop in front of her.

"My dad," Brooke huffed, letting out a deep breath. "His partner was at the house, they were complaining. Something weird is going on at the station and the other cops are picking up on it. They didn't get any notification that the town square had been attacked. My dad straight up said the chief is hiding things from them, they're thinking of going above his head and filing a complaint. They brought Higgins up too, referring to him as the root of the problem. The cops who aren't Renati, I mean."

Lauren leaned against the wall. "So the non-Renati cops have finally caught on that there is corruption in their department?"

Brooke nodded. "He said a lot of stuff is getting swept under the rug or not dealt with properly. The Renati cops aren't as discrete as they used to be. Not getting any of the calls about the attack on town square was the final straw."

Rayn and Nic stepped into the living room from the kitchen. Nic turned to Brooke and hardened his gaze. "If there are more Renati on the force than powerless cops, they'll be dealt with. Your dad needs to watch his back if he doesn't want them preparing his 21-gun salute."

Brooke faced him with wide eyes. "Don't say such things!"

Nic shook his head. "It's the truth and you know it. This is all useful information but stop him from digging too deep if you want to keep him above ground."

Rayn let out a sigh. "Would it be the worst idea for the higher ups to come in and kick the Renati off the force? It can't be that hard to separate the crooked cops from the rest."

"So these higher ups can be charmed or killed? Taking out Erebus is the only solution," Nic replied.

The front door of the cottage flew open and Emery ran in. She wrapped her arms around Nic's waist and smiled up at him with bright eyes. "Happy birthday, Nicky!"

"Oh…" Nic rested a hand on Emery's back and gave her a confused smile. "Who told you?"

"My mommy! We bought you a present." Emery let go of him and jumped up and down with excitement. Emery turned back to Harmony and clapped her hands. "Can I give it to him, Mommy?"

"What's this?" Nic stared down at the wrapped package in Harmony's hands.

Harmony handed Emery the gift and turned to Nic with a soft smile. "I haven't bought you a birthday gift in a long time, but I hope you like it…It's something you would have liked back when…Well, pretend you like it if you don't."

I checked the date on my phone. "Oh, shit. I didn't realize it was the seventh already. I'm so sorry, Nicky." I rushed to his side and pulled him into a hug. "Happy birthday."

Rayn crossed her arms. "I didn't know it was your birthday, Nic!"

He gave me a one armed hug. "I didn't plan on celebrating."

"What?" Emery shrieked. "But it's your *birthday*. Why wouldn't you want to have a party?"

Nic let out a short sigh and took the present from Emery. "Thank you, Emmy."

She beamed with pride and excitement as Nic unwrapped the gift. He tore open the wrapping and revealed a CD. Nic's eyes widened and he let out a short breath as he turned the CD over in his hands.

He glanced up at Harmony and blinked. "Where did you find this?"

Harmony shrugged off a smile. "Some used record store in Falcon Bay. I, uh, I don't know if you ever replaced your copy but–"

Nic shook his head. "No, but I looked everywhere for it." He knelt down and pulled Emery into a hug. "Thank you so much."

Emery wrapped her little arms around Nic's neck and nuzzled into him. "Do you like it?"

"I *love* it," Nic answered. "This album was my favorite when I was younger."

"Can I listen to it?" Emery let go of Nic and took a step back.

"Uh." Nic glanced at Harmony across the room before he smiled down at Emery. "When you're older." Nic turned his attention back to Harmony. "I can't believe you remembered this."

A blush crept across her cheeks as she smiled. "How could I forget? You played it on repeat the entire summer."

I cleared my throat. "You really don't want to celebrate your birthday?"

Nic glanced at me over his shoulder. "No, I really don't. Not after what happened."

"Shouldn't we take the good moments where we can get them?" I pushed.

Nic smiled down at his CD. "This is enough." He looked back and forth between Rayn and I. "You should keep tabs on this Higgins guy."

Lauren crossed her arms. "We don't even have to get that close, I can hear from a pretty far distance."

"The sooner the better. From what I overheard, he and Grady are on nights so they are probably at the station." Brooke urged us towards the door with a wave of her hand. "Like, now. We should go now."

"Not all of you." Harmony stepped forward. "The more people go, the easier you'll be to catch."

Lauren turned to Rayn and I. "Just us three, then. We better hurry up before they leave."

) ·) · ● · (· (

Rayn, Lauren and I hid in the bushes across the street from the police station. A row of hedges along the sidewalk gave us the ability to get close enough to listen without being seen.

"Who is that woman?" I whispered to Rayn.

Rayn shrugged and crouched down further.

A woman with her light blonde hair pulled up into a bun stood in the shadows of the building. She seemed to be ripping Officer Higgins a new one. Higgins appeared relaxed, with his shoulder resting against the brick of the police station. The woman, on the other hand, appeared to be anything but relaxed. She moved her hands as she spoke, clenching her fists as if she would hit Higgins at any moment.

Lauren leaned in closer, tilting her head to listen. Rayn and I stayed as quiet as possible, giving Lauren as much silence as she needed to hear them over the distance.

"She's mad because the hunters are getting out of hand," Lauren whispered to us. "She expected Higgins to partner with Grady and keep them on a short leash, but Ezekiel has gone rogue."

The woman shoved Higgin's chest, pushing him against the building. Pointing her finger in his face before he grabbed her hand and held it tightly at the wrist.

Lauren widened her eyes, watching them intently. "He's threatening to tell Erebus about the wards if she comes at him like that again."

"Abbie was right," I whispered. "Erebus doesn't know the Renati broke the wards and let the hunters into Rifton. Are they working together or is Higgins the one who broke the wards?"

"I don't know, but whoever that lady is, she's insane thinking she can control the hunters," Rayn muttered.

Lauren held up a finger and turned her ear towards Higgins and the woman. The woman ripped her wrist from Higgins grip and fixed her top before she stomped out of the parking lot to her Toyota Camery.

"She threatened to kill him if he doesn't get the hunters under control. She said they were supposed to take us out long ago." Lauren bit her lip and looked at me with worry in her eyes. "If someone doesn't start holding up their end of the bargain, she'll unleash the beast."

"Unleash the beast?" I clarified.

The headlights of the woman's car shined into the brush as she left the police station. Lauren, Rayn and I dropped to our stomachs, making our bodies as flat as possible as she drove away. I let out a deep sigh of relief when she turned at the stop sign and disappeared from sight.

Lauren shrugged. "That's what she said." She pushed herself up off the ground. "If there's division amongst the Renati, they aren't as well put together as they appear on the outside."

"Nothing is," Rayn answered. "Whoever that lady is, she's stirring shit up. She'll be the next one Erebus attempts to publicly execute if she doesn't watch it."

"We may be able to use this to our advantage." I turned to look at her. "Now that we know what's going on behind the scenes, we can exploit their weaknesses. Whoever that lady is, she doesn't trust Erebus."

"Why would anyone be a member of the Renati if they didn't trust Erebus?" Lauren whispered, looking back to the police station, but Officer Higgins had moved out of sight.

I shook my head. "It doesn't make any sense, does it?" "Come on." Rayn motioned for us to follow. "Let's get out of here before anyone realizes we were spying."

Back at the cottage, Bryan, Dmitri and Abe had arrived before we'd returned. Lauren, Rayn and I shared with the crew what we had overheard between Officer Higgins and the mystery woman.

Brooke furrowed her brow. "They aren't as inconspicuous as they think they are, my dad and the others know something weird is going on. Was this blonde woman a cop?"

"I don't think so," I answered. "She wasn't in uniform."

Rayn put a hand on her hip. "That doesn't mean she's a civilian."

Rose nodded in agreement. "These cops aren't even trying to hide anymore. The way none of the police showed up to the attack on town square? How did the police who aren't Renati justify that?"

"My dad said none of the calls made to dispatch were transferred to anyone on the force," Brooke explained. "Only the fire department was notified."

I chewed on my bottom lip, trying to make heads or tails of everything. I let out a sigh. "Whatever is going on with the cops and the hunters, we have to leave for the palace.

Henry Drake won't let our actions go unanswered. We kidnapped his wife and interfered with Emma's punishment."

Lauren scoffed. "We let Bonnie go. We could've killed her."

I shook my head. "I don't think Drake is going to see a difference."

My small backpack began to vibrate. I stared at it in confusion, since my phone sat in my pocket and didn't move an inch. I checked the screen anyway to make sure, but only a photo of Bryan and I met my gaze.

I moved into the dining room and set my bag on the table, digging through it in search of the vibration. It came from the inner pocket.

The blue lace agate.

A chill ran through my body as I unzipped the pocket with trembling fingers and retrieved the stone. The mate had been left with Roberta at the Hallow in case she ever needed to get in touch with me. I couldn't imagine Roberta calling to say hello and catch up.

Fiery images of my vision came to the forefront of my mind. The smell of smoke filling the air. The embers spreading through the air, catching the trees. The shadows crawling through the grounds, attacking the witches.

"Roberta?" I whispered into the stone, praying the connection still held at this distance.

"Whitney," her voice answered through the stone.

I let out a small breath of relief at the clarity of her voice, but the connection also allowed me to hear the fear that trembled my name. Everyone in the living room rushed to my side and huddled around me, eager to hear why Roberta would contact us.

"It's me. What's wrong?" I asked.

"We have a situation here. There are Shadows at the shield again. They aren't digging this time. They don't seem to be actively attacking or even planning to. They are lounging. They are waiting."

"That doesn't sound good," I answered. "How many are there?"

"Another dozen. I hate to ask for help like this, Whitney, but I fear I am left with no choice. We have been preparing and training for another attack the best we can, but we are homesteaders, not warriors. Whatever the Shadows are waiting for, we are not equipped to defend against it alone."

"I'll talk to the others, but we will come." I glanced around at my people by my side. "We, uh, we should get out of Rifton anyway."

"Something has happened," Roberta stated, not a question.

"Erebus attacked town square. He...he killed a lot of people."

Roberta let out a sigh. "A retaliation?"

"Yeah, we have the stem of the key."

"May our loved ones watch over us, Whitney, we are in dangerous territory."

"I will talk to the others. We'll be there soon," I promised.

When Roberta didn't answer right away, I thought she'd ended the connection, but her voice cracked as she spoke. "I feel the end nearing, Whitney."

"Hang in there. We'll need a night to get our things together, but we will be there tomorrow. I promise you."

Chapter Forty-One
Relatively Safe
Lauren

After the conversation with Roberta ended, Whitney whipped around to face us. "We have to help them. I promised we would answer their call."

"Could it possibly be a trap?" Aden wondered.

Whitney shook her head. "I left the other blue lace agate with Roberta for this exact reason. Now that we have the stem of the key, I think it's a good idea to return to the Hallow. We can get their situation figured out and then head to the palace. What do you guys think?"

"Okay, good. Um, I have to stay here. I can't disappear into the woods with Emery." Harmony glanced up at the loft where her daughter slept in bed.

"I'm coming with you this time," Dmitri said, not a question.

Bryan stood up next to him. "So am I."

Abe turned to Dmitri. "You aren't going into the woods without me."

Of course they were.

"Guys, hang on a second." Rose put up her hands. "We don't know what we're walking into at the Hallow, it might be best if–"

"This is what I've been training for." Bryan cut her off. "Besides, after that attack on the town square, do you really want to leave us here?"

"What about Mom?" Rose asked her brother. "What about your parents, Abe? Harmony can't watch over everyone at once."

"I sent my parents away after the tornado," Abe announced. "They are at my aunt's in Reno and they'll be there until I lift the charm I put them under."

I noticed Whitney let out a small sigh of relief knowing Janice and Jeff were out of harm's way, but we still had to make sure Rose and Brooke's parents weren't in danger.

"My dad already left for Idaho, so he's not in any danger," I replied, unable to hide the sadness in my voice.

Saying goodbye to the man who raised me had been hard enough, not knowing for certain if I'd ever seen him again. But saying goodbye when he had no memory of our life together? A new kind of torture I had never imagined.

Dad had barely wrapped his arms around me and quickly pulled away when I wanted to cling to him. I wanted to be comforted like when I was a little girl. Dad didn't hesitate to chase the demons away. Now the demons had gotten into his head and erased all the memories, all the times that I clung to. Losing my mom broke me, but this was almost worse.

I crossed my arms and tuned out the voices of everyone else in the room. The crew planned when and how we'd all get to the Hallow. With my dad safe in Idaho, all I could think about was leaving Ashley again. We weren't exactly talking and I didn't know where we stood, if Ashley would even care. I didn't feel right moving forward with this plan before I at least tried to reach out. I would explain to Ash that I didn't exactly have a choice, I had to go. I'd beg Ashley to be safe and stay the hell away from anyone who could hurt her. Hell, I was tempted to beg Ashley to pack up her family and leave Rifton as soon as possible, to run somewhere safe and far away.

Knowing what I needed to do next, I turned back to the conversations happening around me.

"Mom won't listen because she doesn't remember anything!" Rose argued with her brother. "She isn't going to leave town unless we force her to."

"She's going to get herself killed," I spoke up. "And I'm not saying that to be cruel. You may have to force her hand."

Rose shook her head. "I am not okay with Mom being charmed. Not again."

"I didn't exactly enjoy it either, Rosie, but it sure made things easier. It's kept her safe so far," Bryan argued.

Brooke's shoulders fell and she stared across the room as if a realization had washed over her. "I should charm my dad to stop asking so many questions. If he is playing along, then he won't be a target and maybe the Renati will think he's useful. There aren't enough witches in Rifton for them to drive all the powerless out, they need people who can help keep the town running."

Rose turned to look at her. "What if they don't want to keep the town running?"

"The Drakes have no interest in burning down Rifton," Dmitri pointed out. "We've known that for a while now." He turned to Brooke. "I know it's hard, B, but it's probably your dad's best bet."

She nodded and glanced across the room at Nic. "You're right. If he keeps digging around, they'll kill him."

Rose directed her attention back to Bryan. "What about Mom?"

He sat in silence for a moment, chewing on the inside of his cheek. "I don't know, Rosie. I don't have a solution for this one. Even if we sent her away from Rifton, where would she go? We don't have extended family out of state. If she leaves her job, how is she supposed to support herself?"

"None of that matters if she's dead!" A tear escaped the corner of Rose's eye.

Whitney stepped forward and placed a hand on Bryan's shoulder. "The Renati didn't mess with anyone the first time we went to the Hallow, maybe they won't this time either."

I shook my head. "I wouldn't put that much faith in them."

"I know, but Harmony is staying and so are the trio of witches who came to Ostara. We aren't leaving our families completely unprotected." Whitney straightened her back, as if that would make her point stronger. "The Renati wanted your talisman, Lauren. The Renati didn't attack your parents for no reason."

I opened my mouth to speak but no words came. I blinked at the group for a moment. "I don't care what you do with your parents, or who comes with us. We need to do *something*."

"We are coming." Dmitri crossed his arms. "I don't care what anyone has to say about it. I'm staying with my sisters."

Nic groaned, visibly annoyed with the extra travelers for the trip. "It's ultimately up to the girls. If they say no, it means no."

"And if they say yes, you can't argue with them." Dmitri pointed out, crossing his arms.

Nic looked at Whitney sideways, waiting for input.

Whitney took a deep breath. "The Hallow is relatively safe. We'll go help fortify their shield and then head out. They have two Archivists. It might be good to introduce Dmitri to them, maybe they can give him some guidance in that regard."

"Okay, so how do we get everyone to the palace afterwards?" Rose asked.

Nic shrugged. "I don't know. Plane? Car? Whatever. I really don't care." He ran his fingers through his hair. "We can't open a portal because none of us have been there."

"We'd need a bus to transport all of us there," I muttered.

"Then maybe we shouldn't be taking everyone," Nic said through his teeth.

"Nicky, that's enough. They're coming with. Rifton isn't safe anymore, not for them," Whitney snapped.

Nic took a step towards Whitney. "But I'm expected to leave Harmony behind?"

Harmony let out a defeated sigh. "Nicky, I can't take Emery out into the woods. We'll be okay. I'll keep an eye on things. We have a few more boots on the ground here." Harmony took his hand in hers. "I don't know how I'll keep CC up and running without you guys but that's my problem. It's important we get the key before they do, and now that we have the stem, it's probably best you all leave town before they retaliate."

"I don't want to leave you and Emmy," Nic whispered.

"You need to go, keep an eye on the kids." Harmony tilted her head, putting up a brave front. "We will be here waiting for you."

Nic silently nodded.

Abe spoke up. "We have tonight to get ready."

"The backpacks are still enchanted and since we've already made a much harder trip there, packing this round should be quicker." Rayn turned to the fireplace. "Only the essentials."

Whitney grabbed Bryan's arm and pulled him aside. She kept her voice low but I could hear their whispers from across the room. "Babe, what are you going to do about work?"

"I don't care about work," Bryan answered. "I've already dropped out of school, it doesn't matter."

"It absolutely matters, this is a big deal."

"Whit." He put his hands on her shoulders. "I never intended on waiting tables forever, okay? And we already talked about FBU. This is my decision. I'm coming with you and Rose."

"Okay," Whitney whispered. "Uh, we should go home and start packing. My backpack fits…well, I haven't reached the limit yet so we can fit all of our things in one bag."

Everyone dispersed, heading to their homes to prepare for our sudden departure. Rayn and Nic disappeared down the hall to start gathering their things. Harmony stood at the dining room table, shuffling through paperwork. Brooke and Rose left to make sure their parents would be safe in our absence.

I stood frozen in place, chewing on the inside of my cheek. I knew it was hard on Brooke and Rose to leave their parents behind, to be worried about them and doing everything they could to ensure their safety, but I couldn't ignore the pang of jealousy that ran through me

"You feeling okay?" Whitney asked, coming up next to me.

I nodded. "I'm trying not to feel anything."

"Fair enough," Whitney hesitated and turned to face me. "So, uh, Ash is over at our place."

"Oh yeah?" I tried to mask the desperation in my voice. "Good for her."

Bryan put his hand on my shoulder. "Why don't you come over for a bit?"

I nodded. "Yeah, okay. I can't leave again without talking to her. Has, uh, has she said anything to you about our last conversation?"

Bryan shrugged. "She asked me not to say anything."

"Of course she did," I muttered.

"I *will* say that she cares about you, and her confliction has more to do with internally freaking out that magic exists than you being part of it."

I blinked at Bryan before I replied, "Well, if she wants to end things, now is her chance."

Nerves took over my body on the drive to Whit and Bryan's. By the time I parked along the curb, I had accepted two things. One, I had no control over what Ashley chose or accepted. Two, I was leaving either way. Maybe a clean break would make it easier to leave Rifton and not have to worry about coming back. My dad left and if Ashley was out of the equation too…Maybe I would kill Erebus and then leave Rifton for good.

When I walked into the house, I didn't bother knocking. They knew I followed them. Dmitri and Abe stood at the dining room table with Bryan and Whitney, all three of the guys asked Whit continuous questions.

"How many of these witches actually support us?" Dmitri asked.

"Are you sure the shield is strong enough to keep out the Renati *and* the Shadows?" Abe wondered.

"There's a lot of us going, should we bring our own supplies? Food and all that? I don't want to overwhelm them," Bryan said.

Whitney ran her fingers through her hair. "Uh. Not as many as I would prefer. Yes, the shield will hold. I hope. We should pack nonperishables."

"Don't expect much of a warm welcome from the Hallow either. They're very hot and cold," I informed them.

Dmitri nodded and turned to Abe. "Let's go get packed and then we'll get what you need from your house."

"Take the car and watch for Shadows." Whitney handed Dmitri the car keys.

I had no idea how long we would be at the Hallow before we left for the palace, but I knew it wouldn't be as long as last time. Nearly three weeks felt like an eternity to be away from home. I reminded myself that I needed to pack for more than a few days at the Hallow. We needed to think about the journey to the palace, and who knows how long we would end up having to stay there. Would we be able to stay with Maggie? She may have been a member of Amilia's coven, but could she put up all of us? Probably not. Would we have to get a hotel room?

"I don't know if we've thought this through well enough. I feel very unprepared going on a trip like this with so many of us. We have no real idea of how long we'll be gone or if we'll be welcome at the palace," I admitted.

Whitney turned to face me. "Roberta knows we are coming. As far as the palace is concerned? I don't know. Mia at least maintained some sort of communication with Roberta, but from my understanding Maggie Daniels hadn't spoken to my mom or Mia in years."

"We'll figure it out as we go," Bryan reassured us.

I huffed. "Is this the kind of thing we want to wing?"

"Ideally, no." Whit shook her head. "But nothing about this has been average so far."

Ashley came around the corner into the kitchen and froze when she saw us. She took a step back and cleared her throat. "Oh, hi."

"Hi." I turned to face her with a brave face. "Can we talk? It's important and time sensitive."

Ashley nodded.

"Let's go outside." I led the way to the backyard. Once the sliding glass door closed behind us, I jumped right in. I had no time to waste and I had to take advantage of my courage while it stuck around. "Remember when the girls and I all disappeared a few months ago?"

Ashley nodded again.

"We didn't have the problems everyone told you we did." I ran my fingers through my hair. "There are witches living in the woods on a compound and we need their help against the man who attacked the town square. We were there with them. They need our help, so we're leaving again."

"Oh," Ashley whispered, she looked down at the ground with heavy eyes.

"I couldn't leave without telling you. I don't know where we stand right now, but I know that I still care about you and I respect you too much to disappear again without a word." I let out a quivering breath. "You...you need to be safe while we're gone. I don't know how long it'll be, but probably longer than last time. Is there any way you can leave Rifton? Take your parents and go?"

Ashley nodded. "My parents are in Tacoma for the weekend."

"Keep them there as long as possible." I took a step towards her. "Go to Tacoma with them. Please, Ash, don't stay here."

"And leave my friends?" Ashley furrowed her brow. "I'm not doing that."

"Bryan is coming with us." I crossed my arms.

Ashley paused, opening her mouth to talk but only a huff came out. She closed her eyes for a moment and nodded. "Emma and Troy are still here. I'll be fine."

"Fine." My shoulders fell as I accepted defeat. "I know this isn't what you signed up for. I'm not what you thought. I should have...I did consider this before I asked you to be in a relationship so I'm sorry for the deceit. I regret it."

"You regret asking me to be in a relationship?" Ashley moved away from me.

"Of course not." I stepped towards her. "I regret dragging you into this before you knew the truth. I should have known you'd want to back out once you learned about magic."

Ashley crossed her arms and...Did she smirk at me? "When did I say I was backing out?"

I paused. "I assumed..."

Ashley chortled. "You know what they say about assuming? Makes an ass out of you and me?"

I blinked at her. "I'm confused. You haven't talked to me since the attack."

"I've been processing, and it's heavy. I don't know what's going on but you...you I know."

Clenching my fists, I did everything I could not to grab her face and kiss her. "Even though I kept things from you?"

"Is there anything else?"

I shook my head.

"Then I see it all, and I still know you." Ashley reached out and took my hand in hers. "I still...you are precious to me. I won't pretend like I understand all these layers that have built up around the situation, but as far as you and I go?" She ran her thumb along my knuckles. "You do what you need, you go where you need to go. I will be here, right where you left me."

I squeezed her fingers. "Are you sure?"

"I'm not sure about much," Ashley admitted. "But I'm sure that there isn't anyone else in my life who means what you do. So, as long as you and I both still feel that way, I will wait for you to come home."

I grabbed Ashley's beautiful, freckled face and pulled her into a kiss. I backed Ashley up against the table, where Ash reached back to steady us. I wanted to grab her thighs and pull her onto that table. I wanted to do a million different things, but time was not on our side. We held one another close with the tips of our noses brushing together. I felt the tears on Ashley's face and couldn't tell who they belonged to, but it didn't matter. We would share these tears as we'd share our uncertain future.

When Ashley and I went back into the house, Emma sat in the living room whispering to Whitney and Bryan. Emma's shoulders were slouched and she looked small, caving in on herself. She barely lifted her head to make eye contact. Emma's heartbreak reflected in her heavy eyes.

"You're all leaving?" she asked softly.

I nodded.

"We have to get the next piece of the key," Bryan told her.

Ashley stepped forward. "I'm not leaving you, Em. I'm with you until the bitter end."

"Good," Emma wiped a tear from her face. "I thought about staying at the apartment, but at least here I'm not alone."

Bryan apologized. "I'm sorry. I never intended on you getting so caught up in all this, and I never meant to leave you alone in the apartment."

"Bynie, you have to do what's best for you. My family are the ones who fucked all this up. You didn't do anything wrong." Emma reached for his hand. "It's a good idea for you guys to leave. I don't want you to, but I understand you need to stay safe."

"I hate leaving you behind," Bryan admitted. "Rifton isn't safe."

"No, but the house is protected and we are going to make sure to fortify it before we go. Troy and Ashley know the truth now," Whitney paused. "We, uh, we'll figure it out."

"Now that we know what to look out for, it should be easier to avoid it," Ashley replied.

I hoped with all my heart that was the truth.

"Have you heard anything from your family since the attack?" Whitney asked Emma.

Emma shook her head. "Not even from my mom." She wiped another tear away. "I'm pretty sure the final nail has been driven into the coffin. Don't worry about me. We'll be okay. Is anyone staying behind or are you all going?"

Whitney reached out for Emma's free hand. "Harmony is staying, our friend who's been running the Corner Cup. She'll be at the cottage, it's where the rest of our crew lives. You two and Troy are welcome there anytime, okay? If you need anything, Harmony will help you."

"I wouldn't want to impose." Ashley rubbed her arm.

"You aren't," Whitney reassured her. "I own the house. Well...my siblings and I all own the house, but the point is, it's our house and Harmony will help you. Honestly, she needs help too. We have a few witches loyal to us, but she'll be alone and...I'm worried about her. She has a little girl and she'll need help taking care of her."

Emma nodded. "I will do what I can here, but I don't think we stand much of a chance unless you do whatever you can to kill that mother fucker," Emma paused. "And my father."

"I know you're angry, Em, and you have every right to be, but–"

Emma cut Bryan off, keeping her eyes locked into Whit's. "He doesn't deserve to see the other side of this."

"He won't," Whitney promised.

Emma let go of Whitney's hand and pulled Bryan into a hug. She nuzzled her face into his chest and let out a sigh. "Please be safe. I don't know what I'd do if anything happened to you."

"I could say the same to you." Bryan squeezed his arms around her.

Emma surprised me when she let go of Bryan and wrapped her arms around Whitney. Whit turned and hugged Emma, gently rubbing her back.

"I'm sorry about everything," Whitney whispered.

"Me too," Emma sniffled. "I wish we were able to do a lot of things differently."

"We'll have the chance to start over."

Emma sighed, dropping her arms and taking a step back. She wiped the tears from her cheeks. "I really fucking hope so."

Ashley reached out and took my hand, lacing our fingers. I squeezed back, a silent promise that I'd fight like hell to get back to her.

Chapter Forty-Two
Quick to Trust
Whitney

The following evening, the girls and I made our way into the backyard of the cottage with backpacks secured. I glanced around at our new additions to the trip. The guys all seemed ready to go, despite having no idea what they'd face in the middle of the Dark Star Forest.

"Whit," Harmony whispered as she took a step towards me. She wrung her hands together and let out a deep breath. "I will admit this only to you, but I hate that I'm staying behind."

"I know, I understand why you need to." I knew that staying behind was about as safe for Emery as joining us, but I understood the decision Harmony had made.

She chewed on her lip. "Please take care of Nicky."

I tilted my head, surprised that she felt the need to ask. "I always do. I try to at least."

Harmony nodded. "You're the only one I trust to make sure he comes back in one piece."

I attempted to hide my smile. "Does this mean you two are officially back together?"

Harmony rolled her eyes. "Keep his head on straight and attached to his body." Her voice dropped to a whisper. "I'm not losing him again."

"I will, Honey," I promised. She lifted a brow and tilted her head. "Oh, I'm sorry that just slipped out. I know that's only for your closest people to call you."

Harmony reached out and took my hand. "That includes you now."

I pulled Harmony into a hug. "You be safe here too. If you need anything, please reach out to Emma Drake. I know you don't want to and it feels weird because of her family, but she will be there for you if you need her."

Harmony gave me a final squeeze and stepped back. "Okay."

I joined the others around the patch of grass where the dormant portal lay. Rose poured the potion over the grass and we cut our hands to reopen the portal to the Hallow. I felt Bryan wince watching us perform blood magic, but he didn't say a word out loud. The energy began to swirl in front of us and the portal became visible.

"Okay, so." I turned to Bryan and laced his fingers in mine after Brooke healed my hand. "Going into a portal kind of feels like falling but you can walk out the other side if you keep your feet on the ground."

"It feels like you're going down a drop on a rollercoaster," Dmitri explained further. "Hang on to someone and you'll be okay."

"Is there any way that someone could get separated in a portal and end up somewhere else?" Bryan asked, staring down at the swirling magic before him.

"Um, no, I don't think so." I looked at the girls over my shoulder.

Lauren shrugged, unsure how to answer.

Rose stepped forward to reassure her brother. "We opened this one ourselves, it's safe."

"Okay," Bryan's voice cracked as he spoke, tightening his grip on my hand. "Okay, I'll be fine."

On the exterior, he looked solid and confident. But nerves rattled his core. I gave his hand a gentle squeeze. I didn't need to say anything and he knew I could feel his uncertainty. But he put on a brave face and I didn't want to feed into his doubt.

This felt heavier than leaving Rifton the first time. Before, leaving Dmitri and Bryan behind weighed on my heart. But taking them into the forest unsettled my soul. They'd be with us, and we'd be able to keep them safe. On the other hand, they'd be with us and they'd be in the line of danger. After the whirlwind Erebus unleashed on town square, we weren't left with much choice.

I took in a deep breath and stepped into the swirling magic of the portal, bringing Bryan with me. When we stepped through to the other side, Bryan's hand slipped from mine and he fell to his knees on the ground.

"Babe, are you okay?" I knelt next to him and wrapped my arm around his shoulder.

He took a shaky breath and rested his palms on the ground. "That was *not* like a roller coaster."

"I'm sorry, are you okay?" I asked again.

He nodded and took another deep breath before he leaned back, resting on his knees. "I'm fine, just give me a minute."

"Byn?" Rose knelt down next to him. She reached into her pocket and pulled out a small potion vile. "I had a feeling it would give you motion sickness. Here, drink this."

Bryan took the vile from Rose and downed it. Rayn and Aden came through the portal after Rose and Brooke, with Dmitri and Abe close behind them. Abe plopped over on his ass, holding his forehead. Dmitri kneeled down next to him and put a concerned hand on his shoulder. Abe nodded, letting out an unsteady breath. Seeing his reaction, I remembered that Dmitri went through the portal in the meadow alone. Abe and Serenity were already at the lake when Mit fell.

"First time through a portal?" I asked Abe.

Rose handed him a vial of the same potion she gave Bryan. Abe nodded and took the vial. Lauren and Nic came through last, neither of them phased by the twists and turns of portal travel.

Once everyone was out, the girls and I all held our hands up together and closed the portal. The weight of protecting the Hallow hung heavy on my shoulders. We couldn't keep the portal open and risk Renati members finding it. If we were going to keep traveling back and forth safely, we had to cover our tracks. Though I didn't like the idea of cutting Harmony and Emery off from us, in case they needed a quick escape. I silently hoped that wouldn't be the case.

Nic took a deep breath as he looked up at the big wooden gate of the Hallow entrance. He stood planted in the dirt like he had never expected to be back there. As if just the sight of the Hallow brought back every dark emotion he'd spent the last decade burying.

I watched it all surface across his face, in his wide eyes and his unsteady breath. The way he didn't start moving towards the gate, even after everyone else did. Marin appeared in the open entryway and Nic still didn't budge.

Marin stood with their arms crossed, watching us carefully. Even though they knew about our arrival, their mouth still twisted as if they tasted something sour.

"Coming, old man?" I asked over my shoulder, watching Nic carefully.

He nodded. "Go ahead, I'm not far behind."

I took Bryan's hand and walked behind Rayn as we approached Marin. Aden stayed towards the back of the group, grumbling under his breath about how irritated he was to disarm again.

"Welcome back." Marin pushed the gate open further for all of us to walk through. "Though I will admit, I'm surprised to see you."

"We said we would answer if you called." Rayn walked past them, unphased.

Marin furrowed their brow. "What people say and what they do are oftentimes two different things."

"Yeah, well, we keep our word," I answered.

"And you've brought...friends?" Marin looked at the crew we brought over my shoulder.

Even though we only had four extra bodies with us, ten people instead of six was definitely a lot to accommodate when resources were limited.

"We brought our own provisions and are not expecting more than the one guest house that was offered to us. We planned ahead to avoid being an inconvenience to your community," I explained.

"That's considerate of you." Marin raised their eyebrows in surprise and glanced towards the back of the group. "Now that's certainly a face I never expected to see again."

"Marin, charming as ever." Nic came up behind me.

Marin reached out and placed their hand on Nic's arm. "It's good to see you, Dominic. You look good."

He smiled at them. "You too."

Roberta waited for us in the center of the compound near the gardens. Large chickens clucked and ran around her feet as she waved.

"The Elementals are back!" a voice echoed through the Hallow, bouncing off the small buildings.

People came out of their tiny houses to watch us pass by. While many of the Hallow's residents were still skeptical of our presence, most of them seemed pleasantly surprised to see us return.

Roberta smiled as we approached her. She opened her arms, welcoming Nic into a hug. "I'm so happy to see you again," she whispered into his hair. "You've grown. Where is Harmony?"

"She stayed behind." Nic stepped out of the embrace. "I'm not happy about it."

A smile sparked in Roberta's eyes. "She is a capable woman. She knows what she's doing." Roberta turned towards the girls and I. "Thank you for coming. I know things are dire in Rifton and your attention is required there but the darkness is spreading through the forest. If the Shadows are trying to get inside again, it means the Renati are aware of our presence here." She scanned the compound. "I'm fearful of what could happen if they get through without proper defenses."

My vision of the Hallow on fire came to my mind. "I won't let that happen."

Marin chortled. "We never had any close calls like this until this new generation popped up out of nowhere. They trudged through the forest so loudly, attracting hunters. They nearly led the wolves straight to our gates, actually bringing one with them." They crossed their arms and glared at Aden.

"I won't waste time arguing about Aden's loyalty when there are real problems to sort through." I snapped at Marin, my patience already stretched thin. "Have any witches been seen with these Shadows?"

Roberta shook her head. "Not yet, but my gut tells me they aren't far behind. Whether we were hiding in the woods or not, the darkness is spreading. Since the last Shadow attack, we have been preparing. Those who are physically able have been training and learning to defend themselves." While that news felt reassuring, it also appeared too little too late. Roberta continued on, "I'm worried that Erebus is closer to getting the pieces of the key, and if he gets all three, he will be coming for the Shepherd's talismans next."

"He'll have to take them from our cold, dead hands," Lauren said through her teeth, crossing her arms.

Abe turned to her. "That would be his preference. If Erebus carried all three of the manifested generation's powers inside of himself, he'd be unstoppable."

"Can one body hold that much magic?" Rose asked curiously. "Wouldn't that kind of power kill a person?"

"We don't know," Roberta admitted. "It's never been done, but Erebus has spent so much time in the Shadow Realm, I genuinely wonder how much humanity is left in him. Any luck on finding the piece of the key Amilia had?"

I shook my head. "No, but we have the piece Bonnie Drake was in possession of."

Roberta's gaze wandered over to Nic. "Every day that passes gives us a disadvantage."

"You still trust me, don't you, Berta?" Nic crossed his arms.

Roberta nodded. "I do, Nicky."

"We need you to fight with us," Lauren stated, matter of factly. "If the Shadows are knocking on your front door and you worry the Renati are right behind them, then it doesn't sound like you guys have the luxury of hiding here any longer. This is everyone's fight, not just the Elementals."

"We said we weren't–" Marin started, but Roberta cut them off.

"There is truth to your words, and I realize the gravity of the situation. We'll discuss this further in the town hall. I wish to gather the residents so we can hear everyone's concerns and opinions before we make a confirmed decision."

"I think that's fair." I nodded at Roberta. "If we are expecting everyone here to take part in the fight, then they deserve a say in it too. They need to hear how things have changed in Rifton and that we are here to put things right. They need to talk directly to us, not to us through anyone else."

Nerves coursed through my entire body. We faced a make or break moment in our battle against Erebus. If we stood any chance of taking him down, or even holding our own against the Renati, we needed the witches of the Hallow. They may have been smaller in number, but these witches had been surviving on their own in the middle of the forest for over a decade. They had survival skills and determination that many of the pampered Renati witches only dreamed of.

Roberta and Marin gathered the members of the Hallow in the town hall building. Once everyone gathered in one place all sitting together in one room, it felt like there were more of them than I had originally anticipated. Only twelve may have left Rifton in the first wave, but there were easily two dozen people sitting before us. The girls and I stood in the front of the room with the rest of our crew off on the sidelines.

Dmitri scanned the room nervously, stepping further into the wall, as close to the wood as he would get without crawling inside of it. He always hated being in a crowd. Abe stood close to my brother, resting his head on Dmitri's shoulder. Nic leaned against the wall with his arms crossed, chewing on the side of his mouth. Aden was nowhere to be found. I looked down the line at each of them until my eyes landed on Bryan.

He already looked at me, a soft and encouraging smile on his face as our gazes locked. Adoration swelled in his chest as he nodded, silently letting me know that we could do this.

"Attention, everyone!" Roberta addressed the crowd. "The Elementals have returned and they wish to speak with the compound. Please give them your full attention."

I straightened my back as I scanned the crowd. I was an Elemental. One of the strongest witches in documented history. I was the product of centuries of regenerated magic; a living compilation of the hopes and dreams of every Water Elemental that came before me. A goddamn queen. It was about time I started to act like it.

I projected my voice. It echoed off the walls of the town hall, silencing the muttering crowd. "Erebus attacked Rifton. He tore apart town square with a massive tornado and killed dozens of people. He exposed magic to the town's powerless and attempted to publicly execute my friend, the daughter of a town councilman, who stood by and watched." I held my head high. "As many of you know, my generation and I have come to seek your assistance in battling the Renati. They have done as they pleased in Rifton for too long. It's time the town returned to a safe haven for witches and powerless alike." I paused to collect my thoughts when my sister took over.

"I know many of you heard the news of Erebus' resurrection and believed it to be a rumor, but I assure you it's true. We saw the resurrection with our own eyes. We have seen him in his physical form. We fought against him as he attacked our homes and killed our loved ones. We fought against him to protect our town and the innocents who live there. We cannot maintain this fight if we continue to fight alone." Rayn looked to Rose to continue our speech. If the witches of the Hallow were going to believe in us, all five of us needed to convince them.

Rose nodded, calculating the right words in her mind. "We know this isn't a fight any of you wanted. We know you left Rifton to keep your families safe. The Renati destroyed your livelihoods out of spite, but the fight has found you regardless. The darkness has spread through the forest and is knocking at your front door. We will do whatever we can to protect you, but you have to help."

Brooke took over. "We cannot fight the Renati alone. The shadows have evolved in ways we never could have imagined. We were able to close a portal to the Shadow Realm that was opened to bring Erebus back to our world, but the Shadows that already came through are getting stronger every day. You saw this yourselves when they attacked the gates of the Hallow. You may not believe it, but you are powerful enough to stand against them. We will stand together."

"The Shadows, the Renati and Erebus will not rest until they have ended not only us but every single one of you for supporting us. They are ruthless and they will not discriminate against your children or your elderly. They will burn the forest to the ground before they show an ounce of restraint or weakness," Lauren announced. "We will do everything we can to keep the Hallow safe, but you have to protect yourselves too."

Murmurs broke out amongst the crowd. Residents leaning over to whisper to their neighbors. Concerned looks and worried thoughts consumed the town hall. I glanced over at my sister, moving only my eyes to see her eyebrows raised in concern.

"Why should we trust you?" A man stood on his seat. "We left Rifton for a reason. How do we know the Shadows at the shield didn't follow you here? No one found us until *you* led them here."

"Yeah, that's right," a woman raised her voice. "We never had any trouble with dark magic until you showed up."

The first man nodded at the woman. "Maybe it's a trap. We should have never let them in here, Roberta! They brought a hunter with them, for generation's sake!"

"We are a generation!" I raised my voice to be heard over them. "We are the same Elemental magic you read about in those books next door. We aren't here to deceive you."

"We wouldn't be in this mess in the first place if the Elementals had taken better care of their people. You're the reason the Renati exist!"

I caught Nic flinch at those words out of the corner of my eye.

"We are a new generation, a different one!" Rose argued back. "We are trying to correct those wrongs."

"We should exile them!" the first man shouted. "Fortify the shield and cut off communication with Rifton all together. It's the only way to keep us safe."

"That's enough!" Jake's voice boomed through the town hall. He stood up on his chair with his hands around his mouth, amplifying his voice. "I said that's enough!"

The crowd began to quiet down to listen to one of their own.

"I know you're all panicked and scared, but we have to listen to them. The Elementals have always been in charge for a reason. They are the most powerful witches in our world, plus they have first-hand experience fighting off the Renati *and* the Shadows. They know their weaknesses and their strengths in ways we could only guess. If they have ideas on how to keep the Hallow safe, they are our best bet. I trust them and you should too."

"And why are you so quick to trust?" a different man asked Jake, crossing his arms.

Jake laughed under his breath. "Because I actually took the time to get to know them, unlike the rest of you who hid in your houses and watched from afar. I took the opportunity to share knowledge and they did the same. They came all this way and risked their lives to come to us for aid. We asked them for help and they didn't hesitate to answer. Their intentions are pure and we owe it to ourselves to fight. We can't keep running forever. Even if we could, we can't let our community be remembered as the cowards who hid when Erebus came back. We'd be no better than the ones who resurrected him in the first place."

The first man to speak out against us turned to look at me and held out his hands. "And what exactly do you have planned to protect the Hallow?"

"We take the fight as far from the community as possible, that way none of your homes get caught in the crossfire. We strike first. The most success we've had in fighting the Renati has been when we catch them off guard." I steadied my voice. "Their Shadows are hard as stone so you can't fight them one on one, you have to keep your distance and hit them with magic. Fire works best but they can be disoriented with energy waves."

"How close are the Renati to the Hallow?" someone in the back of the crowd asked.

"There is no evidence that they've penetrated the shield yet," Lauren reassured them. "Only Shadows have been seen on the perimeter, no witches yet. There's no reason to panic, we have the upper hand here."

"We will be staying here at the Hallow with you in the meantime." Rayn looked out across the crowd. "If anything happens, we will be here to help defend your homes."

"What about Rifton?" someone else asked. "Is the town left defenseless while you're here waiting for an attack that may not happen?"

Oh, so *now* they gave a fuck about the safety of Rifton? When it was their town to defend, they ran and hid in the forest. Now that it's our town to defend, they act like we left our supporters in Rifton helpless against the Renati.

"There aren't many Elemental supporters left in town," Brooke answered. "None that the Renati know about. Those that are left are safe for the time being. One of the other Elementals stayed behind."

Our words seemed to be enough to keep the crowd from breaking out in a complete panic. Roberta thanked everyone for taking time out of their evenings to hear us out and dismissed everyone. Those who spoke out against us were the first to leave but there were some stragglers that wanted to talk to us more. They wanted to hear more about what life had been like in Rifton since they'd left or what we needed to take down the Renati for good.

It was hard listening to them talk about the Renati like they were all inherently evil, that this fight between us was black and white. Nic and Roberta tucked themselves into a corner of the town hall and whispered to one another, neither of them looked very satisfied with how us addressing the witches of the Hallow went over. While there were still some who were hesitant to trust us, we had won over quite a few more than last time and for me, that was a victory in itself.

Chapter Forty-Three
ANCHORED
Whitney

The never ending questions from the Hallow witches left me drained. I hid in the corner of the room with the guys huddled close to me like a barrier. Bryan, Dmitri and Abe all stood close enough to make me feel protected but far enough away to let me catch my breath. Once I finally had a moment to breathe, Jake made his way over.

He picked at his cuticles as he spoke. "Hi. I'm really sorry I interrupted you like that, but I just–"

"Don't you dare apologize, you saved our asses." I put out my arm and welcomed Jake into a hug. "Thank you for having our backs."

He smiled. "That means a lot. Having you here means more than you'll ever know."

"Jake, these are our people we brought with us. This is Bryan, my boyfriend and Rose's brother." Bryan shook Jake's hand as they exchanged pleasantries. "This is my brother, Dmitri, and his boyfriend, Abe." A smile curved up Jake's lips as he turned to Dmitri and Abe. He shook their hands and held onto them a bit longer than he did Bryan's. When he let go, he ran trembling fingers through his hair. "Sorry, I've never been around guys my own age."

I motioned towards my brother. "Dmitri is actually an Archivist now. He took over for Amilia Burnett."

"How is your Archivist training going?" Jake raised his brow and turned to Dmitri.

"Uh, nonexistent." Dmitri shoved his hands into his pockets. "Amilia never told me that she intended for me to take over so I'm not really sure what to do. I've been keeping her books safe with a cloaking spell but I honestly don't really know what an Archivist is supposed to do."

"Wait, you had no idea you were taking over?" Jake clarified. Dmitri shook his head. "Oh, wow. Okay. I've been in training for years, but that's just Amanda. I always figured I'd take what I knew and move on to another coven somewhere." Jake perked up. "I could help, you know. I could give you an Archivist 101 kind of thing while you're here. I've learned a lot from Amanda and honestly, I don't even need training anymore. I know how to translate and care for the books without her."

"That would be fantastic! Thanks." Dmitri smiled.

"If you're free, I could take you over to the library. It's quiet right now, I'll show you the books," Jake offered.

"Yes, I'd love that," Dmitri said before Jake had time to finish his sentence. He turned to Abe. "Is that something you'd want to do?"

"Yeah, if it'll help your training, we should go." Abe put a hand on Mit's shoulder.

Jake gave me a reassuring glance as if silently saying that he would keep my brother safe. "I can show them where the guest house is afterwards. We won't be long, I promise."

"Go on, then."

The three of them rushed to the door.

"So that's our Allurement guy?" Bryan wrapped his arm around my shoulders and gave a gentle squeeze.

"Years worth of research. It's incredible. Maybe Jake can actually help Mit get excited about his new role as our Archivist."

Bryan smiled. "I hope so. I know it seemed rough having those people yell at you guys but I think ultimately you made good progress tonight. They'll all come around, even the most skeptical of the bunch."

I leaned into him, closing my eyes as the heat from his body radiated into me. "I'm glad you came. I feel a lot less anxious than I did the first time we were here, and this time there is an actual threat on the horizon."

Amanda stepped up next to me, keeping her voice low. "I see Jake is dragging our newest guests to the library?"

I let out a short sigh. "My brother is an Archivist. He took over for Amilia."

Amanda nodded, as if the information didn't surprise her. "As long as they keep their hands to themselves. I have a system." Her gaze wandered up and down Bryan's tall body. "Hello. Is this your boyfriend?"

I tightened my arm around his waist. "Bryan, this is Amanda, the Hallow's Archivist. Amanda, this is Bryan."

They exchanged pleasantries before Amanda turned back to me. "Thank you for coming back. When we heard more Shadows were seen on the other side of the shield...I wondered if you'd actually keep your word."

"Thank you for having so much faith in us." My voice dripped with sarcasm.

Amanda flashed me a smile before she strolled off. "Let Marin know if you need anything."

Bryan chewed on his bottom lip. "We need eyes on the perimeter of the shield. Just in case. If the Shadows or anything else get through, we need to know before they're at the gates."

I nodded. "You're right. I don't really know what Roberta and Nic are talking about but hopefully it's something along those lines."

"I can take a shift," Bryan suggested. "I don't know if asking the residents here to watch the border is the best idea. Some of them might think you guys lied about the likelihood of an attack."

"I don't necessarily want *you* out there either," I admitted. "Aden would love to. He does everything he can to stay outside the gate. They don't let him have his crossbow while he's in here."

"I don't blame them."

"Hi." Nic came up behind us, his voice barely a whisper. "Sorry to interrupt. Roberta got news of more Shadows along the outside of the shield."

"More?" My eyes widened.

Nic let out a tired sigh. "Who knows what they've already reported back to the Renati in Rifton."

Bryan leaned in. "Who has been watching the perimeter?"

"The birds," Nic replied, as if his words weren't completely off the wall.

"What?" Bryan tilted his head.

"Like, literal birds?" I specified.

"Yes," Nic answered. "Roberta has a thing with the birds. I don't know if it's a spell or what but that's how she keeps an eye on everything going on in the forest. The Renati can't be more than a few days out."

"Fuck." I rubbed my face. "This is not what I wanted to hear."

"Yeah, me either, but it's what we're stuck with." Nic rubbed the back of his neck. "I'm going to get in touch with Honey through our blue lace agates and see if there's anything weird going on back home. Maybe she'll be able to give us a heads up if the Renati are moving out. We've got people watching them too." Nic patted Bryan on the shoulder. "I'll meet you guys back at the guest house. Be good." He ran his fingers through his hair as he weaved through the remnants of the crowd.

"This is not ideal," I said to Bryan as he put his hand on the small of my back.

"It's gonna be okay. We have a heads up and can prepare." He pressed a kiss to my forehead. "But we should get some rest."

"Yeah, not a bad idea." I found my sister and the girls across the room and made my way over to them, Bryan close behind. "We're going to get some sleep."

"We were talking about getting in touch with Jennifer, the herbalist. We can make sure the greenhouses and the apothecary are stocked." Rose scanned the stragglers. "If something does happen, I want to make sure we have enough healing potions and tonics to take care of everyone. If they don't then I need time to grow everything."

"We need to replenish our own stock anyway," Brooke pointed out. "I did what I could before we left Rifton, but we didn't have as much time to prepare as we did the first time."

"Do you need help with anything?" I asked, but the four of them shook their heads.

"No, we got this under control. You two get some sleep." Lauren smiled.

"Oh, okay, sounds good." I remained unsure.

Bryan grabbed my hand and pulled me towards the door. His whispers sent sweet chills through my body. "I selfishly want to have as much alone time with you as possible."

Even though we lived together, it had been a while since Bryan and I had any decent alone time. A moment to talk without being interrupted. Our attention had both been in high demand for weeks now. I couldn't even remember the last time we talked about something that wasn't related to Erebus and the Renati.

I took Bryan down the row of tiny houses to the one on the very end. "Here's the guest house." I opened the door. "This is where the girls and I stayed."

"It's, uh, cozy." Bryan ducked his head and stepped inside.

"Roberta said there's a second story below us. Uh, right about here?" I moved across the little house to the back by the bathroom, searching the floor for the door. "Oh, here it is." I grabbed the handle and pulled the door up, revealing a staircase leading down under the ground. "This is cool. She didn't tell us about this the first time. We all took turns sleeping in the loft together."

"Well, this is handy." Bryan followed me down the wooden stairs. "We definitely have a crowd with us this time." He paused, gently grabbing my shoulder to turn me to face him. "It's really nice to be alone with you."

"It is." I smiled at him. "I'm sorry this whole shitshow has consumed everything. It's hard to be in a relationship with someone who is in my situation."

"Hey, listen to me." Bryan took my chin in his hand and lifted my gaze to his. "There is nowhere else in the world I'd rather be, okay?" His heart swelled in his chest as our eyes locked. He meant it. Bryan didn't need to tell me how he felt and I didn't need an empathic connection. He showed me everyday how much this mess I'd gotten into meant to him. How much keeping me safe meant to him.

I pushed myself up on my toes and brought him into a kiss. He cupped his hand around the back of my neck and deepened the kiss, gently nibbling at my bottom lip as I wrapped my arms around his back. I took a step forward, inching him closer to one of the bedrooms.

"We don't have to do anything if you don't want to," Bryan whispered against my lips. "I'm happy to be with you."

"I want both," I admitted, kissing him again. "Can I take your clothes off and then maybe we can talk a bit?"

"Yes." He pulled me back in, kissing me harder than before. He snaked an arm around my waist and set me on the small dresser in the bedroom. He took off my boots and unbuttoned my jeans, lifting me to slowly slide the denim down my legs. His fingertips dragged up the length of my thigh as he got down on his knees and threw a leg over each shoulder.

I expected him to take his time, to go agonizingly slow but Bryan was a man on a mission. He moved my panties to the side, and licked up my center. Heat overcame my body, spreading through every inch of me. I closed my eyes and rested my head against the wall, the rest of the world melting away. I let out a low moan and arched my back, giving him more room to work. He grabbed under my thighs and spread my legs, opening me up. He wrapped his lips around my clit and sucked gently, twirling his tongue as I shuttered.

My fingers gripped hard at the roots of his hair. I felt like I could float above the room, my entire body weightless but Bryan kept me anchored. His hands dug into the skin of my thighs, enough to feel it in my muscles but never enough to hurt. There was nothing before this and nothing after this. Nothing else in the world mattered in that moment but Bryan's mouth.

My body rushed towards the edge. My desire and anticipation had been building since we snuck off together and I knew I only had moments left. I gave in, letting go of any control over my body, my mind, or my vocal chords. My breaths came out in heavy pants and Bryan's name slipped from my lips. The louder I got, the more his excitement grew and I felt his need burn throughout his entire body.

He got off on pleasuring me and that sent me over the edge. My thighs tightened around his head as my orgasm pulsed through my body. Pure ecstacy ran through my veins and I cried out. Bryan rode out the climax with me, slowing his rhythm as I peaked, but he didn't come up for air as my breathing leveled out like he normally did.

Instead, Bryan slid two fingers inside of me, curling them as his lips wrapped back around my clit.

Oh.

He thrust his fingers in and out, picking up his pace as my body responded. I ground my hips against him to match his rhythm when another orgasm crashed through my body, unexpected and unannounced. My hips bucked and I screamed, my voice straining my throat. This time when I came down from the high, he lifted his head.

I opened my mouth to speak but my throat burned, dry as sandpaper. I coughed into my arm, looking around for my bag.

"Are you okay?" Bryan rose onto his feet.

"I need water." I cleared my throat.

Bryan picked me up and set me down on the bed before he rummaged through our backpack. "How far down is it buried?"

"To the left."

"Got it." Bryan brought me the refillable bottle and sat down next to me. He bit his bottom lip, attempting to hide a smile that swept across his lips.

"What?" I took a drink, the water soothing my aching throat.

"Enjoying the effect I have on you." Bryan smiled. "The effect we have on one another." He cupped my cheek and brought me into a kiss. "I love you."

"I love you too." I dropped the water bottle and pushed him onto the bed, slowly running my fingers down his chest. I hooked my fingers into the waistband of his jeans and undid the button.

Bryan watched me slowly undo his pants. I took my time undressing him. He raised his arms to pull his shirt over his head and lifted his hips as I slid his jeans down his legs. His body reflected the work he had been putting in with Aden. The muscles of his legs were more toned and hardened from the morning jogs. His arms were bigger, the muscle definition had always been there but now it was more apparent.

I ran my fingers down the hard muscle, tracing the bare skin. I ran my fingers through the blonde hair that grew on his chest and made little constellations out of the freckles. His skin began to perk up in little goosebumps under my touch.

Bryan finished undressing me and flipped me onto my back without warning. He hooked his knee under mine, spreading my legs open. I wrapped myself around his back, hooking my ankles together. His soft lips kissed the corner of my mouth as his hips ground against mine.

I angled my hips and he nudged at my entrance, gliding inside. He moved slow and sweet, taking his time. Moving every single inch of himself in to fill me and then back out again, stretching me with every thrust.

Our bodies moved in perfect sync. Enough force that I felt him at my core but still gentle and caring. We made unhurried love as our hands explored one another. We acted like we had all the time in the world, as if when the sun rose the next morning we would have the rest of eternity to lay in that bed and worship each other. No impending threats from the other side. No Shadows at the edge of the shield. The other witches of the Hallow disappeared as he groaned against my neck, burying himself deep in me with one final thrust.

Bryan placed a kiss on my neck and collapsed beside me. We lay there in silence, panting and sighing. He ran his fingers through his hair and reached for my hand, lacing our fingers. We lay in silence until our heartbeats fell into an even, steady rhythm. His pulse echoed through my body along with my own. I had reached a point where I didn't feel at home unless I could feel both of those heartbeats.

"What's going on up there?" Bryan moved a loose strand of hair from my face. "Talk to me."

"Trying to memorize every little detail," I whispered. "To take advantage of the quiet moments. There aren't many of them anymore."

Bryan kissed the top of my head. "It won't always be like this."

"It's hard to look past it all and see the other side."

"Hmm." Bryan tightened his grip around me. "I see it all the time, it's what keeps me going. Me and you grocery shopping, making dinner, fussing over the bills. I'm going to buy you a house and we'll sleep in on Sundays."

"Do you want to stay in Rifton?"

"We'll go wherever you want."

"I want to be close to everyone. I want us all to stay together."

"Then that's what we'll do."

I nuzzled into his chest and closed my eyes, taking in a deep breath of cedarwood and vanilla. The steady beat of his heart against my cheek as my body relaxed. Bryan wrapped his arms around me and held me close, pressing a kiss into my hair.

"Get some sleep," he whispered.

Chapter Forty-Four
DISTRACTION
Whitney

Whitney! Rayn's voice echoed through my mind. My eyes flew open to darkness.

What? I answered back, sleepily. Unsure if the urgency in Rayn's voice was actually there or if sleep blurred my perception.

The door to the bedroom flew open and Rayn flipped on the lightswitch.

"Get up!" she shouted. "They're trying to break down the shield!"

"Who?" I silently thanked the universe I had the urge to put on Bryan's t-shirt before I fell asleep.

"The fucking Renati! Drake and everyone else. Roberta's birds reported. We need to distract them away from the shield and kick their asses."

Bryan sat up in bed, luckily covered up to his waist by the blankets. "What do you need from me?"

"Stay here, keep things under control. Take care of my brother. We're taking the witches who can fight with us but someone needs to stay behind with the kids." Rayn moved her hands to rush me along. "Put on your fucking pants! Let's go!"

"Okay, okay, okay," I repeated as I slipped my jeans on and fumbled for my shoes. "We'll meet you upstairs."

Rayn left the bedroom door opened as she ran up the stairs, cursing as she sprinted. Bryan jumped out of bed and dressed quickly. I raced up the stairs with my boots still untied and Bryan right behind me. I knew the Shadows were at the shield, but I had no idea the Renati were this close.

Upstairs was pure chaos. Aden strapped his crossbow to his back and filled his quiver with bolts before he checked the magazines of his guns. I only saw the back of Nic's head as he ran out the front door, leaving it wide open behind him. Rose, Lauren and Brooke were all tying their shoelaces.

Rose turned to us with her mobile apothecary open. "Grab some vials. Healing and energy. I have all kinds of stuff in here." I reached for a dark midnight blue vial but Rose stopped me. "Not that one, that's a sleeping potion."

I grabbed an energy potion and a healing potion, shoving them into my pockets.

"You're staying here?" Rose asked Bryan.

He nodded. "Yeah. Be safe, understand?"

"Yeah, you too." Rose paused halfway out the door and looked back at her brother. "I love you. Take care of this place. Dmitri and Abe are staying too."

I couldn't tell if them staying behind while the rest of us ran off to fight fueled my anxiety or gave me an ounce of comfort, but I didn't have the luxury of time to figure it out.

"Love you." I pushed myself up on my toes to give Bryan a kiss before I ran out the door after the rest of our crew.

"I love you!" he yelled after us as we sprinted across the lawn towards the main gate of the Hallow.

Roberta and Marin were already gathering witches at the gates to join us. The atmosphere was uncomfortable and chaotic. Everyone mumbled about how we promised this wasn't supposed to happen at all, let alone tonight. They argued that we had led the Renati to their front gate.

"Bryan, Dmitri and Abe are staying behind to help here, so if you need anything, utilize them," I told Roberta, who I imagined would be staying as well.

"Marin will be joining you in the fight." Roberta's eyes moved around, trying to focus on everything happening around us. "I will put a shield up around the Hallow itself, in case the fight comes to our doorstep." She reached out and put her hands on my shoulders. "I have faith in us. We will survive the night."

I smiled at her, seeing my mom and Amilia in her eyes. "We'll stop them before they get too close. The Renati won't reach the Hallow."

"Be safe, dear." Roberta's eyes welled over with tears. "Your mother would be so proud of you."

My generation, Aden, Nic and six witches from the Hallow ran off into the night. Birds squawked in the sky, flying low to guide us to where the Renati and their Shadows hit the shield. The birds led us the long way through the woods. When we finally reached the edge of the shield, Marin waved their hand and let us through to the other side.

Over a dozen Renati witches faced the shield, throwing energy waves repeatedly at the barrier. Magic bounced off the shield but as the Renati continuously hit it, the more visible the shield became. Glimmers of gold reflected off the moonlight, sparkling against the night.

Rayn and Nic combined their powers and a massive fire ball flew through the air over our heads. The attack landed in the middle of the Renati. Dirt and rocks scattered into the air as it crashed into the ground like a meteor, throwing the Renati back. Only half of them got back up.

Henry Drake and Big Boy were towards the back of the pack, as if they were awaiting our arrival. If Drake knew anything for certain, it's that my generation would come to the defense of our supporters.

Slowly, Drake turned and smiled, holding his arms out as if to welcome us to the party. Big Boy stepped in front of Drake and snarled.

Rayn hit Big Boy with a blast of flames to his face. No longer under the shield, Rayn had full control of her powers.

With the winged Shadow distracted, I set my sights on Henry Drake. I hardened my second skin of ice and charged, getting within a few yards of Drake before the Shadow moved into my path. I took a step back, unprepared to have to get through the demon to get to Henry Drake. I threw a sharp icicle over Big Boy's head, aimed right for Drake's heart. The moment I released my attack, Big Boy pounced at me.

My heartbeat pounded in my ears as I ducked for cover and threw a shield around me. When I glanced up, a massive, steady flow of flames hit the demon's side, knocking it over. Big Boy fell to his side and yelped as Nic came into view. The flames did not stop when the Shadow hit the ground. Nic kept his hand out, a stream of fire flowing from his palm.

It wasn't endless though, he'd run out of energy eventually. So would the rest of us. We had to end this fight before that happened.

With Big Boy down, I sprinted at Drake again. He turned to run, but I threw my magic at him and he froze. His face stuck in a gasp of fear. I left his surprised gaze and watched half of the other Renati members fighting against the witches from the Hallow and my crew.

Rose and Rayn stuck close to one another, combining their powers. Rose levitated a thick branch into the air as Rayn caught it on fire. The two of them thrusted their energy, sending the branch flying at a group of Renati members who were ganging up on some Hallow witches.

Marin picked up a Renati witch, levitating them into the air towards the top of the trees before they slammed the witch to the ground. Another Renati came up behind them, attempting to take Marin by surprise. I opened my mouth to shout a warning to them when Marin turned and punched the witch square in the face. The sheer strength Marin put behind that punch only came as a shock because of their usual calm demeanor, but taking a second look at their muscular arms, I should've known better.

Nic appeared at my side, panting. He glared at Drake's frozen form and a wicked smile crept across his lips.

"He's all yours, Nicky," I said to him.

Nic stepped forward, and I left Drake frozen in place. He didn't deserve to fight back. He didn't deserve another chance to try and hurt Nic. He deserved to remain paralyzed in his body while Nic took whatever kind of revenge he'd been dreaming about for years.

I left his side and ran to my sister. Rayn and the girls were fighting off Renati members by the shield, but the witches of the Hallow were not doing well. Whatever they had been doing in regards to training had not been enough. Many of them were already injured, pulling Brooke away from the action in order to keep everyone alive. She scrambled back and forth, stretching herself too thin. Only Marin and a few other witches remained on their feet, sending energy waves and levitating fallen branches or rocks to throw at our enemy.

Aden released a bolt from his crossbow, dropping a Renati member to the ground. I smiled, knowing we weren't losing. Unfortunately we weren't overwhelming the Renati either.

A cry of pain echoed into the night and I caught a glimpse of Nic on top of Drake. His hands burned into Drake's skin and Nic showed no intention of letting up. Nic's hand covered Drake's face as he screamed again.

"I've waited a long time for this," Nic gritted through his teeth, tightening his grip on Drake. Nic's voice broke as he glared down at him. "You ruined my life, you sadistic son of a bitch."

Drake began to snap back. "You sh-"

Dominic grabbed Henry Drake's head on either side and snapped his neck.

Nic stumbled getting up, but when he stood, he stared down at Drake's body. I expected to see tension leave Nic's shoulders, to see some kind of relief wash over him but he looked the exact same. He still clenched his jaw, his hands were still curled into tight fists. Big Boy scrambled to his feet and charged at Nic. He barely turned, grounding the Shadow again with another blast of flames.

Seeing Henry Drake's neck flopped to the side, the Renati witches went feral. One threw themselves at me, screaming at an octave I was certain could shatter my eardrums. My hardened second ice skin broke my fall as the witch tackled me to the ground. I let them land on top of me, knowing they would claw and punch against the ice. I barely felt their attacks until two more witches joined them.

The spell protecting my body became overwhelmed and the ice around my skin cracked. I threw out an energy wave, knocking the three of them off of me, but one of the witches tripped on my leg and landed next to me. Barely a foot away they struck me in the face with a closed fist before I could blink. A second blow followed right behind and my nose cracked.

Pain erupted across my face in a burning throb. My eyes filled with tears from the impact of my nose breaking. I wouldn't let this fucker get in a third hit.

I put up a shield, allowing myself to get my bearings. When he punched against the shield, he pulled his hand back and hissed.

"Use your powers and fight me like a witch, coward," I hissed through clenched teeth and threw an energy wave at the man.

He stumbled backwards and fell at the base of a tree. I no longer cared about whether I injured Renati or killed them. I would no longer allow their deaths to cause me emotional turmoil. I would no longer lose sleep over their humanity. Only so much empathy could be felt towards people who would not stop attacking me and the people I loved. The Renati witches made their beds, they could sleep in them.

I grabbed the man around the throat and froze his skin. The ice crystals spread from my fingertips and covered his entire body. I felt my powers sink down into his blood, into his organs; his entire being turned to solid ice. As frozen as their hearts had become.

A chill crept up my own spine and before I could turn to look, Erebus towered over me.

His dark eyes burned holes into my soul as he glared at me. His long, slender frame crept closer. He took his time, moving as if to savor every moment. He had been waiting centuries to finally kill me and his big moment had arrived. He wanted to remember every last little detail of my demise.

I wouldn't give him the satisfaction.

I threw my hands out in front of me and ice shot from my fingertips. Erebus waved his hand as if swatting a fly, his flames melted my ice with ease. His other hand extended out towards me as an energy wave knocked me over. His magic slapped against my face, punching me square in the nose.

I stumbled backwards but kept my footing as tears stung my eyes. I thrust my own energy wave at Erebus, pouring all my hatred into the attack. My magic knocked him back but distracted me enough for another Renati member to hit me from behind. Our crew was spread too thin, everyone focused on taking down a Renati member or a massive Shadow. Erebus and the man behind me teamed up on me without any protest from my friends but I could handle them.

I threw my hand out behind me and a thick row of ice shot up from the ground, impaling the Renati member. Crimson blood dripped down the spikes of ice, pooling on the forest floor.

Turning my attention back to Erebus, I took the stance Harmony had taught me and prepared for another blow. My muscles screamed at me from the punches I'd already received. I knew my body couldn't take much more and my energy buzzed in my head. My magic was not as strong as it had been when I first ran into the forest, but I still had enough to deal with the king of shadows.

I attacked with another row of ice, breaking through the ground, but Erebus quickly melted my attack with flaming hands.

"Those flames are *mine*!" Rayn growled and threw a fireball at Erebus, hitting him in the back. "You stole that magic and I want it back!"

"You were undeserving then, and you're undeserving now," Erebus hissed.

He opened his hands and lifted his arms slowly, palms up to the sky. His head tilted back as he smiled; his fingers trembled and his body stiffened. I couldn't feel his magic, but he had something up his sleeve.

I threw another attack at him, but my powers bounced off a shield that protected his body. Erebus had cracked our shield when we were fighting to protect the town square. I knew he had an entire generation's worth of magic in his blood but my entire generation stood by me too. If we threw enough magic at him, we could break his shield and end this whole thing here.

I kept my eyes on Erebus, preparing another attack when the crackle of snapping bones echoed through the trees.

The limp body of a dead Renati member convulsed. Their limbs twisted as the bones broke, their fingers digging into the earth as they pushed themself onto wobbling legs. The corpse snarled and took a step.

All the dead witches came back to life.

"Are these fucking zombies?" Lauren spun in a circle, watching the dead rise.

My blood turned to ice as Henry Drake's corpse stood up and turned his snapped neck towards me. His head hung to the side as Drake growled, taking his first step in our direction. I sent an energy wave flying towards Drake's corpse, but he got right back up.

"Shit..." I muttered, trying to calculate a plan.

"What do we do?" Marin's voice shouted from behind me.

Rose waved her hand and the dirt under one of the corpses opened wide, swallowing it whole. It screeched as it fell into the ground. A dozen more corpses still remained, limping their way towards us.

Brooke put a shield up around the injured witches from the Hallow. She scanned the trees frantically as the corpses surrounded us. "How many times are they going to come back?"

"Only one way to find out." I levitated a fallen log and threw it, knocking four corpses onto the ground.

Rayn lit the corpse closest to us on fire as Erebus turned and left the forest. The Shadows sulked after him, moving out like a pride of lions following behind their master. Erebus didn't look over his shoulder to see if any of his followers survived. He hadn't so much as batted an eyelash when Nic snapped Henry Drake's neck. He simply didn't seem to care who he sacrificed on his conquest as long as he got what he wanted in the end. Those who had offered their own children to be the blood sacrifice for Erebus to open the labyrinth were left to die in the woods alone.

This moment solidified the difference between Erebus and the Elementals. The girls and I could never...if it had been Rebecca or Jane or Kelly out here in the forest, I'd fight for them until the bitter end. If any of the Hallow witches were trapped out here, the girls and I would never leave them at the mercy of Erebus. Nic and Harmony would never leave an innocent person to die in the woods to preserve themselves. I had no idea how Erebus convinced the Renati witches that his choices were righteous, but I'd never forget this act of selfishness.

A corpse moved into our personal space as Nic lit it on fire. The corpse hissed and screamed, collapsing to the ground. It writhed and jumped around until the flames set in and the corpse grew still. I held my breath waiting for it to jolt back to life, but it lay motionless.

"We only have to kill them one more time!" I shouted to my crew.

Aden got to work, pulling his pistol from its holster and taking out two of the corpses with head shots. Rayn lit three more on fire. Lauren sent two more flying into the air, thrusting them into the trees where they were impaled by low-hanging branches.

My generation's powers swirled under my skin as I threw an icicle straight through Henry Drake's eye. His corpse fell motionless to the ground with a snarl. Nic may have been the one who killed him, but it felt gratifying getting to kill him again myself.

I licked my tongue over my lip, tasting the metal ting of blood. I touched the side of my face and the blood leaking from my ringing ears. I blinked, bringing my vision back as it sunk in that we had not only survived the fight but won. I looked up at the shimmering gold magic before me. The shield was damaged but it remained intact. Erebus was much stronger than he had been when he attacked the cottage, but so were we.

"Whit?" Rayn called out, rushing to my side to help me up. Blood dripped from her nose and a massive gash ripped open the skin above her eyebrow.

"Are you okay?" I assessed the rest of her but ultimately she seemed unharmed.

She nodded. "Lauren broke her arm but Brooke healed her. B is exhausted, I don't think she can walk back to the Hallow."

"We'll carry her if we have to." I wiped the snot and blood away with my sleeve.

Rose and Rayn each took one of Brooke's sides as Brooke wrapped her arms around their shoulders, putting her weight on them. Her head hung to the side, resting on Rose as we moved through the forest back to the Hallow. The witches who came with us from the compound were bloodied and bruised, but they all lived and they were able to carry themselves back home.

I smiled at them. "You should all be so proud of yourselves." I turned to Marin, who limped behind the group. "Are you okay?"

They nodded and winced. "I'll be fine." Pausing, they studied my face. "You followed through."

I forced a smile. "Don't sound so surprised."

"Thank you." Marin put their hand over their chest. "For everything." They turned and continued back to the Hallow.

I took in a deep breath, swallowing my pain as I moved my feet. The toe of my boot caught on a rock and I stumbled to my knee.

"You took a beating, kiddo." Nic put his arm around my shoulder to stabilize me and helped me onto my feet.

I rested my weight on him, knowing we had all used too much magic at once. I felt the magic hangover wash through my body in the pounding in my temple and the ache in my muscles. "I'll be fine." I turned my head to look at Nic. "You killed him. Drake's dead."

"I did," Nic answered simply, his eyes void of any emotion.

"Are *you* okay?" I searched his face for any reassuring sign. For a soft smile to curl the edge of his lips or a gleam in his hazel eyes. Nothing.

"I thought..." He paused. "I thought I would feel something, but I'm empty." Nic shook his head and tightened his grip on me.

"Killing him was never going to bring Abbie back." I grabbed his hand on my shoulder.

He nodded. "It's over now. It doesn't matter how I feel about it."

"The way you feel always matters to me. It matters to Honey."

Birds flew over us, flying low as their desperate squawks echoed through the trees. They sounded distressed, crying out repeatedly. One flew so low, the wind from their wings blew my hair into my face.

"What?" I looked up, as if the birds could answer me in plain English what they were so upset about. "Are those Roberta's birds?"

"Yes," Nic said under his breath. "Something's not right."

We picked up our pace, rushing as quickly as our tattered bodies would let us go. When the Hallow came into view, I couldn't see the shield Roberta had put up as soon as we left. It wasn't invisible – it had vanished. Not a hint of magic lingered in the air. The Hallow wasn't missing the extra shield Roberta erected when we left, no shield protected the compound at all.

A cloud of black smoke and ash hung over the Hallow as flames licked the sky.

The entire compound was on fire.

Chapter Forty-Five
BITTER DEFEAT
Whitney

"M it! Bryan!" I screamed, running to the charred wood that once made up the gate. My pounding heart filled my ears and my whole body tingled. The pain that once filled my core was instantly replaced by fear. "Abe!"

"Whit!" Rayn screamed after me, the sound of her boots on the ground close behind. She threw her hands into the air and split the fire that circled the Hallow, creating an opening for us to get through.

The heat of the flames licked my face as I jumped through the opening and ran into the Hallow. The moment I stepped foot within the boundary, a bolt shot into the ground inches from my boot. I jumped out of the way and tried to take in a good look at my surroundings when another bolt came rushing in my direction.

"Hunters!" a male voice cried out from across the compound. Jake sprinted towards me as fast as his long legs would carry him, holding his hand up over his head to shield himself from the bolts. He grabbed my hand and pulled me behind one of the smaller buildings still left intact.

"What the fuck happened?" I coughed as the smoke crept into my lungs.

"They came out of nowhere." Jake covered his mouth with his sleeve, his voice muffled in the fabric. "Broke right through the shield. It doesn't make any sense."

I looked around the corner of the building, trying to get eyes on any of my people. We had taken most of the witches who were able to fight with us to attack the Renati, leaving the rest of them defenseless.

Screams echoed off the trees. The sorrowful, pain filled, terrified screams. Everything around me lay in ruin. The town hall building had been completely demolished. Half of the tiny houses were destroyed, including the guest house and Roberta's cabin. The greenhouses and the apothecary were destroyed as well with nothing but scattered debris remaining.

I choked on the scent of burnt plants and charred flesh.

I caught sight of Aden with his crossbow out. He aimed for a hunter that stood at the top of a tiny house, shooting down at the helpless witches looking for refuge. Aden pulled the trigger and pierced through the hunter's armor. He fell to the ground with a thud.

I swirled my hands up above my head, mustering all the energy I had left. The clouds above the Hallow darkened and a crackle of thunder boomed across the sky. Rain poured down, smothering the flames and stirring up all the ash and dust that had settled on the ground. Jake and I coughed into our sleeves as the fire slowly began to die.

"Where's my brother? Where's Bryan?" I asked Jake.

"I don't know," Jake admitted, his eyebrows low with worry. "It all happened so fast I don't know where anyone is. I can't find my dad."

I grabbed Jake's dirt-caked hand and squeezed. He cleared his throat, as if attempting to hide the tears that already smeared his ash-stained face.

"We'll find your dad," I promised him. "But we have to take care of these–"

"Whitney!" Rose's voice screamed across the compound.

I left the shelter of the garden shed and ran out into the open. Jake moved behind me, staying close. A bolt flew through the air and bounced off a shield over us that I didn't erect. I caught a glimpse of Jake's hand up over my shoulder, keeping us both safe as we dashed toward the cries for help. I spotted Rose and Brooke near the collapsed town hall building.

"Whitney!" Rose yelled out again.

I ran to them as fast as my body would allow, falling to my knees once I reached them. Roberta lay under a fallen beam, her face covered in blood. Rose waved her hands and her magic swirled underneath my skin. Jake moved his hands to help Rose lift the beam from Roberta's body. Brooke got to work quickly, resting her hands over Roberta and squeezing her eyes shut, using the last bit of her magic to heal her.

"Roberta, can you talk?" I asked as the golden glow of Brooke's magic covered her body.

"Yes." Her voice came out gravely and thick.

Brooke collapsed onto her side, unmoving.

"B!" Rose cried out, grabbing her arm. She pressed fingers into the side of Brooke's neck, checking for a pulse. "She's never used this much magic before, but she's alive."

Jake moved to Brooke's side and gently rested her head on his thigh. He hunched his body over hers and scanned the compound while Rose and I tended to Roberta. No one would catch us by surprise with him keeping guard. This guy deserved the fucking world.

I let out a sigh of relief and grabbed Roberta's hand. "What happened?"

"T-the wolves," she muttered, closing her eyes.

From what I could see, Nic, Rayn, Aden and Lauren killed the remaining hunters still in the compound. The sense of urgency had flickered out and my sister fell to her knees, holding her head in her blackened hands. Nic put his hand on Rayn's shoulder, scanning the compound but his shoulders relaxed. Aden put his crossbow away.

"Where's Byn?" Rose searched the area. "Where's Dmitri and Abe?"

"Roberta, where are our brothers?" I asked. "Jake said he didn't know. Where was the last place you saw them?"

"There is an underground shelter by the houses, th-they were taking the children…" Roberta struggled to speak.

"I need help over here!" I shouted to the group and Lauren ran over, her hair a wild mess. "Stay with Roberta and Brooke. B passed out, but make sure Roberta doesn't die."

Rose jumped up and ran to the torched tiny houses as I followed close behind. My entire body trembled with the rush of adrenaline. My muscles and bones screamed at me to slow down; that if I didn't take a rest, I would be the next one to pass out but I kept pushing. I pushed myself with each step, each movement. I protested and shoved the pain deep down in my core, ignoring it. If I paid for it later, so be it.

Rose waved her hand, using her magic to move some of the burnt wood out of the way but she was exhausted too and the beams barely budged. I went around the charred tiny houses, searching the grass for anything that looked like an entrance. The foliage behind the buildings was burnt and black, but one patch remained green.

"Here!" I called, using the last bit of magic I had to remove the shield and pull back the wooden door that appeared in the ground. "Mit! Bryan!" I screamed into the hole.

"We're here!" Dmitri called back. "Abe and I have all the kids. We're down here."

"Where's Bryan?" Rose demanded.

"He stayed up there," Dmitri answered. "The hunters saw us with the children and started attacking. He shoved me down here and closed the door."

Of course he did.

"Bryan!" My voice echoed throughout the dead compound.

No answer.

"Bryan!" Rose screamed out, running past me towards the destroyed greenhouses. I ran after her, desperate for something, *anything* that would indicate his safety. Rose halted in front of the wreckage. "Oh fuck. Amanda, are you okay?" Rose knelt down on the ground and reached out her hand. A bloodied and blackened hand reached out from the debris. Rose helped Amanda climb from the wreckage.

"He's a stubborn ass. Brave but so stupid," Amanda groaned, trying to put weight on her knees but toppled over.

"My brother?" Rose's voice broke as a sob escaped her lungs. "Where is he?"

"The leader of the pack," Amanda struggled with her words. "As soon as you guys got back." She coughed. "As soon as he saw you, they retreated, but they grabbed him."

"Wait, my brother? You're talking about my brother? Tall blonde?"

Amanda nodded. "I'm sorry. I'm so sorry. It all happened so fast. He took the children underground and next thing I knew, they were all over me. I tried to get to the library to save the books but they shot me with this dart and I couldn't use my powers. I don't know what the fuck he thought running over here like that."

Tears fell down Rose's cheeks. "What do you mean they grabbed him?"

"They took him into the woods with them."

I blinked slowly, letting her words wash over me. "They took him?" I clarified. "The hunters took Bryan with them into the forest?"

"Why would they do that?" Rose demanded as if Amanda had any answers.

"I don't know. It's not the first time they've taken witches back to the den for questioning. I think they question them, at least." Amanda shook her head, a tear fell down her cheek against the ash. "I'm so sorry."

"No, absolutely not." I shook my head. "What direction did they go?"

Amanda pointed behind her. "They went through the back clearing."

I took off running. I didn't even realize my body moved again until the low hanging branches of the pine trees slapped me across the face. There had to be a clue, a sign, anything that gave some kind of idea where the hunters had gone. Something to lead me back to their den. I'd flood the place, rip it to the ground to get Bryan out of there.

Something caught on my foot and I hit the forest floor hard, my face bouncing off the dirt. I tried to push myself back up but a shooting pain in my ankle took over my entire body and I collapsed again.

"Whit!" Voices came up behind me.

The search party. Good. They could help me track down the hunters. We still had time to get to them before they reached the den. We still had time to save him.

"Whitney, your ankle is broken," Nic said above me.

"I can keep going." I got back up on my feet but one step on my right ankle sent me back down on my knees. I crawled across the foliage and wet earth until tattooed arms wrapped around my waist and lifted me.

Good. We could go after the hunters and rescue him. We still had time.

Only he carried me in the wrong direction, back to the Hallow.

"Put me down!" I screamed. "They have him! The Hunters have him! We have to go after them! We have to." I tasted the salt on my lips from tears I didn't realize I shed. "Nicky, please, put me down!"

"No." He refused to look me in the eye.

"PUT ME DOWN!" I screeched, straining my voice. My throat burned with every word.

"So they can kill you too? No. I'm sorry, but we would be running into a trap. We can't go after Bryan. I told you not to bring him." Nic tightened his grip on me as I flailed, doing everything I could to make him drop me.

I threw my fist, meeting the side of Nic's face as hard as I could. His head flew to the side. He finally looked me in the eyes, fire burning behind his gaze. He let out a huff through his nose and dropped me on the ground. I scrambled away from him, crawling in the opposite direction when Nic flipped me onto my back.

"I am not letting you get yourself killed." Nic reached into his pocket and pulled out a vile. He grabbed my chin and forced my mouth open, pouring the midnight blue potion into my mouth.

I choked on the liquid, trying to spit it back out but he covered my mouth with his hand and pushed down on my face. I had never seen him this angry before. Nic had never been this rough with me before.

He clenched his jaw as he scanned our surroundings. He blew some of the anger out in a deep sigh and closed his eyes. "I'm sorry, kiddo, I really am."

My vision began to blur and my body grew weightless. Nic finally removed his hand from my mouth but I was too limp to move.

"No," I whispered as my vision went black.

The hunters had Bryan, and they had no reason to keep him alive.

EPILOGUE

Rayn

I sat under the moonlight next to the ocean. The tide slid up the beach towards me in gentle waves, as if even the sea itself felt as exhausted as I did. The stars shone down on me from the cloudless sky, the light reflecting off the water. I wanted to admire the beauty of it all, but that was impossible to do when my sister had been asleep this long.

The last twenty-four hours remained a blur. A swirl of the zombie Renati members crawling towards us mixed with the scent of the fire that destroyed the Hallow. The terror in Whit and Rose's voices as they screamed for Bryan. I barely had time to process any of it when Nic opened up two portals, one to send the Hallow survivors to Rifton and another to bring our crew to this house on the coast. The older woman who lived in the house rushed outside and tended to the blood dripping down Nic's fingers from the cuts as if she expected us.

Now Whitney lay in a bed towards the upper levels of the house behind me, still passed out from all the sleeping potion Dominic had poured down her throat. The other members of my Elemental generation were furious with him. When she saw Whit passed out, Rose had attacked Nic, screaming that he was going to let her brother die. Nic burnt the vines she had wrapped around him but he didn't fight back. He had only picked Whitney up off the ground and carried her back to the charred remnants of the Hallow.

Rose and Lauren had been ready to lead the search party, frantic to go into the woods after Bryan, but I had stayed in place. My mind raced as I attempted to process but I couldn't keep up. Whitney and Brooke were unconscious. None of us were in any state to go after the hunters. Instead, we retreated and Rose cried the entire way.

Rose had been locked in a bedroom with a sleeping Whitney and I sat on the beach trying to wrap my head around it all. I loved Bryan. I wanted to rescue him. I wanted

EPILOGUE

to bring him back to this house we'd been brought to and keep him safe, but Nic had been right. We'd be running into a trap. Whit and Rose didn't care. They would've gotten themselves killed, and then everything we had already lost would be for nothing.

The steady throb of a headache had taken over my temple since the middle of our fight with the Renati. The moment Erebus raised his hands to bring the fallen back from the dead, I thought that would be the end of us. I thought I would never hug my brother again or laugh with my sister. I thought I'd never get the chance to tell Aden I loved him.

I glanced over my shoulder at the place Nic had brought us to after the Hallow attack. Behind me stood an old, three-story Victorian style house with long windows. The tall, winding staircase felt like it went up higher than three stories when I'd climbed it to see my sister. The house had been enchanted – that's what the owner told us when we'd arrived. I stared at the peeling white paint on the exterior from where the house had weathered storms and the salt of the Oregon coast. Vines grew up the first level, partially covering one of the windows that showed the dim glow of the fireplace in the kitchen.

Our crew remained inside, probably still yelling at each other, scattered and scared. Erebus and the hunters had done exactly what they'd set out to do. We were not a united front, we couldn't even be in the same room without a fight breaking out.

The sound of footsteps crunching in the sand sent a chill up my spine. I spun away from the house to see a tall, dark figure making its way towards me, shoulder length hair swaying with every step.

"Aden," I called into the darkness.

"It's me," his deep voice replied.

I let out a short sigh of relief and turned back to the ocean waves. Aden sat in the sand next to me, pulling his legs towards his chest.

"How's it going inside?" I dared to ask even though I could sense the tension flowing from the house all the way from the beach.

Aden huffed. "Words have been exchanged."

"You know the hunters better than any of us, I trust your opinion on the matter above anyone else's." I glanced over at him, his gaze staring out over the dark horizon.

"I want to tell you that because Bryan holds valuable information about the witches, Ezekiel and his pack will not kill him. But I can't predict what Zeke will do anymore, I don't know how far gone he is now. All I know is, they counted on us coming after him right away. They will expect us to come eventually."

"And should we?" I turned my body to face him. "I want to but...I also understand why Nic did what he did. Whit would have gotten herself killed."

Aden nodded. "Yes, she would have." He turned to face me, the heat from his body sending electric chills through my entire being. "And yes, we should go after him. Whenever your sister wakes. It was smart to bring the crew to a place where we can recover and prepare. None of us were in a condition to fight after the Renati. Not when your healer lay unconscious."

I trilled my lips and blinked away the tears that threatened to overwhelm my system. "You're right." I paused, daring myself to share my true feelings out loud. "Can I say something that feels so insensitive that I'm ashamed to even think it?"

Aden didn't speak, but he kept his eyes locked into mine, waiting.

"I just keep thinking...I'm terrified for Bryan and heartbroken for Whitney, but there is this little voice in the back of my head that..." I swallowed my fear. "That feels relieved it wasn't you."

Aden froze, barely seeming to breathe. Maybe it had been a mistake to admit that intrusive thought to him but I couldn't take it back now. I turned away as a heated blush took over my face. My throat constructed as a panic took over me. I had pushed too far. Would he leave if I made him uncomfortable? Aden stayed to protect us against the hunters, to fulfill the life debt he felt he owed us. How stupid of me to form a girlhood crush on a man much older than me, a man with no interest in me whatsoever.

"Rayn," Aden whispered my name like a prayer. "I would have killed every last one of them to get back to you."

The words slipped from my lips before I could process his sentence. "There were too many of them."

"Then I would've died trying."

Finally, I met his gaze once more, a heat in his eyes that hadn't been there earlier. A flicker of hope that maybe...just maybe he felt the same heat in his chest that I did. "Back to *me*?" I clarified.

"Maybe I haven't been as obvious as I thought," Aden paused and licked his bottom lip. "Tomorrow isn't guaranteed, you know. Not all of us will walk away from this fight in the end."

I stared back at him, waiting for the words. Begging him to finally say what I'd been dying to hear, but he waited. He waited for me to speak, but I couldn't breathe with him this close.

EPILOGUE

His heat radiated into my body, raising my core temperature in a way that I'd never experienced. I let out a short, quivering breath and my gaze wandered down to his lips, only for a second. Long enough to wonder but maybe I'd looked away quick enough that Aden hadn't noticed.

Aden's eyes burned into mine. "I didn't spare you in the meadow that day because of a sudden moment of clarity." He inched towards me, leaning closer than he'd ever been before. "It's not that I couldn't kill...It's that I could not kill someone I found so beautiful, so captivating. Rayn, I looked at you and time stopped."

I closed the space between us and crashed my lips to his without thinking. Aden seemed to be waiting for the kiss because his fingers tangled in my curls and he pulled me close, the side of his body flush against mine.

My entire being could have erupted in flames and I wouldn't have noticed. A spark in my chest exploded, igniting a burn in me that had threatened to go out a long time ago. A small pilot light, barely flickering in the darkness until Aden stumbled into my life.

Aden cupped my cheek with his free hand and his teeth scraped against my bottom lip. I opened my mouth, but Aden held back. His lips pressed against mine once more, soft and gentle before he pulled away. My mouth followed, hoping I could catch him before he spoke, but I wasn't quick enough.

Had something felt wrong? Was I a bad kisser and no one ever thought to tell me?

I reached out and placed my hand on his thigh, his muscles tensed under my fingers. "I'm not fragile, you know." The words left my lips in a whisper. "I can handle this. I can handle you."

Aden's honey-colored eyes met mine. "I don't think you're fragile." His gaze wandered down to my mouth, the feeling of his teeth against my swollen bottom lip remained. "If I don't walk away right now...If you say yes to us, I won't be able to stop myself."

"And if I say yes?" I watched his eyes wander back up to mine.

"I'm going to fuck you until the only word you remember is my name."

A chill shot through my body, causing my limbs to tremble. My heart skipped a beat as the heat in my blood all pooled between my legs. The magnetic force around Aden yanked on me and I subconsciously leaned into him, our faces inches apart. He stayed perfectly still, with the precision and concentration of someone who had been trained their entire lives to be stealthy.

Our lips barely touched, only a whisper of a kiss. Aden didn't move, waiting as I whispered, "Yes."

Finally, Aden unleashed.

His lips crashed against mine, the force of his body shoved against me and knocked me over. He followed, the weight of his muscular physique pressed me into the sand. Finally, I knew how his body felt on top of me. I ran my fingers through his hair, much softer than I ever dreamed it would've been. My tongue swept across his bottom lip and a deep groan vibrated in his chest before he parted his lips. He plunged his tongue into my mouth and it swept against mine as my thigh rubbed against something hard.

I pressed my thigh against his erection and Aden rolled his hips, grinding against me. A moan escaped my mouth as his lips left mine, trailing down my cheek to my neck. He bit the nape of my neck where the skin met my shoulder. I gasped and angled my head, giving him more space as I held onto the back of his head.

"You are everything." His lips moved up to whisper in my ear. "I need to taste you."

I should've suggested we find somewhere more private but the new moon cast a shadow on the earth. Everyone else was busy arguing in the house, and I wanted Aden inside of me as soon as possible. I waved my hand and cast a shield around us, something that would not only keep us out of sight but also keep any noise from reaching the house. I had wandered far enough away for privacy and I didn't want to risk this ending prematurely.

I leaned forward as Aden pushed himself up on his hands, watching me carefully. I reached behind my back, up my shirt and undid my bra, sliding the straps down my arms. I grabbed the fabric from under my shirt and tossed it to the side. Before I could even think about lying back down, Aden grabbed the bottom of my shirt and yanked it over my head. The cold, ocean air kissed my skin, hardening my nipples. Only a moment after the chill crept across my skin, Aden's warm mouth wrapped around one of my nipples and his tongue swirled around it.

Groaning, I arched my back. A throb appeared between my legs, begging to be satisfied. Begging for his hands, his tongue, his cock. Any part of him as long as Aden was the one touching me.

His hand massaged my other breast, his thumb ran little circles around the nub. I bit my bottom lip and reached down his back, grabbing a handful of his shirt, yanking it up. His mouth left my skin long enough to rip the shirt from his body, quickly returning to my other nipple. The wet skin he left behind chilled in the night air, only heightening my senses.

I ran my fingers up his back, to the center of his shoulder blades where his hunter mark permanently etched his skin. Aden shuddered as I slid my fingertips across the little lines of raised skin, but he didn't stop me. I followed the jagged lines up to his hairline. It took a moment for my brain to register that my hand did not travel up, Aden traveled down. He kissed down my stomach, swirling his tongue around my belly button, until he reached the hem of my jeans. Aden did not take his time as the sound of ripping fabric filled the air.

I couldn't see him in the dark, but his hands never left my body, taking in every inch of my skin. I moved my feet, kicking off my shoes as he removed whatever was left of my jeans. I reached down to slide my panties off, but Aden's hand caught mine. Our fingers laced together and he squeezed, gently rubbing his thumb against the side of my hand.

I lay back in the sand, letting him ravish my body. His tongue glided up my core, over the cotton of my panties. A deep moan escaped my lips and my entire body trembled, overwhelmed with the unsatisfied desire for him. The fabric between us was enough to feel the pressure of his tongue, but I didn't want anything separating us.

I wrapped my fingers in his shoulder-length hair, gripping the roots as Aden threw my thighs over his shoulders. He licked over my panties once more and I shuttered. His thumb replaced his tongue, running up and down the wet fabric; pressing hard enough that I knew he could make me come without ever removing my underwear. He teased me, sweeping his thumb up and down.

"Aden," I moaned, tightening my grip on his hair.

"Again. Say it again." His breath was warm against my inner thigh.

"Aden," I groaned louder, arching my back.

Finally, the cold air rushed against my skin as Aden removed my panties and slid his tongue into my core.

I shattered. Every molecule of my being dispersed and slowly came back together as Aden closed his lips around my clit. He slid a finger inside me as my hips rolled with his movements. Aden ate like a starved man, someone who hadn't felt lust in years. I had never been devoured like this. No one had ever been gentle yet firm at the same time. He tightened his grip on my hand, clinging to me as he replaced his finger with his tongue.

I barely had time to register the build of an orgasm as I came crashing down. Aden held me firmly in place, riding out the waves of passion with me until my breath came out ragged. He placed a wet kiss on my inner thigh and I yanked on his hand, pulling him towards my face.

"I need you inside of me. Now." I grabbed for the buckle of his jeans and undid them as quickly as my trembling fingers could move. I slid his clothing down his hips as his freed erection slapped against my thigh. I left his pants and wrapped my fingers around it. My eyes widened as my fingertips barely touched the edge of my thumb. Aden's entire body trembled as his weight shifted, sliding his jeans down.

His body covered me once more and his lips crashed down to mine. He cupped my cheek and kissed me tenderly, gently running his thumb across my cheek as his other hand grabbed my thigh. He spread my leg open and I directed him to my opening. Without warning, Aden thrust his hips and filled me. He stayed buried in me for a moment, as if giving me a chance to acclimate to his size.

I moaned into his mouth, kissing him deeply, wanting to be joined with him in every way possible. "Yes," I whispered into his lips between kisses. "Yes."

Aden's hips began to move, thrusting deeper into me with each move.

"So wet," he groaned against my mouth. "So tight. Fuck, you're perfect."

As perfect as this felt, I wanted to show him how badly I'd been craving his body all this time. I put a hand to his chest and Aden's movements stopped immediately. I gently pushed him into his back and straddled his waist, lowering myself down on his erection. Aden gripped my hips as I slowly joined us once more. A moan vibrated in his chest as his fingers dug into my skin.

I moved my hips, riding him slowly at first to get into a rhythm. Once I found my pace, I picked up speed. I angled my hips, rubbing my clit against his pelvic bone. Both of us were a mess of pants and moans until words slipped from Aden's lips. "Close. I'm close."

I kept my pace, not wanting to alter a single thing about this euphoria we existed in, only me and him. My fingers dug into his chest with each roll of my hips, all of my weight bearing down on him. Aden didn't seem to notice, all his attention on where our bodies joined as his hips thrusted up to meet my rhythm.

Aden's head fell back onto the sand and a deep moan escaped his lips as his muscles tensed under me. He pulled my hips down onto him and held me in place as he came. I collapsed onto him and Aden wrapped his arms tightly around my back, both of our heartbeats pounding against the other.

His labored breath warmed the side of my neck, the two of us clinching to one another. The water from the ocean kissed our sides, alerting us to the rising tide. Aden didn't budge, either not caring about the water inching closer or unaware of it all together.

"We should head inside," I whispered into his hair. "The tide is rising."

EPILOGUE

Aden hummed against my neck. "To your bed?"

I ran my fingers down his side. "I haven't actually picked a bedroom yet."

"Now is the time," he replied, peppering soft kisses across my skin. "You're still able to form sentences. My job isn't done."

A jolt shot through my body, swirling with excitement and anticipation. "Someone seems to have ripped my jeans."

Aden huffed. "You're lucky that's all I ruined getting to your perfect body."

"I love you," I announced before I could talk myself out of it.

Aden stilled, turning his head to look at me as his muscles tensed under my fingertips.

"I-I know it's..." I stammered, trying to find the right words. "Anything could happen tomorrow, and I don't want anything left unsaid. I love you, Aden Owens."

His lips met mine in a hungry kiss that took my breath away. "I love you too."

I let Aden pick our bedroom. No sense in him staying elsewhere when I had decided on that beach he would never spend another night away from me again. We lay in bed, tangled in the sheets. I had lost track of the hour, stopped counting the number of times Aden had moved inside of me. I only realized any time had passed at all by the meals Aden snuck into the kitchen for. His most recent trip, he brought back some homemade bread, butter and some cheeses. The platter remained half eaten, sitting on the dresser as I pressed my lips against Aden's. His hands grazed down my bare back, leaving goosebumps behind.

Nothing in my life had ever felt this right, this perfect. I shoved the guilt out of my mind, not wanting to think about Bryan with the hunters or that my crew fell apart on the other side of the bedroom door. The moment Whitney woke up, everything would be thrown back into motion. Reality would sink in and we would be right back at it. The hunt for the last pieces of the key. The long journey to the palace.

No, I didn't have the capacity. All I wanted was the weight of Aden's body on top of me, the feel of his calloused fingertips on my skin. His lips on mine, hungry and needing, soft and savoring. Anything he willingly gave, I would take and thank every god and goddess to ever be worshiped that I had this man in my arms.

"You know," Aden whispered against my lips. "The hunters set up arranged marriages."

I lifted my brow, silently wondering where he planned to take this story. "Do they?"

Aden nodded and nudged his nose against mine. "The pack leaders had asked, several times, to set something up, to assign me to someone." He shook his head. "I couldn't stomach the thought."

"Arranged marriage is so medieval," I replied.

"Not everyone is miserable. My parents were in an arranged marriage and they loved one another very much. We do get a say in the matter, but I shunned it all together. I had accepted that I would spend my life alone." His gaze burned into mine as his fingers traveled back up my spine. "Now I know why my heart held off."

A smile spread across my face and I pressed my lips to his, kissing him deeply. "I didn't think anything like this would ever be mine."

"I'm yours," he whispered and kissed me again. "I know things in the past have been unfair, but as long as your heart is mine, it'll never be broken again." His hand wandered to the front of my body, sliding up my stomach to cup my breast when a knock pounded on the door.

"Go away!" Aden shouted over his shoulder, his lip curled into a snarl.

"Rayn," Lauren's voice called through the crack in the door. "Whitney's awake."

I froze in place as the words seeped into my bones. My sister.

Ray? Whitney's voice appeared in my head and a chill ran through my body.

I jumped out of bed, scrambling to put my clothes back on. I answered her, *I'm here. I'm on my way.*

I slid on an intact pair of jeans and threw on a long sleeve shirt, not bothering with a bra. Aden moved behind me, slipping back into his clothes with haste.

My heart pounded throughout my entire body. I couldn't wait to see Whitney's eyes open, to feel her embrace and tell her that Aden and I had finally given into one another. Everything I had to share with my sister about my personal life would probably have to wait. As excited as I was to see her, I knew Whitney would be out for blood.

ABOUT AUTHOR

Meg Lynn has been writing for most of her life. She wrote her first short story in third grade and has been creating fantasy worlds ever since. Meg is a Northern California girl married to her high school sweetheart, they have three beautiful children and three cuddly cats. She received a bachelor's degree in Social Science from CSU Sacramento and loves coffee, books, and witchcraft. When Meg isn't writing, editing, or marketing you can find her binge-watching TV, playing videogames, or shuffling a tarot deck.

www.meglynnbooks.com

@meglynnwrites

Also By
Meg Lynn

Tidal Wave (Mystical Elements 1)

Wildfire (Mystical Elements 2)

The Calm Before the Storm: A Mystical Elements Novella (Audri's Story)

Whirlwind (Mystical Elements 3)

Rogue Wave: A Mystical Elements Novella (Nic and Harmony's Story)
Coming 2025

ACKNOWLEDGEMENTS

Dave, thank you for everything you do to make my dream of being a published author a reality. You have been so supportive, and I cannot begin to express how much I appreciate you. You are the only person besides me who knows how this series will end, so thank you for still loving me knowing what will happen lol.

Mom, thank you for always supporting my dreams. Thank you for listening to all my ideas and reading all the different versions of my books. You're the best proofreader and I appreciate your feedback.

Kerry, thank you for always reminding me that my voice matters. Whitney and Rayn's story is a love letter to our friendship, and I couldn't have asked for a better person to go through all these stages of life with. You're my day one and I wouldn't be where I am today without you.

Sarah (and Pierce), your friendship is the best thing to come out of this series. I never thought I'd grow so close to an ARC reader in the beginning of this journey, but the universe knew how much we needed each other. I love you and I cannot wait for our next adventure!

Ashley, thank you for letting me use your name and beautiful face for one of the sweetest characters in the series. Bryan couldn't ask for a better friend in Ash and I couldn't ask for a better friend in you. And thanks for being so cool about Ash becoming a love interest lol but I mean, can we really call each other best friends if I didn't write sex scenes involving your likeness?

Sydney, the best editor anyone could ask for. Thank you for putting so much care and attention into my book babies.

My friends, the ones who have been listening to me talk about publishing these books for years and order the first round of signed copies every release. Thank you for everything.

And as always, thank you to Starbucks, Taylor Swift, and Noah Kahan for giving me the drive and motivation to continue this journey.